CAMB

24 HOURS RENEWAL HOTLINE 0845 6070 6119
www.cornwall.gov.uk/library

one and all   onen hag oll
CORNWALL COUNCIL

CONTENTS

Prologue	1
1. Guest of Honour	5
2. Papa	11
3. Schloss Dragenberg	17
4. Dreams	27
5. The Woodcarver	36
6. The King	47
7. Strangers	55
8. A Gift	61
9. The Luxury of Time	68
10. Thwarted Schemes	75
11. Flight	83
12. Henchmen	90
13. Swanstein	97
14. Swan Maiden	108
15. The Friend	120
16. New Encounters	127
17. The Winter Garden	136
18. A Night of Drama	143
19. Maiden's Blushes	151
20. A Carriage of Birds	159
21. Rumours	169
22. Isle of Swans	180
23. Gundelfinger	187
24. New Power	194
25. Warnings of War	201
26. Rising Power	208
27. Temptation	221
28. New Moon	228
29. Shadows	239
30. Revelations	249
31. Treasure	260
32. A Way Out	268
33. Decisions	277

34. Three Wishes	284
35. Moonshine	292
36. Endings	297
37. The True Story	302
38. Changeling Child	314
39. The Third Wish	320
40. Something Magical	329
41. King of the Swans	335
About The Swan King	343
Keep in touch	347
Books by Nina Clare	349

For Ruth
My fellow Bavarian explorer,
who also knows that the best royal kingdom
is yet to be seen…

I wish to remain an eternal enigma to myself and to others.

King Ludwig II of Bavaria

PROLOGUE

München, Bayern 1866

HANSI GRIPPED his fingers around the carving he carried. The feel of the light birch wood comforted him. The magic liked wood. It flowed gently through it; kind, protective magic. Nothing like the powerful stuff that the mountain held. Or did until some days ago.

The room was very formal. A score or so men were crowded against the wall, watching the proceedings. Although he was taller than most, Hansi still had to bend his neck to one side to see her. She sat on a chair on the platform. He was glad they'd given her a chair and not made her stand.

She looked very pale. She'd been through so much since he'd first met her. But she had a new look of confidence about her, the kind that comes from knowing who you really are.

The chairman shuffled his papers, adjusted his monocle, and cleared his throat to show that he now meant to begin. The room quieted from loud chatter to whisperings. The chairman began.

'The Government Committee of Enquiry is now assembled, and charges all witnesses to give true testimony, answer all questions faithfully, and assist in this enquiry as to the whereabouts of the king, and in ascertaining if His Majesty is of sound mind and fit to rule, once he is found—or otherwise.

'Fräulein...' the chairman rummaged through his papers again, 'I do not appear to have a name for you. You are listed merely as a distant relative of the queen mother's.' He looked pointedly at her, but she did not speak. 'The Committee of Enquiry requires your testimony, but first we must know who it is who testifies.'

Hansi strained to hear her voice, which was clear, but muffled by the whisperings of the crowd. He wanted to tell them to be quiet, but they were of the upper classes; it was a wonder they had not thrown him out yet, seeing as he was the only man in the room not wearing a tailored suit.

'You may call me...' her hesitation was so brief, only Hansi heard it, 'Fräulein Opel. And I have already given statements of what I know and what I have seen, but no one believes me.'

She wore unfamiliar clothes. She gave a shiver, and he hoped she hadn't caught a chill from the water. Poor Herr Haller was in the sanatorium recovering from hypothermia.

'Dr Mensdorff affirms that shock influenced your first testimony, Fräulein Opel, and thus must be discounted. Now you have recovered, you must tell us what you witnessed.'

She looked at the window, staring past the chairman and the dark-suited men of the committee. The rain was hammering on the glass; it had rained all morning. The snow would be muddy slush in the streets.

'What do you want to know?'

'Everything. How did you become a member of the king's entourage? Who are you, Fräulein Opel, where did you come from, and how was it that you were one of the last persons to see the king? We must know everything.'

'The last person in this world,' she murmured.

'I beg pardon?' said the chairman. 'What did you say?'

She did not reply, but looked at Hansi. He gave a nod of encouragement. He knew she could not speak freely. He knew this, but the men sat watching her did not. And must not.

Every word she shared with the committee she must choose with care; she was not safe yet. She might never be safe if they did not believe her.

'Very well,' she said at last, turning her eyes from Hansi, to look back towards the window, as though she were looking out at a vista of memory; as though remembering was a labour. 'If you want to know all, then it is not only my own story I must share. My own is intertwined with another's. I cannot separate them.'

'Very well, Fräulein Opel. Proceed from the beginning.'

CHAPTER 1
GUEST OF HONOUR

'THE STORY STARTS WITH A GIRL. *A girl who had lived a quiet life near a small town, all of her seventeen years.*'

'*Of what class was this girl, Fräulein Opel? What was her name? We must have particulars.*'

'*She was the daughter of a baron.*'

'*She was the happy child of fortune, then.*'

'*Fortune had not been kind to the baron. His second marriage was costly, in every way imaginable. He kept his manor. He kept servants, a carriage, horses. Beautiful horses. But there were debts. The story began the evening the young baroness met the count.*'

'*Fräulein Opel, which baron and which count do you speak of? Are they of Bayern?*'

'*Yes. And I will reveal their names in due course.*'

'*We have enough mystery already in this investigation, Fräulein Opel. I adjure you to speak plainly.*'

Her eyes glazed a little. Hansi knew she was seeing the past. She was recalling all that she had once forgotten.

SHE HAD STAYED OUT RIDING TOO LONG. SHE RAN INTO THE house, up the back stairs, taking them two at a time. Her maid's young face looked anxious as she met her in the door of the bedchamber.

'Quick, my lady, the mistress has been in to hurry you along—I said you was in the bath!'

The baroness threw her hat on the bed and struggled with the ties on her winter cloak. 'The wretched thing's knotted!'

Her maid freed the knot. 'Oh, my lady, your boots!'

A trail of mud sullied the floor.

'I was in such a rush I forgot to take them off at the door. Have the guests arrived?' the baroness asked, lurching onto the nearest chair to unfasten the long row of buttons on one boot, while her maid worked to unbutton the second.

'More than half an hour ago.' She tugged one boot off, almost falling backwards with the effort.

The baroness groaned, got up, and stepped out of her skirts. 'Don't waste time changing my petticoats, Ziller, just give me the gown.'

'But there's mud on your hem!'

'Only a spatter, the gown will cover it. There are no handsome princes downstairs, are there?'

'Princes? What would a prince be doing here?'

'Exactly. If there's no princes to dress for, I'm not worrying about a bit of mud.'

'I don't understand, my lady, I think you're making one of your jokes. But what shall we do with your hair?'

The baroness stood in her fresh gown, her dark hair lying windblown round her face and in tangles down her back.

'That new turban thing that Tante Emmeline sent,' she said, snatching up her hairbrush from her dressing table. 'It's ugly, but there's no time to dress my hair.'

Ziller hurried to fetch the turban from the rows of hatboxes in the dressing room.

'It's not a good match,' Ziller said, looking from the purple turban, with its cluster of dyed feathers to the baroness's green gown.

'Never mind. Put the thing on me and tuck my hair under it. I'll pretend it's the new fashion to wear contrasting colours.'

Ziller did not return her grin. She burst into tears when the turban was on. 'You can't go down in that—the mistress will say I am the worst lady's maid and send me to the scullery!'

The baroness turned to the mirror and surveyed herself in her deep green gown with what looked like a laundry pile of purple silk piled on her head. She groaned again.

'Let me put your hair under a net and set this hair piece on top,' begged Ziller. 'Mistress said to take care you looked well this evening.'

'Oh, all right, but do stop crying, Ziller.' She plucked off the turban and sat at the dressing table. 'Hurry. Oh, why did I ride so far this afternoon?'

Ziller worked with quick, nimble fingers, twisting the waist-length hair into a fat roll and encasing it under a decorative net. She jabbed the pins in and clipped on the hairpiece. The baroness now had sleek, fashionable curls falling neatly at each side of her face. She flew out of the room, her soft-soled shoes running noiselessly down the stairs to the hall. She paused outside the drawing room to catch her breath, patted her false curls to check they had not moved out of place, folded her hands demurely, and made her entrance.

'And here she is,' said her stepmother. 'At last.'

Her stepmother came gliding across the room, her hooped skirts swaying gently.

'You're late', she hissed when she reached her.

'I beg your pardon,' the baroness said. 'I was riding, and—'

'No time for excuses, Elisabeth. Redeem yourself by being most agreeable this evening to our guest of honour.'

Elisabeth glanced across the room at the guests and wondered which one was the guest of honour.

'Lift your head. Breathe in. You are a lady. Smile. A *natural* smile.' Her voice faltered as she gave her stepdaughter a second look, 'But what have you done to your hair? It looks as though you've stuffed it under a net. Is that a false front? Wait until I see that maid of yours.'

'It was not Ziller's fault, I—'

'Hush! No time. Shoulders back. *Smile.*'

The guests stood talking in the window alcove with the baron. His daughter pasted a smile on her face and hoped it looked less false than her curls.

'My lord,' said the baronin sweetly, ushering Elisabeth towards a tall, unfamiliar man. 'Allow me to introduce you to my stepdaughter, Elisabeth.'

Elisabeth made her curtsey to the tall, lean man with greying moustache and hair. She noted the white silk waistcoat, the jewelled pocket watch chain. Above the orderly folds of an ice-blue cravat she encountered the face of the count. She had never met him before this introduction, but she knew of him. Everyone knew of him; he was one of the wealthiest and most influential men in the kingdom. His hooded eyes raked over her, lingering on her figure. He took her hand and bent to kiss it in greeting. She wished she had worn gloves.

'Would you do us the honour of taking Elisabeth into dinner, my lord?' said the baronin.

'I should be delighted.' He held out his arm, and Elisabeth was obliged to take it. She searched for her father, wanting a look from him—to reassure her that the baronin could present her to as many middle-aged men whose pomade smelled of camphor as she liked, but Papa would always take her part and say that she was young yet. Plenty of time. But her father was talking with Herr Lenbach, a business associate of his.

The count seated her at the long dining table. The daylight had faded, and the wax candles were lit. The best tableware was displayed that evening: the Augsburg silver, and the Meissen porcelain. The baronin certainly wanted to make a good impression.

'I hear you are an excellent horsewoman, my lady,' said the count.

'I enjoy riding very much,' Elisabeth replied.

'I hear you have a gift with horses.'

She was startled, and put her glass down quickly, for fear she would spill its contents.

'Gift? I ride well because I practise.'

He smiled. His teeth were yellow from smoking. He bent his head towards her to speak quietly. 'Do not worry, my lady. I can keep a secret.'

She shot a look at her stepmother across the table, and flushed with anger. Who but the baronin would tell this man of her gift? But why? No one was to know of it. She might be called a witch if they did.

'You must come and see my horses.' The count drew back again. She took a deep breath to steady her voice.

'I understand your horses are of the highest pedigree, sir.'

'Everything I acquire is of the highest quality, or will help me achieve the highest.' He tilted his raised glass towards her. She flushed again, this time with unease, as his eyes swept over her. His gaze ended with a slight frown as it settled on her hair. She tossed her ringlets like a rebellious horse tossing its mane.

'Shall we say two days hence, my lord?' said a voice from across the table.

What sharp ears the baronin had.

'I should be so glad to bring Elisabeth to see your famous stables. Perhaps we may have a peek at your equally famed art gallery?'

'That would be my pleasure, Baronin. And I will show you not just my prize horses and art, but all that is worth seeing.'

'Elisabeth would be delighted,' said the baronin, arching her eyebrows at her stepdaughter to remind her of her manners.

'Delighted,' Elisabeth murmured, turning towards her

father in appeal. But he was still engrossed in talking business with Herr Lenbach.

She would not get out of it that easily.

CHAPTER 2
PAPA

Papa's study was her favourite room. Next to the kitchen, the study had the best smells: rows of leather-bound books, many of them inherited from previous barons, the antique smell of old paper, fragrant bowls of dried orange peel and cinnamon sticks which the housekeeper placed about the room to dispel the smell of Papa's evening pipe. She liked the way the aromatic pipe smoke mingled with the dried orange. She even liked the mustiness of the fur rugs on the floor, mixed with the smell of a contented dog, for Magni, the aged mountain hound, was usually found stretched out on one, dreaming of his youth.

No one entered Papa's study without permission; not even his wife, only his daughter held that privilege from her earliest childhood. She always took Papa his second cup of coffee before business took him away for the day.

He was at his desk poring over papers, so engrossed that he was unaware of her until she put the cup down beside him. He started and hastily turned over the papers before him. She saw a flash of red ink on the overturned document.

'Is everything well, Papa?'

He nodded, but he looked tired.

'You work too hard. I've barely seen you for weeks.'

'You see me every morning, Elsa.'

'Briefly, and you seem distracted of late.' She put a hand on his shoulder and he reached up to pat it.

'Nothing for you to worry your young head about.'

'Are those the plans for the new dining room?' She pointed at a folder with the embossed sign of *Tauffenbach & Sons* on the cover.

'They are.' Papa pushed the folder towards her.

'You don't sound pleased. Are they not to your liking?' She leafed through the drawings. 'They're very…ambitious.'

The dining room was now too small for the baronin. She wished to entertain on a grander scale. In the four years since Papa had married her there had been a steady schedule of change and expansion under her direction: a new carriage, built to her specification, an extension to her own wing, for the existing dressing room was not big enough to house the wardrobe of a child, let alone a baronin. So she said. The kitchens were updated to make them fit for the new cook, who had cooked for Margravine Wilhemine. Elisabeth and her brother had concluded that the margravine must have greatly favoured horseradish, for it seemed to be in every dish. Or perhaps the margravine had not liked horseradish any more than they did, they joked, and that was why she had let her cook go.

The baronin had re-dressed every window, re-upholstered every chair, purchased new furniture, new plate, new liveries. Only the baron's study was forbidden from alteration.

Elisabeth folded up the plans and returned them.

'You've had to work very hard to pay for so much…'—she wanted to say, 'so much *extravagance*', but that would sound like criticism— 'for so many improvements, Papa. I hope this is the last, so you can rest more.'

He brushed her concerns aside with a wave of his fingers. She moved to the window and looked out at the gardens beyond. They were looking very tidy. Another improvement of the baronin's.

'Papa, must I go to the count's schloss tomorrow?'

There was a silence. She turned around. Papa looked thoughtful.

'He is a great man, Elisabeth. A man of influence. The invitation is an honour. Your stepmother has talked of nothing else since.'

'But I don't like him.'

'Why not?'

She put her clenched fists together, searching for the words to describe how uncomfortable and exposed she felt when the count's eyes were running up and down her, as though she were a horse he was thinking of purchasing. How could she say this without sounding foolish or vulgar?

'Everyone knows he is a harsh man.'

'Everyone? Who is everyone?'

'The servants. They say he was cruel to his wife. They say he *killed* her.'

Papa shook his head. 'Don't listen to servants' talk. His wife died of illness, and if he runs his house with a firm hand, that is how these great men often are, particularly military men. Look at me—I am so slack in running my house that the servants have everything their own way, running up what trade bills they like. If it were not for your stepmother taking over the household, we should be poorer than our potboy by now.'

He was trying to elicit a smile from her, but she did not feel like smiling. She had pinned her hopes on him disentangling her from the unwanted attentions of the count.

'Also…' she said slowly. 'He knows.'

'Knows?'

'About…my understanding. With horses. Or some of it.'

A frown rumpled her father's forehead. 'He cannot know much. Doubtless your stepmother alluded to it in some manner, but she would not have disclosed it openly. You will visit for an afternoon, and then come home again. You won't be left alone with him. And if the count should speak of you, I will tell him you are too young to be thought of. You won't have to go a second time.'

'I don't see why I should go at all, then.' But her fists relaxed a little.

'Do it to keep your mama happy.'

Her fists clenched again, and she glowered. She hated it when he called her *mama*.

Papa sighed. He knew her thoughts. 'Please, Elisabeth. I have enough to worry about at present without having to negotiate another conflict between you and my wife.'

'I knew something was wrong!' Her anger melted at Papa's admission of worry.

'It is only temporary business matters.' Papa sank against the back of his chair.

'All right. I'll go if it makes you happy,' she said.

'Thank you. Now leave me. I have a mountain of work. I shall be away next week on business and there's a lot to prepare.'

'Going away again? You get so tired on long journeys.'

'It's just a week or two. I would not go if it were not essential.' He rested a hand upon the pile of documents with the red ink. 'I shall return with a new shipment of goods; a very profitable consignment. Someone must pay for all the new gowns your stepmother has ordered for you.' He was trying to make her smile again.

'I'd sooner never have a new gown again. Why must I have six of them suddenly?'

'Because you are come of age, child.' He sighed. 'So I am told. But your stepmother knows best about these things. Now go. I am very busy.'

'May I see Alexis today? Nurse wouldn't let me yesterday.'

'I believe he is much better this morning. He will rest till noon, then you may see him. Go now.'

She left to prepare for her morning ride.

As she was returning home, she passed a man tramping

up the hill with a large leather sack. He doffed his cap as her horse walked past.

'Excuse me, Fräulein,' he called. 'Am I on the right road to the baron's manor?'

'You are,' she called back. 'What business do you have there?'

'Carpentry work.'

'It's at the top of the hill. Not too far.'

'Thank you, Fräulein.'

He has that smell, her horse said, as she rode on, passing a meandering line of more workmen, trudging up the hill with leather bags of tools on their backs.

Who does? she asked soundlessly. *The man who just spoke to me?*

Who else?

What smell?

Pumpernickel gave a blurry reply, but Elisabeth knew him well enough to understand.

We call it a gifting. Like my brother has for knowing things, and I have for talking to you. I wonder what his gift is. What smell is it?

It smells of... Pumpernickel did not know the word, but a series of images came into her mind as he tried to describe it: birch trees with silvery bark and whispering leaves; bouncing cones as they dropped to the ground; the smell of pine and new-cut wood; beads of sap, like an amber necklace resting on a trunk.

His gifting must be something to do with wood, she concluded.

A cart rumbled ahead of them bearing lengths of wood. So, the work on the new dining room was beginning. And Papa must go away to pay for it.

She felt a flare of resentment at the baronin for this. Why couldn't she leave things alone? She felt another surge of anger at Papa. Why had he married her? All that talk of Alexis and her being at a disadvantage without a mother—they could have managed just fine as they were.

She recalled how elegant and gracious the baronin had appeared when first Papa had brought her to meet his children. She had not been a baronin then, she had been Frau Richter, childless widow of a business associate of Papa's. There was no denying that Frau Richter had been a charming woman. That was why he had married her, she concluded; he had been charmed. How ridiculous to fall for someone based on appearance and glamour; she would not do the same.

She asked Pumpernickel to quicken his pace and overtake the rumbling cart. The baronin had warned her not to be late back, there was a final fitting for one of her new gowns, and she was determined to see Alexis before the seamstress arrived. No doubt the wretched gown was for the visit to the count tomorrow. Well, she'd make the visit, for Papa's sake, but then she would refuse to see the man ever again.

CHAPTER 3
SCHLOSS DRAGENBERG

THE BARONIN WAS in a good humour at dinner that evening.

'Brunn will dress you in the morning,' she told Elisabeth. 'You will wear the new light green moiré—no, the rose taffeta. And I will lend you my pearls.'

'But the new pink one has hoops.'

'Of course it has hoops.'

'But we shall be in the carriage for hours, then walking around the count's grounds. Hoops will be a nuisance.'

'Don't be ridiculous, child. All the ladies are wearing hoops in the city now. Do you want to look like a mountain cottager? You will look like the daughter of a baron. You will look like the future wife of a count.'

Elisabeth glared at her. 'But I am not the future wife of a count.'

The baronin's eyebrows arched higher. 'If you shame your family by behaving like a recalcitrant child, Elisabeth, I will —' She stopped and recovered her even tone. 'I will be most disappointed. As will your father.'

'Whatever I do will not disappoint my father,' she said stoutly.

The eyebrows arched again. 'Vexing me will disappoint him greatly. Is that not so, Gilbert?'

Papa looked between them and threw up his hands.

'Why will Brunn dress me in the morning?' Elisabeth asked. 'Why not Ziller?'

'Ziller made an appalling mess of your hair the other evening. She will go to the laundry room.'

'She shall not!' Elisabeth's knife and fork clattered onto her plate, making everyone, including the footman opposite, jump. 'It was not her fault that my hair was bad!'

'Do not raise your voice, Elisabeth,' said the baronin. 'Brunn has been most kind in agreeing to take over Ziller's failed duties.'

'Papa!' she implored. But her father shook his head to say he would not interfere in his wife's domestic arrangements. He never did.

'I'm not hungry,' said Elisabeth, her face tight with anger. 'If I may be excused.'

She did not go straight to her room, however. First, she peeped in at her brother's bedroom. Ten-year-old Alexis lay on his side, watching the flame on his bedside lamp. His languid eyes brightened when he saw her.

'Elsa, I wondered when you'd come.'

'Nurse wouldn't let me in earlier. She said you needed rest.' She sat down on the bed.

'She's in the kitchen having her supper.'

'Good, she'll be gossiping with Cook for at least half an hour then. Shall I talk to you or read?'

'Read! I want to know what happens after Telmarund tries to kill Lohengrin.'

'As if you hadn't heard it forty times before.' She got up to fetch the well-worn book.

Alexis struggled to sit up against his pillows.

'Lie back down, little brother, or I'll be in trouble for getting you all excited.'

She had just reached the part when Lohengrin's magic swan turned into Gottfried, whom all had thought murdered—and the witch had burst in to see her wicked enchantment undone—when Nurse returned and shooed her away.

'Please, Nurse,' begged Alexis, 'just to the end of the story.'

'My lady can read it when you're stronger. Look at you, your eyes all wild, you'll be burning up like a pig on a spit, and mistress will have my hide for garters for calling out the doctor again.'

'See you tomorrow, Alexi,' Elisabeth said over her shoulder as Nurse bundled her out.

THERE WAS THE SOUND OF BANGING AND SCRAPING AND unfamiliar voices next morning. Elisabeth peered into the dining room. A workman was taking measurements and calling out numbers while others carried out furniture. Through the open windows came the sound of sawing and chatter and the deep baritone of a man singing a folksong.

'Breakfast is in the drawing room, my lady,' advised Griffin, the head footman. She stepped back to let him pass into the room with his heavy-laden tray. A small cheer sounded from the workmen at the sight of the jugs of small beer and platters of bread and meat. She went to find her own breakfast.

The baronin scrutinised her as she approached the table.

'Stand still, Elisabeth,' she ordered. 'Now turn around.'

Elisabeth caught Papa's eye as she turned. He gave a wink of solidarity, but she was still angry from the previous evening, and looked away.

'Very good,' pronounced the baronin. 'You look exactly as you should. Brunn has done well with your hair.'

Elisabeth stifled the urge to run her hands through the carefully piled up ringlets and ruin them. It had been an uncomfortable night with her head tightly bound up in rags. Perching on the edge of her chair was also uncomfortable; the hoops made sitting difficult. And Ziller never tied her corset so tight.

'So the work has begun on the dining room,' Elisabeth said dryly as she placed a napkin across her lap. The lace cuffs on her gown trailed irritatingly over everything as she reached for the butter dish.

'Let the servants wait upon you, Elisabeth,' said the baronin. 'Do not stretch across the table.' Anselm, the footman in attendance, stepped forward to move the butter dish closer to Elisabeth's hand.

'The work has indeed begun,' said the baron. 'There shall be no peace for me in my study now.'

'Fortunately, you will leave within the week,' the baronin reminded him. 'And shall avoid all the fuss and noise. By the time you come back it will be completed, and we shall enjoy our first dinner there. I have begun drawing up the guest list.'

'How long will the work take?' Elisabeth asked her father.

'The foreman thinks a month.'

'A month! Will you be gone so long, Papa? You said a week or two.'

Her father raised a palm as though to express that he had no hold over circumstances. 'I must travel farther than I thought. Now don't look like that, Elsa. I would not be going if it were not necessary.'

'There are a lot of things I don't see as necessary,' she retorted. 'Such as a new dining room.'

'Of course it is necessary,' said the baronin evenly. 'We cannot take our proper place in society without the space to entertain. An excellent table and wine cellar are essential for establishing and maintaining connections.'

'But we don't have a wine cellar,' Elisabeth replied, thinking of the wine pantry which the butler kept the key to.

'We soon shall. Eat quickly, we must be on our way. It is a long journey to Dragenberg.'

· · ·

SCHLOSS DRAGENBERG WAS VERY IMPRESSIVE, THAT MUCH Elisabeth could not deny, as its towers were first glimpsed, emerging out of a forest of pines. The carriage climbed the mountain road, through the villages, past the scattered hamlets and farms, every turn in the road revealing another glimpse of the count's home. She craned her neck at the carriage window to better view the red brick towers, topped with conical, grey roofs.

'This is merely his country estate,' the baronin said. 'He also has a magnificent manor house in München. But this is where he keeps his famous horses.'

The entrance to the schloss was imposing and dark. A pair of stone dragons guarded the gateway, curling round the gateposts and baring their fangs at those who entered. The driveway was flanked by massive yew trees, casting a gloomy aspect. But the yews in the gardens beyond were well cultivated, shaped into orderly walls and neat topiary.

'Magnificent gardens,' said the baronin. 'I imagine they are delightful in the summer, do you agree?'

'Very stiff,' Elisabeth said.

'Stiff? What do you mean, child?'

'I mean everything is shaped so rigidly. It's all so formal. So stiff.'

'Keep all demeaning adjectives to yourself, Elisabeth. A guest only ever compliments her host's home and grounds.' She arched her eyebrows. 'Sit back, we are almost there.'

The count stood at the top of the steps of his home, cigar between his teeth, awaiting their arrival.

'Such an elegant figure,' said the baronin, as the carriage came to a halt. 'Such upright bearing. One can tell he was a military man.'

Elisabeth did not reply; the door had been opened, and she was busy trying to negotiate the task of alighting from the carriage. She was experiencing some difficulty, for the carriage door was too narrow for her hoops to squeeze through easily.

'Keep your skirts still, they are swinging unbecomingly.'

'Welcome,' called the count. 'I trust your journey was not too tedious?' He kissed the baronin's hand, and Elisabeth obediently put out her own. She thought he lingered over it longer than necessary.

'Such a beautiful house, my lord,' said the baronin. 'We are honoured to be here.' She tilted her head towards her stepdaughter to prompt her to speak.

Elisabeth had decided she would be merely demure and polite that day. She had no intention of being interesting or entertaining.

'Honoured,' she murmured.

The count bowed in reply and ushered them inside for refreshment.

Ornate panelling and gothic carvings lined the walls inside. Heavy red drapes shrouded the windows.

'Magnificent,' breathed the baronin. 'What exquisite woodwork. It is just the style I hope to achieve in our little dining room. None of that petit-bourgeoise Biedermeier for me, I much prefer the traditional style. So aristocratic.' She inclined her head towards Elisabeth.

'Magnificent,' she mumbled.

'So glad you like it,' said the count. 'Come into the gallery for tea.'

The baronin expressed her admiration at everything, and Elisabeth echoed her when prompted, never saying more than one word if she could help it. They sipped tea and nibbled kipferl.

'Would you care to look around the grounds before we dine for luncheon?' offered the count.

'That would be delightful,' answered the baronin. 'Would it not, Elisabeth?'

'Delightful,' she said into her teacup.

'But if you do not object, my lord,' said the baronin, 'I confess the journey has induced some fatigue. Would you excuse me if I sat here quietly before luncheon? Elisabeth, however, would love to walk in the grounds.'

'Oh, but I would not dream of leaving you alone,' Elisabeth said quickly. 'I am quite content to sit here also.'

'Don't be ridiculous, you darling child.' The baronin gave a tinkling laugh. 'I won't hear of it. Off you go.'

They exchanged sharp looks, and Elisabeth put down her cup a little harder than required.

'Do not hurry on my account, my lord,' said the baronin. 'Show Elisabeth everything. She has been so looking forward to it.'

'THE GARDENS ARE A LITTLE BARE AT THIS TIME OF THE YEAR,' the count said, as he and Elisabeth stepped outside. He paused to light a fresh cigar. A wreathe of smoke curled about her before they walked on. 'You will like them in the summer. Today I will show you what I know will interest you most.'

Elisabeth did not enquire as to his meaning; she did not want to engage in conversation.

He led her to the stretch of stables, with tree-lined meadows behind, and courtyards to the front. Everything was immaculate and well ordered; the count certainly took good care of his horses.

'Here he is.' The count stood before a stall, pointing with the end of his glowing cigar. 'Bring him out,' he ordered a groom. 'I want my guest to see him properly.'

The groom scrambled to do as he was bid, and Elisabeth watched as a young horse was led out of his stall and paraded before her.

'What do you think?' asked the count. His eyes gleamed as he watched the sleek horse walk by. 'Seventeen hands already. Next year he will race at Hamburg, won't you my beauty?'

The count moved to the horse to run a hand down his side

as he walked past. The horse tightened his jaw and lip and threw his head back.

Elisabeth was somewhat surprised at the change in the count's voice and expression. He seemed to really love his horse. Or did he? Was the shining look in his eyes admiration or just avarice? She did not know how the count really felt about his horse, but she knew how the horse felt about the count. 'He does not like me,' said the count, as though hearing her thoughts. 'He does not like anyone much. Why is that?'

'Why do you ask me?' Elisabeth replied. The horse was led round the courtyard, his flattened ears and grumblings evidence of his displeasure. Twice the groom had to duck out of reach to avoid being nipped.

'Your mother tells me you have a remarkable affinity with creatures.'

'Stepmother,' she corrected.

'His name is Comet. He was born at midnight, while a comet fell from the sky. So it is said. An appropriate name, don't you think? Seeing as he is the star of my stables. Kings and emperors will beg for his stud services once he has proved himself at the courses. His lineage is impeccable. But he must be more compliant or he will never fulfil his purpose. And I have a great reluctance to break him. I want to harness that spirit of his.' His eyes gleamed as bright as the end of his cigar as he spoke.

The count beckoned the groom to bring Comet near. Elisabeth could not resist moving close to lay a hand on the colt's neck. He was so beautiful, and horses were her favourite animals.

'Take care, my lady,' said the groom. 'He's prone to biting.' But to the groom's surprise Comet only snorted softly at her.

'If our usual methods of training continue to fail, I suppose we will have to resort to more forceful ones,' said the count languidly.

Elisabeth looked sharply at him. 'What do you mean?'

The count narrowed his eyes in return. 'Sticks. Whips. The usual tools.'

Elisabeth felt her stomach lurch; the thought of violence being used on such an animal, any animal, made her sick.

'Sometimes one has to break the spirit. For the good, of course. If there were any other way…'

'What's wrong?' she murmured to Comet, turning her back to the count as she scratched the horse's chin. Comet exhaled from his nose, then nuzzled into her hand.

'Remarkable,' breathed the count. The groom's mouth dropped open.

'He doesn't like being stabled for long periods,' Elisabeth said after some minutes. 'He wants to be out in the grass. And he wants more of the green stuff in his feed. I think he means alfalfa. And…' she hesitated.

'And what?' said the count.

'And…he thinks you smell like mould. That's why he doesn't like you.'

The groom gave a snort of laughter before stifling his mirth; Comet snorted too. Elisabeth took a sly glance at the count to relish his displeasure, but was chilled to the quick by the look on his face. Such a cruel look. But it passed as quickly as it came, and the count's voice was smooth as he said, 'Tell him he can have more time in the meadow and more alfalfa if he ceases his bucking and biting when he is saddled.'

Elisabeth turned back to the horse, stroking his face as she wordlessly communicated pictures to him, as she had always done with her father's horses, for as long as she could remember.

'Well?' demanded the count.

'The saddle irritates his skin. Try putting a softer blanket underneath it, and don't saddle him until he's worked off some energy first. And he prefers apples to carrots.'

'Rather cavalier, isn't he?' the count drawled, but he looked gratified. Elisabeth grew cold again at his look, for it was no longer on the horse, but resting on her as he took a long draw on his cigar.

'Take him to the meadow,' the count instructed the groom. 'Come, my lady. You have been most helpful.' He held out his arm, but she would not move close enough to take it; he was still regarding at her in that hungry manner.

'Of course,' said the count, 'I never use sticks or whips on my horses. Only for people.' He smiled, showing his yellow teeth. She was not certain if he were joking. 'You are wasted on your father's little brood of mares. You should be riding and working with the best horses in the kingdom. What breeder and trainer has such a gift as you? It is remarkable. It is priceless.'

Elisabeth felt a sinking feeling in her stomach. What had she done? She should never have demonstrated her ability before him.

CHAPTER 4
DREAMS

'Did you have a good day, my lady?' Ziller enquired when Elisabeth returned home and reached her room.

'No.'

Ziller looked up from folding laundered undergarments, laying them neatly in the chest of drawers.

'Help me off with this dreadful gown!' Elisabeth said, straining to reach the buttons at the back.

'Dreadful? Why, it's a gown fit for the queen.' Ziller unfastened the tiny silk-covered buttons that ran down the back of the bodice.

'All day it's been pinching me and making me feel like I can't breathe properly.'

'That's the corset. Not the fault of the dress.'

'And these wretched hoops.' She could hear the peevishness in her own voice. Perhaps it was not really the dress that was bothering her so much as the feelings she had been straining against all day.

She stepped out of her crinoline and flung herself backwards on her bed in her chemise, stretching like a cat.

She rolled onto her front and watched Ziller at work, hanging up the discarded gown and tidying away the accoutrements.

'I'm really sorry, Ziller,' she said.

'Sorry?'

'About you being sent to the laundry.'

Ziller shrugged. 'Can't be helped. Was my own fault. I didn't do my job properly.'

'It was my fault you didn't have time to dress my hair that night.' She propped her chin on her elbows. 'I will speak to Papa about it.'

Ziller looked up from rolling up the silk stockings that had been discarded on the floor. 'Thank you,' she said in a voice so full of relief that Elisabeth felt a fresh pang of remorse.

'Besides,' Elisabeth added, 'Brunn is a sour old bat.'

Ziller gave a rueful smile. 'But did you have a good day? Despite the dress.'

'No!' She rolled over again, looking up at the bed canopy. 'I spent a whole two hours alone with the count, being shown around his gardens and stables.'

'But you're fond of horses and of being outside.'

'Not when it's *his* horses and gardens. Oh, it was all very fine. Very grand. And his horses are beautiful.' She thought of the sleek thoroughbreds and the well-kept stables. She thought of Comet. But then she recalled the movements of fear the horses showed when the count approached them. The way they flattened their ears at him and backed away with their tails clamped down. Every servant they had passed acted in a similar fashion. Even the friendly stable dog that had come to meet her with a thumping tail had slunk away as soon as the count appeared.

She roused herself from unpleasant thoughts and sat on the end of her bed.

'Give me my blue muslin, Ziller. I need something comfortable.'

'It's not here,' Ziller said, after rummaging through her wardrobe.

'It must be.'

Ziller looked again. There was a rap at the door, and

before Elisabeth could respond, the door opened and Brunn appeared.

'Excuse me, m'lady,' she said in her blunt voice. 'Mistress sent me to see if you need any assistance after your journey.'

'No thank you, Brunn. Ziller is assisting me.'

'Ziller is wanted in the laundry.'

'Ziller has been doing her duty in putting away my clean laundry,' Elisabeth said, standing up and trying to look like a mistress with authority, but feeling at a disadvantage in her bare feet and chemise. 'And now she is engaged in finding my blue muslin.'

'It's not the place of a laundry maid to be dressing her mistress. I will see to such matters from now on.'

Ziller dropped a curtsey and scurried out of the room. Brunn moved to the open wardrobe and pulled out a gown. 'The blue muslin is gone, m'lady, along with the other outmoded gowns.'

'Gone? Who has had the audacity to go through my wardrobe without my consent?'

'I removed them this morning. Orders of the mistress. Now that you are a young lady all inappropriate clothing has been replaced with suitable gowns. May I suggest the peach satin, m'lady? Very proper for this evening's quiet family dinner.'

Elisabeth glared in reply. The blue muslin was her favourite, slightly loose fitting, and admittedly, a little outgrown in length, but so comfortable. She almost snatched the gown from Brunn,

'I'll lace up your corset for you,' Brunn said, picking it back up from the chair.

Elisabeth slipped into Alexis' room once she had escaped the ministrations of Brunn. He was sat on the window seat with his legs stretched out, and a blanket across his knees.

'You're out of bed,' she said with pleasure. 'You must be feeling better?'

He nodded. But he still looked pale with dark shadows under his eyes. She could not remember a time when he had not looked pale and hollow-eyed. He had never enjoyed good health.

She sat at the other end of the seat, picked up his slippered feet and put them on her lap.

'I wondered when you'd come,' he said. 'Tell me all about it. Was the count's house a gloomy old castle with a big dungeon?'

'There was no dungeon. Or, not one that I saw. It's a very grand schloss. It is rather gloomy. His horses are very nice.'

'Did you see him beating his servants? Did he carry a stick with him?'

'He wouldn't very well beat them in front of guests, would he?'

'You should have followed him when he wasn't looking, or crept up into the attic rooms, like in Bluebeard.'

'With our stepmother watching my every move?'

They pulled a face at one another.

'You can't marry him.'

'Marry him! Who said anything about marrying him?'

'Nurse and Brunn were talking about it when they thought I was asleep.'

'They have no business discussing me. What were they saying?'

'That The Step wants to marry you to the old count, because he's rich and has lots of high-up friends.'

'She can want all she likes, but Papa won't make me marry him. I doubt I shall marry at all.'

'But Mama said you would.'

'Seems to me that when girls marry, they don't get to do anything much except keep house and do what their husband wants. I'd like to climb mountains, and swim in lakes, and ride as far as I can, without a groom reminding me it was time to turn back for dinner.'

'But you'll marry a rich prince and won't have to do anything you didn't want to,' said Alexis. 'But I'm glad you won't get married yet. If you did, you'd have to go away.'

'Exactly.'

'Papa says he's going away again.'

'I know. Business trip. Hopefully the last one for a long while.'

Alexis' voice dropped to a subdued tone. 'I had a dream about you and Papa going away. You were on a boat, being pulled by a giant swan. I was shouting at you to come back, but you left me behind, standing on the bank.'

'You've been reading too much Lohengrin. Papa will be back as soon as he can, and I am going nowhere.'

'It was such a real dream, Elsa. You were all soaking wet, and your hair was all down and blowing around everywhere.'

'What a picture!' She laughed. 'Was the Swan Knight in the boat too?'

'I don't know. There were other people, but it was misty. I couldn't see them.'

'It was just a dream.'

'It was so real.'

'It was just a dream.' She pulled off a slipper and tickled his foot until he laughed himself out of his grave mood.

'Have you heard all the banging and racket the workmen are making?' she asked, wanting to change the subject.

Alexis nodded. 'Wish I could watch them. Papa says they will knock down a wall and then build it again down the garden.'

'That's right. And they'll make fancy carvings to go around the walls. There's that much wood stacked up in the stable block it's a wonder there's any forest left. I'll take you down tomorrow to have a look if Nurse lets me.'

'Please!'

'Well, eat all your supper and show Nurse you're feeling better.'

Alexis nodded.

'Tell you what, I'll speak to Papa now about it. If he says you can leave your room tomorrow, then Nurse can't keep you.'

Alexis nodded again. 'Then come back and read to me before bed.'

'I won't be reading Lohengrin tonight. Not if it gives you bad dreams.'

She moved his feet aside and stood up. 'Perhaps a bit of *Wholesome Tales for Little Boys*,' she said, lifting the unread book from the bookcase.

Alexis rolled his eyes.

The door to the baron's study was ajar; Elisabeth was about to rap upon it and push it open when the sound of voices arrested her.

It was the baronin's voice. What was she doing in Papa's study?

'She will never get a better offer, Gilbert. Never. He is even wealthier than I first understood. He has an estate near Berlin and a mansion in München, not to mention numerous lodges. He has shares in all the new industries—the railways, this new electricity that everyone is talking of, as well as overseas investments. There is talk of him being offered a senior position in the government later this year, possibly that of Cabinet Secretary, if old Pfiffermeister finally retires, as he ought. He has an income of more than a quarter of a million gulden, Gilbert, think of it!'

'Very impressive,' murmured Papa's voice. 'But, Sabine, money is not the only consideration in a marriage. I would not see Elisabeth married without affection.'

'You must be practical, Gilbert. Think of the connections

such a marriage would make. I have worked hard these past years to raise the standing of this family.'

'Sabine, my dear,' Papa sounded weary, 'I value all you have done, and I appreciate that you take the welfare of my children seriously and would see Elisabeth well married, but I tell you again that I will not force her into a marriage without affection. I will not.'

'Then you're a fool!'

The hostility in the baronin's voice startled Elisabeth. She had never heard her speak in such a tone to her father.

'We are on the brink of ruin, thanks to your misguided investments, and a lifeline comes along—a man of wealth and excellent standing, who will help us, invest money for us that we might get back on our feet and take our rightful place in society, and you talk of affection?'

'Why would he help us? Why is he so interested in Elisabeth? He must know she has very little dowry.'

'He does not need to marry for money. He would help us as part of the marriage agreement.'

'Is that what he said?'

'In so many words. He is not likely to speak candidly of it to me, is he? That is for you to discuss. But he has made it very clear that he will do all he can for her family once we are related.'

'Such a man always marries for advantage. We are far beneath his notice.'

'Exactly! That is why this chance cannot be lost.'

'It makes no sense...she is very pretty, but, no great beauty, except in my eyes...'

'If you must know, I believe it has to do with his horses.'

'Horses?'

'He values his horses above all other interests. He is famed throughout the continent for his horses.'

'Even so...it makes no sense. Elisabeth is an excellent horsewoman, to be sure...'

'It's not because she is an excellent horsewoman, it's because of the way she can…you know…'

'Communicate with them. You told him.'

The baronin did not reply.

'We agreed not to speak of it beyond our family, Sabine.'

'Oh, what does it signify? Honestly, Gilbert, what is the point of such a useless skill unless it attracts such a man as the count?'

'You told him of Elsa's ability because you thought it would draw him in. I wondered why such a man would condescend to dine here.'

'I did well in drawing him here. You should thank me, not sit there with that insipid look on your face.'

'We agreed never to talk of it. It could cast a slur on her as being something unnatural. She could be castigated by society.'

'Gilbert, when one reaches the heights of society that the count moves in, one is far above such superstitious nonsense. The further one gets to peasantry the stronger the ignorance, but in the circles that the count moves in, no one cares about such things.'

'I care what people think of her. And even if it is her ability that the count wants, he does not need to marry her for it. He could simply invite her for her counsel. It is not as though such a man can be refused.'

'And have his horse-breeding rivals hear of her and pull rank in making use of her? Sometimes I wonder if you have any faculties of reason left, Gilbert. Too many hours spent poring over accounts have addled your brain.'

'Insult me all you like, Sabine, I understand your disappointment with me, but if Elisabeth dislikes that man then there will be no marriage, and that is the end of the matter.'

'That daughter of yours is as much a fool as you are! She does not know what is good for her. You have indulged her every whim and—'

'Now that is enough! Elisabeth is a good girl. She has always minded you, and I have always encouraged her to.'

'No, she has outwardly minded me, but inwardly she despises me. Both your children do. I'm not a fool, I can see it in their spoilt little faces–'

'I won't hear this. I won't hear my children abused. This trip will put our finances back on an even keel. We shall recover. I have let you have your way in everything, Sabine. You've had a free hand and an open purse for all you desired to do. I've worked hard to pay for the expense of it all, but whether I am a rich man or a poor one, I will not force my only daughter into a marriage she does not want. I promised her mother that very thing, I made her a solemn vow. Now oblige me by leaving me in peace. There is nothing further to discuss on this matter, and if there were, I should refuse to discuss it in this room.'

Elisabeth heard the baronin's heels clicking on the floor, so she turned and fled back upstairs.

CHAPTER 5
THE WOODCARVER

'FRÄULEIN OPEL, can you tell us your relationship to the young baroness you speak of? The committee cannot yet see any connection to this investigation. Thus far you have stated that she was introduced to a Bayern count, whose name you will not supply. What is the connection with this young woman to the whereabouts of the king?'

'Both the baroness and the count become involved with the king's affairs. Their actions had great significance with regard to him.'

'And what is your relationship to her? Why do you hesitate?'

'I hesitate because I cannot tell you everything at once. I know of her story because I knew her very well. If you will allow me to continue, I will explain all.'

FOR MOST OF THE NIGHT ELISABETH TOSSED AND TURNED, WITH her stepmother's words replaying in her mind and seeping into her dreams.

Early next morning she dressed herself and went first to the kitchen, and then to her father's study. He was already at work, as she knew he would be. His expression when she opened the door smote her; she hadn't seen him look so unhappy since her mother had died.

He managed half a smile, however, and she padded across the room to his desk to put his coffee down, then put her arms about him and clung tightly.

'What's all this?' he murmured, patting her hands at his neck.

'I just wanted to give you a hug, Papa. You look tired this morning.'

'I've been up a long while going over accounts.'

She withdrew her arms. 'I wish you'd let me do more of your accounts and letters. I could do more than just general things, Papa.'

'I'm sure you could. But sitting at a desk is no life for a young lady. Especially a young lady who likes to be out riding half the day.'

'I'd like something more to do. The days seem so long sometimes. If you won't let me help you, then let me take care of Alexis. He's out of danger. For now. Please tell Nurse that I may take him out for some fresh air each day, it would do him good. We will only go in the grounds, I can push him in the bath chair.'

'I'll have a word with Nurse,' her father promised. His seat creaked as he sat back and sipped his coffee.

'Also, Papa…please say I can have Ziller back. She has done nothing wrong.'

Papa shook his head over his cup. 'I will not interfere with the household matters. It would cause all manner of resentment. If there is one thing I need at present, Elsa, it is harmony in my home.'

He looked so sorrowful as he said this that she could not argue. She said nothing more for the time being but moved around the room, looking and touching all the familiar objects. She ruffled the dried orange peel in the big china bowl to release its fragrance. She bent over the old sofa and kissed Magni's big, furry head. He thumped his tail against the cushions. She moved past the shelves of books. There was a gap in the shelf where the beautifully illustrated copy of *Lohengrin* once sat. Alexis had commandeered it long ago.

She paused in front of the cabinet where the family documents were kept. The large, brass key was in the lock.

'I've been going through my papers,' her father said, seeing her touch the key. 'Ensuring all is in order before I leave.'

Those words alarmed her. People put things in order before they went away in case they didn't come back again. But she forced the thought away. It was too horrible.

There came a rap at the study door, it opened, and the baronin's face appeared.

'Ah, you are here, Elisabeth. I thought you might be. Brunn said you were not in your room when she went to dress you.'

The baronin's eyes slid around the room, from her husband to Elisabeth, as though she were gauging what had passed between them. All the harsh words of the night before sprang fresh into Elisabeth's mind, and she could not bring herself to meet her stepmother's eyes as they settled on her.

'You have no corset,' her stepmother said flatly. 'Get dressed properly before you come down to breakfast.' And she closed the door again behind her.

'Best do as she says, Elsa,' said Papa, pushing his empty cup away. 'I have much work to do.'

ELISABETH ANNOUNCED TO NURSE THAT HER FATHER HAD GIVEN permission for her to take Alexis for a walk. The weather was dry, the bath chair was at the door, and she would brook no resistance.

Nurse grumbled about pneumonia and pleurisy setting in for sure, but assisted with bundling Alexis beneath a mound of blankets. Elisabeth took charge of the chair and set off.

'We'll go around the shrubbery to the back of the house,

and then I'll show you where the workmen are,' she told her brother. 'One of them has set up a workshop next to the stables, and I want you to see what he's doing.'

She guessed correctly that Alexis would like to see the work of the carpenter, who sat at a bench with a long length of cherry wood before him; onto the wood he was chiselling out the most exquisite designs of flower garlands and cherubim. He looked up at the sound of the bath chair wheels, whistling and squeaking as they rolled over the paved path.

'May we watch?' Elisabeth asked. 'We won't distract you with talking.'

'Talk all you please,' the woodcarver replied, beckoning them to come and sit near him. 'Been talking to the horse in the stall yonder, but she don't talk back.'

Alexis laughed. 'She does to Elsa. May I touch them?' he asked, stretching a pale, thin hand towards the carved shapes.

'They're beautiful,' Elisabeth said. 'Where did you learn to carve?'

'Carpenter's apprentice for seven years,' said the man. 'Showed a liking for the fancy work, so studied under a master for another five years. Been working out on my own since.'

'You must have started your apprenticeship very young,' Elisabeth said, gauging that the man was not much more than twenty-five.

'Twelve. Worked on a farm to get money for an indenture. Went to München, asked at every carpenter's workshop in the city till one took me on.'

'Where did you live before you went to München?' she asked.

'Little mountain village. Füssen. Close to Swanstein.'

'Where the castle is?' said Alexis.

The woodcarver nodded.

'You travelled all the way from Füssen to München on your own at the age of twelve?' Elisabeth marvelled.

'And you worked every day when you were a boy?' asked Alexis.

'Been working since I can remember. Sister worked at a farm since she was six.'

They sat with the woodcarver until another workman called that it was time to eat. It had been pleasant sitting with him, listening to him talk in his mountain-region accent. Elisabeth had not realised it was noon already.

'May we come again tomorrow?' Alexis begged.

'Wish you would.'

'What's your name?' Alexis asked, as he was wheeled away.

'Hans,' called back the man. 'Friends call me Hansi.'

'See you tomorrow, Hansi.' Alexis waved. 'I like him. He's clever. Do you think he'd let me try at carving?'

'Perhaps. Though we mustn't keep him from his work.'

Hansi did not mind at all showing the siblings how to carve using the little chisels he kept rolled up in a leather wallet. Wood carving was more difficult than it looked. But those hours passed pleasantly with the three of them sat around the stove, feeding it the wood shavings that fell around their feet.

Hansi liked to talk as he worked. He answered questions about his home in the mountains. He and his sister had been born in München. Their father had been a carpenter with a little shop, but he'd only made simple furniture, and they'd lived in the poorer part of the city. They lost both parents to the typhus that had swept through the neighbourhood. Two hundred people died, and the king ordered work carried out to improve the drains and sewerage. But the improvements had come too late for them. Their only living relative was their father's sister, Tante Trudy, a midwife and herb woman, and a very skilled one, Hansi said. If she lived in the city, she could make a good living, but she hated the noise of the town, so she lived in a tiny cottage in the mountains.

'Imagine living so near to Swanstein Castle,' Elisabeth said dreamily. 'I'd like to see it. Have you ever seen the king and queen, or the crown prince?'

'Seen the queen and prince many times in my youth. They were fond of riding and hiking.'

'What were they like?' she asked.

'Queen's a tiny lady. Marched up the mountain faster than any of the young attendants.' Hansi laughed. 'Should see them, red faced and panting, while she flew up, like a mountain goat, ordering them to keep up.'

'And the crown prince?' she asked. 'Is he as tall and handsome as he looks in his pictures?'

'Folk do like to see him.'

'I wish I could see him,' she said. 'Alexis has a book with pictures of Lohengrin. We think the prince looks like the Swan Knight.'

'I'll show you the picture,' said Alexi.

'Show me,' said Hansi, resuming his work, 'and I'll tell you.'

THE BARON LEFT WHILE IT WAS STILL DARK.

'You should be in bed,' he said when Elisabeth appeared in the entrance hall. The carriage was at the door, and Gerling was strapping the baron's boxes to the roof. 'We said our farewells last night.'

'I wanted to see you off, Papa.'

He opened his arms, and she moved into them, pressing her head against his shoulder, letting him envelop her within his greatcoat. She felt like a little girl again, held in such a way, and could not prevent a childlike tear from rising.

'Now, none of that, Sisi,' chided her father, seeing her tears when he released her. He had not called her Sisi for years.

That had been her mother's name for her. 'You're the strong one, remember? You'll take care of Alexi.'

She nodded.

'I'll be home again in two months at most. What shall I bring you? New silks, like your stepmother, or books, like your brother?'

'Just bring yourself, Papa. That's all I want.' The lump in her throat made her voice sound choked.

'Bless you,' said Papa, kissing the top of her head. 'You're a good girl. Now let me go. The trains won't hold if I'm late.'

She watched the carriage until it was long out of sight.

ALEXIS CARRIED HIS LOHENGRIN BOOK CAREFULLY ON HIS LAP that morning as Elisabeth pushed him through the grounds. They were eager to see if the woodcarver thought the crown prince looked like the heroic Swan Knight.

Hansi examined the pictures, carefully turning the pages with his work-rough fingers.

'Prince is very like him,' was his conclusion. 'Same look about them, like they're from another world. See here,' and he turned the page to where the princess and Lohengrin were saying their anguished farewell. 'Who's that like?'

Alexis and Elisabeth leaned forward to see.

'She looks like you, Elsa,' said Alexis. 'I never saw it before.' Then he sat back in the bath chair looking troubled.

'What's the matter?' she asked.

Alexis pointed at the picture. A boat, pulled by a great white swan, with a golden crown encircling its neck, lay by the waterside. The Swan Knight was stepping into the boat, and the princess was pleading with him not to leave. Her white gown fluttered in a breeze as she moved towards the boat. She was up to her knees in water, and her hair was blowing in a wild mass about her pale face.

'My dream,' said Alexis. 'That's how you looked. Except

you were in the boat, and it was me shouting for you not to go.'

She was feeling heavy-hearted at her father's departure that morning, so Alexis' melancholy images unsettled her more than they ought.

'It was looking at these pictures that caused the dream, Alexis. That's all.' She plucked the book from Hansi and closed it with a snap. 'Let's talk about something cheerful. Hansi, tell us again about your life in the mountains. Tell us about the trolls.' She knew the mention of trolls would rouse Alexis from his brooding, and she was right.

'Did your aunt really see one?' said Alexis eagerly.

Hansi resumed his work. While he carved, he spoke in a low, rhythmic voice.

'Would that be the time Tante Trudy came across a cave in the mountain, as she was coming home?'

'She'd been to a house high up—higher than any house she'd been to before,' said Alexis.

'You know the story, young sir.'

'What did it look like? Tell me again.'

'Were a small thing, size of a child that's found its feet. Maybe a child-troll, hard for Tante Trudy to tell, for it had such a wrinkled face.'

'A brown, wrinkled face, like a sun-dried berry,' added Alexis.

'Hair the colour of mulch, in tufts, all over its body,' said Hansi.

'And no clothes!' said Alexis gleefully. He dropped his voice. 'Was it a boy troll? Did it have—?'

'That will do, Alexis,' Elisabeth said.

'There it sat,' continued Hansi, 'upon a rock. Tante Trudy pulled out her bell and shook it. Trolls hate bells.'

'Who would be scared of a little bell?' said Alexis.

'Some say it sounds as church bells, which they can't abide. Others say it's as the sound of the fair-folk king and queen, driving in their sleigh.'

'And why don't they like the fair-folk king and queen?' asked Alexis. 'Are trolls not fair folk?'

'Trolls are darkling, not fair. The fair and the dark are often at war. The fair always win in the mountain of Swanstein that's why it's a good place to dwell. There's more light than dark. That's what Tante Trudy says, although there have been strange things happening these past years, and life has been hard.'

'What kind of things?' said Alexis.

'Animals taken, sightings of darkling creatures. Poor crops. Food scarce. Even Tante Trudy's found it hard to find herbs. The mountain is not happy. Something is amiss.'

'Darkling creatures?' Alexis's eyes were wide with interest. 'What things?'

'Can't say. Some kind of goblin or troll. They dig holes in the mountainside, like they're looking for something. Wherever a hole appears folk take care to keep away, that's when their animals disappear. One time a goat herder went into a hole in the mountain to see what was there.'

'And what was there?'

Hansi shrugged. 'Can't say. His fellow herder said he didn't back out again, and he wasn't going in after him.'

'How dreadful,' said Elisabeth.

'Did he ever come back?' Alexis said.

'Never.'

'Don't you wish you could see a troll or one of the fair-folk?' asked Alexis. 'I wish I could.'

'Few people do. Tante Trudy has a special feeling for such things, and she sees more than most. Of late folks see more evidence of the darklings than the fair.'

'I wonder why,' said Alexis. 'I wish I could meet her. I bet she can tell lots of stories about things she's seen.'

'Oh, she's full of tales of Faerie.'

'Did you say she was a midwife?' Elisabeth asked. She was whittling away at a small block of wood, trying unsuccessfully to shape it into a bird.

'Best midwife in all Bayern. The queen was at Swanstein to birth the prince so as to have Tante Trudy on hand.'

Elisabeth ceased whittling to stare at Hansi. 'Do you mean that your aunt was at the birth of the prince?'

He nodded.

'You mean your own aunt delivered the crown prince?' She exchanged looks of wonder with Alexis. 'She's a royal midwife, and yet she lives in a tiny cottage in the mountains? Why, she could make a fortune in the towns and cities—all the noblewomen would want her at their births.'

'Don't doubt it,' said Hansi. 'But Tante Trudy can't abide towns and cities. It's not much talked of, her being at the birth. Folk in the city think it a whim of the queen's having a local midwife present. They're known to be fond of the villagers, respectful of their way of life. It's said the prince hates the city, wants to live in the mountains always. City folk think that's a strange fancy of his.'

'Your aunt must talk of it all the time,' Elisabeth said. 'What an honour for her.'

Hansi paused for a moment. 'Never talks of it.'

'Never talks of it?'

Hansi did not answer, and she concluded, with puzzlement, that it was not a subject that he wanted to talk about either.

'Elsa's going to marry a prince one day,' said Alexis. 'Aren't you?'

'Really?' said Hansi. He blew wood dust from his work.

'Yes, really. And live in a castle, and everything, aren't you, Elsa?'

'Who knows? Perhaps it's just a fairy tale.'

'Our mother said it was true.' Alexis looked upset as though she had denied something important.

'Mama always said it was so,' she agreed. She felt embarrassed talking about it in front of Hansi. It was something only spoken of between Alexis and herself. 'Our mother had a kind of gift for knowing things. But I don't know if this was one of them, or just a story.'

'I have the knowing gift too,' Alexi said. 'Just a bit. Elsa's gift is different.'

'We don't usually talk about it,' Elsa said, giving her brother a pointed look.

'It's alright to talk about it to Hansi,' he said.

'How do you know?'

'Because I know things, remember? Tell Hansi what Mama said about you.'

Elisabeth was reluctant, but to please Alexi she repeated the old childhood story. 'Mama liked to say that when she first held me, she knew I would one day live in a castle and marry a prince.'

Hansi paused in his work to make a playful bow. 'Your Highness,' he said.

She laughed. 'It's just a story.'

'You said it was true,' said Alexis. There was reproach in his voice.

'Mama said it was true,' she admitted. 'But Papa doesn't believe it.'

'I believe it,' said Alexis. 'So long as I get to live in your castle.'

'As if I would be happy, even in a castle, without you.'

'And If your fine castle needs carpentry or carving, I'm your man,' added Hansi with another droll bow.

CHAPTER 6
THE KING

ALMOST SIX WEEKS had passed since the baron left. The dining room was nearing completion, but the baronin kept finding new jobs for the workmen: the bricklayers built walls for new storerooms, the carpenters replaced shelves in the pantries; the general labourers widened the carriage road, and the stonemason carved ornamental coronets into the gateposts.

Hansi was now commissioned to carve decorative panels for the drawing room.

'I'm glad Hansi isn't leaving yet,' said Alexis. He and Elisabeth sat together in the hour before his bedtime. 'And he's glad about the extra work. He'll have more money to take home. He's going to build a chicken house and a new room, so his sister can keep hens and have her own bedroom'

'I know,' she said. 'He's a kind brother.' She was on the window seat, watching the small, white moon climb the evening sky. Alexis chattered, but she was only half attending to him. Her thoughts were of her father, and other related matters.

'I would let you have all my money,' said Alexis.

The following pause roused her to look at him. His eyes were too big in his pinched face, making him look younger than his ten years.

'I know you would.'

'But you'll be living in a castle when you marry, remember? With your true love.' He pulled a face. 'So you won't need me to build you a cottage room.' She didn't reply. 'Do you think it's true?' he pressed. He asked her this a lot of late. She wondered why it was so important to him.

She shrugged. 'Who knows? I always believed it when I was younger. Perhaps it's just a fairy tale Mama liked to tell me.'

She turned back to the window. The moon seemed cold and indifferent that night. Usually she thought of it as a friendly light.

'There are lots of fairy tales about ordinary people who become princes and princesses and live in castles and are happy,' said Alexis slowly. 'They've just got to be brave enough to go on an adventure. Even if they're scared. It's only the ones who stay at home who are the ordinary ones.'

'You're right. And as we both have to stay at home, I suppose we will only ever be ordinary.'

She felt a sudden pang as she spoke. The feeling must have shown in her expression, because Alexis asked, 'You don't want an ordinary life, do you?'

She brushed the question off with a little laugh.

'I think what Mama said was true,' said Alexis. 'But I wish you didn't have to go away.'

'I'm not going anywhere, Alexis. I'm staying right here with you. If any adventures come knocking, I'll tell them to go away. I have a brother to take care of. And besides him, I would miss my father. And my horse.'

She got the smile she was trying to elicit.

'I wish I didn't sometimes know things that are going to happen,' he said. His smile faded.

Elisabeth felt a prickle of fear.

'I know you'll have to go away, Elsa. Like in my dream.'

'Enough of that, Alexis. Dreams are not real, they're just

stories we tell ourselves when we're asleep. I'm not going anywhere.' She was trying to convince herself as much as him.

'Something bad is going to happen, Elsa.' Alexis leaned forward, his big eyes wider than ever, his voice low and urgent.

Goosebumps broke out on her arms. It was all she could do to keep from shivering. There was a sudden feeling of foreboding in the room. Then she realised that the foreboding had been there before Alexi spoke.

'I'm scared,' he whispered.

She moved from her side of the window seat to his and put her arms round him. 'Don't be scared, Lexi. Nothing bad is going to happen. I won't let it.'

THE NEXT DAY WAS TUESDAY. SHE REMEMBERED THIS ON WAKING. So why were the church bells tolling so early in the morning when it was not a Sunday?

The bedroom door opened and Ziller's flushed face appeared.

'Ziller,' she murmured. 'What is it? Are you allowed to wait on me this morning?'

Ziller shook her head. Only her face and one arm were showing; the rest of her remained behind the door. 'I'm not supposed to be here.' She glanced behind her. 'I wanted to tell you the news.'

'What news?' She would have scrambled out of her sheets, but it was cold outside of the covers. 'Come in.'

'I can't. Brunn made me promise not to step one foot inside your room. And I've not, have I?' She lifted a foot up to show it was still behind the bedroom door.

'What news? Is it my father?' A moment of panic seized her, and she sat up, although reason told her that the tolling of the church bells could not be related to her father.

Ziller shook her head again. 'It's the king. He's dead—that's what the bells are for!'

And then she fled.

The king was dead. That was news to cause dismay, for the king was not an old man. No one had thought of him dying for many years yet. She dressed quickly, wanting to get downstairs to hear everything.

The kitchen was full of talk. Cook was weeping into her apron, for she loved the royal family, and kept a faded print of them on the top dresser-shelf; the head-housemaid was doing her best to comfort her. The footmen were talking of the crown prince, and what a lucky fellow he was to become king at his age. They imagined what they would do with such wealth and power. The scullery maids were sighing over the crown prince's famous good looks, his tall, athletic figure, his skin like smooth marble, his piercing blue eyes, his lovely, wavy hair. Then the housekeeper came in and ordered the maids back to work, and the butler came in to see what the footmen were about. Everyone dispersed to their duties. Cook wiped her eyes and began making the morning's bread.

Elisabeth could get no real news from the servants; they knew nothing beyond the fact that the king was dead, which they'd heard from the dairyman when he dropped off the milk that morning. She went to seek Hansi in the workroom by the stables; the workmen had lodgings in town, so would be sure to know something more. But Hansi was not yet there; it was too early. She thought of running back to the house and changing into her riding gown and going into town. The baronin would not approve of her leaving without permission, but how often did it happen that one's king died? She would go and learn the news.

THE TOWN FELT DIFFERENT THAT MORNING. EARLY THOUGH IT was, it seemed that everyone was on the streets, talking over the news. Some shops had already hung black drapes in their windows, and people wore black ribbons on their hats, or round their arms.

She walked her horse through Hohenloe Park where she usually met with family acquaintances. Frau von Bülow and her daughter, Margarita, sat in their open carriage talking to a young man on horseback.

'Baroness Elisabeth!' called Margarita, catching sight of her. Elisabeth returned her wave and directed her horse to the side of their carriage.

'What dreadful news,' said Margarita. 'Our poor king! Mama almost met him several times. She is quite distressed, are you not, Mama?'

'Dreadfully distressed,' said Frau von Bülow. She wore black ribbons on her hat and had pinned a miniature of the late king to her cloak. 'Who could have dreamed it? He was so young, so dashing.'

'And now we have a boy for a king,' said the gentleman on horseback. 'What will become of the kingdom?'

'He is hardly a boy,' replied Margarita. 'He is nineteen, and well educated for his position, I am sure.'

'Eighteen,' corrected her mother. 'But I am sure he will do very well, for he is his father's son.'

The gentleman on horseback pulled a face to show that he did not agree, and bid the ladies good morning.

'How did the king die?' Elisabeth asked. 'It is such a shock. We had not heard he was unwell.'

'Oh, but he has been dreadfully unwell,' said Frau von Bülow. 'They hushed it up, but those of us acquainted with his circle knew. Rheumatic fever. Dreadfully painful. So very brave. His doctor urged him to go to a warmer clime, but our poor, dear king, so committed to his people, so diligent in his duty, he left Italy against his doctor's orders, and returned home to sort out this dreadful Schleswig-Holstein business.' She dabbed at her eyes with a large, black-bordered handkerchief. 'So dutiful,' she murmured. 'And of course, it has been so cold this winter. München has been covered in snow until the end of February. He should not have come back until spring, but he felt it was his duty, and now he is dead!'

Margarita patted her mother on the shoulder. 'There, there, Mama.'

'The poor queen,' Elisabeth said. 'And the crown prince. They must be distraught.'

'They say the crown prince was at the opera the night his father died,' said Frau von Bülow accusingly. 'Why was he not at his father's bedside? He was watching *Lohengrin* while his father lay dying.'

'Oh, Mama, the prince must have believed his father was in no danger or he would not have gone,' said Margarita. 'The king's death was most unexpected even to his physicians. We heard he was making a good recovery from his fever, did we not?'

'I see Countess Fugger von Glott's carriage coming into the park,' said Frau von Bülow. 'She has dined at the palace, and once she danced with our beloved king at a ball. She will be glad to commiserate with me.'

Elisabeth bid the two ladies good morning and rode on.

She met other acquaintances as she rode through the park. She learnt from elderly Herr Klein that the crown prince had turned white when a pageboy first addressed him as "Your Majesty" and almost fainted. 'Worrisome business,' declared Herr Klein. 'Here we are, pulled between that grasping Bismarck on one side, and Österreich and Preußen on the other, and we have a boy-king to lead us. We need a leader. A man!'

Young Fräulein Paulina Voelk had heard that the crown prince had been wonderfully dignified on learning he was now king, and had looked so handsome when he appeared in his regimentals to address his government. 'He will be as good to us as his father was,' she assured Elisabeth. 'Dear King Max was so good to his people; he loved us, did he not?

Surely his son will be just as good. We shall go to München to pay our respects on the day of the funeral, shall your father take you to München to see it?'

Elisabeth could not say. It was unlikely, and Papa was away on business, though expected back any day now.

After speaking to a few other people, she decided she ought to return home. Hopefully the baronin had ordered her breakfast to be served in her bedroom, as she often did when the baron was away, and Elisabeth had not been missed. But as she rode up the entrance path, she saw a figure at the window of the morning room, watching the pathway. The baronin was watching for her return.

She dismounted and gave the reins to Gerling who had attended her on her ride. She shook out her skirts, squared her shoulders, and entered the house, ready to face the consequences of her impulsive ride into town.

She was startled out of her composure by the presence of another person.

The count stood by the fireplace, one arm resting on the mantelpiece.

'Where have you been?' asked the baronin. Her voice was even, but she looked peculiar.

Elisabeth curtsied to acknowledge the count. 'I rode early into town to learn of the news.'

'The news?' her stepmother repeated. 'How could you learn of it there? The count has only just related it to me.'

'Allow me to offer my deepest condolences, my lady,' said the count, bowing his well-groomed head.

'Thank you,' Elisabeth said. 'It is very sad news.'

'How can you speak so lightly, you hard-hearted child?' said the baronin.

Elisabeth blinked in astonishment. 'I do not speak lightly of it, I assure you. I am very sorry for his death. It was most unexpected. Everyone is sorry. The whole town mourns for him.'

'I think you refer to the king, my lady,' said the count. He crossed the room and took Elisabeth's hands before she could resist. He leaned over her, his eyes boring into hers as she looked up at him in surprise.

'My poor young lady, the death we refer to is that of your father's.'

CHAPTER 7
STRANGERS

THE HOUSE WAS AS STILL as a tomb. For the first week all the curtains were drawn, every mirror shrouded with black crêpe, and all the clocks silenced. The workmen were sent away, told to return in one month to finish their work and receive their wages. The servants tiptoed about the house, their voices low, and taking especial care to close the doors soundlessly behind them.

To add to Elisabeth's sorrows, her brother's health was failing again. Even now, more than a fortnight after the news of the baron's death it did not seem real to Elisabeth. She haunted the windows overlooking the entrance to the house, watching the road, willing her father to be riding along it. She almost convinced herself that she saw him walking up the path, his grey greatcoat mantled about his shoulders, his black travelling cap on his head.

A train crash, the count had said. Close to München. Many bodies still missing. The carriages tumbled down a hillside, breaking up and flinging passengers out into the undergrowth or into a lake. There were some survivors, but the baron had not been found.

Elisabeth forced away every image of her father being

thrown from a train. She would not allow him to be rolling down a hillside, with cruel rocks and briers tearing at him—and certainly he was not to be flung into the lake, to have his final breath cut off by the wintry waters. It could not be. It would not be. It must not be true.

The days merged, long and grey. Visitors came, bringing condolences. A stranger carrying leather folders full of documents frequently called. He was shown into the study, where the baronin ordered that no one disturb them. Elisabeth watched the closed doors of her father's room jealously. The baronin was notably terse after these visits. The servants spoke of such days as a "black suit day" and kept out of the mistress's way.

After the sixth "black suit" visit, Elisabeth determined to search for evidence as to the man's identity. She slipped into her father's study, hunting for some clue. A card was on the desk, partly hidden by a small sheaf of documents: *Herr Schack. Lawyer. 61 Grubenstraße, München,* read the card. She glanced through the documents, but they were old papers of Papa's. There was a second card underneath the last document: *Herr Dollinger. Pawnbroker. 102 Kaufinger Straße, München.*

'What are you doing?' said a sharp voice.

She started, knocking the cards to the floor. The baronin's face looked pale, the black ribbons from her cap and at the neckline of her gown intensifying her pallid skin and her dark eyes.

'Are you snooping?' She crossed the room swiftly and bent to pick up the fallen cards. 'Yes,' she said. 'He is a lawyer. Even a sheltered girl as you must know that when a man of property dies there are many legalities to work through.'

'But we do not know if Papa is dead,' Elisabeth countered. 'There has been no body.'

'Of course he is dead. No one could have survived by

now. That is why my lawyer is working to get a death certificate issued.'

Elisabeth did not trust herself to say what she thought about that. She clenched her fists and pressed her lips together, looking away from the baronin, who seemed like a grim figure in black, standing there urging the finality of death upon her father.

'Will there be a funeral?' she asked in a tight voice.

'No. Not without a body. Perhaps a memorial service of some kind. I cannot think about it now, there's too much else to consider. There is no family beyond this house to attend any service.'

'There is Tante Emmeline,' said Elisabeth.

'I don't know of any Tante Emmeline.'

'My mother's sister. She is reclusive. But she always writes to me on my birthday.'

'She has never written to me, or shown me the courtesy of acknowledging me on my marriage into this family,' said the baronin. 'I owe her nothing. Write and tell her of your father yourself.'

'I will,' said Elisabeth stoutly, suddenly feeling defensive of her sole remaining relative apart from her brother.

'Life must go on, Elisabeth,' said the baronin in a flat voice. 'Do you think it gives me any satisfaction to have to force my way through all these legalities and difficulties? Did I marry only to be left as I am, with this uncertainty and ruin hanging over me?'

'There must be people who can help us?' Elisabeth said. 'Papa had friends.'

'Friends whom he owed money to,' said the baronin. 'He let everyone down. He must be certified as dead. Only then can I begin to untangle the mess he has left behind him.'

'Mess?'

'Yes! A dreadful mess. Unpaid accounts, notes and loans, so much debt.' The baronin swayed a little, and Elisabeth moved towards her to help, thinking she might faint, but she flashed such a fierce look at her that she stepped back again.

'And not only has he left me burdened with debt, he has left me burdened with *you*. Not to mention that invalid child upstairs.'

A surge of anger filled Elisabeth at the mention of Alexis. She was about to retort, but the baronin sank down onto the desk chair, dropped her head onto her arms and let out a wail of misery.

Never had Elisabeth seen her stepmother cry. It dissipated some of her anger, and she moved to lay a hand of comfort on her shoulder. The baronin snapped up her head and glared at her.

'Get out,' she hissed. 'Leave this room and do not enter it again.' Her look was filled with something so like pure hatred that Elisabeth gasped and fled from her.

OTHER STRANGE MEN CAME TO THE HOUSE. THEY ARRIVED VERY early, as though they were not to be seen. They too wore black clothes, but not tailored suits with silk cravats and polished shoes, they were ruddy faced and burly with heavy boots and shabby coats. Elisabeth first saw them from her bedroom window. She quickly dressed, desiring to see what was happening, but on opening her bedroom door the stern face of Brunn met her.

'Mistress says you are to stay in your room,' said Brunn. 'I shall arrange your hair and dress you properly in the meantime.'

She moved to enter, but Elisabeth swiftly closed the door again, saying, 'Not now, Brunn. I will call you when I need you.' She returned to the window, watching for signs of the men's departure. When they reappeared, they were carrying items wrapped in sheets and blankets.

. . .

Elisabeth had barely said a word to the baronin since the scene in the study. She did her best to avoid her, but there was no escaping her at mealtimes.

She took advantage of the servers being out of the room for a moment at breakfast that day, and asked, 'What were those men carrying away this morning?'

She thought her stepmother would not answer. She continued eating as though she had not heard. Griffin returned and took up his place by the serving table.

'I have had some extraneous furniture removed,' answered the baronin in a voice that carried clearly to Griffin. 'I need to make room for the new furnishings for the dining room. The workmen shall return next week to complete the final decorations.'

Elisabeth was astonished. Her father had been gone barely a month and his widow could think of refurbishments? She stared at her, then pushed her plate away and said coldly, 'I shall see how Alexis is this morning. Excuse me.'

She marched about the rooms, looking for missing items. What had the men taken? Two paintings were gone from the sitting room, and a pair of vases. A bureau desk was missing, also some ornaments and a carriage clock. An awful thought struck her, and she ran to her father's study. At first glance everything was as it always was. But just as she was about to leave, her eyes fell upon the oak bookcase adjacent to her father's desk. She rushed to it, touching the topmost two shelves, running her hands over the empty spaces where her father's leather-bound books should have been.

A cold voice sounded from the doorway. 'What are you doing in here? Did I not forbid you to enter this room?'

Elisabeth glared at the baronin. 'His books! Where are Papa's books?'

'Everything in this house belongs to me.'

'Alexis is the heir to Papa's property!'

'Not until he is of age. As his guardian I will do as I see fit with the estate. Now go. This room contains important papers. I do not permit you to enter it.'

Elisabeth paused as she passed the baronin in the doorway. 'You never loved him, did you?' she said, surprised at how steady her voice was when everything else inside her was quivering.

The baronin stared back at her with cold, dark eyes.

'Get out and stay out.'

CHAPTER 8

A GIFT

THE WORKMEN RETURNED MID-SPRING. There was no return of the whistling and singing that had previously accompanied their work; they were respectful of the house being in the second month of mourning. Seeing Hansi in his old spot by the stables brought back memories of happier times. He looked well: bright and full of life. The past month Elisabeth had been surrounded by subdued servants and visitors dressed in black. Hansi looked as though he had marched down from the mountains, his body strong and his mind as fresh as the mountain air.

'It's good to see you again,' she told him, as these thoughts passed through her mind.

'Was heartily sorry to hear of the loss of your father,' said Hansi, removing his cap to bow his head in greeting. 'Often thought of you both. Made you something. Hope you don't mind.' And he took something from the deep pocket of his apron and held it out. 'For your brother. Sorry to hear he's sick again.' It was a little figurine of a man in armour.

'It's Lohengrin, the Swan Knight,' she marvelled, taking up the figurine and examining it. 'It looks just like the picture in Alexi's book. How did you carve his face, it looks so real? I can even see his mail shirt and his fingers on his sword! It's exquisite workmanship. You must have worked long hours on it. Alexi will love it.'

Hansi shrugged. 'It whiled away the evenings. Always whittling at something. Got a whole box of things carved for my sister's children, and she's not got so far as getting married yet. Hope you don't mind, m'lady, but there's something for you too.' And he took another small figure from his pocket.

It was a swan, its wings slightly extended, its neck stretching tall and encircled with a royal crown.

'Lohengrin's swan,' she said.

She turned it around, admiring the intricacy of the carved feathers.

'Tante Trudy says my carvings have power in them,' said Hansi, shrugging as though he didn't like to speak of his own gifts. 'Good power. Nothing as strong as Tante Trudy's, but you'll likely feel some comfort when you hold it. Best not to mention it, though. Some folks get jittery about such things. But you and your brother understand.'

Elisabeth did feel strangely lighter as she held the carvings in her hands. They did impart a comforting power. So this was Hansi's gift; Pumpernickel had sensed he had one when first they passed him by that day on the road.

'They're so beautiful. What could I possibly give you in return?'

'It's a present. For your friendliness. And your loss. Nothing to repay.' He picked up his chisel to begin his work.

'Have you much work left to do?' she asked, still marvelling at her tiny carving.

'A few weeks. Unless the mistress has more for me.'

'And then you go home to the mountains?'

He nodded. 'Snow should be well melted by the end of the month.'

'Alexis loves hearing about the mountains. He remembers all the stories you told him. He likes the one about the waterfall and the buried dwarf's coins best of all. He says he'll write the stories down one day. When he's better.' Her voice trailed away.

A footman from the house appeared at the door of the workroom, rapping on the doorframe to get her attention.

'Excuse me, my lady,' said Anselm, straightening his wig, which had worked loose in his hurry. 'Mistress sent me to look for you to say you're to come to the house immediately and get ready.'

'Get ready for what?'

'She did not say.'

Brunn was waiting in her bedchamber. Elisabeth took in the preparatory signs about the room: the new gown of black silk neatly laid on the bed, the hairbrush and pins and ribbons lined up on her dressing table. From the antechamber came the smell of rosemary, indicating that a bath had been drawn and the usual infusion prepared for rinsing her hair.

'I can bathe myself,' she said, when Brunn moved to follow her into the antechamber where the copper bath gleamed before the small, crackling fire.

'Be quick,' ordered Brunn. 'The mistress wants you ready by noon.'

Elisabeth felt the impertinence of a servant telling her to be quick, and closed the door on Brunn firmly.

It was almost noon when she stepped carefully down the stairs to the great hall. Her new shoes had a heel to them so she took extra care on the polished stairs. Her gown felt heavy and cumbersome, and her head smarted from Brunn's vigorous hair-dressing.

She paused outside the drawing room. She could hear the baronin, speaking with that smooth voice she used with people she wished to charm; she also heard the deeper tone of the count. It had occurred to her that all the preparations were for him. Who else would the baronin make such a fuss for?

'Of course, a period of mourning must be allowed for,' the baronin said. 'Six months is usual.'

'I am not a patient man,' replied the count. 'When I see something I want, I take it.'

'Three months should be quite sufficient,' said the baronin quickly. 'That is only six weeks from now.'

'One month,' said the count.'

There was a slight pause before the baronin's voice resumed its smoothness. 'Just as you wish. It would not do to have a public wedding within the first twelve months, but all can be conducted discreetly. It will do her good to have a period of living quietly at her new home, getting adjusted to running a household. She has been used to being waited on, without responsibility. But she is young, and not unintelligent. She will soon learn.'

Elisabeth turned from the door, feeling sick at what she had heard. She had no wish to see that man. But as if her stepmother had some uncanny sense of her presence, the door opened.

'There you are, dear,' she crooned, reaching out to take hold of her arm. 'I was about to send for you.' She ushered Elisabeth to a settee, and made a fuss of pouring her tea; Elisabeth could drink nothing.

The count was saying something by way of condolence for their loss, and the baronin lifted a handkerchief, edged in black ribbon, to dab at her eyes. Elisabeth could have slapped her. It was one thing to pretend that all was well between them in front of guests, but it was quite another to pretend she actually grieved for her husband.

'We do not know that Papa is dead,' Elisabeth said loudly in response to the count's commiserations. The baronin held her handkerchief mid-air. The count raised his eyebrows over his teacup, which seemed ridiculously small and delicate in his large hands. 'There has been no body.'

'There has been no body, neither dead nor living, though

more than a month has passed,' said her stepmother in a taut voice.

'The search party was most thorough,' said the count. 'I joined it myself; I searched the face of every survivor taken to hospital in hopes of being able to bring you good news. I wish, for your sake, my lady, that your father had been spared. But had he survived they would have found him within a day or two.'

'You speak what is right, sir,' said the baronin, giving Elisabeth a warning glance. 'Let Elisabeth refill your cup while you tell us of the king's funeral. How did the queen and our new young king conduct themselves?'

'The little queen mother was dignified, and the new king managed well enough. He has not much to say for himself, but it is early days. Young people are pliable, they can be taught to behave as they ought.' Elisabeth flinched under his gaze as he spoke these last words.

'He was brought up in a frugal manner, I hear,' said the baronin.

The count nodded. 'The late king believed it his duty to raise his heir to be doughty. No indulgence. Like a soldier. Wise man. I knew the prince's first tutor, was in the same regiment. As a boy the prince had a tendency to be emotive, writing poetry and crying over stories and songs, that sort of thing. His father drove all that out of him. No luxury, bedroom like a monk's cell. Strict regime of study and exercise, no rich foods. Make a man of him, a leader of armies, a king.'

'Such training will stand him in good stead,' agreed the baronin.

'So long as the sudden acquisition of power does not go to his head,' said the count, 'and his father's good work be undone.'

'You may be right, sir, it may well go to his head. Young people often think they know what is best, and delight in doing the opposite of what their elders would counsel. That is why it is our responsibility to impose our wisdom upon those under our charge. It is our duty to ensure they do not throw away excellent opportunities and act foolishly.'

'I quite agree, Baronin,' said the count, returning his cup to the table with a clink. 'The sooner the spirit of folly is subdued, the better.'

'Are you going to marry that man, Elsa?' Alexi asked the following evening. He was lying in bed, looking so frail she could hardly bear it. His hand curled round the carving Hansi had made.

'What man?' Elisabeth knew full well who he meant.

'The count. The servants say you are.'

'Don't listen to gossip, Alexis. And, no. I will not marry that man.' She gave a little shiver. 'Papa said I would not marry anyone I did not care for. And I certainly don't care for him.'

'Good. I don't think he's a nice man. And he's old.'

'You've never met him.'

'Hansi talked to his groom and coachman when he came yesterday.'

'Oh?'

'They told him all sorts of things. They hate him. All his servants do. Except for his henchmen. And they only like him because he pays them so much.'

'Henchmen?'

'That's what they call them. His men who do whatever he wants. They say his wife died because he made her so miserable. Not long ago he beat one of the grooms so bad he couldn't walk for a week, just because he laughed when someone said the count smelled like mould.'

Elisabeth stared in horror at her brother. 'Don't tell me any more. It's too horrible. Hansi shouldn't be repeating such things to you.'

'He didn't. He told Ziller, and she told Lina. They were talking when they were making up my bed.'

Elisabeth was silent; she felt dreadful about the poor groom. It was something of a relief when Nurse came in and shooed her out.

CHAPTER 9
THE LUXURY OF TIME

THE DINING ROOM WAS COMPLETED. Elisabeth hated it. Her father might not be gone if it wasn't for the wretched work that had to be financed. The butler's pantry smelt of new pine shelving. Hansi's panels were hung on the wall. The extra storehouse had been built. But still the workmen lingered. They arrived early every morning to stand in the servants' courtyard, leaning against walls or pacing the length of the yard.

'What are they waiting for?' she asked Ziller. They were at the small window in the laundry room. The room was hot from the fire and the steaming vat of soak water.

'They're waiting to get paid,' replied Ziller, standing on tiptoe to better see out.

'Were they told to come today?'

'The mistress keeps giving them extra jobs, but now they'll do no more 'til they get what they're owed. That's what Hansi told me.'

'They've received nothing for all the work they've done?'

'Not one pfennig. And Hansi needs his for his sister and aunt.'

Elisabeth looked at Ziller closely 'Do you talk to all the workmen, or just Hansi?'

Ziller shifted from one foot to another. 'We've all talked to them. They've been here for ever so long.' Elisabeth wasn't sure if Ziller's deepening flush was from the heat of the room, or otherwise. 'But I like talking to Hansi the best,' she admitted.

'He is very nice. Very kind.' A new thought struck her as she decided that Ziller's deep blush was more than just the heat. 'And quite handsome.'

'He made me this,' Ziller whispered. She pulled something from her pocket. It was a tiny spray of roses carved from wood. Elisabeth would have known it was Hansi's work at once. Someone with a heavy tread was coming down the passageway, and Ziller thrust the carving away and flitted to her ironing table by the fire. Brunn entered with a demand for the baronin's black merino and scolded Ziller for it not being ready yet.

'Old bat,' muttered Ziller, when Brunn had gone. 'She'll dock my pay again.'

'Dock your pay? Who authorised her to do that?'

'The mistress. Ever since...' Ziller's words trailed away, and she gave Elisabeth a stricken look.

'Since my father has been gone?' Elisabeth said quietly.

Ziller nodded and patted away the perspiration from her forehead with a cloth. Elisabeth had heard Brunn's admonitions about not dripping sweat on the clean ironing. 'Things are different now. Brunn's more in charge than she was before. The mistress says we all have to do as Brunn says.'

'What things are different?'

Ziller glanced at the door and lowered her voice. 'No one's been paid. Our quarter wage was due three weeks ago. And Brunn keeps docking us for any little thing, so we won't get much anyhow. Jank and Griffin say they're going to leave once they get what's owed. I think Cook and Lina might go too. They think Brunn's getting too full of herself, ordering them around all the time.'

'I would hate to see anyone leave. Most of you have been

here for as long as I can remember.'

'I won't leave you, my lady,' Ziller promised. 'Even if I do hate being stuck in here. And Nurse would never leave the young master.'

'I suppose if a handsome man offered to carry you away to the mountains and marry you, you might leave,' Elisabeth said, wanting to rouse a smile from poor Ziller. She managed half of one, and another deep blush to go with it.

'The count will be here at noon,' the baronin informed Elisabeth at breakfast, after she had dismissed the servers. 'Brunn will ensure you are presentable. He has something of great importance to speak of.'

'He can have nothing to say of importance to me,' Elisabeth replied.

The baronin gave her an icy look. 'You must know full well what he wishes to speak to you of.'

'Obviously, as a highborn man, he will not be pressing me on any matter of importance so soon after my…loss. That would be disgraceful.'

'As a gentleman of high position he is at liberty to press his matter of importance any time he sees fit, Elisabeth.'

'I did not call him a gentleman. I called him highborn. A real gentleman would consider it disrespectful to impose himself on a girl so newly orphaned.' Elisabeth raised her chin, trying to stare down her stepmother.

'We have not the luxury of time for a long period of mourning,' her stepmother replied, with slow emphasis. 'That belongs to those who have the security of wealth. Your father left his affairs, and myself, in a dreadful position—no money, a mountain of debts, and his two dependent children.'

'Perhaps,' Elisabeth said, her voice quivering with anger, 'if you had not spent my father's money beyond your means these past years such a situation would not exist.'

There was a silence. Elisabeth expected either an outburst of fury, or a cold reply that included retaliation. To her surprise, the baronin tilted back her head and laughed.

It was not a pleasant laugh. It was a laugh that signified a release of pent up emotion. It passed away, and her features resumed their usual composure, though her eyes glittered.

'You are a silly child who knows nothing of such things. It is not your place to question anything I do in this house. I must do what I have to, or there will be no house, and where will your feeble little brother live then?'

Elisabeth pushed herself away from the table and stood up to leave. But her stepmother was not finished yet.

'I will not have you both hanging about my neck. The count has been most generous in offering to take you. He could marry far above a poor baron's daughter, but for reasons of his own he has determined that none but you will do. In taking you, he will spread his wing of provision and protection over this house, he will repay all our creditors as part of the marriage contract. He will save us all, Elisabeth. If you care nothing for yourself or for me, or for the staff that will lose their positions, then consider your brother. If this house is sold, he has no inheritance, and no home.'

She had been cornered. She could argue against nothing her stepmother said. She rushed away, feeling a little light-headed; feeling as though the world she walked in had tilted into a nightmare.

THE COUNT'S CARRIAGE GRATED THE DRIVE PROMPTLY AT NOON. His four outriders awaited his return; Elsa wondered if they were his henchmen. They looked grim enough to deserve the title, sat upon their horses like four giant crows, in their black riding cloaks and hats.

'You are very quiet, my lady,' the count commented. Elisabeth sat at one end of a sofa in the drawing room, the count sat at the other, the baronin had just left them on the pretence of finding some papers she wished the count to look over for her. The sofa felt far too short. She tried to say something, but as usual she felt frozen in his presence.

'I think I understand your reticence,' he said. 'Your mother has related to you my purpose in coming here today.'

'Stepmother,' she corrected.

'You can have no surprise in what I have to say, my dear.'

Her eyes snapped up at the words *my dear*. The hunger in his expression made her skin crawl. He moved closer and she inched away from him, but he reached out and took hold of her wrist and pulled her back.

'Your modesty is commendable. I will speak directly. I ask you to gratify me by becoming my wife.'

He was not hurting her wrist, but his grip was strong, and she knew he would not let her go until he had his answer.

'I…' she faltered. Her stepmother's words were resounding in her ears. If she refused to marry this man, Alexis would have no home. But would he? Was the baronin telling the truth?

'I…'

'Say, *I do*. Two little words, Elisabeth.'

'But… I *don't*.'

His hold on her wrist tightened.

'If my father were here you would not dare ask me in such a manner!'

'Your father,' sneered the count. 'Who left his family behind with a bankrupt estate?'

The count's voice was low and controlled; his words circled her like a stalking animal. 'Do you believe your father would not wish for your brother to keep his inheritance and the degree of care he enjoys? Would your father see you cast into poverty and degradation, your house and everything in it sold, the servants dismissed, your brother stripped of all the comforts his weak, ailing body relies on?'

'Things cannot be so bad as that!' she gasped out. 'I don't

believe it!' She tugged her arm away, but he would not release her.

'Oh, but they are. Your father was not wise in his business dealings. He made errors in recent years. He speculated where he should not have and failed to invest where he should. Your father has left you destitute, Elisabeth, and I, I am your saviour.'

'There must be something that can be done. There must be someone who can help us!'

'Such as his creditors? His business associates, his so-called friends, all of whom financed his latest failed scheme, and are now relying on me to recoup their loss? He has troubled far more families than merely his own.'

She jerked her arm hard enough to pull free from his clutch, and leapt up, moving to a nearby chair and standing behind it, her hands gripping the chair back. Her wrist burned. If the count had not been sat between her and the door, she would have fled the room.

'It's too soon,' she said, wanting to stall him. 'I need more time.'

'Time is what you don't have,' drawled the count. 'Don't be a fool, Elisabeth. I am offering you everything. And I always get what I want.'

Her breath was coming faster now as if the pressure she was under was crushing her chest. Perhaps he was right. Perhaps the baronin was right. Perhaps she was selfish. But she looked at the count, and she saw that hungry look, and remembered the poor groom who'd been beaten, and the stable dog who slinked away in fear, and she felt nauseous at the thought of being yoked to him day and night. The door opened, giving her a momentary respite from the tension. The baronin entered, looking keenly between the count and Elisabeth. What she saw clearly did not please her.

'I hope you have enjoyed an interesting discussion in my absence?'

'It has been enlightening,' said the count, standing up

from the sofa and tugging down his silk waistcoat.

'Enlightening? In what manner?'

'I understand how things stand.'

'And...how do things stand?'

'Your daughter is undecided.'

'Undecided?' the baronin repeated dully. 'What is there to decide?'

'Perhaps the young lady will tell you herself. I bid you goodbye for today. I will return in a couple of days perhaps. There may be some certainty when a little more time has elapsed.'

'So long is hardly necessary. Come back tomorrow, my lord—you know how changeable young ladies can be.'

The count bowed. 'I have business farther south. I will return the day after tomorrow on my way home. We can drive to my estate where my local registrar can conduct the necessary ceremony.'

'She will be ready,' the baronin said, and curtsied as he passed her by. When the count had gone, the baronin strode swiftly across the room, grasped Elisabeth by the shoulders, and shook her.

'You stupid, ungrateful, selfish little fool! How dare you spurn such a man!'

Elisabeth staggered backwards when released. 'I will not consent,' she gasped out. 'I can't bear to be near him!'

'Don't be such an imbecile! What are you expecting? That some handsome prince will come and sweep you off your feet? In real life girls marry the man their parents decide is a good match for them. As your only legal parent I say the count is an excellent match. You will never receive another like it. You will leave with him when he returns—'

'No!' The nightmare grew darker and closed in. 'I won't! I won't! I won't—'

A stinging slap to the cheek shocked her into silence.

'Get out of my sight. Stay in your room until you gain sense. Go!'

CHAPTER 10
THWARTED SCHEMES

ELISABETH HEARD the key turning in the lock of her bedroom almost as soon after she reached it.

She was ready for her stepmother's entrance hours later. She sat near the window watching the sun set, but without seeing it. She had washed her face to remove all evidence of tears, had tidied her hair and smoothed her gown. Resolution brought some degree of calmness.

The baronin's black skirts rustled as she crossed the room. Elisabeth turned to face her.

'I am glad to see you looking so composed, Elisabeth,' she began. 'You must have reached a decision.'

'I have.'

'Good girl.' She moved closer, smiling and reaching out a hand to take Elisabeth's. 'Let me congratulate you, my dear.'

Elisabeth put her hands behind her back. 'My decision—' She took a breath. 'Is unchanged.'

A pause. 'Unchanged?'

'I will not marry him. I don't believe he will be a kind husband. My parents would not wish me to marry him on that account.'

The baronin's face darkened; she seemed to grow taller

and weightier as she stood over Elisabeth, looking down with utter disdain.

'Your mother and father would not wish it,' she said, articulating the words as though they were disgusting. 'Stupid, idiotic, fool—as much a fool as your father ever was.'

This insult gave Elisabeth courage. She stood up, meeting her stepmother's flashing eyes with defiance, half expecting to be struck, but not caring in that moment. But her stepmother did not raise her hand. She withdrew, turning away with a swish of her skirts. She paused at the door before opening it. 'This is not the end of it. If you will not listen to reason, you give me no choice but to do what I must. For your own good.' She left the room, locking the door behind her.

There was no dinner brought that evening. Elisabeth was uneasy as she pondered what move her stepmother would take next. But what could her stepmother do? Starve and beat her into submission? The count could not make her marry him. He could not carry her away and force her. Could he? Fragments of stories she had heard the servants tell of came to her mind—stories of the count and his first wife. They said he had locked her up, did they not…?

Such thoughts haunted her as she tried to sleep; she woke in the night gasping for breath—a dream of being in darkness, somewhere cold, as though in black water, and the count pulling her down, under the water, snarling in her ear that he would break her—drowning, thrashing, trying to gain breath and liberty—such a murderous look on his face.

She lay gasping, staring into the dark with her heart hammering, wishing she had a candle or any kind of light. The fire had long dwindled out; no one had replenished the wood basket the previous day.

Morning dawned. She was hungry, and her water jug was dry. She heard carriage wheels, and she flew to the window, her empty stomach lurching at the thought of the count returning earlier than expected. But the tall figure in black who entered the house was not the count. It was only the pawnbroker from München. What had he come to take away today?

Footsteps sounded outside her room a while later; she hoped it was someone bringing water, but no one came. This was intolerable—she was being treated like an animal. She knocked repeatedly on the door, demanding attention until her hands grew sore, then took up a pewter candlestick, and hammered.

There were voices in the hall. She put her ear to the keyhole to listen.

'Please, let me go in to her. She wouldn't be banging away so if she weren't in need.' It was Ziller's voice.

'Get along with you,' said Brunn's deeper voice. 'It's no concern of yours.'

Ziller sobbed, and her voice and footsteps faded. Elisabeth took up her candlestick and began hammering again, but a great thud against the door startled her away from it.

'Cease your racket,' growled Brunn from the other side of the door.

'I need water!' she called back.

'The mistress says you'll get nothing till you stop that noise.'

Defeated again, she laid down the candlestick and waited.

Brunn came in. She thumped a tray on a side table, looking slyly at Elisabeth out of the corner of her eye. Elisabeth was not brought so low as to shrink before her impertinence.

'The chamber pot in my dressing room needs emptying,' she said. 'And I need water for washing.'

'I'll send Ziller for the pot,' said Brunn with a smirk.

Ziller looked stricken at the sight of Elisabeth. She said nothing while Brunn stood watch at the door, but someone called Brunn's name from the hallway; with a grunt of annoyance she turned away.

'That was Nurse,' Ziller whispered, 'she'll delay Brunn a few minutes so I can speak to you.'

Elisabeth was about to reply, but Ziller put up a hand to silence her. 'I've got to tell you,' she said, her eyes wide. 'Jank heard Brunn and the mistress talking about you and the count. When he comes back, he's taking you with him, and you don't have any choice—he's just going to take you and the mistress and Brunn is going to help him!'

Elisabeth stared at Ziller, absorbing the full meaning of what she was saying.

'You have to get away, m'lady. You have to go before he gets here.'

'But Alexi…' she said, her thoughts going immediately to him.

'Nurse will look after him. She's not afraid of Brunn. And she don't care if she isn't paid, she wouldn't ever leave young master for the world. You'll be back when it's safe.' Ziller's speech poured out as she hurried to say all she wanted to. 'There's laws about being forced to be wed, Jank and Cook says so. But you can't let him carry you off, or Cook says you'll be as good as wed forever, and only the parliament, or something, can get you out of it then, and they won't get you out, 'cause the count is in with them all—he's in with everyone. He'll get papers drawn up and stuff, and then you'll be trapped with him forever!'

Elisabeth's mind raced. She heard Brunn's voice down the hall and knew she would return any moment. Where would she go, and how would she get out? Her bedroom was on the third floor, she could not get out by the window.

'I need a key, Ziller.'

Ziller nodded. 'Housekeeper has a spare set.'

'Would she help me? She might get into dreadful trouble.'

'We all want to help you, m'lady.'

Elisabeth's mind flew over all the people she knew. She had acquaintances in town, but none who had the power, or cared enough for her, to protect her against the count. She had but one relative who lived many miles away.

'I'll have to travel alone.' That was a terrifying thought. She had never gone beyond the town.

'I think I know who—'

Ziller had no time to say anything more, for Brunn's heavy tread approached, and Ziller took up the covered pot and left the room.

All morning Elisabeth paced her room, thinking of what she should do and where she could go. She rummaged through her writing desk to find Tante Emmeline's last letter, written in her pointy, eccentric script. Would her aunt help her? She had not seen her since she was a small child, when her mother had taken her north for a visit. But she was her only hope of aid. She needed somewhere safe to stay; with someone who might help her get legal redress against her stepmother's plans.

Brunn came a second time with a fresh jug of water, more bread, and a small slice of cheese for a midday meal. She set it down on the side table.

'I've orders to change the bed linen,' said a voice from the doorway. It was Ziller, stood with an armful of folded sheets.

Brunn looked at her suspiciously. 'Whose orders?'

'Housekeeper's. Beds must be changed every seventh day without fail.'

Brunn jerked her head to indicate Ziller could enter. 'Be quick.'

Ziller didn't dare speak to Elisabeth; but as she gave one last smooth of the bedding, Elisabeth thought that she flashed her a significant look while her hand rested on a pillow, but it was so brief, she was unsure. Ziller picked up the candlestick Elisabeth had dropped on the floor, and set it carefully on the bedside table, giving Elisabeth another glance before gathering up the changed bedclothes. Brunn followed her out, locking the door behind her.

Elisabeth stood regarding the freshly-made bed. She lifted up the pillow, turning it over; she ran her hands around the edges of the mattress, feeling for anything hidden; she checked the blankets, but there was nothing. Disappointed, she sat on her dressing-table stool, slowly consuming the bread and cheese, while eyeing the bed as if it might have a secret to tell.

The baronin came later that afternoon. Elisabeth turned away from her; now that she knew her stepmother's plans her anger seethed as she heard her silk skirts swishing like the flick of a serpent's tongue.

'There's no use sulking, child,' said her stepmother in a calm tone. 'Tomorrow you will bathe and dress and meet the count with your acceptance. Then there will be an end to all this unpleasantness, and we can all forget it.'

Elisabeth fixed her gaze on the picture hanging on the wall opposite. It was a small watercolour of a lake with blue mountains towering above it in a friendly, protective way; or so she had always thought. She had always liked the picture.

'I trust I have your compliance, Elisabeth?'

She would not answer. There was a rustle of silk and the baronin's face thrust itself between Elisabeth and the mountain lake.

'Answer me.'

Her stepmother's face looked strained. She was so close that Elisabeth could see the dark flecks in her brown irises, the stray silvery hairs at her temples, and the place on her nose and cheeks where her face powder had worn away since the morning.

'And if you don't have my compliance, what will you do?' Elisabeth said with a forced quietness. 'There are laws against forcing a person into marriage, you know.'

Her gathering rage must have shown in her eyes, for the

baronin stepped away from her, looking uneasy. She regarded Elisabeth for some moments and Elisabeth stared back. The baronin arranged her features into a softer aspect and spoke as though talking to a child.

'Elisabeth, my dear. It grieves me that things have come to this. Let us agree together to end this sad state of affairs. I will call for the maid to draw a bath. You shall dine downstairs on whatever you fancy to eat. You will sit with Alexis; take him for a stroll about the grounds in the morning. What do you consider?'

Elisabeth continued her steady glare, feeling her anger grow stronger. This woman was going to separate her from her brother one way or another. This woman was going to send her into a future of misery. This woman had come into her family like a foul spirit, tearing it apart, forcing first her father away, and now herself. Her wrath was close to eruption. The baronin took another step back, then spun on her heel and was at the door in a moment. She turned back and spoke from the safety of the distance between them, the softness now gone from her face and voice.

'You have till tomorrow morning. And I will see the back of you, you ungrateful, selfish little—'

She did not finish her insult for at that moment Elisabeth gave a shout of rage, snatched up whatever came to hand and flung it with all her strength.

The baronin pulled the door shut just in time. The hairbrush Elisabeth had thrown clattered uselessly to the floor, and though she rushed at the door, the key was turned before she could reach it. She threw herself onto her bed, burying her head into a pillow to muffle her cry of vexation.

As she gripped the pillow, something crinkled beneath her fingers; she sprang from the bed, carrying the pillow to the window to see by the waning light.

Her fingers searched the hem of the pillowcase, and sure enough, tucked inside, was a small square of paper. It might be only a note of consolation, though Ziller could not write much herself. She did not recognise the rough writing.

MEET IN THE THICKET, BY THE STREAM.
  Will wait from midnight.

CHAPTER 11
FLIGHT

ELISABETH STARED AT THE PAPER. There was no signature. She paced around the room, clutching the little note as her last shred of hope, trying to think of some means of flight. How would she escape from her locked room? Her eyes fell upon the candlestick at her bedside. It was the last thing Ziller had touched.

There was a dent in the pewter stick that matched the gash in the bedroom door where she had struck it. Underneath the candlestick lay something small and shiny. A key. The spare key to her bedroom door.

WHEN THE HOUSE WAS SILENT, SHE DREW ON HER WARMEST cloak, and took up a small bundle of possessions. She opened her bedroom window; it would cause confusion as to how she had escaped. She would return the spare key on her way out; she didn't want suspicion to fall on Ziller or the housekeeper.

Her heart pounded as she turned the key in the lock; it seemed such a loud noise. She locked it again behind her.

She should hurry from the house as swiftly as possible, but she stood for a moment, filled with a desire to see Alexis before she went. His door was ajar, his night-light glowing in its pottery bowl. Magni lay at the foot of the bed; he lifted his grizzled, old head and regarded her, his tail making a slow thump in pleasure.

Good boy, Magni, she silently told him. *Watch over him.*

Nurse's soft snoring could be heard from the adjoining room; the door was always left open, in case Alexis needed her in the night.

Elisabeth tiptoed forwards to the bedside. The carved figurine of the swan knight peeked out from under his pillow. She touched her own carved swan, which she wore as a pendant around her neck. As if knowing, even in his sleep, that she was there Alexi turned his face toward her and opened his eyes.

'Shh,' she mouthed, putting a finger to her lips.

He raised his tousled head. 'Are you going?'

She nodded. Then she gathered him to her, feeling her heart would break.

'I'll be all right,' he murmured into her shoulder. But he felt so small and frail. Her resolve faltered. Was this a scheme of madness?

'You have to go,' Alexis whispered, lifting his head and reading her thoughts in her face.

'I'll be back to get you as soon as I've found someone to help us,'

He nodded. From the next room, Nurse's breathing pattern altered; the snoring paused. She had better leave before she lost all resolve, and before Nurse came in. She kissed him goodbye.

She knew all the places in the floorboards that creaked, and walked soundlessly through the house, down the servants' stairs, into the kitchens, faintly lit by the glowing embers of the fire. She replaced her key in the little cupboard on the wall.

'Caught you!' came a loud voice, causing her to jump and almost cry out. Her stomach lurched, for the voice was that of Brunn.

'I knew it was you, pilfering from the pantry! I'll have you turned out on your ear in the morning, you thieving good-for-nothing.'

'Oh, please don't, mistress! I just get so hungry! I wake up in the night an' my belly hurts it's so empty!'

It was Hugo, the houseboy, who was apprehended. Elisabeth pressed against the wall, only a few strides from the pantry. She edged back, moving away and crouching in the dark alcove where the brooms and pails were stored.

'Go on with you, get to bed! If it were up to me, I'd throw you out this minute!'

There was the sound of bare feet on the stone floor as Hugo fled.

Brunn did not leave the pantry. Elisabeth strained to hear every sound and was certain she could hear the noise of eating. What a hypocrite! It seemed like an age before she finally left the kitchens, with her heavy tread. She waited until she heard the creak of the wooden stairs from the kitchens to the servants' quarters, and then ran towards the door that led outside.

'Is she gone?' whispered a voice behind her, causing her to jump and almost cry out a second time. She whirled round to see Hugo stood in his bare feet and nightshirt.

'Are you running away?'

'Hugo, please don't tell anyone,' she begged.

He shrugged. 'Why would I? If they shut me up with nothing much to eat, I'd run away too.'

'Will you bolt the door behind me?'

He nodded.

The bolt grated as she pulled it back; she winced at the sound.

'Thank you,' she whispered in parting. 'And I'm sorry about you getting caught in the pantry.'

He shrugged again. 'Never liked working here, anyhow. I'll join the army.'

'Good luck, then.'

'You too, m'lady.'

She slipped out of the door.

'Oh, m'lady?'

She stuck her head back round.

'Watch out for Griffin. He's guarding the front gate.'

'Why?'

'In case of people who come at dawn, to catch folks out who owe 'em money. Griffin says the mistress don't want 'em coming in the house.'

'Has the clock struck midnight yet?' she asked.

'Not yet. But chimed eleven a long while ago.'

She left the porch, hurrying through the courtyard, and out into the grounds.

Hugo's tip about the front gate being watched was a mercy, she thought as she ran beside the walls. She would avoid Griffin by going out the back gate that none but the servants used. It was hidden from the road by hedgerows. It would mean she would have to retrace her steps, however, passing round the outer wall of the house to get to the path that led to where her mysterious helper waited.

It was dark among the trees by the stream; dark and forbidding. Doubts assailed her. What was she doing?

She hesitated, watching the black trees ahead and listening. There was a rustling noise, like that of a sizeable animal. She plucked up her courage and called in a loud whisper, 'Is anyone there?' There was no answer. The rustling noise resumed. Something was moving towards her, not a person, but something large that swished against leaves and made a bulky, black shape among the foliage. Foolish thoughts of Hansi's mountain trolls suddenly gripped her.

'Who's there?' she said, a little louder.

The thing emerged from the thicket—there were two, no three. She stepped back, uncertain of what she was seeing, and then she laughed in relief. 'Hansi!'

'Hello, m'lady.' He led two mules, one either side of him. 'Glad you made it out. Ziller worried you might not find the key in time. These fellows getting a bit restless now we're out of carrots. Climb up. Sorry it's not a lady's horse, couldn't stretch to that, but too far for you to walk.'

Sitting astride the small mule differed greatly from sitting side-saddle on Pumpernickel, but she was glad of anything to ride at that moment.

'I need to go north, Hansi.'

'North is where we're heading, m'lady. To the mountains.'

They travelled most of the night, stopping to rest for a few uncomfortable hours in the shelter of an old barn. Next morning Hansi went into a small market town to buy food. Elisabeth waited anxiously, hidden from the road in a copse of trees outside the town.

Hansi looked worried when he returned. 'What's wrong?' she asked.

He was gathering up their packs and loading the mules.

'Men in town, looking for you.'

A stab of fear passed through her. 'So soon.'

Hansi nodded. 'Best get on. Keep off the roads. Will mean a longer journey, but best be out of sight.'

They passed a second night in a makeshift shelter of canvas and sticks in a little wooded glen. Hansi thought they were far enough from the road to risk a fire. It was some comfort to have the warmth and light from it, but it started to rain that evening, and the fire turned to a hissing, smoky pile as they huddled under their covering.

The following day Hansi had to venture again into the next town for more provisions. He was loath to go, and Elisabeth was equally reluctant to be left alone, but the mules had chewed through the straps of their pack in the night, and eaten every scrap of food stored within.

Elisabeth scolded herself, for it had been she who had tied the mule's ropes while Hansi set up the shelter. She also scolded the mules, but they were indifferent and unrepentant. *Smell food, eat food*, they said, with a swish of their tails.

It was well into the afternoon when they reached the next small town where Hansi could get food. He left her in a little clearing, set back from the road. She walked about waiting his return, it was too cold to sit idly. She wished the sun would come out and warm her a little; it had been a cold, damp trudge all morning, and she was hungry and anxious. Hansi had taken one mule, and the remaining one ignored her as it grazed, only making the occasional complaint about how short the grass was.

Is food all you think about? Elisabeth said crossly to him. *At least you've a full belly, mine is empty, thanks to you.*

Plenty of grass, he replied.

I don't eat grass.

After what seemed like hours, she heard the sound of rustling and twigs snapping beyond the trees.

Someone coming, said the mule, lifting his head and sniffing the wind.

Only our friends, she told him. Hoping that this was true. Someone shouted. She froze, listening hard. It sounded like Hansi. But if so, why was he yelling?

The mule's nose twitched, and his ears pricked forward.

Strangers.

Strangers! Elisabeth ran to the mule to release him so they could hide.

She fumbled over the rope, cursing herself for the clumsiness of her fingers, as fear scrambled her movements.

If it's not Hansi, it will only be a farmer, she told herself. But the fear persisted. She heard Hansi's shout a second time. And this time she heard what he was shouting:

'Run!'

Quickly! She urged the mule. *Run!* She tugged him on, heading out of the little clearing, intending to hide in the trees beyond, away from the direction of the road and the approaching strangers.

They rushed on, reaching the safety of the trees. Only then did she dare to look back.

Strangers! said the mule.

Two men were in the clearing. They were no local farmers. Their black travelling cloaks flapped like crow wings; they had long, thick sticks in their hands, beating the undergrowth, calling to one another in gruff voices, searching for something, or someone... 'Henchmen,' she whispered in horror.

Strangers! said the mule. His voice grew more insistent, escaping as a loud bray.

Hush! Elisabeth urged. *They mustn't hear us!*

Strangers!

'Found her!' shouted a deep voice.

Elisabeth spun round in terror. Ahead, emerging out of the shrubs and trees were two more men, dressed in black cloaks.

She heard herself scream. She let go of the mule, who fled into the woods. She ran also, but her stride was no match for the longer legs of the men. Someone grabbed her round her middle, she thrashed and yelled, and struck at the man's hands with her fists—in the distance she heard Hansi shouting for her—a large hand clamped over her mouth, and her feet were lifted off the ground as she was carried away.

CHAPTER 12
HENCHMEN

'Fräulein Opel, you have just described to us a crime. Kidnapping is a serious offence.'

'Yes, sir. It is a dreadful offence.'

'Have you reported this to the authorities? And what has become of the young baroness?'

'II am reporting it now. I have not had opportunity to do so before. As to what happened to the baroness, I will tell you.'

SHE SAT ON A STOOL WITH HER HANDS BOUND IN FRONT, A CLOTH tied about her mouth, and her back against a wall of wood. A draught swirled round her legs, and she shivered from cold and fear. Four men were in the room, three sat round a newly lit fire. One man paced up and down, casting frequent looks at her from across the room.

'I tell you, we need to get on. He's waiting for us,' said the pacing man. 'We'd have been there by now if it weren't for that broken wheel.'

'We'll never make it on these roads at night,' said one of his comrades. 'I'm not risking my neck riding into a ditch in the dark. I had a cousin killed in an overturned carriage last year. It was lucky only a wheel got broke today.'

'Zetkin's right,' said a third man, the tallest and broadest of the group, a man so large that Elisabeth had felt she was being carried off by a giant when he had grabbed her. He picked up a jug and filled the cup in his hand. 'Bad enough trying to pick our way through in daylight. If we didn't have that blasted carriage it would be easier.'

'We could sling her across a horse,' said the man pacing up and down. 'Leave the carriage behind and ride on.'

'Have a drink, said Zetkin, taking the jug up and pouring himself a cup. 'You're getting irrational. He said not to let her be seen. She's to stay hidden in the carriage. Those were the orders. Now, sit down, you're making me edgy with all that pacing.'

'You should be edgy,' said the man, still pacing. 'We've done a lot of things for him, but this is something else. If we get caught, he'll disown us and let us swing.'

'We won't get caught,' said Zetkin,' his voice grew rougher. 'Now sit down before I make you, you're annoying me, Schrenk!'

Schrenk clearly took the threat seriously and sat on a bench before the fire, but he remained fidgety.

'I'm so blasted hungry,' groaned the giant. 'I can't believe no one thought to bring food. What's a man to work on?'

'Work?' said the man next to him. 'All you've done all day is sit inside a carriage like a little lady. I've been out in the cold leading the horses and keeping look out. It was me who spotted that shifty-looking feller who led us to her, me who tracked them, what have you done except whinge the whole time?'

His hungry neighbour ignored him. 'There must be something here besides beer,' he said, looking about the shadowy room.

'Shall I give the girl a drink?' the fidgety Schrenk asked. 'He said not to damage the goods. Can't let her dry out.'

Zetkin grunted and passed him a cup.

The giant was rummaging noisily through the drawers and cupboards of the furniture dotted about the room of the lodge. The walls, floor and ceiling were all of wood, the furniture simple and without decoration. It looked like a hunting lodge that had not been used in a long time.

Schrenk carried a cup to Elisabeth, sloshing beer into her lap as he leaned forward to pull down her gag and thrust the cup out. She held up her bound hands to show him she could not take it. He put the cup on the floor and undid the knot on the cord. She held her breath as he bent over her, hating the smell of him. She had spent hours crammed between him and the giant in a lurching carriage, with the smell of Schrenk's nervous sweat and the giant's stale breath. The cord was dropped and the cup of beer was pushed into her cold hands. She sipped at it, not much liking the taste, but needing something to slake her thirst.

The giant peered into bins and forced lids from barrels; he threw aside a coil of rope and a pile of horse blankets from a chest to look inside. 'Bring a light will you, Schrenk,' he called, 'can't see a thing.'

Schrenk took up the lantern, the only one in the room, and held it over the chest. 'Nothing,' said the giant in disgust. He slammed the lid down, making Elisabeth jump, her nerves taut and easily jarred.

'What are we to eat?' he roared.

'Go and catch something in the forest,' suggested the fourth man, with a snigger. 'Show us your hunting skills.'

The giant glowered at him, the light of the lantern making his face dance with shadows. 'It's no joking matter,' he growled. 'I need food! I've been on the road all blasted day and haven't eaten since that greasy pile of slop we had for breakfast.'

'We're all hungry, Gass,' said Zetkin. 'Pipe down. What with Schrenk as nervy as a colt, and you whining like a girl,

I'm starting to lose *Patience!*' He roared the last word. Elisabeth jumped again.

'At least we've got beer,' said the fourth man, reaching for the jug to refill his cup.

'Which you're guzzling down,' said Gass. 'Here, give me it.' He snatched at the jug, but it was moved out of his reach.

'There's plenty more in the barrel,' said Zetkin.

'I can't stand this bickering,' said Schrenk, putting his hands to his head. 'I've put up with it all day. I've a mind to set off now just to get away from you all.'

'I've a mind to ride on too,' said Gass. 'At least we'd be there by dawn and could eat.'

'I've told you, the roads are country tracks, you'll never make it at night,' said Zetkin. 'Do you want to break your neck in an overturned carriage?'

'Wouldn't be a bad thing if Gass broke his,' muttered the man by the fire. 'Likely it was his oversized backside in the carriage that broke the wheel.'

Gass glared at him again, his lantern swinging wildly.

'Let's do as Imhoff says, and leave the carriage behind,' Schrenk said, resuming his pacing. Even if we walk the horses, we'll be moving on. We're not safe 'til we get back.'

'And there must be some inn on the way we can rouse up for food,' added Gass.

'We're in the middle of nowhere, you fool,' said Zetkin. 'There's no inn between here and Dragenberg.'

'A farmhouse, then,' snapped back Gass.

'So, we'll rouse up a farmhouse, and of course they're going to open up and welcome four strange men into their kitchen in the middle of the night. Welcome us with a brace of shotguns, more like. You're such a dunce, Gass.'

'His brain's as fat as his backside,' said Imhoff with a snigger. He'd downed the best part of a second jug and was clearly feeling jovial.

'Come here and insult me,' snarled Gass. 'Come on, I've

about had enough of you these past two days,' He put up his fists.

'Pipe down, you idiots,' said Zetkin, but Imhoff was on his feet pushing back his sleeves to ready his fists for a fight.

'Come on then,' he goaded, a beery leer spreading across his face. 'I've had enough of you too, and your whingeing and whining. Let me use that belly of yours for some left hook practice!'

'Let me tickle my knuckles on that ugly face of yours,' growled back Gass. 'That'll shut you up.'

'Sit down!' ordered Zetkin.

But the fight had begun. Zetkin and Schrenk tried to intervene, Zetkin roared in pain as he caught a stray fist on the nose. He doubled over, blood spurting out. Gass threw himself at Schrenk's middle, tackling him to the ground with a crash; Imhoff, who clearly liked a fight, let out a shriek of glee and dove on top while Zetkin remained crouched with his head in his hands moaning and cursing. Gass caught the lantern with his flying foot, and the lamp crashed to the ground and went out.

Elisabeth saw her chance. She wasn't sure her legs would move properly, she was cold and weak from hunger, and almost paralysed with fear, but her senses were heightened by the sudden burst of urgency coursing through her, and she edged along the shadowed wall until she reached the door and lifted the bolt. She was out, she was in the blackness of the night, stumbling along, following the sound of the horses, in the stable beside the lodge.

She released them all, throwing wide the door, urging them to go home, sending them images of warm stables and pails of steaming mash. Only one horse did she retain, the one that she sensed as the most intelligent. The duller horses were too fixed on their own needs to consider anything else. *Will you carry me?* she asked her. *Without saddle or bit. I cannot see in the dark as you do. Will you carry me as far as you can, and then I will release you to return home?*

Will you feed me? The mare replied.
I will lead you to good grass as soon as it gets light.
You may get up, the mare agreed. *It is too cold here. I would sooner move.*

She left with only moments to spare. As the mare rode away, there came a great bellowing of curses as the hapless henchmen spilled out of the lodge. Elisabeth did not dare look back.

WATER, SAID THE MARE. DAWN WAS GREY AND DAMP, AND Elisabeth was numb with cold, feeling she could not hang on to the mare's mane a moment longer. But she must hang on. She must get to safety. They had crossed fields and passed through wooded stretches, but had seen no habitation. They had sheltered a couple of hours in a derelict stone barn, the mare could not walk all night without rest, but there had been no rest for Elisabeth. Each time she closed her eyes she saw the grim face of Zetkin, felt the sweaty palms of Schrenk as he bound and unbound her, heard Imhoff's curses. When exhaustion drove her to snatches of sleep she dreamt of black, suffocating carriages, and always she saw the count. Heard his smooth voice, shrank from the grasp of his fingers, and woke gasping for breath as his hungry eyes moved closer and closer.

Water, said the mare.

I think I see water, replied Elisabeth. *Looks like a lake.* The sun had risen, and the shimmer of water was in the distance. As the morning mist lifted she was surprised to see mountains beyond the lake. She hadn't realised how far she had travelled.

I want to go home said the mare.

So do I. But I can't. I don't have a home.

Take me to the lake, she told the mare. *Then I will go on alone and you can go home.*

It was indeed a lake. A heron lifted its head at their approach, then took flight. A pair of ducks honked, and paddled away.

Another sound reached Elisabeth's ears. One that jolted her out of her cold misery and filled her with panic instead: the sound of men's voices.

She looked around, scanning the trees around the lake, wondering which way she should turn to hide.

There was a loud crack, and her cry merged with the scream of her horse.

Steady! urged Elisabeth, feeling the horse about to lift up beneath her—*Steady!*

But a second crack sounded, and the horse reared up, her forelegs scrabbling at the air. Elisabeth tried to hold on, but she felt so weak, so numb, she couldn't grip the mare's back tight enough with her knees, she couldn't hold fast to the mane as the horse reared a second time. She was falling, she was tumbling through the air.

'Did you hear that?' called a man's voice from somewhere. 'Sounded like a scream, did it not?'

'By the moon's light, Paul, if you've struck a swan, I'll have your trigger finger cut off!'

'It's a girl!'

That was the last Elisabeth heard after she struck the ground. The world filled with blinding stars, then all went black.

CHAPTER 13
SWANSTEIN

'SHE WAKES.'

She could hear before she could see. The voice was close. She forced her eyes open, feeling disorientated and peculiar. She was in a wood, surrounded by trees. No, not trees, but walls of wood and rafters of fir above her head. Something heavy lay upon her: a fur rug, covering her from neck to foot. A face appeared above her. It was the face of an angel. *I am in heaven*, she thought. No face so handsome as this could be on earth.

'Glad to see you awake, Fräulein,' said the perfectly shaped lips in the beautiful face. 'Is there someone I can send word to of your whereabouts?'

Her speech had left her. She only stared at the vision hovering above.

She tried to lift her head, but winced and dropped it back down.

'Don't try to move. You've had a nasty fall. I don't think anything is broken, but we must get you looked at by a physician.'

'Where am I?' she asked, finally finding her voice, which sounded raspy and weak.

'You are safe. As soon as you are well enough to walk, we will see you safely home. Where do you live?'

She looked blankly at him.

'What is your name, Fräulein?'

She could only stare in reply.

'You do not wish to tell me your name?'

'I…' she said in a frightened voice, 'I…do not know my name…'

He regarded her thoughtfully.

'I wish to return, Paul,' said the voice of a second man. She could not see him from where she lay. 'I have meetings to prepare for,' said the hidden voice. It was a clear, voice. Well modulated. Imperious.

'Shall Hausser attend upon you, sir?' replied the angelic Paul. 'While I wait for the young lady to be well enough to be moved. It would not be courteous to leave her alone with a groom.'

The second man emerged into view. She gasped, for while the man called Paul was the most handsome man imaginable, yet he paled in comparison beside this second man. He was tall and slender, and the very skin of his face shone. But it was a cool beauty while Paul's was warm and smiling.

'I will return and send a carriage for her,' said the second man. She cannot stay here, there are not the necessary facilities. I will have the physician awaiting her arrival.'

'Yes, sir.'

The tall man turned to leave, but something caught his eye. 'What is that?' he asked. He looked toward Elisabeth. He did not meet her eyes, and she had no wish to meet his, for they were piercing and unsettling. He pointed a long, slender finger. 'About the neck. What is it?'

Her hand moved to her neck to rest upon something. A pendant, of carved wood.

'May I see?' he requested.

'May I have it, for just a moment, Fräulein?' Paul asked. He held out his open hand. She fumbled with the clasp and dropped the necklace into his hand, taking care not to touch him.

The tall man held the pendant up to the light of a small window. The pendant was a carved swan.

'Where did she get this?'

'My I enquire, Fräulein, as to the origin of your necklace?' Paul asked.

She shook her head, then winced at the pain that the movement caused. 'I cannot remember,' she whispered.

'Perhaps a sweetheart gave you it?' Paul whispered in reply; his eyes gleamed playfully. 'I am trying to prompt your memory, Fräulein.'

She flushed and said nothing.

The tall man ran a finger over the carving of the swan, narrowing his eyes as though he were a jeweller examining a gemstone. 'It is excellent workmanship,' he said. He returned the pendant and left the room.

'My apologies, for your being left alone with me,' said Paul. 'When the carriage comes, we shall find you more appropriate arrangements.'

'Where am I?' she asked.

'We are but five miles from Füssen.'

'How did I get here?'

'You were thrown from your horse. Perhaps you were out riding? You were unaccompanied, so perhaps you lost your attendant?'

'I don't remember.'

'I am sorry to say that your horse bolted before we reached you. We could not recover it.'

'I'm frightened,' she whispered. 'Why can't I remember anything?'

He smiled his beautiful smile. 'Your memory will return. Most certainly it was the blow to the head you suffered when you fell. I have heard of such things happening. His Majesty will see that you are well cared for in the meantime.'

'His Majesty?'

'The king.'

'I shall meet the king?'

'Fräulein, you have just met him.'

'You have no idea who she is?' The physician completed his examination, and now spoke to Paul.

'As yet we have little clue to her identity,' Paul replied. 'She speaks as a well-born lady, and is dressed in clothes of high quality.'

'She has unusual marks on her wrists,' said the physician.

'Unusual?'

'As though she had been bound.'

'Bound?'

'With rope or cord. And the marks are fresh.'

'That is most unpleasant.'

'And she has bruises on her arms that do not accord with a fall, but suggest she was rough-handled. They too are fresh, only a day or two old.'

'Even more unpleasant,' said Paul. 'That would explain why she rode out alone; she was escaping, but from whom? Are there any signs of…violation?'

'No.'

Elisabeth could hear them talking, but the draught the physician had given her made her feel sleepy and dull. She had noticed the raw marks on her wrists herself, and wondered about them.

The physician returned to the bedside. 'Well, Fräulein,' he said in a voice loud enough to make her wince, for her head still throbbed. 'No bones broken, some bruising, and of course, that nasty bang to the head.'

'When will I remember?' she said huskily, struggling to keep awake. She felt as though she had not slept in days.

'In good time,' said the physician brightly. 'You could

wake up good as new, all your memories restored, or it may come back a little at a time over a longer period.'

'A few days?' she asked.

'Days, weeks, months.' He shrugged.

'Months?' That was her last dismayed thought as she drifted into sleep.

EACH TIME SHE AWOKE, SHE FELT BEWILDERED. HER MIND scrabbled to recall where she was, who she was, why she was lying in a great four-poster bed surrounded by tapestries and countless candles. Every time she awoke, she was bathed in perspiration, as the nightmare receded. Always the same dream: she was drowning in black water—someone was pulling her down, she could not wrench free—she tried to push her assailant away—all she could see of him was a mouth with snarling, yellow teeth—he would not let go—her mouth filled with water as she screamed, and then she awoke. Always she awoke just as the water filled her and cut off her breath. She never saw his face; only those yellow teeth. She lay trembling between the soft, white sheets.

'Morning, m'lady,' said a brisk voice. 'Brought you breakfast.'

A maid set a tray down on a little table before the window. 'Shall I open the curtains?'

Elisabeth assented; it was the first time in six days that she had wanted them opened. She had felt too sensitive to the light until now.

'Lovely morning. Spring at last,' said the maid, as the sunshine pooled in. She turned back to the bed, holding out a dressing gown. 'Would you care to sit up and eat? The prince said to see you up and dressed today. Orders of the physician. Get a bit of fresh air and exercise, but just a little, mind.'

Elisabeth permitted herself to be led to the table to breakfast, then be directed in washing and dressing, almost as a child.

'Are these my clothes?' she asked, when a gown was laid out for her.

'They are now,' said the maid. 'The one you came in has been sent for cleaning and mending. Full of rips and caked with mud.'

'So, whose gown is this?'

'The prince went to München to get clothes for you. Nothing hereabouts would fit. Her Highness is too short, Countess Hildebrand is too tall, and that's all the ladies' clothes we have. The Prince said we couldn't put you in a dirndl. I shall pin up your hair for you,' she said, after combing out Elisabeth's long, brown hair. 'The prince said to make sure you were presentable. The king can't bear anything out of the way of neatness and niceness.'

'Who is the prince?' Elisabeth asked. 'Is he a visitor here?' Though she could remember nothing of her own life, she recalled the history of the world around her, and she knew the king had no brothers.

'Lieutenant Thorne. Prince Paul von Thorne. The king's aide-de-camp.'

'His aide-de-camp,' she repeated, wincing as her hair was brushed, even though the maid was trying to be gentle, her head still felt tender. So, the man she knew as Paul was a prince.

'I hear he rescued you,' said the maid. She swung her head round to give her a grin. 'Swept you up in his big, strong arms and carried you in. Lucky you. He's a real charmer, so watch yourself.'

'I think you mean charming,' she replied.

'No. I mean charmer.'

The maid stepped back, her work completed in the form of a thick crown of glossy plaits. 'It's not city fashion,' admitted the maid, 'but you look nice and neat. Now, if you'll follow me, m'lady, I'm to take you to the family rooms.'

She was shown to a room on the first floor. The room was comfortably furnished, as a family room would be, one wall lined with rows of leather-bound books, mostly on history and politics. She sat a while, then felt restless, having been confined for days, and opened the door to peek into the passageway, hoping to see someone—anyone.

She heard voices close by, and curiosity drove her to investigate. An open door gave her a glimpse into a lovely room with walls bearing murals of medieval knights and princesses. The furniture was of gleaming wood, upholstered with purple velvet; golden lamps hung from the plasterwork ceiling.

A tiny woman in voluminous black skirts sat upon a chair near the window, an embroidery frame before her. 'Where has he gone now, Matilde?' the woman asked in a plaintive tone.

'Perhaps he has gone riding, Your Highness.'

A second woman, dressed also in black, though not as sumptuously as Her Highness, sat opposite, sorting through skeins of silk thread.

Elisabeth deduced that she was looking at the queen mother and her lady-in-waiting. The queen mother looked so small; how could so tall a man as the king come from so tiny a woman? She had no wish to be caught observing them, and made to move on, but her eyes lingered over the lovely murals and furnishings a moment longer.

'I did not hear the horses,' said the queen mother in her high voice. 'I do not think he has gone out yet. I fear he was vexed at breakfast with me. Why does he object to my inviting guests here? He never objected before.'

'His Majesty had no power of objection before,' her lady-in-waiting said. 'He was but a child in subjection to his excellent parents until recent sad events.'

'He is still a child,' said the queen mother. 'What can he know at a mere eighteen years of age. He needs firm counsel and guidance, but he shuts everyone out.'

'It is very early days. He must be allowed some period of adjustment.'

'He is the king,' said the queen mother. 'His life is not his own. He cannot please himself in any matter.' She gave a sigh. 'Paul tells me the Cabinet Secretary is due this morning. He must not fail to return to meet him. His father would never keep his ministers waiting. He was so punctual. So well mannered.' She turned her lace-capped head to look out of the window as though looking for her errant son.

'His late Majesty was excellent in all his duties,' agreed her lady-in-waiting, frowning over a tangle in her threads. 'And his son will be likewise, I am sure. It is only His Majesty's youth, and his sudden accession that makes him a little forgetful of his obligations. It will soon pass.'

'That is just what Pfiffermeister says.' The queen mother did not sound much assured. 'But why does he insist on sending everyone away? He should have a full entourage as his father did.'

'He has kept Prince von Thorne. I am sure His Majesty will retain all his attendants when he is in the city. Here he likes to forget the court and ride out and climb mountains as he did as a boy.'

'I had hoped he would grow out of his obsession with the mountains by now. No doubt that's where he has gone. Up to those old ruins he is so fond of. Too fond of. Such an eccentric boy. Mountains and castles and old stories, that is all his head has ever been full of. It does not bode well.'

'All will be well, my lady. He is young. When His Majesty returns to the city in the autumn, he will take up his duties and carry them magnificently as his father did.'

'You are very good, Mathilde,' murmured the queen mother. 'But I have such a foreboding. I cannot shake it off. Now that he is of age he can do as he wills, and I fear he will make irregular choices, for he was always an eccentric child. I never understood him.'

Elisabeth dared not linger any longer and returned to the

little room, taking up the first volume of *The Full and Formal Analysis of The Seven Years' War* in an attempt to distract herself. She had returned just in time, for a servant soon appeared, dressed in breeches and a coat of lake blue and gold and asking her to follow him.

They reached a door with gilt carving and an ornate handle.

'In there, m'lady,' said the footman, bowing his head. He trooped away, the heels on his shoes clicking on the polished parquet.

She rapped on the door.

It flew open. 'Good morning!' greeted Prince Paul. She tried to return his smile, but while his was self-assured, hers wobbled as her stomach made a little lurch at the sight of him. By lamplight, on the day she had met him he was so very handsome, but by the full light of day he was dazzling!

'Come in. I trust you have rested well these past days?' Prince Paul ushered her into a room of panelled walls and rich furnishings and a large desk with neat piles of documents arranged upon it; all was a little dark and heavy, but elegant.

'What is going to happen to me, Your Highness?' she asked.

'In truth, Fräulein, we do not know what we should do with you.' He smiled again. 'You are our mystery lady. But you were found on the king's land, and the king shall take you under his protection. We shall discover the truth of your identity, and restore you to your family.'

'You are very kind,' she murmured, feeling suddenly emotional, as though kindness was not something she had known much of. 'And the king is very kind.'

'His Majesty is coming to greet you,' said Paul. 'When he comes, Fräulein, it is customary not to speak unless directly asked a question by him. Nor should you look directly at him unless he requests it.'

She nodded.

'And one other thing.'

'Yes?'

'Never knock on the door, as you did upon entering.'

'Never knock? I am to walk straight in?' That seemed improper.

'You must scratch.'

'Scratch?'

'Like this.' He rapped with his nail on the back of a wooden chair.

Was he joking?

'The king dislikes any crude noise. All must be refined.'

'Except gun shot,' she said dryly, then gasped. 'I remember gunshot! Do I remember rightly?' She was so overcome by this sudden stab of memory that she had to drop down onto a nearby chair.

'Excellent,' said the prince warmly. 'You do remember right. 'When I came upon you, I was shooting. Not at you, of course, I had no notion of your presence until you cried out, and your horse screamed. It was mere target practice.'

There was a pause, and she realised she was staring at the prince as he talked, watching his mouth shape his every word. She flushed with embarrassment and dropped her eyes.

'We must give you a name,' the prince said. 'I cannot keep calling you Fräulein. The king refers to you as the Swan Maiden.'

'Swan Maiden?'

'On account of your pendant.'

'Oh.' She put a hand to the carved swan at her neck. It always felt strangely comforting to touch it.

'Perhaps we shall call you Fräulein Schwan?' He smiled, spreading golden light around him, or so it seemed to her. He could call her whatever he liked; whatever he said was beautiful. She mentally shook herself of such foolish thoughts. What was the matter with her?

'But what to give you for a Christian name?' he enquired.

Her eyes fell on the mural on the wall behind him. Something about it gripped her, as though she recognised it. He followed her gaze, turning to look.

'Lohengrin and Princess Elsa,' he said. He turned back to examine her face, she caught his eye and blushed again. 'She looks very like you. I think from henceforth we shall call you Fräulein Elsa Schwan, if it does not offend you?'

She did not immediately reply. She was staring again at the mural. Why did it stir something within her?

'You do not agree? Should it be Princess Elsa, or Countess Schwan?'

'Nothing so grand, I'm sure,' she said. 'Fräulein is just fine.'

'Baroness?' he said, smiling his good humour.

She blinked. 'Fräulein is just fine,' she repeated, but her voice faltered slightly.

There was a soft noise at the door. Someone was scratching.

'Enter,' Prince Paul called in his pleasant voice.

A footman opened it. 'His Majesty approaches,' he announced.

Paul gestured her to stand up, offering her his arm as assistance.

The king came in.

CHAPTER 14
SWAN MAIDEN

Despite being warned not to look directly at the king, it was difficult to be in the same room as him and not stare at him.

He was very tall, as much as six and a half feet, she gauged, and his slender figure caused him to appear taller still. His hair was black and glossy, falling in smooth ripples at each side of his face—and his face! —every girl in the kingdom would give a princely sum for the secret of such milky-white skin.

And then his eyes—impossibly blue!

Prince Paul von Thorne stood a little in front of her as though to shield her. What a contrast between the two men: one was all warmth and languid grace, like a sun-basking cat, the other cold and brilliant as a diamond. Her hand moved to her swan pendant as she watched the king moving papers about on the desk; the smooth lines of the swan were becoming a talisman of reassurance.

The king's gaze snapped towards her when her fingers drew out the pendant. She dropped her hand to her side, seeming to hear someone's voice, she knew not whose, telling her to stand tall, shoulders back, head straight, and absolutely no fidgeting with one's hands. A lady never fidgets.

'Good morning, Fräulein,' greeted the king, seeming to see

her for the first time. 'I trust you are making a good recovery?'

She rose from her curtsey, and dared to glance at him, but his eyes looked just above her head.

'Good morning, Your Majesty. I am recovering well, thanks to your kindness in providing care for me.'

'Do we know who you are, yet?' asked the king.

She shook her head. 'I cannot recall, Your Majesty.'

'The physician says it could take some time,' added the prince.

'You will be our guest until you have made a full recuperation,' said the king.

She curtsied again as she thanked him.

He turned back to the large, ornate desk and picked up a sheaf of correspondence.

'I understand the Cabinet Secretary is due this morning, sir,' said Paul, stepping closer to the desk. 'The telegram on the top announces his intentions.'

The king made a gesture of impatience with his hand. 'I cannot see him this morning. I must ride out. The queen mother vexed me greatly at breakfast. I cannot attend to Pfiffermeister's demands until I have exercised.'

'Very good, sir. I will send word to the stables to prepare your horse, and may I suggest that arrangements be made for the Cabinet Secretary to be engaged until this afternoon? It is too late to send word to him to come later, for he will be on the road as we speak.'

The king looked again at the papers, then dropped them on the desk. 'You may accompany me on my ride, Paul.'

'I am at your service, sir. But the Cabinet Secretary…?'

The king's beautifully curved lips pursed in annoyance. 'So disagreeable.'

Prince Paul did not reply, but stood patiently.

'Stay with Pfiffermeister, and inform him that on no account is he to call before luncheon again.'

'Very good, sir.'

'And give word that I shall eat breakfast alone from now on.'

'As you wish, sir.'

The king turned to leave. 'Good morning, Fräulein. I shall be pleased to introduce to you the queen mother, but it must wait until dinner. I hope you will continue your convalescence in the meantime.'

She curtsied a third time as the king left the room.

'I had hoped to show you about the grounds this morning, Fräulein Schwan,' the prince said. 'But now I find I have a disgruntled Cabinet Secretary to appease instead.' He pulled a face that made her smile. 'Ah, that's better,' he said. 'The first smile I have seen from you. And it was worth the wait.'

Her smile turned to a frown at such flattery, but it was impossible to be truly offended when such warmth accompanied the words.

'Let me escort you to your room, and find a maid to wait upon you and show you the grounds. The physician has prescribed short daily walks for you. Nothing strenuous.'

He left her at the door of her guest room. She felt a pang of disappointment at his departure. It was as if the sun had gone behind a cloud. She berated herself for such foolish thoughts. Anyone would think she'd never been flattered by a handsome young man before.

No maid appeared, however, and she desperately wanted to be outside. A cloak was hung obligingly in the wardrobe, so she ventured out alone.

'Where may I walk?' she asked one of the tall footmen who stood at his post in the entrance hall. He looked down at her without moving his head. 'I wish to take some exercise about the grounds. Are there any areas I may not walk in?'

'Not the Queen's Bower without the permission of the queen,' replied the footman in a surprisingly deep voice for one so young. 'Nor the Prince's Walk without the permission of the king.'

'And how shall I know where they are?'

'Because you'll be seen off if you step in them.'

'Most helpful advice.'

The footman opened the door and she stepped out.

She wandered about, enjoying the May sunshine, when the clouds permitted it to break through. A birch-lined walk led her to the lake where a procession of royal black swans sailed across their watery kingdom, their blood-red beaks vivid against their black feathers. For a moment she thought of the king, with his glossy black hair, eyes blue as deep water, and lips as red as the beaks of the swans gliding past.

She followed the direction of the swans, walking leisurely along the bank, beneath the canopy of new leaves on the trees above. The view before her was familiar: the mountains towering up in a protective stance above the turquoise lake and the valley. Perhaps she had been here before? She stood gazing out, hoping that some memory might be prompted, but nothing came.

A movement interrupted her thoughts, and she turned her head to see a swan moving towards her. Not a black swan, but a white one, an exceedingly large one. Had she forgotten what a white swan looked like, she wondered, for she did not recall them ever being so large? Two pairs of smaller white swans swam a little behind it, a pair either side, as though making an escort.

As she watched the magnificent creature moving closer, a series of images formed in her mind. They were vivid, yet fluid, like water; if she poked at them with her thoughts they would ripple and blur. The experience was so quick, she had not time to consider how strange it all was, but somehow it was not so strange. It was as though this was something that had happened before.

The images replayed, and now that she let herself rest into them, they formed meaning, though some images were unclear. She stared at the great swan, and as a shaft of sunlight pierced through a break in the cloud above, the white feathers gleamed like fine porcelain, its beak like red gold, and for a moment she thought she saw a golden crown about its slender neck, but the ray of sun withdrew, and she blinked and the crown vanished.

The images pressed upon her a third time, with more urgency. The swan was speaking to her, it was strange, and yet it was so. She understood the series of images now; they fell into place like jumbled words falling into a sentence.

I will give your message. Such as I understand it. She assured the swan, sending it images of her doing so. A sense of something heavy and binding settled upon her. She had agreed to do something, and she would not be released until she fulfilled her word.

The swan bowed its neck and glided away. Another ray of sun broke through, and where the swan had been there was only golden ripples on the water and the two pairs of white swans sailing by, urging her to make haste and do as she was bid.

A MAID FOUND HER STILL WATCHING THE PLACE WHERE THE great swan had been.

'Oh, m'lady, I've been looking everywhere for you,' said the maid. 'The prince asked me to show you the way round the gardens, but I couldn't get away from the kitchen straight away, or the biscuits would have burned, for no one else was free to watch them, what with the special lunch to get ready for the important minister, and the queen does like biscuits with her tea.'

The maid was young, with rosy cheeks and a pleasant face. Elisabeth thought she reminded her of someone.

'Do I know you?' she asked.

'Know me? I'm Brigit, m'lady.'

'Do you know me, Brigit? Have you ever seen me before?'

Brigit shook her head. 'Never seen you before, m'lady. Sorry I couldn't get away to show you round, but now the prince wants you to come back to the castle for luncheon. Said you was to meet the important minister.'

Prince Paul strode in, lighting up the hall with his golden hair and smile. He now wore the deep blue uniform of the Bayern army, his golden epaulets drawing attention to his broad shoulders.

'I thought it would be good for you to meet the Cabinet Minister, Fräulein Schwan. He may be able to help in solving the mystery of your identity.'

'I need to speak to the king,' she said as she walked beside him down the hall. 'It is very important.'

'Do you remember something?'

'No.' She hesitated. What could she say? That a great shining swan had given her a message for the king. Now that she was away from the lake, it all seemed rather implausible. Did she imagine it? Had the injury to her head sent her a little mad? It had seemed so real at the time, but now she was unsure. 'It does not matter,' she said, feeling confused. 'I forget now...I'm not sure.' But even as she spoke, a heavy burden pressed down upon her. She would not get out of keeping her word that easily. She would suffer under this burden until she spoke the message.

They entered a room of glossy dark wood and deep green furnishings. A fire burned in the shiny grate, despite the mild weather.

'Herr Pfiffermeister is getting on a bit,' said the prince, nodding at the fire. 'He needs his comforts.'

'Where is he?' she asked.

'He will be here shortly. He knows the way. We are not terribly formal here at Swanstein, not as we are at the palace.' He called in the footman outside. 'Bring forward His Majesty's chair from against the wall. Place it about that table with a second chair. A cushioned one. Can you find some extra cushions from somewhere? The Cabinet Secretary has been complaining of his back all morning.'

The room was rearranged, and she stood waiting. The burden was growing stronger, she would know no peace until she had spoken her message.

'Don't be anxious,' said the prince, seeing her face, 'there's nothing daunting about Pfiffermeister, he's only irritable at worst.'

A portly man with a large, scarlet coloured nose and tiny eyes came in.

'Let me sit down, Lieutenant,' groaned the portly man. 'My legs are in revolt against the rest of me today.'

The prince directed him to the seat appropriated for him. The Cabinet Secretary fiddled about with the cushion, arranging it between himself and the back of the chair, panting a little at the exertion.

'Allow me, sir,' said Paul, moving to adjust the man's cushion.

'Thank you, Lieutenant,' murmured the Cabinet Secretary. 'Much obliged. Is this the young lady?' The minister looked up at Elisabeth, standing opposite. She gave a curtsey. 'Pretty,' murmured the minister, bowing his head in greeting. 'I usually remember a pretty face, but I do not recognise her.'

'Perhaps you could initiate an investigation, sir,' said the prince. 'There must be someone looking for a missing young lady.'

'Indeed,' agreed the minister. 'I will speak to the Chief Inspector when I return to München. And you really can remember nothing, Fräulein?' he asked.

'No, sir. Nothing as yet.'

'Most extraordinary,' murmured the minister. 'One hears of such things, but I have never met someone with memory loss until now. Perhaps she ought to see Dr Mensdorff,' he said to the prince. 'He is a specialist in conditions of the mind.'

'I would not wish that upon her,' said the prince. 'And it is not her mind that is faulty, it is a temporary loss of memory. I am not sure they are the same thing.'

'I hear he does all sorts of modern treatments with that new-fangled electricity,' said the minister. 'He might be able to bring her memory back.'

'I should not like to see any young lady subjected to Dr Mensdorff's modern treatments,' said the prince, casting a reassuring smile at Elisabeth, who was looking and feeling alarmed. 'I have heard of his treatments on the aunts.'

'Well, they are rather a hopeless case,' said the Cabinet Secretary. 'Not even Mensdorff can do anything to help them.'

'Speak only to the Chief Inspector, sir,' advised the prince. 'We will not employ Dr Mensdorff and his electrical treatments. Perhaps,' he added, 'we should keep all enquiries strictly confidential for now, sir. There may well have been...' he glanced at Elisabeth, '...foul play involved in the young lady's circumstances. We must get to the bottom of the matter without betraying her presence to anyone who may have malicious designs.'

'Most extraordinary,' said the minister, looking at Elisabeth with fresh interest. 'A mystery and a crime. I shall make all enquiries under a cloak of discretion, you may be sure.'

'If anyone enquires as to Fräulein Schwan's presence, we shall say she is a visiting distant relative of the queen mother's. Niece of a second cousin twice removed, something of that degree.'

The Cabinet Secretary agreed, then was obliged to struggle into a standing position once again, as the king was announced; he strode in, filling the room with his presence.

Elisabeth was struggling with all kinds of conflict; her thoughts swirled with talking swans and urgent messages, and she wondered if she really did require a zealous doctor to repair her mind. But the heavy weight upon her persisted. She must speak to the king. It was not a choice, it was the imperative of something more powerful than herself.

She was also unsure if she should stay in the room, but no

one had told her to leave, so she remained by her seat near the bureau, opposite the Cabinet Secretary, who stood waiting for the king to be seated, so he too could sink back onto his chair.

'Shall we begin,' said the king. His young, striking face looked and sounded annoyed, as though the minister was an intrusion.

'Perhaps, Your Majesty,' said the Cabinet Secretary, 'We might begin with the visit of the Österreichen Emperor?'

'He may go to the palace, but he is not to come here,' said the king. 'I have already had this discussion with the queen mother over breakfast today.'

'But he will wish to see you, Your Majesty. It will be expected. And it will be a mark of respect to entertain the emperor both informally and at the formal palace banquet.'

'Banquet?' said the king.

'The usual state banquet, sir. In honour of such a distinguished guest to our kingdom.'

'I understood there would be no banquets or balls during the national period of mourning.'

'This is the one exception, Your Majesty. The political movements of the allied kingdoms are such that we must demonstrate our own alliance with our powerful neighbour. We must act now. We must confirm solidarity with the emperor, we must honour and welcome him. Our survival may depend on his support in times to come.'

'So be it,' said the king. 'But Swanstein is not a place of business. It is a refuge.'

The Cabinet Secretary frowned at his papers and adjusted his cushion. 'Your Majesty, I know you find formal gatherings unpleasant, and are not fond of the city, but you are now our king, and it is the king's duty to show himself to his people. You have hardly been at court since your accession.'

'I have been in mourning.'

'I understand. But the king's mourning cannot be like other men's, sir, for the king is not like other men.'

'You sound like my mother,' said the king. 'Does she speak your words, or do you speak hers?'

'Her Highness is wise and speaks only what is best for the kingdom.'

'I will return to the palace,' agreed the king. 'But I will not receive the emperor here. If he wishes to be entertained *informally* as well as formally, he shall be entertained at Schloss Berg. He may go fishing while I fish for his support.' The king gave a little sigh as though it cost him greatly to accede to this.

'Very good, sir,' said the Cabinet Secretary resignedly, shuffling through his papers for the next item of discussion.

Elisabeth was longing to escape the room; every time she heard the king's voice, she recalled the urgency in the swan's message. And every time she thought of the swan, she felt a pang of fear that she was losing her mind. Visiting dignitaries were to be rebuffed; applications for meetings were denied or postponed. The king was in his private castle, and would not be disturbed until he returned to the city. The meeting was eventually concluded, without much satisfaction to either party. Cabinet Secretary Pfiffermeister was escorted out.

'Always they must intrude,' murmured the king, moving to the window and looking out

'Her Highness would be glad to receive the emperor here, sir,' Paul said in a mild voice.

'Oh, she would, would she?' The king's eyes flashed dangerously. 'Just as she would have that grasping man from Saxony with his garrulous wife to visit again, but I will not permit it!'

'The Arch Duke and Duchess of Saxony have been great supporters of the House of Wittelsbach, Your Majesty,' Paul said amiably.

'The Arch Duke of Saxony persuaded my father to have me brought up like a monk under penance. I am no longer a child. I will not suffer to be dictated to. I will not be controlled as I was all my youth. I must go!'

'Go, sir?' The prince's perfect calmness was fractured for a moment.

When the king spoke, it was in a decided voice. 'If the king finds himself unable to find refuge at Swanstein with the queen mother, then the king must have a new Swanstein.'

'Sir?' The prince waited for further explanation.

'I must find somewhere else. Though there is no place in all the kingdom I love so well as these mountains.'

At the king's words Elisabeth's heart began hammering. The weight upon her increased. She felt she had to speak the message she had been given, or she would be crushed under the pressure; but how could she dare say such an outlandish thing? And she was not permitted to speak to the king without being addressed first.

There was a soft noise at the door, and the prince crossed the room to open it and speak to the messenger on the other side. Elisabeth's heart still pounded, but she felt compelled to move a little nearer to the king. Unconsciously, she reached for her swan pendant for courage. The king turned his head to look down on her.

'Have you something to say, Swan Maiden?' he asked, not unkindly.

Her voice caught in her throat, but the pressure on her forced the words out, though they were barely above a whisper. 'Do you believe in signs, Your Majesty?'

'Signs?'

'Messages. From the world around us.'

He stared at her, frowning. But when she dared lift her eyes, he was looking at the carved swan between her fingers. The weight on her urged her to continue.

'Perhaps it was some kind of dream, Your Majesty, but I believe I heard a message, and I feel compelled to speak it to you. I have no understanding of what it means.'

'A message from whom?'

She swallowed. 'A...swan.'

She thought he would laugh, or sneer, or stare, or call for a doctor. There was a pause, but when spoke his voice seemed unperturbed.

'Please relate the message.'

There was no going back now.

'You are to awaken the mountain. You are to raise up the ruins of the castle. You are to restore what was lost and recover what was hidden.'

A thick silence descended. But the hammering in her heart abated. She had done what she said she would. She felt lighter; the feeling of something weighty lifted. She felt free, even if she were now to be castigated as a madwoman.

'What is it that is lost and hidden?' he asked quietly.

'I do not know. I could not understand. I...saw a castle... and some object...something small and green...I do not understand what it was.'

'What is this?' said the prince, returning to them, looking at Elisabeth with an inviting smile and a curious look.

The king turned to face the prince, and a gleam was in his dark blue eyes.

'I must build my own castle. I have just seen it.' He turned back to the window and pointed. 'On that mountain peak will stand the king's castle. He shall raise up the ruins. Send for Herr Weimann!'

Paul's smile slipped away. 'Herr Weimann fled the kingdom many months ago, sir.'

'Find him. No one else will do. He is a genius of architecture. All my life I have admired his work. He will build the new Swanstein.'

'I understand he fled due to heavy debts, sir. If he returns, he will be liable for prosecution.'

'Have I not the means to clear all debts? Send a man immediately. Send jewels; send the king's portrait. Such genius should not be lost from the kingdom. He is needed.'

'I understand his debts to be substantial, sir,' Paul ventured. 'But the king's command must prevail.'

'It must!'

CHAPTER 15
THE FRIEND

PRINCE PAUL WAS DESPATCHED to seek the famed—or notorious—Herr Weimann. He was gone ten days. Elisabeth found she rather missed him. He was the closest she had to a friend. She had been introduced to the queen mother the evening before he left, but the queen mother's curiosity towards her had been eclipsed by her dismay at the king's announcement of his new castle. She was so put out that the next day she made her own announcement—she was returning to the palace at München. She would await her son's arrival at the opening of parliament, if he could not be persuaded to return sooner to take up his duties at a close quarter.

The king enquired daily of Elisabeth if she had any new message, but she had not. In fact, she deliberately kept away from the lakeside; the encounter had been so strange, that she half-feared it happening again. But she discovered that it was not merely swans she could hear and speak to. When she stopped to stroke the stable cat and asked him how he was, he told her that he had something in his paw that hurt him, so she obligingly took out the tiny thorn that he had caught between his pads.

When she visited the horses, she found them all eagerly looking for the king. They liked him. Loved him. They would follow him anywhere, that was the general consensus in the stables. The king kept no hunting dogs, for he did not care to hunt, but there were a pair of aged hounds of the late king, who lived behind the stables. One of them had a bad tooth, which she reported to the keeper, making it sound as though she had happened to notice it. The other hound wanted his kennel moved into the shade; the early summer sun was making his kennel too hot.

If she concentrated very hard, when sitting outside, she could just make out a recurring song from the songbirds that dwelt in the hedges and trees of the castle grounds. Birds were much harder to understand than domestic animals; their thoughts were wilder, less easy to follow, but she caught some notes of a recurring chorus, and as she heard them repeated day by day, she began to pick out bits of meaning as they trilled back and forth from dawn to dusk. Their song was of the mountain: *mountain sleeping, mountain stirring, mountain dreaming, he is coming, waking, waking, waking.*

When she did dare to walk by the lake again, she saw only the four white swans, and not the great crowned one. The swans were restless, circling the water before her; *it is time*, they urged, *it must be found*.

What must be found? she asked. But the image she saw was faint and hazy: something green and bright; something jewel-like, but larger than a jewel. She concentrated hard, but the image would not come into focus.

It must be found. It must be found. The message was repeated.

Mountain sleeping, mountain stirring sang the birds in the trees lining the lake. *Waking, waking, waking…must be found…*

It was the tenth day since Prince Paul's departure. The blare of the outriders sounding their horns, and the carriage wheels rumbling up the long drive to the castle, drew Elisabeth to the entrance hall.

The castle doors were swung open by the hand of a gloved footman, and the king stood waiting at the top of the steps, his figure alert with anticipation. Elisabeth watched discreetly from behind a pillar.

'Welcome, Herr Weimann!' called the king to a figure emerging from a carriage. The figure threw back his dark-red cloak over his shoulder, and made a formal bow, sweeping his hat to the ground.

Prince Paul stepped from the carriage, to escort the king's guest up the steps to the entrance. Was it her imagination, or did the prince look more youthful, stronger, taller and his hair a brighter shade of gold than when she had last seen him? Perhaps it was because at his side walked an unfamiliar man, old enough to be the prince's father, with black hair and beard, and a shorter than average height. The man made a second ornate bow on reaching the steps where the king waited.

Prince Paul saw her as he reached the topmost step. She made a curtsey in greeting, and blushed as he gave her a glorious smile of greeting, as though he were as pleased to see her as she was him. He held out an arm, offering to escort her, as the king led his eagerly-awaited guest inside.

The king's presence always filled the room with a kind of awe; Prince Paul's presence likewise filled the room, though with a very different feeling. Herr Weimann was yet another man who filled the room: the air seemed now to pulse with energy as all three men passed through the great hall.

Herr Weimann was dressed in a suit of ruby-red velvet. He wore a, fur-collared cape about his shoulders, despite it now being the month of June, and a feathered hat upon his large head, which seemed out of proportion to his body. Elisabeth wondered that he should dare to keep his hat on in the presence of the king, and she wondered that the king did not object. But the king looked restless and excited as he escorted Herr Weimann through the hall into the king's study.

'Delightful cornices, Your Majesty,' declared Herr

Weimann, sweeping a hand towards the ceiling. 'Charming chairs. The work of Baumgartner if I am not mistaken? Excellent windows. Most pleasing arches. Fine fretwork.' Herr Weimann looked about him; as his gaze passed over Elisabeth, he bent his large head in greeting, his dark eyes with their bushy eyebrows met her own look of curiosity. The bushy eyebrows lifted, then he turned his head away.

'It is the taste of the queen mother,' said the king, dismissing all compliments.

'And that is why it has the elegance of a lady, Your Majesty,' replied Herr Weimann, swivelling round so that the feather in his hat bounced. 'But if this were the castle of a king, there would be ceilings double, nay, treble the height! The fireplace would roar with a great brazier of finely wrought iron.' He waved a hand at the current fireplace which was unlit, and decorated with a tapestried screen. 'Cornices three feet high, carved and gilded; chandeliers descending from chains of gold, windows of coloured glass to flood the room with heavenly light and colour.'

'Yes, yes,' agreed the king; he paced up and down in time to Herr Weimann's words. 'And skilfully painted murals filling the walls with heroes and kings,' added the king. 'And everything must be beautiful, Herr Weimann. *Everything* must be beautiful. From the very stones of the foundations to the candlesticks on the tables, all must be perfection. Can you do this? Can you build a castle of perfection and beauty for the king? Can you resurrect the castle of Gundelfinger?'

'Your Majesty,' exclaimed Herr Weimann, removing his hat to make another sweeping bow. 'You are as a god granting thy humble servant the greatest gift his heart could desire. To build you a castle of perfection and beauty would be a heavenly dream! I have only one greater desire.'

'What is that, Herr Weimann?' asked the king.

'That I would not be merely a servant of my king, but henceforth, I should be known as—*Friend* of the King.'

There was a moment of silence, as the prince and Elisabeth gaped at Herr Weimann's audacity.

'How may an artist discern and interpret the desire of the heart, unless the artist knows the heart in the intimacy of friendship?' Herr Weimann shrugged, as though it were a perfectly natural assumption.

'So be it,' said the king. 'I have long admired your work. Henceforth I call you Friend.'

Herr Weimann beamed, his black whiskers twitching as his cheeks lifted in a grin of delight; he swept off his hat to make another bow.

'Of course,' said Herr Weimann, replacing his hat, 'His Majesty understands that perfection and beauty comes at great price.'

The king lifted his hand. 'Speak nothing of cost, Herr Weimann. You shall want for nothing. Make your requests known to Paul, and he shall see to all.'

'Very good, Your Majesty. I shall go away directly and draw up plans.'

'You shall not go, Herr Weimann,' said the king. 'This room, this castle, is at your disposal to draw up your plans without delay.'

Herr Weimann looked about him. 'I fear the desk is too small, Your Majesty.'

'You shall have a greater desk brought before you.'

'I fear the light is too yellow. I can only work by true north. And the space, Your Majesty, it is cramped. When the Muse comes, she demands expansion, freedom,' he flung his arms wide. 'She insists on high ceilings that she might soar above me.'

The king's bright eyes dimmed some degrees. 'There is not such a room in this castle,' he said.

'The Muse demands stimulus also, Your Majesty. A house in the city would be excellent to invoke her. The music of the opera house, the grand architecture of the palace, the bustle of the crowds as one enters one's own theatre box or rides in one's own carriage through the streets of the finest quarter. Good wine and good food, with all due respect, Your Majesty, cannot be found any place better than in the royal city. And the Muse desires them all. She must be appeased. She must be wooed, if she is to inspire perfection.'

The king looked displeased. 'I imagined a true artist would be too pure, too high to be concerned with such things as food and drink,' he said.

'And so I am!' cried Herr Weimann. 'If it were only for myself, I should be content in a cottage, dining on wild onion soup. But the Muse, Your Majesty, must be treated as one would treat an empress. Should she suffer east facing rooms and low ceilings? Should her vessel of artistic genius be fed on rustic fare? Should she be denied all that man can offer by way of artistry in song and stage? Only a king could understand such things, for he is akin to the power of the Muse, is he not? She inspires, the artist interprets, but the king!—he brings both together, he unites, he makes possible what is impossible with mere man. He is the facilitator of true art, of creation—without the king, there is nothing. Nothing!'

Herr Weimann waved his arms like an orchestral conductor during this speech, his voice like that of a dramatic actor.

It was only then that Elisabeth realised there was a fourth man in the room. She had been dimly aware of another figure, but had paid no heed, assuming it to be a valet or footman. Herr Weimann had so captivated her attention that it had been diverted even from Prince Paul. But a gesture by the figure standing quietly in the corner of the room now caught her eye. It was a young man, perhaps a couple of years older than herself, and he was rubbing his hand across his eyes as though suddenly wearied by what he had just heard. He shifted his step and knocked into a side table, hurriedly grabbing at the vase on it to keep it from toppling.

'Very well,' said the king. 'Give Paul your requirements. I will talk further with you after luncheon, Herr Weimann.'

Herr Weimann bowed with a flourish, and the king strode from the room.

'If you care to direct your requests, Herr Weimann,' said Prince Paul, 'I will draw up a list.'

Herr Weimann sat down upon the king's chair and began his list, which was most lengthy indeed.

CHAPTER 16
NEW ENCOUNTERS

HERR WEIMANN HAD ACHIEVED what the chief ministers and queen mother had not been able to: the king was returning to the city, that he might settle The Friend into suitable lodging where his work of genius would begin.

'I am to go the palace?' Elisabeth said in surprise.

'His Majesty considers it may be helpful for you to view the court,' said the prince. 'You may recognise someone. If you formerly lived in or visited München, you may remember something. I understand the Chief Inspector wishes to speak with you, he is undertaking a discreet investigation on your behalf. Don't worry,' he said, seeing her face fall at the mention of the inspector. It reminded her that there might be some foul adversary of hers out there somewhere. Her nightmares had not yet abated. Every night the faceless man with the yellow teeth pursued her.

The prince put a warm hand on her own and gently squeezed it. He smiled down at her. 'I know this must be disturbing for you, but I promise I will not let you out of my sight. The king agrees. He takes his responsibility seriously as your protector.'

It was only when he removed his hand and turned away

that she realised what a liberty he had taken in touching her as he did. But it was too late to protest against such familiarity now. And, besides, she had rather liked it.

THE CITY WAS BIGGER THAN SHE HAD IMAGINED, AND NOTHING was familiar, leading her to believe that she had surely never seen it before. In the royal district the streets were wide and paved smooth; the buildings were of cool, pale stone, their bricks and arches crowned with decorative stonework and flanked by great heraldic beasts. Statues of past kings and mounted generals stood guard around the walls of the palace, while living guards, only half the height of their stone compatriots, stood with sword and halberd at the palace gates.

Her carriage rumbled into the courtyard, past a great fountain where Neptune pointed his trident at all who passed by. A servant in deep blue livery and a snowy wig, opened the carriage door and led the way to her guest room, first arguing with the coach driver about her loss of luggage, until she explained that she really did only have the one small trunk.

Her room was very pleasant, and larger than the bedroom at Swanstein, but the view of the formal gardens was not so good as that of the lake.

'So you have come!' said a high and quivery voice. She turned to see an elderly lady dressed in an elegant black gown.

'Are you the seamstress?' Elisabeth asked, thinking that she was rather old to be the ladies' maid she had been told would be sent up, and therefore must be the seamstress she had also been told to expect. The prince had thought of everything.

'Let me look at you,' said the old lady, coming forward and reaching out her wrinkled hands to take hold of Elisabeth's face.

'She is quite pretty,' said the lady. 'They would like her.'

'Is she?' replied a second voice. 'Let me see.'

A second woman now appeared, with long, silvery hair, worked loose from its hairnet, and wearing a gown of white. 'She is not as fair as *her*,' said the lady in white, coming forward, leaning on a silver topped cane.

'No one is as fair as *her*,' agreed the lady in black. She released Elisabeth's surprised face. Both ladies stood peering up at her.

'Are you both seamstresses?' Elisabeth asked, she could not think who else they could be. 'Did the prince give you any orders?'

'No orders!' cried the lady in black. 'We want no more, do we, Little Sister? We have so many.'

The lady in white nodded with vigour. 'Come here, go there, sit down, be quiet, eat this, drink that, know what's good for you, don't argue back, and never never go into the cave where the music sings and lives and makes one dance.'

Elisabeth stared at her in surprise.

The lady in black nodded in time to words. 'So many orders. Day and night, night and day. Go to bed, get up, put that away, leave that alone, cease that singing, move from that window, away from that door, and never never go into the cave where the little lights twinkle and shimmer and glow.'

'Your Highnesses!' cried a third voice. 'I have been looking everywhere for you.' A tall, stout woman now appeared, panting hard, and red faced, as though she had been either hurrying or very anxious, or both. 'You've been very naughty again, haven't you? Caused Frau Müller a lot of worry. Shall get Frau Müller into a lot of trouble!' She took an arm of each lady and tugged them away. 'Come along now, this way, be good, no more nonsense.'

'Come here, go there, be good,' echoed the lady in black.

'Let me go, you'll infect my sleeve!' cried the lady in white, shaking her silver topped walking cane at the stout woman, and tugging her arm free.

'Walk nicely beside me, Your Highness, and I'll not need

to hold your arm,' the matronly woman replied. 'Strike me with that stick again and I'll take it away and throw it into the river!'

'Walk nicely, be good, don't speak, don't laugh, and never never step into the water, no never.' The lady in white cast a sorrowful look at Elisabeth as she left her room. 'Follow the dancing lights, the pretty pretty lights, and never come back! Oh, why did we come back?' The lady in white's mournful voice grew faint as she was led away, chanting her words over and over. Elisabeth stood in the doorway watching them go, and wondering at them.

Another woman, now came marching up the hall, as doughty looking as the first. She nodded a sober greeting to the stout woman and managed to bob a kind of curtsey to the elderly ladies without breaking her stride.

'Fräulein Schwan,' she greeted briskly. 'I will wait upon you while you are here. Let me unpack your box, you will want to change out of your travelling gown.'

'Who were those elderly ladies?' Elisabeth asked, still watching them as they were escorted away.

'Princesses Sibylle and Marie,' the maid replied.

'Are they visiting from another kingdom?' Elisabeth allowed the maid to shut the door and direct her to the tapestried screen to undress.

'They are the spinster aunts of the queen mother. And it is palace protocol that no one is to speak of them. It greatly displeases the queen mother for guests to see them. I don't know how Müller let them get away again. Another keeper who will lose her position before the week is out.'

'Keeper? What are they, pets?' She peered round the screen.

'They are mad, is what they are,' said the maid, catching up the discarded skirt Elisabeth placed over the screen. 'A disgrace to the family.'

Elisabeth tossed her jacket at her in reply, deciding that

she did not much care for this stern maid with the gruff voice, who reminded her of someone; if only she could remember who.

'A page awaits at the end of the hall to lead you to the king's suite,' said the maid. 'You are to return here at three 'o' clock to be measured by the seamstress. I shall return at six to dress you. The king dines at seven.' She cast a disparaging glance over Elisabeth's scanty wardrobe before making a perfunctory curtsey and stalking away.

The page sent to show the way to the king's apartments was as cool in manner as all the staff Elisabeth had thus far met. There was certainly a marked difference in the formal air of the palace and the more homely atmosphere of Swanstein Castle.

'If you wait here, m'lady,' the page said, leaving her standing before a gilded door, 'they will call you when they are ready.'

Elisabeth stood admiring the carved roses and cherubs that adorned the white panelled walls and doors. She was distracted from her request to wait and wandered about the room. The carpets were deep red, with woven designs in gold. Mirrors and paintings and gilded panels covered every surface, even the ceiling. She had never seen so much opulence.

'Fräulein Schwan,' came a cheerful voice that made her heart beat a little faster. She returned Prince Paul's smile of greeting, as she walked towards him. 'Please come this way,' he stood to one side with a bow of his head, and she passed by him into a room even larger and more opulent than those she had entered by.

She curtsied to the king, but he did not acknowledge her. He was fully engaged with Herr Weimann; they stood at a large table where drawings and plans were spread out, covering its surface. She stood discreetly beside a cabinet of inlaid wood, and waited, wondering why she was there.

'Make them taller!' the king said, pointing at the plans on the table. He was glowing with enthusiasm. He towered over Herr Weimann beside him, who was dressed in violet trousers, and a waistcoat and bow tie of amethyst silk. 'The spires must soar higher.'

Herr Weimann nodded his large, head and looked pointedly at his assistant. Only then did Elisabeth notice the young man she had first seen at Swanstein Castle. Like herself, he stood to one side. He held a notebook and pencil, and he was scribbling fast. She watched him for a moment as his head bent over his book. He was of average height, taller than Herr Weimann, but not quite as tall as the prince. His hair was of mid-brown; she could not see his eyes. He was not unattractive, just ordinary, but how few men could stand in the same room as Prince Paul and the king, and not look plain? The young man lifted his head as he finished his writing and glanced at her, dropping his pencil as he did so; as he bent to retrieve it, she turned her head away, a little embarrassed to be caught watching him.

'I have given the order for the work to begin,' the king declared. 'The site shall be made ready, the foundations built. Every working villager shall have as much labour as he desires. Have your plans made ready, Herr Weimann, for the time will fast approach when the first stone shall be laid.' The king's blue eyes blazed.

'They shall be completed within three months, Your Majesty,' Herr Weimann promised.

'Three months?' The king glared down at him. 'Within three weeks! I must return to the mountains, I cannot stay here above a month. I cannot breathe in this air. I look out of my palace windows and what do I see?'

'The beautiful city of München?' offered Herr Weimann.

'Walls! People! All of them staring as though I were on a stage for their amusement.'

'The people love their king,' said Herr Weimann. 'They are captivated by his beauty, entranced by his majesty. How can they not gaze in adoration when he passes by?'

'How can they love their king when they do not understand him? My people are in the mountains.'

Herr Weimann raised his hands in a gesture of helplessness as though he knew not how to answer. 'Three weeks is so short to complete such detailed plans. The Muse cannot be rushed, she must be invited, she must be waited upon.'

'The Muse must obey the king! Three weeks, and the initial plans will be delivered to me. The interior designs will follow.'

'I shall have to work through the night, Your Majesty, to achieve such a feat!'

'And what of it? I often read and write through the night. Moonshine is the most beautiful of lights.'

'The Muse shall require greater comfort for such labour,' said Herr Weimann. 'To work night and day shall require a larger account for her humble vessel to draw upon.'

'Paul shall arrange all things,' said the king. 'Do not trouble me with small matters. Only speak to me of beauty and purity and art.'

'And it shall be a work of beauty, Your Majesty.' Herr Weimann assured the king. 'The turrets and towers shall gleam white and dazzling as snow on the mountains. And should the sun hide herself, and the clouds descend, shrouding the turrets like a veil, the mist rising from the lakes to swirl about its base —even then it shall be beautiful, for it will seem to float in the air—a castle in the clouds!

'And when the moon arises,' continued Herr Weimann, his face animated, his arms waving, 'she shall bathe the walls with her pure light, and they shall glow with unearthly splendour, just as they did in days of old!'

'Shall you use white stone, Herr Weimann?' Prince Paul enquired, peering over the shoulder of the architect at the drawings. 'I know not of any quarry in the kingdom that can produce such stone.'

Only Elisabeth caught Herr Weimann's look at his assistant, who stood apart from the group. she saw the young man mouth a word to his master. Herr Weimann frowned darkly as though he could not understand, so the young man mouthed the word more distinctly.

'Lime!' announced Herr Weimann triumphantly, his scowl vanishing. 'His Majesty shall have the stone from his own royal quarries, but the stone it shall be dressed in lime, that most alchemical, most magical of substances that shall cause the king's spires to shine by sun and moonlight!'

The king's lips curled with satisfaction. 'Three weeks,' he said in his musical voice. 'And the work shall begin.'

There came a light noise at the door. The prince answered it, then returned to the king's side.

'The Prime Minister awaits His Majesty's pleasure, sir,' Paul informed him.

The light dimmed in the king's face. 'His Majesty's pleasure does not reside with the Prime Minister. He must wait further. I must show the Swan Maiden my garden first. Farewell for now, Herr Weimann.'

'But The Friend shall see His Majesty at the theatre, shall he not?' Herr Weimann enquired before bowing. 'The Friend has heard the good news that the king permits the first performance since his sad time of mourning descended.'

'Shall The Friend have time for the theatre when he is labouring day and night to create his art?' replied the king, a trace of irony in his voice.

'It shall be a sacrifice to tear oneself away from such labour, but—the Muse, Your Majesty, she must be fed with such art as only royal patronage can procure.'

The king gave a brief nod of assent. Herr Weimann bowed again, looking gratified.

'Come this way, Fräulein Schwan' ordered the king as he

crossed the room with long strides, pushed open a hidden door in the gilt panelling and disappeared.

'Come,' Prince Paul said with his golden smile. Elisabeth followed with interest.

CHAPTER 17
THE WINTER GARDEN

THE DOOR in the panelling concealed a staircase with plain wooden walls, but carpeted in deep red. The king climbed fast, and Elisabeth hurried to keep up. She arrived at the top a little breathless, but her sudden gasp as she looked about her was not due to the exertion of the stairs, but to the sight that greeted her.

She stood under a great dome of glass. High above was the blue of the early June sky; around her and as far as she could see were plants and palms, and great frothy ferns. Exotic flowers glowed among the green, and a stretch of water, like a small mountain lake, sat serenely, with a bridge spanning it.

'Do you like the king's Winter Garden?' Paul asked. 'You are privileged to see it, few are permitted.'

'It's beautiful,' she said, speaking quietly, for the air was very still. She could hear only the sound of trickling water, until a shrill cry pierced the air, startling her.

'It's only the birds,' Paul assured her, pointing at a rustling clump of ferns, which were now parted by an emerging peacock. She sighed with admiration as it fanned out its tail in a perfect arc of iridescent blue and green. It stood before the king and seemed to bow its head before him.

There was a blur of colour, and a sound of soft buzzing and Elisabeth saw a bright flash streak through the air.

'Oh! Are they magic?' she cried as several more appeared, flitting and darting, vanishing and appearing in the blink of an eye.

'Hummingbirds,' said Paul. 'Imported from afar.'

The king walked on and they followed at a respectful distance. She forgot she was in a room of girders and glass, high above the royal palace, she was in an exotic garden, another world. Fish the colour of amber darted to the surface of the water, leaped into the air, and fell back with soft plops. A sudden turn in the path brought her before a fountain. Water flowed from the mouth of a marble dolphin, and the scent of flowers filled the warm air.

'Not enough flowers,' the king's voice said from somewhere ahead, hidden among the foliage. 'More ferns.'

Paul beckoned her to catch up. She lifted her long skirts and hurried down the path. The king stood on the little, ornate bridge, surveying the water. 'And where are my swans?'

'They were to follow on directly, sir,' said Paul. 'I will enquire immediately.'

Paul disappeared into the thick foliage, and Elisabeth was disconcerted to find herself alone with the king. He beckoned her to come nearer to where he stood on the bridge.

'I have brought the white swans with me,' he said.

'From Lake Swanstein?' she said in surprise.

'Yes. They may speak again. They may tell you what it is that is to be found.'

Elisabeth was silent for some minutes, watching the golden fish break the surface of the water, and admiring the water lilies.

'I wonder...' she dared to say, though hesitantly. 'I wonder, Your Majesty, how it is that you believed me so readily, when most would not.'

She thought he was not going to reply. She stole a glance

at him. He was so perfect, too perfect, as though he did not quite belong in the ordinary world. Standing tall and still as he was, he looked as a carved statue of a historical king, or an illustration of a mythic hero.

'I have never spoken of this since I was a small boy,' the king said in a low voice. He did not look at her, but watched the water below them. 'From as far back as I can recall, I heard living creatures speak. If I listened carefully, if there were no distractions, I could hear them. The words came as pictures, as fleeting images, some bright and strong, some soft and small, some so quick they were hard to catch.'

Elisabeth nodded, feeling a gladness bubble up inside her —there was someone else like her!

'What do they say to you?' she asked, her excitement in her voice. 'Do you hear horses and dogs the clearest? Birds are harder to understand, I find, and the smaller the creature the less I can hear, do you find the same?'

'I trained myself not to listen,' said the king. His musical voice sounded a low, sad note. Suddenly he looked so young, and she remembered he was but eighteen. She usually forgot that, for his manner was that of one poised and old beyond his years. 'I once told my nurse that I spoke to the animals, and my father heard of it.' He paused. 'And thus, I was corrected. Children who claimed to speak to animals were to be shut away from all creatures until they were cured of their fancies by isolation and by the rod.'

'How dreadful,' she said softly.

'It has been liberating to me to hear that you have the same gifting, Fräulein Schwan. It has reminded me of many things from my youth and caused me to think over them.'

There was another long pause. Elisabeth felt as if she were being entrusted with great confidences.

'When I was a child, I was quite sure that I did not belong in this world. Nor even in this body. I thought perhaps my birth was some kind of accident, or that I had different parents, another family where I could feel the comfort of belonging, instead of feeling as a stranger, an outsider.'

'And now, sir?' she dared to ask.

There was the ghost of a smile about his lips, but it was a rueful smile.

'And now I find all those old feelings rising up once again. I thought I had trained myself not to believe them. Education, discipline, fear of punishment and of disappointing my father, those were the tools to suppress all that was not… acceptable. But now…something awakens. And I do not know what it all means.'

She could not answer him. She did not know either.

'We are very alike are we not, Fräulein Schwan? We neither of us know who we really are, or where we belong. And yet we *are*. We exist even outside of memory, should it fail, do we not? There is something greater that holds us to life, that defines us beyond our families, beyond who we are expected to be, who we thought we should be. And even if we are cut off from all we have known, yet still we *are*. We have our own destiny to discover, and none can come with us, we must find it alone. We must pursue it even if those around us resist and are offended. We must pursue truth. We must be true. Only then can we know who we are.'

She nodded politely, not fully understanding all he said, and a little taken aback at hearing him talk so earnestly. And then she heard Prince Paul's voice from across the garden, giving instructions to someone. The king's expression altered in a moment. The youth and vulnerability and passion melted away. He was the king, cool and distant once again.

'I found them in the luggage room, sir,' said Paul, when he reappeared. 'I had them brought directly.'

'Luggage room!' the king was indignant.

'They have been released. There they are.' Paul pointed at the water, and one by one four swans appeared, ruffling their feathers and stretching their necks.

'Are they well?' the king asked.

'I think so, sir,' said Paul, but the king was not asking him.

Elisabeth directed her concentration to the swans. 'They are distressed, sir,' she said. 'Hopefully they will settle quickly.'

'You may feed them, Fräulein Schwan,' the king said. 'You may feed all my birds. I will not leave them to the indifferent care of servants. You alone can care for my creatures as I do. To you shall be granted the right of entering the king's Winter Garden,' said the king, crossing the bridge and walking on.

Paul indicated that she should follow on, giving her a smile that outshone the yellow lilies blooming in the ground.

Elisabeth soon found that the peacock was very particular about what he liked to eat: corn was his favourite, but it had better be good; no soggy or old grain for him. And he liked very much to be told how beautiful he was.

She could not understand anything the hummingbirds said, for they talked too fast and had no interest in her. But she put out fruit peelings, and topped up the tiny bowls of sugar water that hung about the garden. The swans were too vexed at first to eat the specially baked bread and green lettuce she had been supplied with to feed them, but they soon settled in and came gliding to the water's edge when she appeared with their food.

She watched the swans one morning. They spoke nothing new to her. They only repeated their insistent refrain: *must be found, must be found.* But they didn't seem to know what it was that was lost any more than she did. She concentrated hard, asking them what it was that must be found. The same image recurred, that of something green and jewel-like. 'What is it?' she spoke aloud, feeling frustrated. 'How can it be found if I don't know what it is?' But the swans had disappeared from view. They had nothing more to say to her.

'Can I help you, Fräulein?' came a voice from behind her. 'Have you lost something?'

'Oh, what are you doing here?' she said, whirling round and speaking more sharply than she meant to. It was Herr Weimann's assistant. He had startled her; she'd thought she was alone.

'I was sent to draw swans,' he said, holding up a sketchbook. 'For the king's designs. I am Herr Weimann's apprentice,' he said with a polite bow. 'I have seen you on occasion, but we have never met.'

'A pleasure to meet you,' she said without enthusiasm. She hoped he would wander off to find the swans, but he came to stand beside her.

'I have heard something of your story,' he said. 'It must be dreadful not remembering who you are. I hope all will be resolved quickly for you.'

'Thank you. But it is not supposed to be known.'

'I heard from the servants at the castle,' he admitted. 'But my master does not know. He does not speak to servants. And no one talks of it here at the palace.'

He had a gentle voice. She softened a little, and forgave him for intruding on her. 'They're round the other side,' she said, 'you'll have to cross the bridge. The swans,' she prompted.

'Oh, yes. The swans. Thank you, Fräulein…'

'Schwan,' she said with a wry smile.

He bowed his head courteously again.

'Mind that—' she called after him as he turned away; she had been about to say, 'mind that peacock!', but it was too late. The peacock screeched and the apprentice yelped as he received a peck on the leg.

'He was lucky I didn't step on him!' the apprentice exclaimed as he edged past the irate bird.

Clumsy, tail-less, ugly, lumbering giant! Is how Elisabeth would have translated the peacock's thoughts. She hoped he'd make a better impression on the swans; they were prone to be irritable too. They missed their lakeside home. There were no tasty frogs here, nor grass to graze when they fancied a wander about. But it was not her concern how the apprentice found the swans. It was not likely she would be seeing much of him.

CHAPTER 18
A NIGHT OF DRAMA

'THAT SHOULD BE good enough for the lords and ladies in their royal boxes,' the maid who waited on Elisabeth murmured. She pushed one last pin into Elisabeth's carefully arranged hair. Elisabeth stood up and smoothed down her gown of dark blue silk. It was demure and simple in design, it had been quickly made, so there had been no time for embellishment. No one would take her for a duchess or princess in it, but the cut and colour suited her. It would do well enough for an evening at the theatre.

A younger maid eyed Elisabeth with a pained look.

'I hear Prince Paul chose the colour himself,' she overheard the older maid saying to the girl in a sly tone. 'Wouldn't we all like to have a new gown chosen by the prince?' In the mirror, Elisabeth caught the flush on the young maid's cheeks. It would seem she was not the only girl Prince Paul could raise a blush from.

THE KING WAS NOT IN GOOD HUMOUR ON THEIR ARRIVAL AT THE theatre. 'What's wrong?' Elisabeth whispered to Paul as they stood outside the entrance to the royal box. The king's face was cold as marble, while his eyes were dark and stormy.

'The queen mother decided to come,' Paul whispered back. 'And invited much of the court. It spoils the king's pleasure to have a large audience. You look radiant, Fräulein Schwan. I knew that colour would suit you perfectly.'

She turned her face away from him so he could not see her expression; she was half pleased and half embarrassed. She looked down over the balcony to the entrance hall below. Across the circular floor of marble glided the tiny form of the queen mother, her black skirts billowing about her, diamonds glittering at her neck as she nodded at those who bowed and curtsied to her.

'What a pleasure this is,' the queen mother declared, as she reached the king. 'I have missed the theatre, have not you, Ludwig, dear?'

The king did not reply, but put out an arm for her to rest her hand upon.

'How well you look, Ludwig. Showing yourself to your people, as a king ought,' said the queen mother as they entered the royal box.

'I come to the theatre for art,' the king replied. 'I come to look, not to be looked at.' He glared about at the audience below. Every eye was turned to him; eyeglasses glittered in the candlelight as they fixed upon him. The queen mother gave a gracious wave to the audience and took her seat.

Herr Weimann, dressed in peacock blue, bowed and waved from the neighbouring box. Beyond him sat his apprentice. Elisabeth caught his eye, and he bowed his head to her.

'Why is that man seated in the king's guest box?' The queen mother asked.

'Because he is the king's guest,' replied the king.

'But who is he?'

'Herr Weimann.'

'The infamous architect?'

The king did not reply. Elisabeth, seated at the back of the box, could tell by the rigidity in his shoulders and head that he was irritated.

'My ladies talked of his return to München. Someone has paid all his shocking debts.' The queen mother gave a little gasp. 'It is not you, my son, is it? Have you paid off that reprobate's debts?'

'Herr Weimann serves me as architect,' said the king. 'That is all I wish to say upon the subject. Speak no more of it, please.'

The queen mother flicked open a fan and fanned herself vigorously. She glanced frequently at her son, opening her mouth, as though she longed to speak further, but the king's stony countenance silenced her.

No one in the audience could see Elisabeth at the back of the royal box, but she had a clear view of the stage below.

'Do you see anyone you recognise?' the prince asked softly.

She looked around the hall slowly, examining faces.

'No. I don't recognise anyone.'

'Is that Lady de la Rosee?' came the queen mother's voice above the hum of the orchestra as they prepared to begin. She was peering at the neighbouring boxes through her eyeglass. 'I heard she was unwell. I am surprised to see her. She looks ill, does she not? Poor woman. She should not have worn grey. And is that Count von Klass?' Her eyeglass swivelled to another box. 'He sits alone. Where is the countess? What has he done with her?'

The curtain was now rising from the stage.

'Ah, Lady Meilhaus! Dear Luisa. I wonder she has not written this week. She is usually so prompt in her attentions.'

'It begins!' the king whispered fiercely.

'Oh, so it does. And there is that singer I like. What is his name?' The king did not answer.

'Herr Leonard, Your Highness,' said the queen mother's lady-in-waiting, who was perched on the chair behind her.

'Herr Leonard. Yes. I am glad he is to be Tannhäuser

tonight. He is an excellent tenor. I heard the Viennese Governor had sent him for, but I am glad to see he has returned. Is not he an excellent Tannhäuser, Ludwig?'

The orchestra began, the sound filling the circular theatre with such power and clarity that Elisabeth felt the notes tingling through her. Surely she would remember if she'd ever had this experience before? Tannhäuser sang, and the hairs on her arms stood up. She sat wide-eyed, gripped with the intensity of the music all through the first act. There was a great pause when the last note sounded, as though no words could do justice to the gift of art that had been poured out. Then the queen mother's high voice pierced the silence.

'That was very nice, was it not, Ludwig?'

The magical moment was broken. All the notes of music dissipated.

The king did not reply. He stood up abruptly and almost threw himself from the box. Elisabeth stared after him, as did everyone. The prince followed him out. Unsure of what she should do, Elisabeth likewise followed them to the balconied hall outside.

'I cannot remain a moment longer—she drives all poetry away!' the king hissed, clutching the balcony bannister. 'How can the beauty of voice and music be *nice*!'

'Your Majesty!' cried a familiar voice. People were coming out of their boxes into the wide hall. Servants appeared with trays of champagne. Herr Weimann already held a flute of wine, he thrust it at his apprentice to be free to make a bow. The apprentice stepped back as he almost spilt champagne over himself. 'A remarkable first act, Leonard was divine!' Herr Weimann gushed. 'But where is he going?' Herr Weimann's voice faltered as the king strode away to the curved staircase.

'His Majesty is indisposed,' the prince answered. 'Herr Weimann, would you ensure the king's guest, Fräulein Schwan, is escorted back to the palace after the performance? I may not be able to return for her if retained by the king.'

Elisabeth looked at him in surprise.

'You would like to see the rest of the performance?' he enquired, turning to her. 'You were enjoying the first act.'

'Yes. Very much.' He had been observing her. That telltale blush crept over her cheeks again.

'If I can return for you myself I will. But I am at the king's service.' He smiled down at her. How thoughtful he was! She realised she was gazing back in admiration, and quickly looked away, her eyes falling on Herr Weimann's apprentice, who stood, still holding Herr Weimann's champagne flute.

'I should like to stay, sir,' she said simply. She curtsied in parting with him and turned to re-enter the royal box.

The queen mother's lady-in-waiting now appeared. 'Where is His Majesty? Her Royal Highness wishes to know.'

'He has left,' Elisabeth replied. 'The prince has followed him.'

The lady-in-waiting clucked her annoyance. 'That will distress Her Royal Highness. And why are you still here? You are not of Her Royal Highness's party?'

Elisabeth hesitated, suddenly feeling out of place and unwanted.

'Fräulein Schwan,' said a voice behind her. It was Herr Weimann's apprentice. 'Herr Weimann requests the pleasure of your company in his box, now that the prince has placed you under his protection.'

Looking between the disdainful face of Countess Hildebrand and the friendly one of the apprentice, Elisabeth felt she had no choice; she turned to accept his invitation.

The guest box was smaller than the royal box, not wishing to sit conspicuously beside Herr Weimann, Elisabeth took the seat near the apprentice, though the corner seats, were shadowy and not well lit.

Herr Weimann held court as men in formal evening attire and ladies in jewels came to greet the new royal favourite. They praised Herr Leonard's performance. They rejoiced that the king had reopened the royal theatre and not prolonged the period of mourning. Herr Weimann's bows and gestures were worthy of the stage behind him, and he outshone everyone with his beautifully embroidered waistcoat, his ornately tied cravat, his diamond cufflinks and pearl buttons.

'A gift from His Majesty,' Herr Weimann was telling his present acquaintance, a lady in blue silk and sapphires who was admiring his cufflinks. He turned his wrist, so the light caught the stones. 'One of many. The king is so very generous. He surpasses all. "My Friend", he said to me, "take this trifle as a mark of my attachment and my recognition of your genius." He always calls me Friend. So generous. How humbled I am by his patronage and deep affection.'

'Most generous,' drawled a deep voice. Elisabeth felt a jarring sensation—that voice—it was familiar, but not in a welcome way. It struck a chord of fear. For a moment she could not breathe. She dared to look. It was a tall, lean man, standing with his gloved hands behind his back as he stood in the entrance to the box. She could not see his face, for his back was to her. She could have stretched out an arm and touched his sleeve, so close was he.

'Fräulein Schwan,' said a low voice. 'Are you well?'

She turned to the apprentice, and realised she was trembling, but she did not know why.

'A man as young as the king, barely out of the schoolroom,' the tall, lean man was saying, 'is easily swayed by those of more mature years whom he admires.'

'What are you saying?' said Herr Weimann, squaring his shoulders and pursing his lips.

'It is no criticism,' replied the man. 'Make the most of what opportunities come your way, that is one of my mottoes.'

The orchestra were preparing to begin. There was a stir as people returned to their seats for the second act. The stranger made a slight bow, his companion, the lady in sapphires, allowed Herr Weimann to kiss her fingers, which sparkled with more sapphires. The smell of pomade caught Elisabeth's nose as the stranger passed her by. It had a hint of camphor, and for some reason the smell turned her stomach.

It was a mercy the man had not turned to look at her, she did not know why, she only knew that she did not want him to see her. She leaned against the back of the velvet chair cushion, willing her stomach to stop churning, and wondering what it all meant.

'Take this,' said the voice of Herr Weimann's apprentice. He held out a glass towards her. 'You seem unwell.'

Her mouth was dry, so she took the glass and sipped. She could barely concentrate on the second act; her thoughts were swirling, and she felt confined and trapped in the darkened box. Before the next interval began, she swallowed her pride and leaned over to the apprentice and whispered, 'Could you escort me back to the palace, please? I feel unwell.'

'Of course,' he said. 'If you care to get your cloak, I will meet you at the entrance. I shall speak a word to my master first.'

'I COULD NOT GET A CARRIAGE,' THE APPRENTICE SAID apologetically. 'Are you able to walk?'

'Yes, perfectly able. It's not far.'

'I'm sorry your evening has been spoiled,' he continued. 'But Herr Leonard is not the best Tannhäuser, in my opinion. Herr Hermann is far better.'

'I would not know. I've never heard him sing. I don't think.'

'I saw him in Berlin. He performs with such honesty, such passion, as though he really is Tannhäuser. Herr Leonard sings as though he is only acting, or so I have always thought.'

'You differ from your master's opinion,' she observed.

He only tilted his head to one side as a gesture of assent.

'I can have no opinion on the subject, I cannot recall having been to the theatre until tonight.'

'All the more pity that you were taken ill.'

'Yes.'

She struggled to talk. She was uneasy and unsettled by her peculiar reaction to the stranger. The worst of it was that she did not know if her reaction was in response to something real or imaginary.

The apprentice tried to make further conversation, but gave up eventually.

'Thank you,' she said, relieved when the entrance to the palace was in sight, lit by large, brass lanterns. 'I can make my way from here.'

He bowed and turned to leave. A pang of conscience assailed her. He had been very kind, and she had been distracted and distant. 'Thank you for escorting me,' she said in a softer voice. 'I am grateful.'

He paused and gave a half smile. 'You are most welcome.'

She put out a hand for him to shake as an offering of conciliation. He accepted.

'What did you say your name was?' she asked; she could not remember if he had told her or not.

He hesitated, as though the question made him uncomfortable, he dropped a glove he had been carrying. He seemed to drop things a lot. But why should he feel discomfort when asked his name?

'Herr Haller,' he said. 'My friends call me Christian.'

'Good night, Herr Haller,' she said, and left him.

CHAPTER 19
MAIDEN'S BLUSHES

THE NIGHTMARE WAS MORE intense the night after the theatre. Now her assailant in the dream smelled of camphor.

She told the prince what had happened next morning; he said he would make discreet enquiries as to the identity of the man. He would not trouble the king directly, as he was with the Cabinet Secretary being persuaded to agree to a date for the banquet in honour of the emperor, as well as contending with worse news—the Duke of Preußen was continuing to press for unification. The duke was preparing his troops, and urging Bayern to make ready her army.

'Is it serious?' Elisabeth asked. 'Might we be forced to go to war?'

'It is serious. And His Majesty hates war. He will do all he can to avert it, although that is not a popular decision with the government.'

'You are right not to trouble him with my concerns,' said Elisabeth.

'He will want to know,' Paul assured her. 'But I shall wait until the right time to tell him, and in the meantime, I will make enquiries and report it to the Chief Inspector. He wishes to interview you as soon as can be arranged, though he is out of the city at present.'

'It may be nothing,' she said. 'I may have imagined it all. The man could be a perfectly innocent stranger. I don't know what is real anymore.' She wrung her hands, feeling strained from her nightmare-filled night.

'Don't worry,' said the prince, taking her anxious hands and smiling softly down at her. 'We will find out the truth.'

His confidence reassured her. 'Thank you,' she said. It was impossible to feel anything but safe and warm with him looking at her as he did. She did not voice the thought that the truth might not be something good. She was half afraid of finding out who she was. She almost wished she could stay just as she was at that moment.

'I have something that will take your mind off last night,' said Paul, still holding her hands. 'A visit to Herr Weimann's, when the king is finished with his meetings. It ought to be entertaining, if nothing else.'

THE CARRIAGE BORE HER THROUGH THE WIDE, ORDERLY STREETS. The city walls soared, ornamented with pillars and arches and festooned with stone wreaths. Stone lions guarded the head of every street, lying atop their stone mounts, or seated, with shield in paw, on stone pillars.

Well-dressed ladies and gentlemen strolled the clean streets, pausing to speak to acquaintances, eying the riders and carriages that rumbled past to see if there were anyone of note travelling by. Prince Paul, riding on horseback ahead of the king's carriage was a sight to draw every admiring eye. Elisabeth was glad her own small carriage was anonymous, without insignia or coronet.

The driver reined the horses to a slow walk as they reached a pair of tall gates, which swung open at the arrival of the prince. The carriages and outriders passed through them, and up a sweeping driveway to a mansion of pale stone, built in the new style.

A columned portico led into a circular hall of marble floor

and walls. Alcoves lined the hall, housing life-sized statues of ancient people. The chandeliers above were grand enough to rival those at the palace, as were the sweeping twin staircases ahead.

From one of many doors a figure appeared. It was Herr Haller, the apprentice. 'If you would care to come this way, Your Majesty,' he greeted the king with a bow. 'Herr Weimann awaits you in the yellow drawing room.'

Paul gave his crop and hat to a footman who stepped forward to take them. Herr Haller bowed in greeting to the prince and then to Elisabeth. 'Fräulein Schwan,' he said pleasantly. Elisabeth thought, as she lifted the short veil on her hat, that he looked pale and very tired.

Herr Weimann stood waiting in the centre of the drawing room. His yellow beret and waistcoat in vivid accord with the yellow silk-hung walls. The carpet was of yellow, a pattern of green leaves woven on it. The long couches and upholstered chairs were of yellow velvet.

'Come and see, Your Majesty!' cried Herr Weimann, opening his brocaded arms to gesture to a round, marble-topped table behind him. 'Is it not beautiful? It was completed last night, and it was all I could do not to send word to come at the hour of four in the morning!'

Herr Weimann stepped aside to reveal a model, standing on a cloth of baize. The king moved to the table, bending to inspect it more closely. Silence fell upon the room as he scrutinised the model of a castle. A castle of white walls, with high towers and turret roofs the colour of the blue mountains of Bayern.

'Stand aside, Your Highness,' Herr Weimann said to the prince. 'You are blocking the light.'

Paul moved away from the window, and the summer sun fell full upon the model. The white towers gleamed.

The king moved about the table, examining the model carefully. His expression was closed, and Elisabeth felt the tension in the air as Herr Weimann waited for his response. It did not bode well, for no smile, no show of pleasure showed upon the king's face.

'Does His Majesty approve?' Herr Weimann asked finally. 'He observes the harmony in the symmetry of the gatehouse? He sees how noble the lines of the windows of the singers' hall are? Perfectly aligned to the west, so the golden evening sun pours in through the coloured glass to fill the hall. And His Majesty's own private suite—see how it commands a full view of the mountains, unimpeded by the towers? Observe the galleried walkways, Your Majesty, their archways framing the views beyond.'

The king was still silent, his eyes passing from the model to the carefully drawn plans laid down beside it.

Elisabeth noticed the apprentice stifling a yawn. He caught her glance and gave a lop-sided smile. She had to suppress a giggle at the contortions his face was making in trying to not yawn. The tension in the air was making her feel the need to yawn or laugh too.

The king stood up from his examination. His face a mask of gravity. 'Herr Weimann,' he said in his musical voice.

'Yes, Your Majesty?' Herr Weimann stood with hands clasped before him, as though appealing for a word of acceptance. 'Does my humble translation of the inspiration of the Muse satisfy the king?'

'Herr Weimann, you are not The Friend of the King.'

'I am not?' Herr Weimann's beret feather trembled.

'You, Herr Weimann, are The *Beloved* Friend of the King. You are his Genius, his True Artist, the only one who understands his soul's need for beauty!'

'Hah!' laughed Herr Weimann, bowing low. 'His Majesty is the divinely appointed Patron of True Art! His Majesty is most Treasured Friend to the Muse. History shall remember His Majesty forever as the Champion of Beauty and Vision! What is the Beloved Friend without his Patron? Who is he but a lowly artist?'

'The work must begin at once,' said the king, marching

around the table. 'Oh, that this wretched banquet did not keep me here when I desire to be surrounded by mountains of everlasting stone, not these temporal bricks of the city. I must return home and begin the work!'

'Indeed, His Majesty must,' agreed Herr Weimann. 'But His Majesty must not forget his duty to his people. The banquet, the ball—are they not works of beauty also? Should not the king extend his patronage to his subjects in the city as well as in the mountains? Will he not spread his light, his love, his radiance to us poor dwellers of temporal bricks?'

'The king will do his duty,' said the king soberly. 'He always does.'

'And His Majesty's most humble servant, The Beloved Friend, he shall bear the honour of a lowly seat at the royal banquet?' Herr Weimann put a hand to his own breast, as though it ached with longing.

'Forgive my intrusion, Herr Weimann,' said Prince Paul, 'but the banquet is strictly for members of state and nobility. The emperor himself is the honoured guest.'

Herr Weimann's face turned dark for a moment, and his hand upon his breast clenched.

'If the king wishes The Beloved Friend to eat at his table, then eat he shall,' said the king.

Herr Weimann's fingers unclenched. 'And does the king wish it?' he dared ask with a quivering voice.

'He does. Among such a table of war-mongering ministers and dragon-tongued courtiers should not the king have one friend?'

Herr Weimann beamed and made his bows while the king made his farewells.

Elisabeth trailed behind the departing men. Herr Weimann was pointing out articles of decor and ornamentation to the king as they passed through the sumptuous rooms.

'I trust you are comfortable in the accommodation supplied,' she heard the king say.

'Delighted, Your Majesty,' Herr Weimann assured him.

'My poor artist's soul could desire nothing more to minister to his small needs as he labours night and day. The only trifle that is lacking, Your Majesty, is the lack of music. There is but one piano, Your Majesty, only one.'

'How many pianos does one need?' enquired the king.

'When The Beloved Friend is pacing through his chambers, night and day, up and down stairs, searching for that image of perfection, sometimes only the sound of beautiful music stirring the air, filling the halls and rooms will entice the elusive Muse to come to him. The sound of the harp, the strings, the ivory keys of the piano—the sweet harmonies of a beautiful voice—only His Majesty can understand how music and song brings forth life and meaning.'

'Paul shall arrange all things,' acceded the king.

'Art thanks His Majesty with all her soul!' declared Herr Weimann. 'Come, let me show you the gallery where I am assembling a collection of busts of every artist and poet and musician throughout history.'

The king and Herr Weimann swept away up a staircase, with Prince Paul following close after.

'Would you care to see the gardens?' a voice behind Elisabeth asked. 'The roses are beautiful at this time of the year. The gallery of artists is quite lengthy. They will be some time.'

She turned to the apprentice. 'Thank you, Herr Haller. I should infinitely prefer roses to dead poets.' She thought privately that he looked as though a walk in the sunshine would do him good, for he was pale with shadows under his eyes.

He smiled and gestured the way, almost walking into a doorframe as he did so.

'What is it you do for Herr Weimann?' she asked as they walked leisurely along the garden pathways.

'Whatever he asks of me. I draw, sketch, calculate, build models.'

'Did you make the model of the new castle?'

He nodded.

'Does he keep you up all night working as he does?'

He pulled a rueful face. 'One of us works all night,' he said. 'The other prefers to dine out and visit concerts and performances.'

'But he takes you with him? You were at the theatre last week.'

'Only if there is something he wishes me to take note of.'

'Take note?'

'A piece of architecture; a style or design that he thinks might be relevant to the project in hand. He wished me to see the theatre to observe the mouldings on the exterior of the balconies. He would like it replicated in the new castle.'

They reached the rose garden, and it was as he had said: beautiful. 'If I were building a castle,' Elisabeth said, inhaling the warm, scented air, 'I should look to such beauty as this for inspiration.' She stopped to look up to admire the trailing roses in the trellis walkway above them.

'As would I,' agreed Herr Haller. Elisabeth was distracted from the hanging roses by him stumbling into a trellis post.

'Are you hurt?' she asked.

He rubbed his forehead and attempted a grin. 'I get so clumsy when I'm tired. Or anxious.'

They walked on, Herr Haller telling her some of the funny names of the roses. They laughed over *Big Maiden's Blush*, wondering if it was the blush or the maiden who was big. He plucked the stem of one climbing rose and held it out to her. It was a spray of white buds. She hesitated. It seemed a little forward to be accepting a gift from a young man, even if the gift was so slight.

'My mother used to say that flowers have meanings,' he said, still offering the cluster. 'White rosebuds are for purity. A man would give such a rose to his sister, or friend.'

She took the spray.

'There you are!' called the voice of Prince Paul.

'I'm sorry, have you been looking for me? I only stepped out to see the gardens.'

'So, I see,' said the prince, reaching them. He looked at the roses in her hand, then glanced at Herr Haller, and back at her.

'Good day, Herr Haller,' she said with more briskness than she intended, unsettled by the thought that the prince had read more into the scene than was really there.

Herr Haller bowed to them, his look of weariness returning; she hurried away to the waiting carriage.

CHAPTER 20
A CARRIAGE OF BIRDS

IT WAS the day of the feast. Elisabeth lingered in the Winter Garden that morning, but not from pleasure—only from anxiety, for she could only find three swans.

She searched every foot of the garden, pacing round the artificial lake over and again, hunting for the missing swan. She asked the remaining three where their companion had gone. They were flustered and scattered in their thoughts, sending hazy images of what looked like men with loud voices and nets.

She searched the palace for Paul, but the prince was excessively busy that morning, and she could not get a word with him. The king was likewise engaged. She found the palace chamberlain, but he looked at her as though she were mad when she explained that she was looking for a missing swan.

'I have no time, madam,' he said, 'to hunt for birds. The emperor is coming!'

She found the Haushofmeister, but he had no interest in ducks—the emperor was coming!

'Swan,' she called after his retreating figure. 'Not a duck,' but he was gone.

She searched the grounds, questioning every gardener she met. But no one had seen a stray swan.

She returned to the palace, feeling defeated, and paused in the great hall, watching the preparations, and wondering where she could look next. She stood near a windowed alcove, out of the way of the hurrying servants, then soon realised she was not alone. There were voices behind her, and she turned to see the two elderly princesses, huddled together, their figures obscured behind the drapes of the window.

'Look, Little Sister, see where they will dance,' said Princess Marie, peeking out behind the drapes.

'As we once danced,' said Princess Sibylle. 'Under the moon, with all the pretty lights dancing with us.'

'And the music, Sister, recall the music, and the singing.'

'Oh, the singing! They do not know how to sing here, they only warble and croak.'

Elisabeth approached them. 'Good morning, Your Highnesses,' she greeted, giving a curtsey.

They started at her voice; Princess Sibylle brandished her silver-topped stick as though to fend her off, but on seeing who it was she lowered it again. 'How do you see us?' she said. 'We are invisible. Sister, it is her. The one who smells of the mountain.'

'Come here,' said Princess Marie, beckoning Elisabeth to her. 'Do not let them see you, or they will take you away and lock the door.'

'Who will take me away?' Elisabeth asked, moving to their side.

'Back!' cried Princess Sibylle as Elisabeth moved near her. 'Do not touch me, you will dirty me!'

Alarmed at her sudden vehemence Elisabeth stepped back again.

'Come by me,' urged Princess Marie. 'You know better than to touch my sister.'

'Who will take me away,' Elisabeth repeated, lowering her voice and stepping farther into the curtained alcove as four footmen filed past, bearing boxes of candles.

'All of them,' said Princess Marie.

'Except our bright and beautiful boy,' said Princess Sibylle, examining her white dress carefully, as though looking for a speck of dirt. 'Did the footsteps of those footmen dirty my gown?'

'Your gown is white as snow, Little Sister,' Princess Marie assured her. 'You come from the mountain,' she said. 'I know you have, for we can hear the flowers upon you, can we not, Little Sister?'

Princess Sibylle ceased examining her gown and looked up to say, 'Oh, yes. Yes, we can. We knew you were coming, for the moonlight told us.' She inhaled deeply. 'And you smell delightful, lightful, full of light Where is that scent coming from?' She sniffed genteelly in Elisabeth's direction. 'It is coming from there,' she declared, stretching out a wrinkled finger to point below Elisabeth's throat. 'What is it?'

Elisabeth pulled out her swan pendant and let it rest against her gown.

'Oh!' cried both sisters, reaching out, so that she stepped back, putting a hand to her necklace to avoid it being snatched at.

'Only let us look!' begged Princess Sibylle.

Elisabeth removed her hand, still wary of any sudden lunge.

'How I wish we could get back to the mountains, Sister,' Princess Sibylle said in a mournful tone. Her eyes not leaving the pendant. 'To see the swans, to follow them once again, into the cave—'

'Hush, Little Sister,' Princess Marie said sternly. 'Do not mention the cave. It is a secret.'

'Oh, yes,' whispered Princess Sibylle. 'Such a secret. When shall we go?'

Her sister did not reply, for at that moment the curtain they stood behind was yanked aside and Princess Sibylle squealed as Frau Müller appeared.

'You naughty, naughty Highnesses, I have been looking

everywhere for you! You will get me into trouble, you will get me fired—is that what you want?'

Princess Sibylle nodded and brandished her stick. 'Do not touch me! Not one speck of dirt, not one!'

'Come along nicely, and I won't touch you,' Frau Müller pledged, ducking back to avoid Princess Sibylle's stick. 'Hit me again, Your Highness, and I will cast it into the fishpond, that I will!'

'Let me touch it once,' Princess Marie said in parting. She put out a trembling hand to reach for the pendant. 'Just a touch.' Elisabeth held up the carved swan so she might touch its surface. Princess Marie's thin fingers suddenly closed tight upon it and a fierce look came into her eyes as she made to yank it from Elisabeth's neck.

'Stop that!' Elisabeth exclaimed, tugging her pendant free.

The fierceness drained from Princess Marie's eyes and they filled with tears instead.

'Come along, Your Highness,' said Frau Müller, taking hold of her arm. 'This way. It's nearly luncheon, you don't want to miss your broth, now, do you?'

'Eat this, drink that,' sang Princess Marie glumly as she was led away. 'Sit there, be quiet.'

'Never never go into the shining cave where the walls glitter and glimmer and sing,' added Princess Sibylle's quavery voice. 'But we want to go, don't we Sister? Oh, why can't we go?'

Elisabeth watched the little figures totter away under the close supervision of Frau Müller.

'Fräulein Schwan,' called a familiar voice. Paul was marching by with a group of young officers. He stood taller and broader and more handsome than all of them in his deep blue uniform with gold epaulets and braiding. 'I hope the mad aunts did not trouble you?'

'Not at all.'

'Very good.' He smiled and bowed his head and passed on, clearly busy with duties.

'One of your latest, Paul?' She heard one of the officers say as they moved away. She did not catch the prince's reply, but she heard his voice and wondered at the laughter that rippled through the group. That did trouble her, and so did the realisation that she had not taken the opportunity to tell the prince of the missing swan, and now he was out of sight.

The mystery of the swan worried her all day; she felt responsible for it, she had been charged by the king to watch over them. She was not of rank to be present at the grand feast, so she had no preparations of her own to see to. She felt adrift in the bustle of the palace, as everybody but her seemed to have something urgent to do. Even the prince, her one ally, had abandoned her; and why had he laughed with those officers about her? She felt very low.

Herr Weimann arrived later that afternoon that he might discuss building plans with the king before the guests arrived. Elisabeth had not seen the king that day. She saw Herr Weimann strutting down the hall to the king's apartments, his apprentice following, bearing an armful of documents. Herr Weimann was dressed in full evening dress with a white waistcoat embroidered in silver. She wondered if his flashing buttons were of real diamonds, if so, they were sizeable indeed.

Later she wandered back up to the Winter Garden, hoping against hope that the missing swan might have somehow returned. But there were still only three fretful swans remaining.

'Do I intrude?' a voice called to her from the little bridge. Herr Haller turned towards her, his sketchbook in hand.

'No, not at all,' she replied. Feeling glad to see a friendly face after her anxious day.

'Are you alright?' he asked. 'You look worried.'

'There's a swan missing. I've looked everywhere. I cannot think where it could be.'

Herr Haller crossed the bridge to reach her. 'Missing?' he frowned. 'There's no way it could wander out of here. I assume you've searched every inch of this place.'

'Many times. I think it's been taken. But I don't know by who, or why.'

Herr Haller frowned again and rubbed his forehead as though that helped him think more clearly.

'There's only one reason I can think of why someone would want to take a swan.'

'What's that?'

He looked grim. 'Follow me. I hope I'm wrong, but we'll soon find out.'

She followed Herr Haller through the palace, away from the king's suite, down to the servants' wings and into the maze of kitchen preparation rooms.

'Why are we here?' Elisabeth asked, as cooks and servers flew about her.

Through the archway to the cold room she saw great pyramids of jellies on silver salvers. She and Herr Haller stood back against the wall as a pair of footmen passed out of the cold room bearing between them a great statue of ice carved into a life-size swan—the king's royal symbol. After them came two footmen with an ice statue of an eagle, the symbol of the emperor.

She followed Herr Haller farther into the kitchens, past the pastry room, the baking room, the fish room, into the main kitchen which was sweltering from the heat of the range. In an antechamber, great platters of roasted meat stood decorated in fanciful displays, served on columns and stands carved from white fat.

'Grand Duchess Soup!' hollered a chef in a tall white hat, red-faced from heat and exertion. 'TAKE OUT THE SOUP!'

Waiters hurried to take up silver tureens, filing out into the servery.

'Queen-style Soufflé!' bellowed the chef. 'How long?'

'Nineteen minutes, sir!' shouted back someone from a distant part of the kitchen.

'Prince's Calves Ears on Torte! How long?'

'Twenty-seven minutes, sir!' shouted someone else.

'Pan-sear of the Duke! How long?'

'Ready to be seared, fourteen minutes before service, sir!'

'Emperor's Swan!'

'Roasted and resting, ready to be served in two minutes, sir!'

'Swan!' Elisabeth said in horror, looking at Herr Haller.

'I feared as much.' He looked pained. 'Sorry.'

Elisabeth rushed into the preparation room. A roast swan sat upon a silver platter, re-clothed in its skin and feathers. It was a macabre sight.

'Where did you get the swan?' she cried, taking hold of the arm of the cook who was pouring liquid green jelly into the base of a platter. He swung round and glared at her.

'Get out of here! I've got two minutes to get this done!'

'Where did you get the swan?' she cried again, feeling frantic.

'It wasn't on the menu,' said another cook, turning his pyramid of carefully balanced roast quails to garnish the back of the platter. 'We got word that roast swan is the emperor's favourite dish, so we had to move fast.'

'Who took it?' Elisabeth's voice was trembling with anger. 'It belonged to the king!'

The cook shrugged. 'I don't know who took it. I just decorate the things.'

Elisabeth couldn't bear to remain in the same room as the swan. She looked about for Herr Haller, but he was nowhere to be seen.

She left the kitchens, desperate to get away from the heat and noise. She slumped against the wall of the hall outside. A hand was placed lightly on her shoulder.

'Where did you go?' she asked Herr Haller.

'I asked around. The head chef had word early this

morning that the emperor was to have roast swan served in his honour as his favourite dish.'

'But why take the king's own swan?'

'He said it was the only one to be got hold of at such short notice. They thought the king would want to please the emperor. At least they left the peacock alone,' Herr Haller said by way of comfort.

'You don't understand,' she said. 'Those swans are important to the king. What will he say?'

'Roasts to be taken out for display!' sounded a loud voice.

Servers swarmed in to take up the platters, Herr Haller pulled Elisabeth to one side to avoid being crushed.

'We can't let them take it out!' she said, pushing Herr Haller's hand from her arm.

'We can't stop them,' he said. 'We don't have the authority.'

'You don't understand!' She rushed after the men bearing the swan to the banquet hall. But it was not easy to follow them through the crowd of servers and cooks and scullery maids. Herr Haller pulled her to the side once again as she was almost mown down by a potboy carrying an enormous pile of copper pans to the scullery.

'You don't understand!' she said again to him, as he held her safely out of the way. The hallways cleared as the servers left. She was tearful with frustration. Herr Haller regarded her with concern.

'No, I don't understand. What is so important about it? There are plenty of others in the king's waters. Do you really think he would begrudge the emperor one?'

She did not answer, but hurried down the hall, she had to stop the king from seeing his swan.

'Fräulein Opel, it has been reported to the Committee that the king's behaviour at the banquet that night was most disturbed. Can you confirm this?'

'I was not at the banquet. I was not of rank to be invited.'

'But you must know of what happened that evening. You were there, in the palace.'

'I know that he left the banquet hall before the meal had ended, yes.'

'In the middle of the soufflé course, was it not? He abandoned the table in the emperor's presence, his most honoured guest. He brought the evening's festivities to a sudden and violent halt, did he not?'

'I believe it was the soup course,' she said lamely. 'But, yes. He did bring the feast to a sudden halt.'

'Can you tell us why? Some report that he had an inexplicable outburst of rage. Some say he was drunk, others say there was no cause whatsoever, but was a moment of sheer madness. Perhaps the first sign of an impending lunacy. Would you agree?'

'No. I would not. He was not mad, or drunk. And he had good cause to be upset.'

'Pray, do explain.'

'They had served his swan.'

'His swan?'

'It was said that the Emperor of Österreich's favourite dish was roast swan.'

'I do not understand. Why would this cause the king to act with such violence? He threw his glass to the floor in front of his guests. He threw back his chair in his fury, did he not? He raged and used the most violent of language. The Countess of Landsfeld fainted with shock. These are attested facts.'

'They should not have taken his swan. He loved all his creatures.'

'He loved his swan. Hmm, does that sound like the sentiment of a rational man? Would a rational man humiliate the Emperor of Österreich and tyrannise his guests with uncontrolled rage because he loved his swan? You do not answer, Fräulein.'

'I have nothing further to say on the matter. They took his swan and cooked it. It was most distressing for the king. They should not have done such a thing.'

'Perhaps they should not have plucked the pea pods from the palace vegetable gardens without the king's express permission!'

'Should you mock your king in such a way?'

'We do not know if we still have a king. We have only a Protector until the king is found.'

'Only a usurper!'

'I see you share the quality of high temper with our missing king, Fräulein. Take care it does not lead you into trouble also. We will remain sensible here as we pursue the truth of the matter.'

'Truth? You will not believe the truth.'

'Enough! I will make allowance for your feminine hysteria to a degree, especially considering your recent trauma, but we must continue in a spirit of rationality. Pray, continue your account. What happened that night when the king stormed out of the banquet?'

'He left. He returned to his mountain castle.'

'And you left also?'

'Yes. I received the order to leave. The carriages drove through the night.'

'And is it true that one carriage contained birds?'

'Yes.'

'You did not consider that odd? A gilded royal carriage with three pairs of horses to transport a peacock and three swans?'

'I considered that the king did not think it safe to leave his birds behind.'

There was a snigger from somewhere in the room, which quickly turned into a cough.

'And what happened when you returned to Castle Swanstein?'

'He began building his own castle. New Swanstein.'

'Describe to us the events of that period, Fräulein Opel. It may shed light on some puzzling facts and strange reports.'

'What do you wish to know?'

'Everything.'

168

CHAPTER 21
RUMOURS

Elisabeth only saw the king once the next day. It was very early in the morning, and the mist still hovered over the lake as she stood watching it.

'Are they well?' said the king, appearing suddenly at her side, looking more like a herald of moonrise than daybreak, with his luminous, pale skin and his deep-blue eyes.

'They are glad to be back,' she replied. The three white swans were ghostly outlines on the water as the mist swirled round them.

'I wish I could communicate my sorrow to them,' said the king, 'for failing to protect them.'

'I wish I could have protected them also.'

'Do they speak any new message? I listen, but I hear only the same thing repeated.'

'Nothing new, sir. There is only the same message regarding the raising of the castle, and of finding what was lost.'

'That is what I hear. I searched throughout the palace treasury, looking for something carved of green gemstone, but I only found jewellery. And it is not jewellery that is sought.'

'No,' she agreed. 'It is not jewellery. It is something large enough to be held, but I cannot see what it is. I will keep asking.'

'And I must begin building. There is an urgency, is there not? A power that grows stronger.' He looked toward the mountain, which was hazy and hidden.

Elisabeth shivered, and wrapped her arms about herself. She too felt the urgency and awakening power, but what did it all portend?

'A MOUNTAIN LAKE ON A SUMMER'S DAY IS GLORIOUS, IS IT NOT?'

Paul's voice startled Elisabeth out of her reverie. It seemed she could not rest at the lakeside at any time that day without someone finding her.

'Where do your thoughts take you, Fräulein Schwan? Or to whom do your thoughts take you?'

He sat down beside her on the grassy bank. He was so close she could feel the warmth radiating from him.

'Beautiful.' He sighed. He was looking at her. 'I have travelled to many places and seen many landscapes, but none can match sitting beside a Bayern lakeside.'

'Nothing can match sitting beside a Bayern lakeside alone,' she said, trying to cover her discomfort at his nearness. She had been deep in thought of the king and his inner turmoil, and she had not forgotten Paul's behaviour at the palace the previous day.

'I will leave if you wish.' He actually sounded hurt, and she looked at him. His deep brown eyes were far too easy to gaze into. 'I thought we were friends.'

'I thought the same,' she replied. 'But If we are such good friends, tell me what you and your companions were laughing at when you saw me yesterday.'

He looked puzzled, and then his face cleared. 'My sweet girl, we were not laughing at you. I am ashamed to admit we were laughing at the mad aunts.'

'That was not kind. They are to be pitied, not laughed at.'

He was silent for a moment. 'You are right,' he admitted. 'What a good heart you have, as well as a lovely everything else.' He took up her hand and kissed it. 'Are we friends again?'

It was impossible not to melt at his warm smile. He took her softened look as an assent.

'May I call you Elsa?' he asked. 'When we are alone. Fräulein Schwan is so formal, and we have known each other for some time now.'

'Twenty-two days,' she replied.

He grinned. 'You have been counting.'

'I have been counting how long it has been since I arrived, and wondering how long it will be before I remember who I am.'

'I never got the chance to arrange a meeting between you and the Chief Inspector,' Paul said. 'I did not expect to be dragged away from München so soon.'

'I suppose it will be the talk of the city,' Elisabeth said, 'the king leaving as he did.'

'I fear it will be worse than mere talk.' The prince said with a shake of his head. He plucked up a daisy and twirled it between his fingers. 'It is a very serious political debacle. I don't know how things will fall out now.'

They were silent a while, looking out at the view, Elisabeth felt the gravity of the king's situation with the emperor, but Paul, it seemed, could not remain serious for long.

'You fit in perfectly in this landscape, Elsa,' he said, his playful tone returning. 'The mysterious Swan Maiden who appears at the royal castle. Where she has come from, no one knows. Is she of this world, or has she stepped out of Faerie? Has she come to enchant and bewitch the handsome prince who finds her?'

'No good ever came to a prince who succumbed to the enchantments of Faerie, is that not what the stories say?' she replied.

'And they are true,' he said with mock tragedy. 'For my heart is haunted by unattainable beauty—I am bewitched.'

'You obviously read too many fairy tales, sir.'

'Call me Paul. I promise to leave you in peace if you say it just once.' He had not let go of her hand. He locked his fingers tightly about hers. 'Say it, Elsa, my Faerie queen.'

'Very well, *Paul*.'

He laughed, released her hand and jumped to his feet. 'Farewell for now, beautiful lady of the lake. Sadly, for me— duties call.' He presented her with the plucked daisy, he bowed, he smiled, then was gone. She turned her head to look after him; he likewise turned and waved.

A black swan neared the bank and looked at her.

'I know,' she said to it. 'I'm being foolish. My life is problematic enough without letting my head be turned by a man, even if he is the most handsome prince in all the kingdom.' She sighed.

The swan gave a little honk, as if to say, *turn your head, is exactly what you just did.*

When she saw the prince later that day his smiles were gone.

A visitor had arrived; Elisabeth, hearing the bustle of someone being announced moved to leave the drawing room where she sat alone. From the hallway she heard Paul telling somebody that the king was not receiving anyone.

'I am not here to see the king,' replied a woman's voice. A few minutes later Paul burst through the doorway, looking dismayed at seeing Elisabeth, as though he'd hoped she would not be there.

'What's wrong?' she asked.

'Is this her?' said a female voice, almost pushing past Paul to enter the room.

Paul spoke with reluctance. 'Fräulein Schwan,' he said, may I introduce to you Lady von Pless.'

Elisabeth curtsied, noting that the visitor was a fashionable lady of around thirty or so years, and a wealthy woman, if her gown and jewellery were a true indication.

Lady von Pless swept in and took a seat on the edge of a settee. 'Please sit down,' she said to Elisabeth, patting the seat beside her and smiling, though not with her eyes. 'Let me look at you.'

Elisabeth took a seat opposite, wondering at the woman's familiarity, and thinking that she had heard her voice before somewhere.

'Paul, darling,' said Lady von Pless, 'find me a glass of wine. Tea will not do after my long journey. I have heard there is a special little stash of bottles from Epernay in the cellars.'

Paul hesitated, and glanced at Elisabeth as though trying to communicate something to her, but she did not know what it was, only that he was not happy at leaving her alone with this woman. He exited the room. Lady von Pless watched him go, then turned to Elisabeth.

'Fräulein Schwan, I have heard of your romantic tale.'

'I would hardly call it romantic. Perhaps you have not heard correctly.'

'Then you must tell me.'

Elisabeth was silent. Something about this woman made her uncomfortable. She had no desire to tell her anything. She wracked her mind to recall where she had heard her voice. Was she someone from her past? Surely not, for Lady Pless did not act as though she knew her.

'Is it true that you know nothing of who you are and where you came from?'

'That is true. But how do you know of it?'

'Oh, I hear everything. It is near impossible to keep a secret in the court. One just has to cultivate discourse with the right servants. But you really do not remember anything?'

Elisabeth did not answer. Lady von Pless examined her

face intently, either to judge whether or not she spoke the truth, or to memorise her features.

'And what do you do here?' Lady von Pless asked, leaning forward and curving her lips into another smile that did not reach her eyes.

'Do?' Elisabeth repeated.

'I heard the king had picked up a girl with a mysterious provenance, but I did not get to see you at the palace. You were not at the feast, were you?'

'Picked up?' Elisabeth repeated her words again, surprised at such a crude expression from this grand lady.

'Aren't you his *amour*? Don't look so shocked. It would be a good thing for him to have a mistress. It would bring him out of his shell. We all think so. Usually the first one is an older, more experienced woman. And usually married. Are you married?'

'No. At least...I don't believe so. But I am no one's mistress,' she added fiercely.

Lady von Pless gave a little laugh. 'Why so angry? Everyone at court has lovers. What a naive little thing you are. Perhaps that is your charm. Ah,' she said knowingly, leaning back and narrowing her eyes. 'If you are not the paramour of the king, then you must be that of his aide-de-camp, am I right?'

Elisabeth glowered at her. 'I told you, I am no one's mistress.'

'But you cannot resist Paul. No girl can. What a trail of broken hearts and reputations lie strewn across the kingdom in his wake.'

Elisabeth was about to get up and leave the room, but Paul now reappeared, his tall figure filling the doorway.

'Ah, you delightful man,' exclaimed Lady von Pless on seeing him usher in the butler bearing wine and glasses. 'So obliging, as always.' Elisabeth caught the quick, knowing look that passed between them.

'I have just been asking Fräulein Schwan what her position is in the king's entourage,' Lady von Pless said, turning her head to Elisabeth, while her body remained turned towards the prince. 'Everyone is talking of it.'

'It is none of their business,' Elisabeth said coldly.

'My dear, the king's business is everybody's business. He belongs to the people. They want to know everything he does. Everything.'

'Fräulein Schwan is a guest,' said Paul. 'She is under His Majesty's protection.'

'Is that so?' said Lady von Pless. 'Protection from whom?' she spoke lightly, but her eyes were sharp. Paul did not answer, he dismissed the butler and busied himself with pouring the wine.

'Thank you, darling,' she said, taking the glass he held out. Her voice dropped to a soft purr. 'Do you remember, that night in Bergen, when we drank champagne until dawn?'

Elisabeth watched the prince's reaction closely. He caught her eye and looked partly irritated, partly disconcerted.

'That was a most interesting evening,' he said politely. 'Now you must tell us the news, Lady von Pless. What has been happening in München since yesterday's fiasco? What are they all saying?'

'What do you think they are saying? They are in uproar. To have walked out as he did, on the emperor of all people, who is such a stickler for protocol and manners. You cannot imagine how angry he has made everyone.'

'I can well imagine,' said Paul gravely.

'The queen mother spent half the night trying to soothe the emperor and make excuses for the king's rudeness.'

'What excuses did she give?'

'She said he was ill. A nervous collapse. That he'd been overwhelmed with the levity of hosting such a man as the emperor. She claimed it was his youth and his deep grief for his father, and so on.'

'He will not like it to be said that he is ill from nerves,' said Paul.

'Better it is said that he's ill with grief for his father than mad with grief for a swan, for that is what they are whispering. And then there is that hedonistic dandy who seems to have our young king in his silk-lined pocket, *he* has not done the king's reputation any good.' She gave a short laugh. 'What peculiar company the king keeps these days. Yourself excluded, Your Highness.'

'Herr Weimann is working on an architectural project for His Majesty,' Paul replied. 'He does not have the king in his pocket, I assure you.'

'Oh, really? Herr Weimann could not show his face in München, nay in the kingdom, this past year, for he had debtors after him in every city. Now he parades through the streets in his new carriage, holding parties at his fine mansion every night. Do you know he has had a fountain installed in his hall that flows with champagne? And he has a whole bottle of Persian Otto poured into his daily bath. A whole bottle! Ten gulden each they cost.'

'Rumours,' said Paul dismissively.

'I have drunk from the fountain myself. He drips with jewels, he minces about in a new suit every day, he has six cooks. And who is paying for all this? That is what people are asking. He was bankrupt, now he lives like a grand duke. People are not happy. They say he has hypnotised our young king. They hiss at him when he comes into the theatre. They throw stones at his carriage as he drives by.'

'Yet they still go to his parties every night,' said Paul. 'Yourself included.'

She lifted a shoulder coquettishly. 'Of course. He may be the most despised man in München, but he does gather about him the best musicians and artists. He is a reprehensible parasite, but he is *interesting*.'

Elisabeth suddenly remembered where she had heard Lady von Pless's voice. 'You were at the royal theatre recently,' Elisabeth said abruptly. 'The night the king reopened it.'

'Certainly, I was. Why do you ask?' She sipped at her glass.

'May I ask who escorted you there? I forget his name.'

'A friend,' she replied.

Elisabeth was not certain how far she could press Lady von Pless, but Paul understood, and took up her query.

'Which friend was that, my lady?' he asked.

'I have many friends,' said Lady von Pless lightly. 'I cannot quite recall which one it was that night.' She put her glass down quickly. 'And now I must go,' she said, standing up and deftly shaking out her skirts. 'Do be a darling, and see me to my carriage, Paul.'

Elisabeth stood up to make the customary curtsey. Lady von Pless gave her one last look of scrutiny, sweeping her humourless eyes from the top of Elisabeth's head to the hem of her gown, then she left, sashaying out on Paul's arm.

Elisabeth followed them out a few moments later; she stood on the balcony, overlooking the castle entrance hall, watching them descend the stairs.

'I don't care what you think, darling,' Lady von Pless's voice floated upwards, as she carefully picked her way down the steps, lifting her gown a little to keep from tripping on it. 'There's plenty more girls for you. It's not as if you've ever settled on one for long, is it? She's as good as married, and you will fare badly if you get in his way. Very badly.'

Elisabeth strained to hear Paul's reply, but they had moved too far away. His voice sounded angry, and not like himself at all. She waited for him to return. When he did his face was taut, the usual glow dimmed.

'Who is she, and what does she know of me?' Elisabeth demanded, when he reached the top of the stairs.

He looked around, as though making sure no one was listening, then ushered her into the drawing room and closed the door.

'Well?'

He ran his hand through his hair and paced the length of

the room before coming to stand before her. The look in his eyes alarmed her.

'That woman was sent to look at you.'

'That was very obvious, but who is she? What is her connection to me?'

'I don't know what her connection to you is. As to who she is, she is a very wealthy widow who moves in, let's say somewhat salacious company at times.'

'But she was here on someone's behalf?'

'Most certainly,' said Paul.

'The man at the theatre—she was here on his behalf, wasn't she? I saw her with him, at least, I heard her voice, I did not see their faces.'

'That is my suspicion.'

'You were going to find out who he was.'

'I am trying. I have a list drawn up of all the men that I know to have been present that night. Herr Weimann is expected tomorrow, I will ask him which of the men entered his box with Lady von Pless that evening.'

'Do you have any clue?' she pressed. 'You seem to know that woman rather well. Quite intimately, in fact.' She tried to keep her voice even; she had no right to be jealous of his past, after all.

'Don't listen to any of her poison, Elsa.'

'But do you have no clue as to who might have sent her here? Don't you know who she is close to?'

'Only to most of the powerful men in the kingdom,' said Paul dryly. 'She changes her friends quite regularly. There are any number of men she could be intriguing with.'

Elisabeth wrapped her arms about herself, feeling that her recurring nightmare was now seeping into her waking world. Paul saw her look and moved nearer to put his arms about her. She let her head rest against his chest. He felt strong and safe. Then she remembered that woman's words as she walked down the stairs. She pulled away again to speak.

'What did she mean, when she said that I was as good as married?'

'I don't know, Elsa. Whoever it is that is looking for you, seems to think he has a right to you.' He gave a wry smile. 'I have been warned off.'

'We must tell the Chief Inspector' she said in a faltering voice.'

'I agree. But we may be dealing with a very powerful man. We must tread carefully.'

'We must tell the king. He is more powerful than this man, whoever he is.'

'The king will certainly protect you. We will get to the bottom of this, Elsa. In the meantime, we must not let you out of our sight.'

She stared at him in alarm. 'In case he tries to kidnap me. Again.'

He nodded. 'It may be speculation, but we can't take the risk. If he was involved in what happened to you, he is a dangerous man. I have my suspicions of who he may be, and I only hope I am wrong.' Paul looked and sounded grim. 'If I am right, it is a man who has men of power and authority as his associates. If that is so, only the king himself can protect you.'

CHAPTER 22
ISLE OF SWANS

HERR WEIMANN ARRIVED in state and splendour in the second-best royal carriage. It flew along with a team of four white horses, four outriders and two postilions, announcing to all between München and the village of Swanstein that there was someone of great importance coming.

A footman ran to unfold the steps at the carriage door, for Herr Weimann's short legs required them.

'Your Majesty!' cried the great architect, upon alighting. He removed his tall hat to make an ornate bow. 'At last I am released from the oppression of walls without sunlight, without sweetness of fragrance. For what life has there been for me in the city once His Majesty withdrew his presence?'

He and the king strolled to the castle entrance, Herr Weimann's raptures booming across the courtyard, while his apprentice was left to follow behind, bearing so many scrolls and folders that Elisabeth was sure he would drop them all. Every footman was laden with trunks, and Paul was busy giving orders regarding the horses, so Elisabeth took it upon herself to assist Herr Haller.

He gave a muffled greeting from behind the piled-up papers. The topmost scrolls wobbled.

'Stand still,' she said, taking four of his burdens from the top of the pile.

She could see his face now. 'Thank you,' he said. 'But you shouldn't trouble yourself.'

'It's no trouble.'

'You look well,' he said with a friendly smile.

'You look tired.'

'I've been working.'

'Watch your step,' she counselled, for he was too busy looking at her to notice the steps before them.

'Ouch!' His foot stubbed the bottom step, and he stumbled.

'Do not drop those scrolls, Haller!' came the deep voice of Herr Weimann from the top of the steps. 'I'll rub your face in the dirt if you foul His Majesty's plans!'

'What a charming master you have,' Elisabeth said as Herr Haller righted himself.

They deposited the papers in the study room and she led Herr Haller to the hall where refreshments were laid out for Herr Weimann's arrival.

The king and his architect stood side by side before one of the arched windows. They made an incongruous-looking couple: the king taller than any man she had yet seen, slim and broad shouldered, his black hair perfectly arranged in smooth waves around his face. Even in heeled shoes Herr Weimann only reached the king's shoulder, his head large and sitting slightly askance on his thick neck. His legs were short, his body squat and dense, his greying hair smoothed down with oil, but still grizzly looking. And yet both exuded an energy that filled the large space of the hall.

'There, my friend,' the king announced, pointing at the view they stood before.

'I see only mountains, Your Majesty.'

'You see the mountain where Tannhäuser once sang in the castle halls. You see the ruins of the castle built by Gundelfinger himself.'

'The magician?'

'So they called him. The Guardian of the Mountain. He who kept the land free of her enemies, who caused the earth to be fruitful, until he transgressed against the Fair, and brought trouble to the land.'

'Ah, the old legends,' rumbled Herr Weimann. 'How I should like to see the place where once the heroes were said to walk.'

'And so you shall,' said the king, his eyes gleaming. 'You shall indeed follow where the great Faerie knight and the magic-wielding guardian once walked. You shall stand amidst the very place where the stones of Gundelfinger's castle stood. You shall feel for yourself the thrum of magic that remains. It echoes around the valley below, it sings to the great firs above, it swirls about the rocks—you too shall feel its poetry. We shall climb there this very afternoon. We shall leave at once, why should there be any delay?'

'Climb?' Herr Weimann's strong voice faltered. 'The Beloved Friend of the king, whose spirit is without weakness, whose heart is that of a sure and solid rock, but whose body —his poor body is but a prison of limitations.'

The king looked down at Herr Weimann, dismay clouding his face.

'This is not to be borne. I have seen you standing beside me in that very place where our new castle shall rise out of the ruins. There, upon that very plateau, hearing the rush of the waterfall that shines with elven light when the moon waxes full. You must see for yourself where your inspired designs shall awaken the power of Gundelfinger once again!'

Herr Weimann stared out at the mountain peak opposite and made a kind of groan. 'I would lay down my life to please His Majesty. But this body is wearied from long hours on the road, it must recoup. It must refill. It must rest.'

'Very well,' said the king. His disappointment was evident. 'We leave at first light instead. You will refresh yourself before dinner while I ride out. I am too restless with anticipation to stay within walls.'

The king strode out of the hall. Prince Paul, who had just come in from overseeing the stabling arrangements, turned around again and followed his master out.

'Climb up there!' Herr Weimann murmured to no one in particular. 'If the Muse gave me her wings perhaps it could be done. Haller,' he bellowed, 'see to my rooms. Ensure they have all that I require. The foul dust of the road clings to me. Tell the servants to draw a bath. And do not forget the Persian Otto.'

WHILE HERR WEIMANN RESTED, HERR HALLER WAS FINDING HIS way around the castle. Elisabeth found him in the servants' wing after dinner, chatting with Schnorr, the king's hairdresser, about his life in the cities he had travelled through with Herr Weimann. Gretel, the housekeeper's niece was tossing her fair plaits and trying to get Herr Haller's attention; Elisabeth was sure she saw her wink at him. The prince came in, and Herr Haller seemed to fade into the wainscoting, as did everyone in the presence of Prince Paul.

'Herr Haller, Fräulein Schwan, please join the king's party at the pier in an hour.' He smiled, looking very different from the anxious man she had seen the previous day after Lady von Pless's visit.

THE SUN WAS SETTING AS THEY REACHED THE LAKE PIER. THE water rippled in golden flecks, reflecting the sky; the mountains were silhouetted against the horizon. Two of the king's gondolas were moored at the water's edge, lit up with hanging oil lamps. The king was dressed in a long cape of blue and silver. By the light of the sunset and lamps, with his tall, graceful frame, and his glittering, flowing cape, he looked like the elf-king from one of Herr Haller's mural designs.

Herr Weimann joined the king; Paul assisted Elisabeth into the second boat, and Herr Haller followed.

Elisabeth leaned back in her gilded seat, enjoying the movement of the boat and the rhythmic sound of the water swishing away as they slipped through it. Out of the dusk appeared dark shapes, passing close by the boat's edge. At least a dozen black swans glided past. They moved to surround the king's gondolier, as if to make a royal escort.

She was so busy watching the swans that she did not notice they were heading for the little island in the middle of the lake, but the soft scrunch of gravel against the prow of the boat told her they had reached the island's shore.

'What are we doing here?' she asked Paul, as he assisted her from the boat.

'One of the king's favourite pastimes,' he replied. 'You will see.'

On the Isle of Swans stood a royal lodge. It was small and plain on the outside, but inside every inch of wall and ceiling was covered in gilding. Countless candles glimmered from chandeliers and wall sconces; it was like stepping into a magical world.

'Ah, champagne,' Herr Weimann said approvingly as a liveried server appeared with a tray of crystal flutes. Paul pressed a cool glass into Elisabeth's hand; the party lingered some time, long enough for her to drink down her champagne and have a second glass placed into her hand, and at some point, a second became a third.

'Is all made ready?' the king asked as a second servant appeared. The king seemed excited, almost childlike with glee. How quickly he seemed to have pushed away all disagreeable memories of the emperor's feast.

'All is ready, Your Majesty,' the second servant replied.

'Then begin!'

The party followed the king into a large courtyard. The sun had set, and all was dark. Shadowy trees whispered above. There was an expectation in the air, as the king seemed to be waiting for something.

Elisabeth was feeling a little light-headed, and concluded that she was not used to drinking down almost three glasses of champagne in quick succession, and probably should not have attempted it; a sudden bang made her jump, spilling some wine. She giggled at herself, then cried out as a great fountain of golden stars exploded in the sky above. More bangs sounded, like rapid cannon fire, more bursts of coloured lights erupted, impossibly bright, hordes of shooting stars falling in trails of light and smoke.

'Do you like fireworks, Fräulein Schwan?' asked a voice very close to her ear. She could smell Prince Paul's cologne, lemon and bergamot, bright and warm.

'I love them! I've never seen anything like it. At least, I don't remember it if I did.'

'You are shivering. You ought to have brought a cloak.'

'I am fine. I'm not cold.'

'I will stand very close to you and share my warmth,' he said, pressing close.

She could not suppress another shiver. An inner voice was telling her that this was not proper behaviour at all, but the scent and feel of him drowned out that voice. The magical lights continued to soar and fall and crash above them. The effects of the champagne took their toll, for all felt warm and fuzzy and pleasant and she leaned back against the strong body of the prince, smiling as he whispered foolish things into her ear. Somehow her head turned to meet his and warm lips were on her own, soft and tasting of champagne, now firmer and insistent. She was in his arms, pressed against him, until a crack at her feet jolted her out of his embrace.

'Are you all right?' called Herr Haller, rushing over. 'A fire cracker shot out at you.'

'Perfectly fine,' said the prince. 'Fräulein Schwan will come to no harm while I am near.'

Herr Haller looked between them. Elisabeth was glad it

was too dark for him to really see her, for her face would betray everything she felt at that moment. And what did she feel, she wondered? Was she happy? Happy was not quite the word. Confused, excited, stirred up by feelings she did not know existed. Was this love?

The firework display came to a finale. The lanterns on the courtyard were lit. More champagne was served, but she refused any more.

CHAPTER 23
GUNDELFINGER

'What changes did you observe in the king, Fräulein Opel?'

'Changes?'

'It is well attested that the king began a descent into unconventional behaviour as first displayed at the emperor's feast. Can you give particulars of these changes, for you were frequently in his presence?'

'I suppose he did withdraw from people more after the emperor's feast. He found comfort and satisfaction in the building of New Swanstein.'

'His new castle. The fabrication of which has almost bankrupted the kingdom.'

'I understand he used only his personal fortune, sir. He bankrupted no one.'

'You say he withdrew from people, is that the reasonable action of a king, a leader, a public figure? He even withdrew from his own mother. Forbade her access to his presence.'

'Perhaps he wanted to avoid criticism.'

'How could he hope to avoid criticism when he squandered thousands of gulden on that wastrel Herr Weimann and buried himself in his mountain retreat while his kingdom floundered in war?'

There were murmurings of 'Hear, Hear,' from the audience.

'There were other forces at work.'

'And what forces do you speak of?'

'Magic.'

'Could you repeat that, Fräulein? You speak in a whisper.'

'Magic!'

'Ah, and now we come to it. All the nonsensical talk of magic that surrounds the king like a sentimental cloud. The peasant folklore. There was no magic, Fräulein Opel, surely even you, young as you are, and with a feminine mind, are too sensible to believe such a thing. There was madness. There was irresponsibility. Negation of duty. Profligacy. Scandal and shame upon the house of his virtuous father and his long-suffering mother.'

'Why do you ask me my opinion then, if you have already drawn your conclusions?'

'There's no need for such a tone, Fräulein.'

'There are always other forces at work,' she said, her voice dropping its anger, *'hidden facts and motives. We ought not to be so quick to judge.'*

Elisabeth groaned the next morning when woken at dawn.

'Orders are to be ready in an hour, Fräulein Schwan,' the maid announced. She had opened the curtains at the window to let the pale light in. It was so early, and the light so dim that the maid was still a shadow moving about the room as she filled up the bowl on the washstand and laid out unfamiliar clothes for Elisabeth.

'New boots,' said the maid. 'To get up the mountain.'

Elisabeth groaned again. Hiking up a mountain after a very late night and little sleep did not seem like an agreeable idea. She sat up, forcing her legs to swing over the side of the bed. She was not going to drink champagne again. Ever.

Her new clothes cheered her a little, for they were lighter in fabric and looser in fit than ordinary daywear. Her outfit was completed with a wide-brimmed straw hat.

Her thoughts were of the prince as she waited outside for

the party to assemble. Her stomach fluttered disagreeably every time she thought of him and last night's kiss. Was she a fool, taken in by his charm? Did he really care for her? She would know when she saw him, she told herself. But it was Herr Haller who appeared first. She smiled to see him in his lederhosen. Suddenly it felt as though they were on a holiday. Ugly nightmares, sinister assailants, threats of war—all seemed impossible in that moment, in the early morning sunshine.

'Nice hat,' he said, grinning back.

'Same to you,' she replied, looking at his Tyrolean hiking hat, complete with small feather.

'I hope you slept well, Fräulein Schwan.'

'Do I look tired?'

He gave a little shrug. 'It was a late night. I would have liked more sleep myself.'

'The king seems to have boundless energy,' she noted. 'He stays up late most nights and is still out riding and hiking half the day. I don't know how he does it.'

'I agree. This mere mortal could do with learning his secret.'

They caught each other yawning and laughed.

Prince Paul appeared, striding down the steps, looking fresh and golden and like a young god of the mountains in his hiking clothes.

'Good morning,' he beamed. A servant followed him bearing an armful of walking sticks. 'Let me equip you with these,' said Paul. Elisabeth looked up at him as he handed her a pair of sticks, hoping for an affectionate look in return, but he did not meet her eyes. The fluttering in her stomach turned heavy. But there was no time to wallow in disappointment, Herr Weimann and the king now appeared. The king marched down the steps, brandishing his carved walking sticks and striding on with a clear expectation that everyone would soon follow on his swift moving heels.

. . .

It was almost midday when they reached the plateau where the ruins of the ancient castle stood, and the king's new castle was to be. It had been a gruelling climb, for the closer they got to the site the more the king's energy increased. While Elisabeth grew tired and in need of rest and water, the king marched on at a furious pace, as though new power coursed through him. Herr Weimann had turned back some time ago, claiming he would gladly lie down and die on His Majesty's beloved mountain should the king command it, but die he surely would if he was pressed to continue any farther. Paul negotiated Herr Weimann's release from the expedition, and a groom was tasked with assisting the perspiring architect back to the castle.

Eventually the king disappeared from view as even the athletically-built prince could no longer keep pace with his master. Elisabeth would have been left alone, with the king and the prince far ahead, but Herr Haller stayed close, offering a hand when they reached a steep part, sharing his water flask and his large supply of sun-dried fruit which he had purloined from the castle kitchen.

They had been hiking through dense fir trees, which provided welcome shade while obscuring the view, but at the site of the castle ruins they were above the trees, in a vast clearing where only the odd fir grew between the stones. Now the view was unhindered.

The blue mountains were all the grander for being a little closer. Far below, the lake they had rowed across last night looked like a sparkling blue pond, and Swanstein castle, its pale-yellow walls and red-tiled roofs and turrets was as a toy fort below.

The king stood amid the ruins with his arms spread wide, his face turned to the sky as though in some kind of trance.

'What is he doing?' Elisabeth said to Herr Haller. 'Are my eyes playing tricks on me, or does he seem even taller than usual?' She rubbed her eyes and blinked.

'He does look peculiar,' Herr Haller answered. He pulled

out a sketchbook and pencil from the knapsack on his back and began swiftly sketching a picture.

She peered over his shoulder. 'How well you've caught him,' she said. The drawing was of a picture of a king from the old legends when magic surged through the land and dragons still roamed.

'This is a strange place,' she said, turning round. 'It makes me feel odd. It's beautiful, but there's something...' she searched for the right word.

'Mysterious?' Herr Haller offered. He blew graphite from his paper. It floated away in a little cloud.

'Yes. But that's not the word. It's as though the air holds a different charge.'

'Mountain air is different from the air in the valley,' said Herr Haller.

'But it's not like ordinary air. Can you feel it?'

He looked around thoughtfully, then turned back to his book and sketched again, this time his pencil flew over the white pressed paper, and yet he was hardly looking down at his work, he was looking out at the ruins before them. In a few minutes he was done, and he held out the sketchbook for her to see.

'Yes!' she said, taking hold of the book. He had drawn a castle, in medieval style, complete with fluttering pennants and a knight in armour tramping over a drawbridge. A robed figure stood in the castle courtyard with staff upraised and swirls of stars about him.

'Gundelfinger,' she said. 'The great magician.'

In Herr Haller's picture there was a moat, fed by a waterfall that coursed down the rocks behind the castle. In the moat sailed three pairs of swans with golden crowns about their necks.

'This is how it was,' she said. The depiction Herr Haller had created resonated with what she felt around her.

'Do you think the magic of Gundelfinger lingers?' Herr Haller said with a smile; he held out his hand for his book.

'Why not?' Her hand sought out her swan pendant. Touching it made her feel less strange, so she kept hold of it. 'It's rather charming and romantic to think of the past still lingering in the present."

'I wouldn't use the words charming and romantic where Gundelfinger is concerned,' Herr Haller said. 'Fearsome and powerful perhaps. He had a dragon at his command and was the only mortal who once passed in and out of Faerie without losing his wits. He was said to have stolen the royal cup from the Swan Knight, he thought that to drink from it every day would give him immortality, but stealing from the Faerie prince only brought trouble to the land, and led to his downfall. If only he had given the cup back, but in his wrath, he hid it instead.'

He put his drawing materials away and swung his bag over his shoulder. 'I'd better get some sketches done for Herr Weimann,' he said, and bounded away, seeming energised by the strange air. Elisabeth sat upon a rock, still needing a little more rest after the hard climb.

'At last I've found you alone,' a warm voice said behind her. She did not turn her head, but her breath caught in her chest for a moment.

'I have not had a chance to speak to you all day.'

'You said good morning,' she replied, keeping her voice cool.

'Why so unfriendly?' He had the cheek to look hurt as he sat down beside her.

'I think you took advantage of me last night,' she said primly. 'A gentleman would not have taken the liberty you did.'

'I am sorry if you think it was a liberty, Elsa. I thought it was something that simply happened between us. Something magical.' He smiled.

'I drank too much champagne. That is what happened. I lost my head. I have no interest in becoming another of your paramours.'

'My paramours? He almost laughed, but stopped himself.

'I have been warned of your reputation.'

He pressed against her arm by leaning closer. 'You couldn't possibly be just anyone's paramour, Elsa. You're too special for that.'

She looked up at him, examining his eyes for a moment, searching for evidence that he spoke the truth. It was always a dangerous thing to allow herself to look into those eyes. He took hold of her hand and she did not pull away. This pleased him and he smiled, bending his head towards her as though to kiss her.

'Oh no you don't,' she said, jumping up from her rocky seat. 'I've a clear head now, so there's no excuse.'

He laughed, standing up and holding out an arm, as a gentleman to a lady. 'Let me show you the castle ruins before the workmen arrive to receive their orders from the king. I promise I will make no attempt to cloud your clear head. For now.'

CHAPTER 24
NEW POWER

THE SOUND of dynamite blasts resounded like muffled thunder through the valley. It did not take long before a wide road had been cleared to the new castle. Even Herr Weimann had no excuse now not to accompany the king by carriage.

Herr Haller was given a desk in the study, where he spent long hours working on plans, directed by Herr Weimann's orders.

One restless, sultry night Elisabeth crept through the sleeping castle, down to the kitchens to refill her water jug. She'd heard the clock in the hall strike midnight, yet the light in the study was still shining beneath the door. She wondered if the servants had left a lamp on and opened the door to check. Someone was hunched over the desk, a dark head bowed upon their arms.

'Herr Haller,' she whispered. 'Is that you?' There was a soft sound of deep breathing in reply. She crept in and stood looking down at the sleeping Herr Haller, debating whether or not to wake him. He looked crumpled up and uncomfortable with his neck twisted to one side. Beneath him lay a thick pile of papers covered in drawings and notes. She bent to look a little closer. He was drawing designs for furniture and friezes, murals and lighting for the new castle. His notebook, the one he carried everywhere, lay precariously at the corner of the desk, ready to fall at the smallest nudge. She picked it up to make it more secure, as she did so a loose sheet fluttered down. She was startled to see what was on it, and lifted her lamp to better look.

It was the drawing of a young woman. She stood beside a lake, watching a white swan. Her hair was loose, falling down her back, and lifted slightly by a breeze. The profile of her face showed a look of care as though something troubled her. She looked vulnerable, lonely, and Elisabeth suddenly felt very exposed.

The deep breathing ceased and a sleepy voice said, 'What are you doing?'

She jumped away, dropping the drawing on the desk as though it burnt her fingers.

'I saw a light on. I was just checking—' she did not finish her sentence; she was too embarrassed at being seen in her dressing gown, with her hair mussed up. 'I was going to wake you,' she murmured, moving away. 'You looked uncomfortable.' She darted across the room. 'You should get to bed, Herr Haller.'

She was out of the study, and halfway up the stairs before she remembered she had forgotten the water she came for. She turned around and headed back.

It seemed the whole castle was awake that night, for on reaching the kitchen she found the cook with his voluminous apron tied over his night shirt, cutting furiously at a slab of goat's cheese, then ripping apart a loaf of bread.

They eyed each other across the kitchen table.

'Hungry?' she enquired, as he slapped pickled salad onto the bread.

'At this time of night?' he growled back. 'His Majesty requires a basket made up. Midnight picnics indeed!'

She took her water and retreated. It was quicker to reach

the guest wing via the servants' stairs. Coming down the stairs towards her was another figure.

'Elsa!'

'Paul,' she mumbled. Being half dressed and unkempt was bad enough in front of a sleepy Herr Haller, but in front of the prince!

'Why are you up at this hour?' he asked. He seemed flustered. He was tucking in his shirt as though he had dressed in a hurry.

'Why are you?' she retorted.

'The king has sent word. I am to prepare his horse.'

'Is something wrong?'

'No. He simply wishes to ride out. He is fond of moonlight.' There was no corresponding smile. Paul seemed as put out as the cook.

'Well, good night,' she said, hurrying past him up the stairs. 'Enjoy the moonlight. And sandwiches.'

It was only when she reached her guest room and sat on the bed that it struck her as odd that Paul should have been hurrying down the servants' staircase, when his own apartment was adjacent to the king's, on the other side of the castle.

'CAN YOU SHED LIGHT ON HOW THE NEW CASTLE WAS BUILT SO *quickly, Fräulein Opel? Unimaginably quickly, according to the reports.'*

'If I did, you would not believe me.'

'You are being obtuse again.'

'It was a magical castle. It was built, in part, by magic.'

'I think you mean that great and new technological advances were made that enabled the construction to be completed so quickly. It is of great interest to many people to learn such secrets.'

'I know nothing of great and new technological advances. I only

know that I saw the stones being carried up the hill and by the next morning they were in place.'

'There must have been some new kind of machinery?'

'There were horses and carts. Scaffolding. Hammers and chisels.'

'You seem determined to wear thin our patience, Fräulein. It would serve you better to be candid.'

'I speak of what I have seen. I can do no more.'

'Why do you only hire peasants?'

Herr Weimann was dressed all in green, looking like a hillock of spring grass with green-dyed feathers in his cap as he surveyed the site of the new build.

'You should send for the best workmen that the kingdom can offer. Men trained at the academies in stone dressing and carving. What can these rustics know of such things? Have they ever seen great works of art? Have they studied under the masters? How then can they produce them?'

'No one may take stone from these mountains and build from it save those who love it,' answered the king. He stood towering over Herr Weimann, his pale skin the colour of the dressed stones, his eyes the colour of the lake that glittered below. He looked as a true king of the mountains while Herr Weimann was as an artificial tree beside him.

There was a remarkable atmosphere at the site. Elisabeth was both fascinated and fearful of it. It was exciting, as though full of boundless possibilities, but it was also weighty, as though it must be treated with respect.

Paul seemed uneasy, his usual smiling presence dimmed, but Herr Haller bounded about, sketchbook in hand, invigorated by the power that thrummed through the place. She knew Herr Haller still stayed up working late, for she often heard the creak of his step as he passed her room to his own at the other end of the guest wing. He still looked wearied and spent, but once he reached the site of the new castle he was renewed, refilled with energy, she saw it in his face, as though he emptied himself out like a vessel each night to be replenished to the brim the next day.

The energy that hummed through the site poured through the workmen from the mountains; they sang in deep harmonies as they laboured as with one mind. Their songs sounded nonsensical to Elisabeth, sung in an old, mountain tongue that was unfamiliar to her. But as their music swirled about her, words formed in her mind, as they did when she listened to animals, and she found herself humming along.

AWAKE, AWAKE, THE TIME HAS COME
The king must return to his land
Build a bridge, build a bridge
Let him cross over
The king will return to his crown

THE WORDS WERE FROM THE SONGS OF THE OLD LEGENDS—THE Swan Knight who came into the world from Faerie and once sang within the enchanted walls of the great wizard's castle. Down on the lake below he was said to have sailed away back to Faerie, but the wizard of the castle had stolen something from him. Something precious, that the Faerie prince would return for one day.

THE HORN, THE HORN, IT CALLS HIM HOME,
The king must return to his land
Build a door, build a door
Let him now enter
The king will return to his throne

· · ·

Birdsong trilled in harmony with the folksong; if she listened hard, remaining very still and very quiet she could hear it as a chorus, weaving between the workmen's song: *mountain sleeping, mountain waking, mountain stirring, he is coming, waking, waking, waking...*

'Your Majesty, I really must insist on calling for the best stonemasons and woodcarvers of the city. These little mountain men are all very good for heaving up bricks and planks, but for true art, for the beautiful carvings the Muse has designed, we must have men who have studied, who are highly trained, who are famed for their skill. There cannot be any such man among these dwarvish rustics.'

'I know of just such a man,' said the king. 'I have heard of him from the villagers. He is the nephew of the village midwife who birthed me, and is said to be unrivalled in artistic carving. I will send for him.'

Elisabeth felt that strange things were unfolding around them in those days. Sometimes it felt overpowering, and she wished she could have an ordinary life, but other times she felt herself yielding to the new, yet ancient, power that gained strength every day in the mountain, and the villages about it. Each brick, each block of stone that was laid strengthened the power that flowed through the site, spilling down the mountain paths below, seeping into the ground beneath, flowing into the lake. There was the feeling of awakening, of something rising up, something coming.

Herr Weimann only dressed in red now for he said the Muse was scarlet with shame and anger at the crude and crass hands carrying out the vision she had bestowed. His powers had dried up, he declared. He must return to his house in München. The silence of Swanstein was deafening. He could not hear the voice of the Muse, and the coarse food and rustic beer was dulling his artist's soul. If the king would not send for a replenishment of champagne from the city, then Herr Weimann must leave until the wine cellar was restocked.

And he was all out of Persian Otto.

Back to the city went Herr Weimann to renew his inspiration. In the meantime, his apprentice would oversee the work on his behalf. Black bread and beer were good enough for him.

CHAPTER 25
WARNINGS OF WAR

'Another telegram, sir.'

Paul added the missive to the pile of unopened letters on the desk.

'Shall I read you the contents, sir? It's marked urgent.'

'Nothing in this wretched world of men is urgent,' said the king, not looking up from the drawings he was examining on Herr Haller's desk. 'Their schemes and grasping for power go round and round, and all that is urgent today is forgotten the next. I shall not get caught up in their petty machinations and dramas. Only beauty lasts forever,' he murmured, touching the designs of his new castle interiors. 'It is the only truth.'

The prince looked troubled. He picked the telegram back up, turning it around in his fingers as though trying to decide what to do.

'Read it if you must,' the king conceded. 'But not aloud. I won't have my morning clouded over with government business. It can wait till later.'

The troubled look on the prince's face only deepened as he scanned the telegram.

'I shall ride into the villages to see how the weaving and

embroidery work is advancing,' said the king. 'Has the order of gold thread arrived?'

'Not yet, sir,' replied Paul distractedly.

'Why not? Write to them. Tell them to hurry it along. I shall be in my new suite by winter. The fabrics must be ready by then. What about the slate tiles?'

'They are not yet arrived, sir.'

The king frowned with annoyance.

'I can stay and write to the suppliers this morning, sir,' the prince offered, 'while you are at the site.'

'Do so. The Little Prince shall wait upon me.'

The "Little Prince" was the king's name for Herr Haller, who had grown in the king's estimation since Herr Weimann had left, for it was Herr Haller who sketched out the king's ideas as they came to his imagination, and they came in abundance.

The king swept out of the room with Herr Haller following, folders full of drawings in his arms.

Elisabeth still felt the same fluttering sensation whenever she chanced to be alone with Paul, a mixture of danger and pleasure. But there seemed no need to worry about his attentions that morning, for they were far from her.

He paced up and down between the window and the desk, pausing to look outside as though he could find the answer to what troubled him riding up the drive.

'Is something wrong?' she asked. He did not reply. He was too engrossed in thought. She asked again, a little louder.

He turned his fair head, his eyes focussing not quite upon her, but in her direction.

'Have you ever had to abandon someone you had always intended to be loyal to?' he asked in a grave tone. There was a pause. She did not know what to answer. But he didn't seem to expect one. 'Of course you haven't,' he murmured. 'How could one so young know of such things as abandonment and the torments of a divided heart?'

'I think no one escapes suffering,' she said. 'No matter

their age.' She wondered who his heart was divided between. An image of him hurrying from the servants' wing in the middle of the night came to her mind. Was his heart divided between her and someone else? Was his heart hers at all?

'But what if you are the person causing the suffering? Or appearing to. What if you are about to cause suffering to the few that you may deter it from the many?' he said, still not quite focussing on her.

'If you care to explain the situation, then I might be able to answer.'

He gave a little shake of his head. His usual smile replaced his serious look, though the smile did not quite reach his eyes.

'I would not sully your innocent heart, my sweet Elsa.'

She frowned.

'Forgive me. I think of you as my sweet Elsa, and sometimes the words spill out.'

'Well kindly restrain them from spilling, sir.'

He laughed, looking like himself again.

'How I love that little spark of yours. It's almost worth vexing you on purpose to see it.'

She was about to leave the room, feeling confused by his changeable behaviour, but he drew near, and suddenly she was enveloped by the scent of bergamot and lemon.

'Dearest Elsa,' he murmured. 'Is not affection the only balm to us in this sordid world? I am sorely in need of it at this time.'

His right hand was on her cheek, his left upon her shoulder, turning her gently towards him and tilting her face to meet his. The sudden nearness of him was intoxicating.

The door to the study flew open, and she jumped away. Herr Haller dashed across the room to his desk to snatch up a leather folder.

'I forgot some drawings,' he explained, then he saw them. She had moved away from the prince, and Paul had likewise taken a step back, but Herr Haller's eyes took in the scene in one glance.

'I beg your pardon,' Herr Haller said. 'I did not mean to intrude.' He nodded curtly and left as quickly as he had come.

'Now look what you've done,' she groaned, pushing past Paul and putting as much distance between them as she could.

'Don't worry about him, sweet Elsa. He won't say anything. It's of no matter.'

'I am not *sweet* Elsa, and it matters a great deal to have my reputation compromised!'

'Darling, I would never compromise you.'

'Then what is it you are doing now? And I thought you had been warned off me?'

Those words caused the softness to drain from his expression. 'You are right,' he said quietly. 'This is madness. It is all madness. And yet…' He did not finish, but bowed his head, and left the room, leaving her in a whirl of conflicting emotions.

The feelings she had for Paul were as strong and wild as something else she had lately felt: the power that swirled about the site of the new castle. The power that was getting stronger with every stone laid in place. Was love a force like magic, she wondered? If it was, she was both entranced and afraid. She feared being swept up by something stronger than herself. She did not want to be out of control of her own feelings. There were enough aspects of her life that were out of her control as it was. And was it even love? How could she tell? What could she compare it to?

She stayed out of the castle that day, wandering about the lakeside and following trails into the forest beyond. Hunger pangs drove her back to the castle in the afternoon. There was a carriage in the stable yard, and the grooms were busy seeing to the horses. She soon learnt whose carriage it was, for as she passed behind the hedge between the queen mother's rose garden and the kitchen gardens, she heard a familiar voice. She could just glimpse the Cabinet Secretary through a gap in the hedge. He was seated upon a bench, mopping his brow. 'I tell you I cannot go away again without speaking to him,' he said.

'And I tell you he is refusing to see anybody at present,' replied the voice of Paul, who was out of her sight.

'He is the king! He must speak to his ministers. He will not reply to letters, telegrams—I have had to drive all the way here, so do not say I cannot see him!'

Herr Pfiffermeister looked very red in the face. He snatched at a glass of elderflower water and drank deeply. 'Don't you have anything stronger?' he said, looking disdainfully at his glass.

'I'll send for wine,' the prince replied.

'First, tell me where I can find His Majesty. It is imperative I speak with him.'

'He is at the site of his new castle, sir. I can order a carriage, but I warn you, he will consider it a violation of his privacy if you appear without him granting an audience.'

'Your Highness we are on the brink of war!' sputtered the Cabinet Secretary. 'Does the king not care? Our only potential ally is the Emperor of Österreich, and despite repeated pleas for His Majesty to make reparation with the emperor, he has not so much as written him one line of apology! The queen mother has been tireless in her diplomacy to smooth things over, but the time has now come for us to act! Either we send troops to join the emperor's or we sit here and wait for that wolf to strike us like a field of lambs whose shepherd has taken off to the mountains and left his flock to their fate!'

Elisabeth was dismayed by what she heard. She almost rushed round to the gate to enter the garden to demand if what Herr Pfiffermeister was saying was true—were they on the brink of war? But the next words held her rooted to her spot behind the hedge.

'Prince von Thorne, I speak plainly and with a heavy heart when I say that His Majesty's government is most distressed, and outraged, by the king's behaviour. He refuses to see anyone, reply to anyone, make any decisions. In short, sir, he refuses to do his kingly duty, and there are calls for him to be deposed.'

'I know,' said the prince. 'I have heard such things.'

'I must speak to His Majesty today. He must return with me to the city and direct his government and army. He must!'

'I will ride up to the king myself,' the prince replied. 'And urge him to return here.'

'Very good, sir. But first, if you please—send for that wine.'

It took three long hours before the prince returned. Elisabeth had made herself known to Herr Pfiffermeister, offering her assistance in making him comfortable by keeping him supplied with edibles.

At last Paul came. But alone. The Cabinet Secretary had retreated to the queen mother's sitting room, to make use of the daybed. Long hours on the road and too much wine required a nap.

She met Paul in the castle entrance, having watched for his arrival.

'Is he coming?' she said. 'Does the king follow?'

'Where is Pfiffermeister?' was Paul's reply. He looked hot and dusty from the sun-baked roads.

'This way.'

'Does he come?' asked the bleary minister, waking up to swing his heavy legs to the floor and fumble about for his spectacles. 'Does he come?' he murmured again, putting his spectacles on his nose and blinking up at the prince.

'His Majesty consents to the mobilisation of his army to join with the emperor in protecting our borders, if such action is required. He trusts that his uncle, Prince Luitpold, will carry out his duties as commander.' The prince pulled a creased letter from inside his riding jacket and held it out.

One edge was torn as though it had been ripped from a notebook.

Herr Pfiffermeister snatched at it, adjusted his spectacles to read the few lines. 'And this is all?' He stood up, waving the letter. Elisabeth recognised the thick, white paper as that of Herr Haller's sketchbook. 'He will not take his place at the helm of his government at such a time? He does not even speak to me in person on such a monumental matter? He only gives consent to go to war via his adjutant on a scribbled note!'

'His Majesty deems his word to be all that is required on this occasion. He is too busy to travel to the city at present. If war does break out, he will return.'

'Too busy!'

'Herr Pfiffermeister I tried my utmost to persuade him to return with me.' The prince sounded weary.

'Outrageous. Irresponsible. Madness!' Herr Pfiffermeister snatched up his frock coat and struggled into it. 'Send round my carriage. I return to government this instant. I have been delayed a whole day while the kingdom teeters on war, and for what? For this!' He shook the letter in the air.

'I will see to your carriage, sir.' Paul left the room.

Herr Pfiffermeister followed after him, but paused and turned to Elisabeth, softening his tone to a plea. 'If the kitchen would make up a little basket for me,' he said, 'I should be grateful. It is a long journey back, and I shall get no dinner.'

CHAPTER 26
RISING POWER

'Fräulein Opel, can you explain why all the men who came away from the building site of New Swanstein had such terrible stories to tell?'

'Terrible stories?'

'They could not work. They were oppressed. They speak in peculiar language of tools being too heavy in their hands and stone resisting them. We would dismiss such odd accounts, but so many of the workers gave the same story independently; at least those who talked. Many refuse to speak of it.'

'You ask me to explain?'

'I ask if you know of any explanation. Was there an oppressive foreman? Were the working conditions unacceptable? How was it that not one man remained?'

'You mean that not one man from the towns and cities remained.'

'I do not follow, Fräulein.'

'The men who came from the towns and cities all left at the start of the building work. Only the mountain people built the castle.'

'I see. No doubt they could endure the working conditions, being less civilised, perhaps. Why do you laugh?'

'What do you call civilised, sir? An absence of imagination? A *denial and rejection of what is unseen, even when there is evidence of it?'*

'You are descending into riddles, Fräulein. Pray, keep to the facts.'

'The facts are, sir, that only the people who loved and respected the mountain and the king of the mountain could live and work and thrive in that land. Those who had no sympathy for it could not stay.'

'So, it was a patriotic difference.'

'It was a difference of spirit, sir.'

'Perhaps that is the same thing.'

'Perhaps.'

THE KING GREW STRONGER, BRIGHTER, AND TALLER. His hairdresser complained he had to trim the king's hair every day, for it grew so fast. The change was imperceptible, yet sure. Elisabeth knew that everyone at Swanstein saw it, and felt it, and it did not trouble them, for the power that awakened in the mountain, in the foundations of the new castle, became the air they breathed.

Hardly any servant or worker who was not a mountain dweller remained. Prince Paul could hardly bear to be at the castle, he went back and forth to the city, carrying letters and reports between the king and his ministers and the queen mother.

But the villagers rejoiced. The harvests that month were abundant. The curse had been lifted, they said. Livestock and children flourished and grew hearty and strong. The craft workers made their goods at an unprecedented level of production and quality. Even the swans and peacocks at the castle multiplied and grew more lustrous; the peacock's iridescent feathers glowing as jewels, the black swans as polished jet. And though it was the end of September, the meadows were brighter than any summer meadow with thick carpets of flowers. Elisabeth thought it a wonder to see them and walk through them, the flower heads reaching her knees where usually they would only reach her ankles.

She often pulled Herr Haller from his work to walk through the meadows; she had to share them with someone, and he made no objection. But the mountain idyll came to an abrupt end. Prince Paul returned with the message that the war had begun, and it was impossible for the king's ministers to make the constant rapid decisions required without his presence. He must return and lead his government. He must be the figurehead of the kingdom for the troops to rally to. He must do his duty. In the name of the house of his fathers—he must return immediately.

The king thundered, his eyes midnight blue and fierce. Even the prince turned pale in his presence, for there was new power in the king these days. He cursed the ugliness of war—he did not belong in this world of strife!

But his anger abated. The fierce King of the Mountain retreated, and the young King of Bayern, with the weight of a kingdom on his shoulders, mourned for the troubles of the land; the order was given. They were all to leave at first light. He must take up his duty

---

RETURNING TO THE CITY WAS LIKE RETURNING TO ANOTHER world, a flatter, emptier world. Everything felt hollow; everyone seemed asleep, though they scurried about, busy with their duties and their pleasures.

'Is everyone behaving as though you're an unwanted foreigner speaking gibberish?' Elisabeth asked Herr Haller, the second morning of their return to München. She found him in the king's antechamber, awaiting Herr Weimann.

'I feel exactly like a foreigner,' replied Herr Haller. 'What's happened to us?'

'Could it be the magic of the mountains? Now I know

why the king hates to leave them. Everything seems more real there.'

'I'm fed up with being stared at,' Herr Haller admitted. 'What is it about me that looks strange?'

She regarded him. He looked taller and fuller somehow, yet he was the same height and size as he had always been, his clothes fitting him the same as they did before. It was a kind of radiance that had settled upon him that made him seem larger; he glowed a little, and his eyes, which she had not much noticed before, were now a luminous hazel. She had always thought him plain-looking, but now, with his features infused with light and life, he was, in fact, rather attractive.

She was a little taken aback at this thought, the more so because as she examined Herr Haller's face, she realised her admiration was reflected in his own eyes as he looked back at her. This would not do! This was no time for getting attached to anyone. It had been something of a relief to see so little of Paul of late, and to feel herself gradually released from constant thoughts of him, but there was pain mixed with the relief; she felt confused and somewhat abandoned by his absence. And she certainly was not going to add to the confusion by falling into feelings for someone else. She looked away, and forced herself to speak in a cooler voice than she felt.

'Life has been strange. It must have rubbed off on us. But it doesn't alter anything. We are still as we have always been, Herr Haller. Nothing can change in that regard.'

He did not miss the coldness in her tone.

'I understand, Fräulein Schwan,' he replied quietly. 'You reject what is real just as everyone around us does.'

'What do you mean?'

'I mean what I say. Things have been different between us these past weeks.'

'I don't know what you mean,' she said, knowing as she

said it that it was not the truth. Things had been different between them.

'You're the only friend I have, Elsa. And I'm the only one you've got at this moment in time. Don't push me away just because we're back here with Prince Charming on the prowl.'

'Prince Charming! You don't know what you're talking about. Don't speak to me like that!'

She fled the room, taking the wrong direction. Instead of leaving the royal apartments she went farther in. Not wanting to turn around and go past Herr Haller again she slipped through the hidden door and up the stairs into the Winter Garden.

She paced around the artificial lake. There were no swans or peacocks anymore; only the hummingbirds still darted between flowers, but she barely noticed them. She could only see Herr Haller's face and hear his voice.

How dare he! She muttered over and over as she marched along.

'How dare who?' came a small, invisible voice, followed by a giggle.

'Hush, Little Sister, they will find us.'

She paused, examining the shrubs and trees either side of the tiled path. A bush near the marble fountain quivered. She moved towards it, parting the leaves to see the aunts sitting on a bench in a little alcove.

'Get away!' cried Princess Sibylle, her silver topped cane jabbing at her like a rapier.

'It is her, Little Sister,' said Princess Marie, dressed in black. 'We are found!'

'Lost and found! Found and lost!' sang Princess Sibylle, jabbing her stick in time.

'How did you get up here, Your Highnesses?' Elisabeth thought of the steep stairs that had to be climbed to reach the garden.

'We flew,' said Princess Sibylle. 'We can fly, you know. Sometimes.'

'People must be looking for you. They will be worried.'

Princess Sibylle suddenly looked fierce, which was alarming, for she was such a delicate looking thing until she lifted up her cane like a queen with a sceptre of command. 'You shall not betray us!'

'I have no wish to betray you.' Who could blame them for wanting to escape the confines of their dour keeper? She had great sympathy with their desire for freedom at that moment.

'Come close and let me smell you,' said Princess Marie, beckoning. 'Can you smell it, Little Sister? Is it not the most beautiful smell of all?'

'Oh, yes it is, I smell the mountain!'

Elisabeth moved towards them.

'Do not touch me!' Princess Sibylle squealed. 'You will dirty my gown.'

'Sit beside me, Mountain Princess.' Princess Marie patted the bench beside her. 'Oh, you smell divine. The mountain is alive again, it has awoken, can you hear it, Little Sister? Can you hear the music in her hair?'

Princess Sibylle laughed and then began to sob. 'Oh, Sister, when shall we return? I want to go home! Take me away! Where are they? What have they done with them?'

'Done with whom?' Elisabeth asked, alarmed at her sudden sobbing.

'The guardians. The keepers. The guides. Where are they?' She stood up, looking about her; her sobbing became a long moan. Elisabeth thought perhaps she should go for help and relay their whereabouts.

'Do not be upset,' Princess Marie said, putting a hand on her arm. 'She will be well again in a moment.'

Sure enough, Princess Sibylle's grief abated as quickly as it came, though tears still lay on her wrinkled, pale cheek. She sat down again and began to hum a melody. Elisabeth recognised it. She had heard the workmen on the mountain sing it. Princess Marie swayed to the sound, and her voice quavered the words of the song:

Awake, awake, the time has come
The king must return to his land
Build a bridge, build a bridge
He will cross over
The king shall return to his crown

'Have you seen it?' Princess Marie touched Elisabeth on the arm again. 'Have you heard the horn? We heard the horn, did we not, Sister?'

'We did! On the day he was born we heard it. Long before the bells.'

'Oh, it was so silvery a sound, was it not, Sister?' Princess Marie closed her eyes as though listening for something. Elisabeth could hear only the trickle of water from the marble fountain.

'I can smell the sound on her. She has been close by. Oh, take us with you, Mountain Princess, you are to lead the way!' Princess Marie's eyes opened, fixing on Elisabeth a pleading look. 'We have waited so long, so long.'

'And we know the way,' added Princess Sibylle. We know the way but we cannot find it. You can take us.'

'Take you where?' Elisabeth asked.

'Home!' wailed Princess Sibylle.

'This is your home. And people will be looking for you. Shall I help you down the stairs?'

She received a sharp poke on her knee from Princess Sibylle's stick at this suggestion.

The sound of another voice resolved the dilemma, it called loudly through the foliage, 'Halloo! Your Highnesses! Are you there!'

'No!' squeaked Princess Sibylle. 'Not here! Not there!'

'Let us fly away,' Princess Marie said solemnly. 'They will never catch us.'

'Yes, let's!'

They closed their eyes tightly, and for one odd moment Elisabeth half expected them to turn into butterflies or hummingbirds and flit away, but they stayed as they were, and the steps of the servants sent to search for them grew closer.

'Found them!' called out a liveried young man. 'By the fountain!'

She watched with sadness as they were led away, Princess Sibylle poking at the footman with her stick lest he touch her, despite his protests that his gloves were clean on that hour.

'THE GOVERNMENT COMMITTEE OF ENQUIRY NOW CALLS *Lieutenant Gustaaf von Varrentrapps to give testimony.*

'Lieutenant von Varrentrapps, were you present in the king's presence chamber on the day he signed the agreement to join the United Empire?'

'Yes, I was, sir.'

'The chief psychiatrists are puzzled by testimonies from several ministers and military officers of the king regarding that meeting. The king was said to darken the room and transform himself into a terrible being. Dr Mensdorff believes such a phenomenon of communal false memory could be accounted for by the collective anxiety on that day as the kingdom feared for its defence. Can you affirm or comment on this occurrence?'

'I cannot, sir.'

'But you said you were in the audience chamber that day, Lieutenant.'

'I was, sir. But I was urged by my commanding officer to go quickly and alert the queen mother. So, I left the room. The incident you speak of happened while I was absent, sir.'

'But your military colleagues spoke of the incident to you?'

'A few words were said, sir. No one could say for certain what happened. It was not clear in their minds, sir, and no one cared to talk of it. It was considered... inexplicable.'

'So, the accounts remain... unaccountable.'

THERE WAS THE SOUND OF UPROAR IN THE KING'S AUDIENCE chamber when Elisabeth returned downstairs.

'There you are,' said Paul, accosting her the moment she stepped through the hidden door. 'You ought not to be wandering about in public.' Paul looked uneasy above the collar of his blue military coat. He glanced around over her head. 'He might be here.'

'Who?' But she knew who he meant. A chill stole over her, and she likewise glanced around, half expecting a spectral figure with snarling yellow teeth to appear and snatch her.

'Have you learnt anything?' she asked, as he steered her across the room to an antechamber. 'You said you would speak to Herr Weimann?'

'There's no time to talk of it now,' said Paul, looking over his shoulder before opening the antechamber door. 'I have only suspicions at present. Wait here,' he said. 'I am only in the next room. I'll come for you as soon as the meeting is over.'

Paul left by a different door, a private one, set into the panelling. She heard the sound of raised voices from beyond. Her curiosity got the better of her, and she cracked open the door to peek through it.

The king sat upon a gilt chair on a dais, beneath a tasselled canopy. He sat tall and straight, his hands gripping the armrests. Two great bowls of white lilies flanked him on a pair of tables.

A crowd of men in either black morning suits or military uniform stood as near to the dais as they could get; from every man radiated anger or anxiety, their voices raised as they called out above one another. Their anger cloyed the room like a sharp, unpleasant smell. For the first time Elisabeth understood the king's need for scented lilies, it was to drown out the smell of men's darkness, how was it she had not noticed before that every emotion had a scent? What was happening to her? All her senses seemed heightened by the air at New Swanstein: smell, sight and sound, overlapping together, as though all things were connected in a way she had never noticed before. In the mountains it was perfectly natural, but now she was in the city she felt unsettled, disorientated and out of place. She did not belong. Neither did the king. His eyes were dark and his mouth was grim.

Prince Paul looked less golden than she used to think him. He looked strained as though he were being pulled in different directions, and he did not know which to choose.

Herr Weimann was dressed in yellow and also looked as though he did not belong, standing among the dark suits of the ministers and officers. She looked for Herr Haller, who stood behind his master. He too looked out of place; he had already knocked into a picture frame and a chair while she watched. Suddenly she yearned for reconciliation with him as the only one who understood how she felt. He turned his head towards the doorway, as though he sensed her eyes on him, but he could not see her.

'Your Majesty,' said the deep voice of General Hogenstaller. 'We cannot rely on aid from the emperor, he has proved inconstant, and his defeat is imminent. We must ally with the chancellor. We must join the new empire.'

'Ally with that warmonger,' replied the king. His voice rang out over the murmur and grumble of the assembly. 'That trickster. That dragon-tongue.'

'We do not argue with Your Majesty's opinion of the chancellor,' said Prime Minister Schamberger, bowing his head in a nod, then shaking it from side to side as though he were indecisive. 'But without the emperor's support we have not the men nor arms to withstand the advance of the enemy.'

'Either we retreat and lose our borders,' said the general, his large hands clenched into fists to punch the air as he spoke, 'or we join the empire and save them!'

'I fear we must join.' The prime minister shook then nodded his head.

The ministers and officers murmured their agreement.

'Or, by Frost's breath, the king could wash his hands of

you all!' roared the king. There was a shocked silence at his outburst. One of the men closest to the door slipped out.

'Why should the king not rid himself of the burden of these double-minded, faint-hearted, lily-livered worms! Why must he stay here to suffer these black and bloodthirsty panhandlers? Where is the heart of these people? Why do they cower and wither under the words of despots and curs! Oh, for a kingdom of true and noble hearts!' The king was on his feet now, standing tall above every man. As his voice grew louder and his words more impassioned a strange thing happened: the room seemed to darken while the king grew brighter. Elisabeth threw a glance at the window behind her, thinking that something had darkened the early autumnal light, but all looked normal outside. It was only the air in the room beyond that grew shadowy.

The men about the dais drew back. The prime minister shielded his eyes as sparks of light shot out from the king with every movement. It happened so quickly, like a flash of lightning and a clap of thunder—for just one moment the room turned black—despite the gilt and mirrors on every wall—and then the moment of thunder was gone, and everyone blinked and rubbed their eyes.

The men looked at one another with bewildered expressions, then shook their heads and looked about them as though to reassure themselves that the world was as it should be.

The king resumed his seat, and there was a new bustle at the door.

'Your Majesty!' cried a woman's voice, and the queen mother came hurrying in, the black silk ribbons on her cap fluttering behind her. 'I beg you not to abandon us—sign the agreement, do!'

Herr Weimann pushed through the ministers and flung out his arms, hitting the prime minister and the general's adjunct with his yellow sleeves. He dropped to one knee in a dramatic gesture of appeal to the king.

'The divinely appointed bearer of the name and honour of Wittelsbach shall never fail his people,' the queen mother declared in a pained voice.

'The beloved of the Muse shall not abandon her to the fate of defeat, for he is the highest patronage of art and beauty!' insisted Herr Weimann.

The prime minister looked dazed. The general clenched and unclenched his fists. 'Only give the word, Your Majesty, and we shall crush all enemies under the combined might of the empire!' he promised.

'Do as you must,' acceded the king in a deep, slow voice. 'But I'll not stay a moment longer. This audience is at an end.' The men bowed and walked backwards three paces before dispersing from the chamber in a rumble of murmuring.

'My son, how could you say such things?' the queen mother implored, when the audience had left. 'These are your people. How can you insult them so?'

'It does not feel as though they are my people,' he replied. 'I do not belong here. It would be better for all if I were to leave. It would be the honourable thing to do, when I cannot bear to be around them.'

'Oh, Ludwig, I thought you had grown out of such foolish thoughts!' cried the queen mother. 'Always, as a child, you were so…odd. Your father tried so hard to instil a kingly discipline into you, to drive all those peculiar thoughts of yours away. Oh, we have failed!'

The king's voice softened. He reached out and placed a hand upon the queen mother's shoulder.

'There was nothing more you could do. I have a different destiny from that which you desire from me. I cannot change it, and neither can you. In the meantime, I shall do my duty. I shall sign their treaty.'

'What destiny?' wailed the queen mother.

'That is what I must discover.'

He rose from his throne, bent to kiss his mother's hand.

'Farewell, Your Highness,' he said softly, and left the chamber.

'Where are you going, Ludwig?' the queen mother called after him.

'To the mountains. Paul, make ready! I leave while the ink is fresh—I will sign their blood-stained treaty, they can have their war—they can have their fill!'

CHAPTER 27
TEMPTATION

'The Government Enquiry Committee now calls Herr Hartwig Schnorr to the testimony stand.

'Herr Schnorr, tell us your profession and your connection to the king.'

'I was the king's personal hairdresser, sir.'

'For how long?'

'Since he was old enough to have a personal hairdresser, sir.'

'And what age was that?'

'The age he was too old to have a nursemaid arrange his hair, sir.'

'Herr Schnorr, in which precise year did you become the king's personal hairdresser?'

'In the year the king turned eleven, sir.'

'Thank you. So, you were in daily attendance upon the king for eight years?'

'I was, sir. Until the day before he…was lost.'

'Tell us, Herr Schnorr, how would you describe him?'

'He had hair like silk, sir. Black as shoe polish and shiny as a mirror. And it always grew so quickly and needed a trim every five or six days, but at the—'

'No, Herr Schnorr, I meant describe his disposition. His general behaviour. What was he like as a person? We are trying to ascertain

the king's state of mind at the time of his disappearance. We are trying to establish whether he is of sound mind or not, that we may know what action to take when he is found.'

'Well, he was like…a king.'

'A good king?'

'A kingly king.'

'Would you describe him as a rational man? A rational king?'

'What do you mean by rational, sir?'

'Was he lucid, logical, reasonable?'

'As long as his hair was waved just as he liked it, he was perfectly reasonable, sir.'

'And if his hair was not as he liked it, what then?'

'Then he'd say, "That bit isn't even, Schnorr." And I'd wave it again.'

'Did he ever fly into a rage?'

'Not at me, sir.'

'At whom?'

'At no one in particular, sir. Just at general things sometimes.'

'What kind of general things?'

'Things he didn't like.'

'Such as…?'

'War. He hated war.'

'Did you ever experience anything peculiar about the king during the last months of his life, Herr Schnorr? Anything that could be called fantastical or extraordinary.'

'Do you mean magical, sir?'

'If that is the word you choose to use. Did you experience anything you would describe as "magical"?'

'Everything about the king was magical. He was always special and different from anyone else. He was the king.'

'I require specifics, Herr Schnorr. Specific events, occurrences. Unusual patterns of behaviour.'

'Well… there was his ears… though I was told never to mention them.'

'His ears?'

'The shape of them. That's why his hair had to be left long and *waved and curled just so about his head. To hide his ears. The queen mother did not care for them.'*

'The only unusual thing you have to say about the king was that he had unattractive ears.'

'They grew more pointed when he moved to the new castle.'

'Pointed?'

'And his hair grew so fast when he was at the new castle. I had to trim it every day. And his eyes…'

'What of his eyes?'

'Oh, they were quite something, sir. Not that I looked him in the eye, sir, I was always mindful of my manners, and he was particular about manners, but sometimes I would catch them in the mirror as I worked, and they were quite something. Bright blue, except when he was angry about war, and then they were almost black. But at the end they changed.'

'Changed?'

'To green.'

'I see. That will be all Herr Schnorr unless you have anything relevant to say on the matter of the king's sanity in the last months of his life? The council is not much interested in eye colour or the shape of a man's ears.'

'I have nothing to say except how I wish I had saved a lock to remember him by!'

'You may step down now, Herr Schnorr.'

'I SHALL MOVE INTO NEW SWANSTEIN IMMEDIATELY!'

'But, Your Majesty, the work continues every hour of the day.' Prince Paul stood with an opened letter in his hand.

'Are the king's apartments complete?'

'Very nearly, sir. But not finished.'

'Then they shall be finished this week. Send the order. I take possession by Friday evening.'

'Shall not the noise of the building work be an annoyance, sir?'

'Why should it? It is a glorious sound. The strike of the chisel, the song of the king's devoted servants; the very ground and air rejoices to see the ruins rebuilt, and the splendour restored. The spirit of Gundelfinger awakes! The spirit of Tannhäuser and Lohengrin lives!' The king's humour was restored from the blow the letter in Prince Paul's hand had caused a few minutes earlier.

Paul made no further protest. 'Shall His Majesty inform Her Royal Highness of his plans ahead of her arrival?' he held up the letter with the queen mother's crest and seal.

'You may send word,' replied the king. He left the study room.

Paul turned back towards the desk where Elisabeth was looking through Herr Haller's new designs. She had hoped to find him at work that morning; she missed him, and hoped to restore their friendship, but he had already left for the new castle.

'I have hardly seen you for weeks,' said Paul, drawing near.

'That's because you choose to be at München most of the time,' she replied.

'I find it oppressive here. And someone has to liaise between the king and the cabinet. I cannot do it easily from here.'

'I thought you liked riding and hiking in the mountains.'

'I used to. I still do like riding and hiking. But that new castle has such an odd feel to it.' He gave the smallest of shivers. 'Don't you feel it?'

She shrugged. 'Yes. But I rather like it. It makes me feel alive. It's as though the mountain and the land about has been woken up.' She shrugged again, feeling that she was talking nonsensically. But she meant what she said.

'You look different,' he said. His eyes travelled over her face inch by inch until she blushed and felt annoyed for blushing. 'Your eyes look brighter. I always thought they were lovely, but now they are beautiful.'

She turned her head so he could not examine her eyes. But it was rather nice to hear them called beautiful.

'And your skin has a glow about it.'

'Mountain air,' she said. 'And fresh goat's milk, I daresay. All the mountain girls have lovely skin, haven't you noticed?'

'Not like yours. And your hair has glints of copper and bronze that were not there before.'

'Too many walks in the sun this past summer. I really ought to carry a sunshade, like a real lady.'

'He had moved closer while he spoke, seating himself on the corner of the desk. He was close enough for her to smell lemon and bergamot. He took up a loose tendril of hair that had escaped from her pinned up plaits, and wound it about his finger, his hand grazing her cheek. 'Would you come away with me, Elsa,' he said softly. 'If I accepted a new commission I have been offered?'

'You are leaving?' she made the mistake of turning her head towards him. He was far too close.

'Can you see us on our adventures? We could travel the continent. See all the kingdoms.'

'How can you leave? The king relies on you. Has he sent you away?'

'He does not know. Don't speak of it to anyone. Nothing is to be made public yet, but come with me.'

'Come with you as what?'

'Only come with me.' His head was bending closer. She pulled back just in time, putting out a hand to ward him off.

'I am not in a position to go travelling about the continent. I need to know who I am. I need to know that I am safe.'

'If you came with me you would be safe.'

'How do you know?'

He did not answer, but the usual glow faded from his face, leaving him looking harder and colder than she had been used to see him.

'Do you know something? You do, don't you?'

He dropped his hands to his knees, clenched them tightly

and said, 'I only have suspicions. But if I am right, you will not remain safe even under the king's protection.'

'Why not?' She was alarmed by his gravity.

'The king...' Paul looked pained, 'chooses to withdraw himself from the seat of power. There is a growing movement amongst men in authority to remove him.'

'Depose him?'

Paul nodded. He rubbed a hand over his jaw.

'Does he know?'

'I've tried to warn him, over and over, but all he thinks of is his wretched castle. I can't get through to him how serious the situation is. The trouble is, I don't think he really wants to be king. It would be safer for him to abdicate than be forced from the throne; he doesn't know who he's dealing with.'

'And is that why you are hardly ever with the king anymore?' Elisabeth asked. 'Because he is a sinking ship. You are leaving before it goes down.'

'Do you think I should stay and drown?'

'I think you should remain loyal to the end. I thought you were his friend.'

He gave a wry smile. 'I wish life were that simple, Elsa. But it's not. It's complicated. He's not the same person anymore. I don't know this man who thinks of nothing but his obsession with building castles. I've tried my utmost to give him good counsel, but he won't hear me. What more can I do? If his reign ends in disgrace, so does my career.'

Elisabeth folded her arms tightly across her chest, regarding Paul coldly. He saw her look. 'I know you're disappointed with me, Elsa. Heaven knows I never wanted things to be as they are. But it is though... as though he is going *mad*.' He spoke the word in a near whisper, as though it were too dangerous to speak loudly. 'It is his own behaviour that condemns him, and I cannot change it. They are calling for him to be deposed on the grounds of madness. It is in the family, as you know, for you have met his great aunts.'

'What will they do to him? Shut him up in an asylum?'

'Quite possibly. If not worse. But Elsa, what concerns me most is what will happen to you. The man driving this movement may be the very one who is seeking you. He is working discreetly, moving through other people, which is why I cannot bring any evidence against him yet, I have only my suspicions based on what I am witnessing and what I can piece together. I even wonder if this movement to remove the king is purely to remove his protection from you.'

Elisabeth gasped in horror. 'You mean that I might be the cause of the king being deposed! Then I must leave, I must go, I must not let this happen to him!'

Paul leaned forward and took hold of her arms, which were still wrapped tightly across her chest. 'Yes! That is why I ask you to come away with me. I have been approached with an offer of a promotion that will take me far from here.'

Elsa's thoughts swirled. 'But who is to say I will be any safer with you? If the king cannot protect me, how can you?'

Paul sat back again, releasing her. She studied his face, trying to read the thoughts passing over his.

'You don't know, do you?'

'No. I don't. But it's worth a try, is it not?'

'I cannot think straight,' she said, gripping herself more tightly. 'I need some time to think. Oh, that I could remember everything, and this nightmare be over!'

'Don't spend too long thinking, Elsa,' Paul warned, standing up and tugging down his coat. 'We have not the luxury of time.'

'What did you say?' she asked. His words had jolted her, as though she had heard that exact phrase spoken before.

'I said we have not the luxury of time. The queen mother arrives tomorrow, in hopes of persuading the king to take up his duties, while I will try once more to advise him to abdicate and flee the kingdom if he will not. But my fear is that he will do neither. He has become obsessed with that castle of his, and will attend to little else. Time is running out. It is running out fast.'

CHAPTER 28
NEW MOON

THE QUEEN MOTHER arrived the next day. A second carriage followed her own, though no one had been told to expect a second guest.

The household stood to attention to receive their mistress, the servants in two orderly lines. Prince Paul waited to assist the queen mother.

'Paul, my dear, I am so glad to see you here. I thought Ludwig had sent everyone away,' she said as stepped down from the carriage, her full, black silk skirts remarkably voluminous for so small a person. Her lady-in-waiting looked rather crumpled, as though there had been little room left for her next to the royal skirts.

'But where is he?' The queen mother looked around, as though expecting the king to materialise from behind a garden wall or pillar.

'His Majesty is at New Swanstein, Your Highness. He desired that you enjoy a period of rest after your long journey, and he will join you at dinner.'

'He cannot even greet his own mother these days. Why are you not with him, Paul? He never goes anywhere without you.'

'He has a young architect with him, Your Highness. I am not required where tesserae and gilding are the subjects of attention.'

'He has not got that profligate with him, has he?'

'If you refer to Herr Weimann, Your Highness, then he is in München. Only his assistant is here.'

'I thought he would have been hounded out of München by now. My ladies tell me shocking things of him.'

The second carriage now rumbled to a halt. A footman moved to open the carriage door.

'Wait!' the queen mother called to him. 'Open it carefully. They may jump out.'

The carriage was opened, and from it spilled a figure in black with silvery hair, closely followed by a lady in white, who jabbed at the footman with a cane to keep him from taking her arm.

Princess Marie turned to the left and Princess Sibylle turned to the right, and for a few minutes there was confusion as the footmen attempted to herd them back towards the castle entrance. No one could approach Princess Sibylle without being struck; the upper floor footman lost a button for his impudence in trying to grab at her.

'Oh, I knew they would be troublesome!' said the queen mother. 'Tante Marie, is this how you repay me for my kindness in bringing you for a little holiday?'

Princess Marie now spied Elisabeth and surged towards her, her silver hair coming loose beneath the square of black lace she wore pinned to it. 'Little Sister, she is here!'

Princess Sibylle made a trilling noise and ceased her assault upon the footmen. She too advanced upon Elisabeth. 'The one who will lead us home!' she sang. 'Sister are we really there.'

'We are here, and we are there. We have arrived and now we may go!'

'May I escort Your Highnesses inside for refreshment?'

Elisabeth asked. She wondered that their warden was nowhere to be seen. Surely they had not come alone?

Princess Marie took her arm with both hands, clinging tightly. Princess Sibylle took a snowy handkerchief from a little pocket on her gown and placed it over Elisabeth's other forearm that she might take her arm without touching her.

'Is there beer?' she asked, looking up at her sweetly. 'They have no mountain beer at that dreadful place we have come from.'

'The butler can provide you with beer, Your Highness,' Elisabeth assured her.

She trilled again with happiness. 'Home, home. To be here, to be there. Oh, I can hear the singing, when shall we go?'

'You must rest,' Elisabeth said. 'I will take you to the swan room where you can sit at the window and look out at the lake.'

'Well this is marvellous,' Elisabeth heard the queen mother say behind her as she slowly made her way into the castle. 'Do we know who she is yet?'

'Not yet, ma'am,' replied Paul.

'What a relief to find someone who can manage the aunts,' continued the queen mother. 'I had to send Frau Müller away, she let them get into the aviary, they set free all my finches, and they were wearing my tiaras and pearls at the time—how they took them unseen from my own chamber I cannot imagine. But that was not the worst of it. They are a pair of fiends. I really do despair of them at times. But look at them now, meek as a pair of lambs!'

THE KING DID NOT SEEM MUCH PLEASED TO SEE HIS MOTHER AT dinner, but he was more gracious to his great-aunts.

'Our beautiful king,' cried Princess Marie. 'Lovelier than ever!'

'He smells of lilies,' declared Princess Sibylle, looking as a lily in her white gown and white lace head covering. 'Will you kiss me?' she said, lifting her hand. Elisabeth was surprised, for Princess Sybille permitted no one to touch her. Her hand looked so frail and small against the long, youthful fingers of the king. He bent down to put her fingers to his lips. She gave a little whimper of happiness. 'So clean. So pure. So perfect. White as a lily, white as a swan, white as the moon, white as—'

'That will do, Tante Sibylle,' the queen mother said. 'No singing at the dinner table.'

'Be quiet, sit still,' murmured Princess Marie. 'Drink your broth, eat your bread, take your tonic—'

'That will also do, Tante Marie. If you care to dine at the family table there must be no singing or chanting. Otherwise I will ask Fräulein Schwan to take you to the kitchen.'

'Where there is beer?' asked Princess Sibylle. 'Yes, let us dine in the kitchen!'

'I have no objection to singing,' the king said, his own voice very musical. 'And if Princess Sibylle desires beer, it shall be brought.' A server turned away to fulfil the request.

Princess Sibylle clapped her hands. She had draped herself with linen napkins, that no drop of food might spoil her gown.

'Ludwig, it does no good to indulge them,' the queen mother scolded. 'They require a firm hand. And why are you not eating?' The king's plate lay untouched. He did not reply but drummed his fingers on the arm of his chair. Elisabeth watched him discreetly; it was hard not to, his presence filled the room, overriding even that of the princesses and the chatter of the queen mother. Energy thrummed through the king; she could feel it, like warmth radiating from a fire, although it was not as strong as when he was at New Swanstein, where the power was thick and heavy as deep snow.

The king could not keep still. While the queen mother

scolded her aunts and talked of the latest news of the people in her acquaintance, the king fidgeted, fingering an undrunk glass of wine.

'You want to go,' Princess Marie said, addressing the king. 'So do we.'

'We are so close, Little Sister. I can taste it in the air. That is why our Beautiful One does not eat,' said Princess Sibylle. 'How can he?'

'No nonsense-talk at the table, Tante Sibylle,' the queen mother reminded her. 'Are you unwell, Ludwig?' she asked for the fourth time. 'You eat nothing.'

The king stood up abruptly as though he could bear no more. The footman hurried to take his chair, but blinked in confusion, as the chair seemed to move backwards by itself. A ripple in the air flowed over the space where the chair had been. It spread as a concentric circle; the braiding on the footman's coat glowed like burnished bronze as it passed over him, the candles in the candelabra against the wall flared brighter for an instant, the flowers in the vase upon the sideboard released a burst of scent as though someone had opened a jar of perfume.

'You will excuse me, ma'am,' said the king with a bow. 'I must take the evening air. I shall go out upon the lake.' Before his mother could protest, he was gone with long strides from the room.

'The council now calls upon Countess Hildebrand.

'Countess Hildebrand, in your position as lady-in-waiting upon the queen mother you saw the king in close proximity, did you not?'

'I did. I accompany Her Royal Highness wherever she goes. I am ever mindful of her comfort.'

'And you accompanied Her Highness to Swanstein Castle on the last occasion that Her Highness saw the king there.'

'Of course. Her Royal Highness would not go without me to wait upon her. I am the only one who can administer her Sal Volatile correctly.'

'How would you describe the king's behaviour during that visit? Did he seem well?'

'He did not. Her Royal Highness was most concerned for the king.'

'What, in particular, was she concerned about?'

'He did not eat. He did not sleep. He could not be still. It was most worrisome to Her Highness. I had to administer much Eau de Cologne to her temples during that visit and send for much chamomile tea.'

'Would you say the king was disturbed in his mind, Countess?'

'Not as disturbed as Her Royal Highness. No one has so tender a heart as Her Royal Highness. I had to send the carriage to München to get secret supplies of sausage. Her Royal Highness needs sausage when she is in the mountains. It is the air. It stimulates her appetite.'

'Sausage? I do not understand. Surely the castle pantry was well stocked with sausage.'

'Not after the king banned the cook from serving it.'

'He banned sausage?'

'He forbade every meat. He said it was barbaric. He said we were all warring, flesh-tearers . No fowl either. Nor fish. No goulash, which is Her Royal Highness's favourite. The cook at Swanstein always made excellent goulash. No sausage for Her Royal Highness's luncheon. It was most distressing.'

'This is very interesting, Countess, and certainly a sign of an unhinged mind, is it not?'

'Most certainly. Only a madman would refuse his mother sausage.'

'Where is Fräulein Schwan? They have disappeared!'

Elisabeth heard the queen mother's shrill voice and hurried down the hall to the morning room.

'They are gone again!' the queen mother cried when Elisabeth appeared in the doorway. 'I left them here for just a minute—only one minute!'

Elisabeth assured the queen mother she would join in the search, curtsied, and hurried back the way she had come. The aunts could not be far. She had found them in the queen mother's rose garden yesterday when they disappeared during their afternoon nap. They had plucked the heads of every late rose and scattered the petals into the fishpond. The pond did look very pretty, but the queen mother had not been pleased.

She hunted throughout the gardens, in every little arbour and nook, but could not find them anywhere. As she passed the study window it opened and a head appeared.

'Have they lost them again?' enquired Herr Haller. They had not spoken since their arrival at Swanstein, other than murmured polite greetings as they passed each other by.

'I've been all over the gardens,' she said. 'The footmen have searched the stables and boathouse, the maids have searched the castle, I don't know where else to look.'

'I'll help you.' He pushed the window wide open and swung a booted leg over the sill.

'Careful,' she warned, 'don't stand on that—'

Herr Haller landed with both feet on the pottery peacock that stood to the side of the path.

'Dash it!' he exclaimed as he heard the loud crack. 'Something else I'll have to mend later.'

'Something else?' She stifled down a laugh at his flustered face.

'I broke a cup at breakfast.' He ran his hand through his hair as he regarded the peacock. 'I hope it isn't valuable.'

She did laugh now. She couldn't help it. She almost said aloud, 'Oh, I have missed you, Haller, you great clumsy oaf,' but she didn't. Their last conversation still lingered unpleasantly in her mind. Then she remembered that he only became clumsy when he was tired or unhappy; perhaps he had been missing her as much as she did him.

'Any idea where to look?' she asked.

'Are you sure they're not inside?'

'Every room's been searched.'

'And you've been round the gardens?'

'Twice.'

'Then we'd better check the lakeside. They can't be far.'

'Don't be so sure. They only pretend to be frail and helpless. They're a pair of wily foxes under those little lace veils.'

He put a hand on her arm to stay her a moment.

She looked at him questioningly.

'I've missed talking to you, Elsa,' he said. 'I'm sorry for what I said about Prince Charming. I know you're too intelligent to let him fool you.'

'Don't call him that. He hasn't tried to fool me. Why do you hate him?'

'I don't hate anyone. But I do hate seeing a girl without protection being preyed upon by a...a...philanderer.'

'A girl without protection!' she spluttered. 'I'm not a child, Haller. I can take care of myself, and what's it to you if Prince Char— I mean, Paul likes me? And he's not a philanderer, he's a good man. He's done nothing wrong.' Even as she spoke the words, she doubted them. She marched on, but he caught her up and kept pace with her.

'If he's not a philanderer then why do I see him coming out of Gretel's room in the early hours of the morning? And I never said you were a child, but you don't have the protection of a father, and that snake would never dare take advantage of you if you did.'

'Gretel! What would he want with that yellow-haired, red-faced thing? And he hasn't taken advantage of me!'

'So, he's never sidled up to you, got you tipsy and stolen kisses?'

She blanched, stopping dead in her tracks. 'You saw?' Her

voice emptied of anger. She felt only embarrassment that she had been seen that night.

'I would *never* kiss you,' he said fiercely.

That seemed an odd thing to say.

'Why not?'

He did not answer. His usually amiable expression was aglow with fierce emotion, and she had to admit that he looked quite handsome with his jaw squared and his eyes flashing. But she would rather have him as he usually was. She had grown to like his easy-going calmness.

'You go that way,' he said, not looking her in the eye; he pointed to the left. 'I'll follow the lakeside path this way. If I find them, I'll give a long whistle three times.'

'And if I find them?'

'I'll catch you up. You won't be going as fast as me with the aunts.'

He strode off and she stood for a moment watching him. She told herself she didn't care that he didn't like her anymore. What did she expect? A real friendship? If Paul's example with the king was anything to go by, real friendship was a rare thing indeed. And it couldn't be true about Gretel. That had been a low thing to say. It couldn't be true. Could it…?

She must have walked as fast as Herr Haller, for they met again coming in the opposite direction. Between them, on a shallow pebbled beach were the aunts. Princess Sibylle stood with her gown lifted almost to her knees, presumably that she might not dirty her hem, while Princess Marie was at the water's edge, her hands cupped about her mouth, making a strange sound across the water.

'Your Highnesses,' Elisabeth called out, 'we have been looking everywhere for you!'

'They won't come,' said Princess Marie. She turned and there were tears in her eyes.

'Who won't come?'

'The guardians. We want them to take us home. Why won't they come?'

'We know they're near,' Princess Sibylle sang out. 'We can feel them in the smell of lilies.'

'We've been forgotten,' said Princess Marie sadly. 'No one wants us. We can't go home. Outcasts. Castaways. Strangers. No one loves us. No one understands. We are all alone. All alone. Alone.'

Elisabeth felt strangely moved by Princess Marie's words.

'You know how it feels, don't you?' Princess Marie said, stretching out her arms towards her in a pathetic pose.

Elisabeth felt tears welling up. Then she caught Herr Haller watching, and blinked them away. 'We must go back to the castle now, Princesses,' she said, her voice not as firm as she wanted. 'Can you walk so far, or shall Herr Haller go for a pair of ponies?'

'Can he get a boat?' Princess Sibylle asked brightly.

'A boat would not reach the castle, Your Highness,' replied Herr Haller. 'Ponies are an excellent idea. I shall hurry back for them.'

'We can walk,' Princess Marie said. 'Come, Little Sister. They will not come today. Perhaps tomorrow.'

'Perhaps tonight, Sister,' answered Princess Sibylle. 'When the moon is over the lake.'

'Oh yes, they love the moon!'

'There is no moon tonight, Your Highnesses,' Herr Haller said. He walked at the side of Princess Marie, while Elisabeth brought up the rear behind Princess Sibylle, who walked carefully, mindful of any overhanging tree branch that might touch her. They made a slow party wending their way back along the path.

'No moon? What have they done with it?' cried Princess Sibylle.

'It is a new moon tonight.'

'New moon, blue moon, old moon, full moon,' sang

Princess Sibylle. She kept up the song all the way back; only Elisabeth heard the birds in the trees trilling the very same tune.

CHAPTER 29
SHADOWS

'DARLING SOPHIA!' The queen mother stretched out her hands to the vision in lavender silk who came gliding across the parquet floor. Princess Sophia was so lovely, so sophisticated, Elisabeth felt like a scullery maid in comparison.

'Your Highness, dearest Euphemia,' gushed the beautiful princess kissing the queen mother's cheeks.

'Come and tell me all the news, Sophia. How glad I am to see someone normal in this place. Fräulein Schwan,' said the queen mother, 'come and meet my young cousin, Princess Sophia, she is passing through on a visit from Hesse.'

Elisabeth moved nearer to curtsey and exchange polite greetings. The Princess's beautiful eyes passed quickly over Elisabeth in her simple gown with her simple pinned-up braids, and though she smiled graciously, Elisabeth felt that she was immediately dismissed as being of no one of rank or much interest. Elisabeth returned to the aunts in the windowed alcove, as the princess sank gracefully down upon a chair by the queen mother.

'Let me smell her,' Princess Marie said, moving to leave the table they sat round.

'We must finish our flowers, Your Highness,' Elisabeth

said, putting a hand on her arm to restrain her. 'Her Highness may not wish to be touched. Or smelled.'

'She's so pretty,' sang Princess Sibylle. Their table was strewn with the wild flowers they had gathered in the meadow that morning. Now they were making up little posies. Elisabeth was quite proud of her initiative in keeping the princesses out of mischief.

'She's as fair as an alpenrose,' sighed Princess Marie. 'But not as fair as *she*.'

'Oh no,' agreed Sibylle. 'No one is as fair as *she*.'

'Make her a posy,' Elisabeth suggested, diverting Princess Marie from her attempts to leave the table.

'A posy of alpenroseys!' Princess Sibylle chanted.

'Why are your aunts here?' Elisabeth heard the princess ask in her piping clear voice.

'Oh, darling Sophia, I have had a dreadful time of things. I had to dismiss their keeper, first she let them get at my finches, and then she lost them a whole day. They were found sitting on the great lion statue in the public square. How they got up there is a mystery, they claim they flew, but, Sophia, there was such a crowd! It was dreadfully vulgar. I could not find another keeper before I came away, so I brought them with me. Mayer is interviewing new ones, I had a telegram to say she will send one on in two days.'

'But it looks as though you have found a new keeper here,' said the princess. Elisabeth shifted uncomfortably on her chair, disliking being talked of as though she were not there, even if she were out of view behind the alcove wall.

'She is a guest of Ludwig's,' said the queen mother. She lowered her voice, but not low enough not to be heard. 'She fell from her horse and injured her head, and now she cannot recall who she is. The Chief Inspector is investigating, but no one has reported a missing young woman in the kingdom, so we think she may not be from Bayern. But it is all to be kept secret.'

'Oh,' said the princess, leaning forward and dropping her

voice even lower, but still not low enough. 'I think I have heard something of her. Is she the mistress?'

'Whose mistress?' said the queen mother sharply.

Elisabeth was finding it hard to sit still, hearing herself talked of. She wanted to leave the room, but she could not abandon the aunts. Princess Sibylle touched her hand with the stem of an orchid and smiled sweetly up at her. 'They do not see us,' she said and gave a little giggle.

'Baronin von Puttkarmerreinhart says she is Paul's,' continued Princess Sophia. 'The gossips say the king's, but I do not believe them.'

'Monstrous idea!' exclaimed the queen mother. 'Scandalous! Ludwig is above such vulgarity. He is not like his grandfather.'

'Indeed, he is not.' The princess laughed merrily. 'My dear Euphemia, let us not dwell on the turpitude of court gossip, we are in the lovely mountains now, away from all that. Let me tell you all the pleasant news.'

'Please do, Sophia. I need cheering up. Everything is so out of sorts here.'

'Out of sorts? Is Ludwig well? I have not seen him for such a long time. Of course, I know all about the incident at the emperor's feast.'

'Oh, do not speak of the emperor's feast, I beg you! Such a dreadful evening, and everything has gone badly since. The emperor has still not forgiven him. Ludwig sees no one these days. All he cares about is his new castle.'

'I have heard it is being built at an astonishing speed.'

'He says he is moving in at the end of the week.' The queen mother gave a little groan.

'So soon? And while you are here?'

'He wants to get away from me, Sophia. What have I done to deserve such treatment?' She groaned again and her lady-in-waiting moved to her couch to dab cologne on her temples.

'You have done nothing to deserve it, Euphemia. You are

the most attentive and affectionate of mothers. Has Ludwig resumed his duties?'

'No. I fear he has not. Every day telegrams and letters arrive, and Ludwig barely reads any of them. He leaves Paul to pass everything on to Niklaus, who speaks with Schamberger.'

'To Prince Niklaus? Why him? Surely Pfiffermeister is the only mediator between Ludwig and the prime minister?'

'Niklaus has been making himself most helpful. But it is all dreadful, Sophia. Why will not Ludwig do as his father did?'

'Remember how young he is. He just needs a little time to grow into his duties. Once he has got this castle project finished, he will be fine, I am sure of it. But is Prince Niklaus the best person to be taking up such authority?'

'He is weak and vulgar you mean, Sophia.'

'I do not wish to call your brother-in-law anything harsh.'

'Call him what you like, Sophia. I have never liked him.'

'So why is Ludwig giving him such power?'

The queen mother lifted her hands in a gesture of despair. 'Exactly! I ask him that myself.'

'And what does he say?'

'He says that a city of warmongering pettifoggers deserves such a man to lead them.'

'Oh dear, it really is worse than I had realised. Is he losing his senses?' There was a pause. Elisabeth knew exactly what she was thinking: was the king becoming as mad as his great-aunts?

The queen mother gave another little groan and her lady-in-waiting hurried forward to administer more cologne.

'Perhaps I could speak to him,' said Princess Sophia. 'I am terribly fond of Ludwig, I think of him quite as a brother. I could call again on my way home.'

'Do come back and speak to him, Sophia, darling, do!'

'I hear Pfiffermeister is retiring from office soon. His

replacement is a former captain and said to be very efficient. Perhaps he could liaise with Paul instead of Prince Niklaus.'

'Is the new Pfiffermeister a pleasant man?' asked the queen mother. 'I have not yet met him, and I hear differing accounts of him.'

'I have not met him either, but my brother has, he is wild to have one of his famous horses. And I know he is a great favourite of Lady von Pless, not that *that* is much of a commendation. But there are unpleasant rumours regarding his late wife.'

'So I have heard. But what did you hear?'

'It is said he was unkind to her, but it may not be true. What is his name...? Wolff...Wulff...Wuelffen. Count von Wuelffen. He has a very good estate in the south, I understand, with famous stables, Schloss Dragenberg.'

Elisabeth froze with an orchid held mid-air. The room seemed to expand then contract in a dizzying lurch. She could not say why, only that the name of Wuelffen made her feel suddenly ill.

'I have not heard of him,' replied the queen mother. Her voice seemed small and far away.

'I will invite him to Poffenhoffen before I leave Bayern,' said the princess. 'I will find out where his loyalties lie. If he will be faithful to Ludwig then you can gather him into the fold as an ally, can you not? Now on to more interesting things—what do you think the Countess of Landersfeld wore to the ballet the other night?'

'Elsa? Did you hear me? Elsa?'

Elisabeth was jolted out of her thoughts and blinked up at the face of the prince. 'You have been elsewhere,' he said. 'Have you heard anything of what I have been saying?'

'Sorry,' she murmured, putting down the uneaten breakfast roll. Paul had found her breakfasting alone that morning.

'You were talking of His Majesty's plans to remove to the castle tomorrow.'

'I was asking you if you would care to inspect the room that has been made ready for you at the new castle? I am sorry you have to remove there. If you find the idea disagreeable, I will speak to the king.'

'Why would you be sorry?'

Paul raised a perfectly shaped eyebrow. 'Surely you cannot wish to be immured up there in that uncanny fabrication? No one will ever see you, save the mountain dwarves and the ghost of Gundelfinger who is said to appear every moonlit night to hasten, or hinder, the work, depending on which story you listen to.' He gave a wry smile.

'I shall go up there directly,' she said. A solitary drive was exactly what she needed. She'd had little time alone since the arrival of the aunts, and her nightmares had been particularly bad the night before, leaving her anxious and troubled.

'You take it very well. I thought it would displease you,' he said.

'Not at all. Quite the opposite. I like it there.'

'You do? You have peculiar tastes. As does Haller, he seems to like it too. I will accompany you,' he added as she stood up to leave.

'No thank you,' she said firmly. 'I don't require a chaperone. I'm sure you have more important things to do this morning.'

'I see you are still angry with me.'

'I'm not angry. But I am confused about many things at the moment, and I need to be alone this morning.' She paused. 'Do you know of a man of the name of Wuelffen? I believe he is a count.'

Paul suddenly paled. 'Where did you hear of him?' he asked quickly.

'The queen mother and her guest were speaking of him.'

'And you recognised his name? You remembered his name?'

'I don't know if it was a remembrance. I just know that I felt very strange when I heard it. It may be nothing.'

She looked more closely at Paul. 'Do you know him?'

'I…er…have heard of him. I understand he is being considered for a senior position in the government.'

Elisabeth wondered at Paul's reaction. But she was so tired from her nightmare-troubled night that she had not the energy to press him. She left him looking as uneasy as herself.

THE PROGRESS ON THE NEW CASTLE WAS ASTONISHING. ELISABETH could see the gleam of white turrets peering above the dark firs above her as the road wound upwards.

She stopped the carriage the last mile of the steep path, and got out, saying she would walk the rest of the way.

Autumn was well advanced now, but the walk made her warm enough to throw back the hood of her cloak. Dark firs were a wall either side of the path, but in places she glimpsed the lake below. The morning light fell softly on the golden crocuses nodding in the earth.

Golden crocuses she thought, standing still a moment to admire a cluster. They did not belong here. They belonged to springtime. And they were so large and so very golden. The closer to the castle she got, the thicker and brighter the flowers grew, until great gold swathes of them stretched away into the forest—and the smell! She did not think crocuses had much of a scent, but these certainly did. Another scent wafted towards her, she had reached the outer wall of the castle, and clambering freely around its base was a riot of jasmine. Was she imagining things, or did new tendrils stretch out and little white buds form even as she watched? She laughed, delighted with the audacity of the little flowers, they had no business to be flowering in profusion in this place at this time of the year.

The thick presence of the castle now swirled about her, enveloping her in another world, far from the cares and concerns of the one below. She welcomed it. Here she was lifted up above her heavy feelings—the anxiety of her situation, the confusion and the feelings of betrayal she felt over Paul, the loss of Herr Haller's friendship, the fear of what the future held. Here was comfort and escape. No wonder the king wanted to be nowhere else.

The gatehouse was almost complete. The courtyard was still busy with workers; the four corner towers had not risen far above their foundations, but the central hall stood proudly as the castle's heart. Limed walls glowed as pearl, turret roofs the colour of the blue mountains beyond soared high, glass windows within tall, elegant arches caught the sun and glittered. The sawing and hammering were rhythmic instruments accompanying the workers' song. Their deep voices rebounded from the castle walls, the air was alive with music and rhythm and a pulsing, living force that made her feel as though anything was possible, anything could happen.

She climbed the grand staircase of the central hall, her eye following the tree-like columns, rising up to a vaulted ceiling of deepest blue, with countless gold stars adorning it. Life-size swans perched proudly on newels and greeted her on the final step.

She stood in the doorway of the king's chambers, watching the construction of the king's bed of carved oak. The intricate carvings of swans and flowers were as detailed and beautiful as that of her pendant. An enormous golden chandelier, shaped as a crown, hung from the ceiling. Mirrors and candelabras and glossy polished wood caught and threw back the light from the windows. The window and bed curtains were patterned with embroidered silver swans. Everything felt alive.

After viewing the few rooms that were completed, she returned to the courtyard and castle grounds.

The feeling of otherworldly power was stronger when she walked on the ground, as though something invisible seeped from the mountain rock beneath, charging the air. It was heady and a little frightening. Whatever it was, it was not tame. There was beauty, but not softness. It was not a friendly power, but if she was respectful, it would not harm her; that was what she felt as she stood watching the activity of the mountain folk working away, singing in deep voices.

She saw a man at work, beneath a constructed shelter, chiselling away at a block of oak. Out of the wood emerged the shape of a heraldic swan, four times the size of a real one, with a crown about its neck. She put a hand to her own carved swan and felt a small pulsing sensation pass through her fingers. A score of men worked under the carver's direction, and the site was filled with woodwork, ready to be set in place.

'What beautiful work,' she said, approaching the great swan, and tracing the lines of the carving. The woodcarver turned to see who spoke and dropped his chisel with a cry of surprise.

'M'lady!' he cried, staring at her as though amazed. 'You are well! You are alive!'

Elisabeth stared back at the man. Was there something familiar about his blue-green eyes?

'Who are you? Do you know me?'

'Know you! M'lady, it's me—Hansi!'

She shook her head, trying to say that she did not remember him, but the shock of his recognition of her made her words fail. Her eyes moved over the carved swan behind him, and her hand reached up to the pendant at her neck. A warm, pulsing sensation flowed through the wood. She looked from the swan to the man stood before it.

'Did you make this?' She whispered, unsure how it was that she knew; she lifted up her pendant.

'Yes, m'lady,' he looked as amazed as herself. 'Don't you remember?' He studied her face, as though puzzled by her lack of recognition.

Images passed through her mind; she did not know what was memory or what was not. The sound of a lathe, a child's voice, *I had a dream, Elsa,* said the child's voice. *You were leaving me...*

'Say no more!' came a voice.

The king came across the ground towards them. 'Whatever you say must be confidential.' He looked about at the workmen, who were watching the scene with interest. 'Do you know this lady?'

'Why, of course—but I thought—'

'Say no more!' the king ordered again. 'Come with us, whatever you say must be told in private.'

The workman took up his discarded cap, and pulled it on to follow the king as directed. Elisabeth followed the king in a dreamlike walk, throwing glances over her shoulder at the man behind, who was likewise staring at her. She felt almost light-headed with the anticipation of possibly hearing who she really was.

'I DEMAND THIS WOMAN BE REMOVED FROM THE WITNESS STAND *immediately!*'

'Excuse me?' the committee chairman swivelled round, adjusting his monocle to better see who it was that dared disrupt the investigation. The new Cabinet Secretary stood in the entrance way, looking dishevelled, his eyes bulging with fury at Fräulein Opel.

'Remove her now!'

'On what grounds, sir? She is giving a vitally important testimony; the committee must hear her.'

'Every word she says is a lie!'

'Sir, you cannot bodily remove her! Guards! Guards, restrain him!'

CHAPTER 30
REVELATIONS

'ORDER! ORDER!' *bellowed the committee chairman, his monocle slipping from his eye as he swung between Fräulein Opel, who stood white-faced on the testimony dais, and Count von Wuelffen, who had to be restrained by two guards to keep from lunging at her.*

A young man, dressed as a worker, pushed his way through the uproarious crowd to reach Fräulein Opel. A third guard moved to block his approach, but Fräulein Opel called out that the man was a friend—please let him pass that he might speak to her.

'You're shaking, m'lady,' said the man. 'Here, take hold of this, it'll help.' He gave her the small carving he held, she clutched it in one hand, her other holding the pendant at her neck.

'Do sit down, m'lady, I won't let him near you. Can a glass of something be brought for the lady?' he asked, addressing an attendant. 'She's had enough shocks these past days.'

The chairman finally regained control of the room; the crowd was quieted, but the tension was palpable.

'Make your statement with the decorum due to the committee,' the chairman said, addressing the furious count.

'Do you know who I am?' the count snarled. 'I'll have you stripped from your office, all of you! How dare you question me. That woman is a liar and must be removed immediately!'

'M'lord Chairman,' called out the young man. *'May I give testimony?'*

'And who are you?'

'My name is Hans, and I was the head carpenter at the king's castle.'

'And what testimony can you have that is relevant to this unseemly turn of events?'

The young man looked at Fräulein Opel, as though questioning her. She met his eyes, then nodded, as though to give him consent to speak.

'I knew m'lady before she was at the castle, sir. I was employed by her stepmother, Baronin von Winterheimer. That man wanted to marry m'lady—that man had her kidnapped—him and m'lady's stepmother between them arranged it—that man tried to kill the king to get her back and cover his crime.' He jabbed his finger in the direction of the count.

The crowd exploded again. The count was shouting, straining against the hands of the guards who held him fast, but his voice was lost in the uproar. The chairman raised his hands in vexation and shouted in vain for order.

I HAVE HAD SO MANY NAMES. ALL OF THEM TRUE IN PART. EVEN now when I recall those days, those days when I could not remember the name of my birth, could not recall my real place in the world, or who my people were, even now there is a hazy cloud over that time, as though I lived a different life in a different world. If I did not have those who shared those memories with me, I might think I dreamt them all.

The night after I learnt my name I dreamed of other names. People calling me by different things: daughter, sister, mistress, someone called me Sisi. I woke with an ache, knowing that there were people I missed and loved, and yet I could not see their faces, I only heard their voices in my dreams. At least I had been spared the usual nightmare for one night.

I woke up to find a sheet of paper slipped under my bedroom door. It was a picture, a watercolour scene of the wildflower meadows as they had been in the summer. The colours glowed, capturing the colours of the columbines, wild orchids and edelweiss. I grew tearful looking at it, not just because it brought back memories of the wonder I had felt in seeing such beauty, but because I understood what the painting was: a request for reconciliation. Herr Haller and I had been at odds for some days, and I had missed his friendship.

'Thank you,' was all I needed to say when I found Herr Haller at breakfast.

He grinned back, looking relieved that I had accepted it. 'Glad you liked it.'

'I love it. You have such talent. I could almost smell the flowers.'

'If I had the time and materials, I'd paint it in oils, then I could really make it come alive. Perhaps one day.'

I was about to say, 'Yes, one day.' But I said nothing. How could I know what was to come in the days ahead? I knew from the carpenter that I had a younger brother, and a stepmother, who, if the carpenter told the truth, was a danger to me. The king had counselled me to remain under his protection while the Chief Inspector made investigations regarding my alleged identity. Baroness von Winterheimer. Only daughter of the late Baron von Winterheimer. The name sounded strange. Surely it ought to resonate in some way if it were really my name? If only I could remember. If only I knew what was true.

'Something wrong?' Herr Haller asked. 'You look troubled.'

'Only the usual troubles. What are you working on today?'

'A design for murals, for the Singer's Hall.'

'Come and take a walk with me first,' I said. 'Something happened to me yesterday that I want to tell you of. I met a man who claims to know who I am.'

WE WALKED ALONG A LITTLE TRAIL ON THE MOUNTAIN SLOPE. A stream ran by, making its way down to the lake below.

'What a strange tale,' Herr Haller said, when I had told him all that the carpenter had said. 'Does it prompt any remembrance?'

I shook my head. 'Very little. Some images, some sensations. But it's like listening to a hummingbird talk, it's all too faint and fast.'

'A hummingbird talk?' Herr Haller sounded baffled.

'It's just a saying,' I said quickly. Then I caught myself; why was I lying to Herr Haller? That was not what friends did. 'Actually,' I said. Because you have felt the magic at the castle, you will not be surprised when I tell you that I can speak with some animals and birds.'

He stared at me for a moment as if trying to determine from my expression whether or not I was joking.

'What are the birds saying?' he said, looking upwards at the canopy. I didn't have to listen hard to hear.

'They're singing the same song they've been singing since I got here. But no,' I listened again, the words had changed. No longer was it, *Mountain sleeping, mountain dreaming, mountain waking.* 'They're singing, *mountain waking, mountain stirring, mountain rising.*'

'What does that mean?'

'The mountain has awoken. That's the power we feel.'

'Why has it awoken? What's it going to do?'

'It's been holding something. The magician who built the first, ancient castle, took something from the Fae and hid it in the mountain and sealed it with magic.'

'Like in the legend?'

'Exactly. Except it would seem it's not a legend. It's true.'

'And in the legend,' said Herr Haller, frowning with thought, 'the Swan Knight was to come again, rebuild the magician's castle, recover the treasure, and return it to Faerie.'

'The king has been searching since he began building,' I said. 'But we don't know where to look. We don't even know what to look for. The legend only says that it was some treasure of the Fae.'

I was partly surprised by how easily he accepted as truth that the story was real; but then nothing was surprising when one was on the mountain, with the otherworldly magic suffusing the air we breathed.

'The king has been searching for caves and clefts in the mountain every day that he rides out,' I said, 'He searches day and night. But he cannot find it.'

'I wonder what the treasure is?'

'Something green as emerald, that's what the swans say. Like this pool.' We stopped short as we entered a little glade.

'I've never seen this place before,' said Herr Haller in surprise, looking around him.

'Nor have I. Though I've often walked this way. We must have taken a different turn.' I knew even as I spoke, that we had taken no turn, for the woodland trail only ran in one direction.

The pool lay beneath the trees, green and shiny as an emerald.

'Careful,' said Herr Haller, putting a hand on my arm to stay me from moving any closer to the pool. 'The magic feels strong here.'

He was right. The air was thick with it. It lay over everything; the trees thrummed with life, I could almost hear the stretch of branches, the rising of sap, the unfurling of leaves. The water in the pool was shimmering, but the birds above were suddenly silent; they were listening.

'I think this pool is a border into Faerie,' I whispered. I did not know how I knew this, but I felt it strongly.

Herr Haller nodded, still looking around us. 'We must be careful,' he whispered back.

There was a swoosh of air behind us, and I cried out in surprise. Herr Haller reached for me and we clung to one another as for one moment our senses were overwhelmed, just as when one is blinded by a bright sun when stepping out of a darkened room.

I opened my eyes to see where the brightness came from: a great, white swan, with a golden crown about its neck had flown down to settle on the emerald water. It folded up its massive wings and fixed a black, glittering eye upon me, willing me to pay attention. I held my breath, still clinging tightly to Herr Haller as I listened hard. I couldn't say how long the swan remained; time fled away in its presence.

'I will tell your message,' I said, when it had finished speaking. I bowed my head, for I felt that I was in the presence of something or someone that demanded respect.

The swan bent its crowned neck to the water; in one graceful movement it dove beneath the surface, and was gone. I blinked, and there was no emerald-green pool in a hollow where the songbirds held their breath. We were on the mountain trail, beneath the pines, and the usual passing of time felt restored. The birds above resumed their song with more urgency than before.

'What did it say?' Herr Haller asked, still holding me protectively.

'The time has come for the king to recover the treasure. The mountain is now fully wakened. He must look to where the water falls.'

'CHIEF INSPECTOR ECKSTEIN, THE KING INSTRUCTED YOU TO MAKE *enquiries with regard to the young lady, who we now believe to be Baronin von Winterheimer. A young lady who was taken under the king's protection following her unfortunate loss of memory.*'

'Yes, sir. It is as you say.'

'And what report have you made on the case? What are your findings?'

'Until recently, sir, I had very little to go on, and very little to find, and very little to report. I instructed every constable in every town to investigate any reported disappearances of any young ladies, but every report that was followed up was found to be unconnected with the young lady concerned.

' I had concluded that the young lady in question must not be of Bayern, but His Majesty, and His Highness, Prince Paul von Thorne, both insisted that she spoke as a native of Bayern, so the mystery thickened, so to speak, sir. However, one of the reports that had been followed up and found initially to be unfounded, has since been investigated further, following fresh findings.'

'What was this report, and what are these recent findings, Chief Inspector?'

'The report was made by a young working man, a carpenter who gave his name as that of Hans Bauer of Füssen. Herr Bauer made a statement to the constable at Vogt on the seventeenth day of May claiming that he had been journeying with a young baroness who was fleeing from a forced marriage to a notable man of the name of Count von Wuelffen. Herr Bauer claimed that the young baroness had been abducted by four men that he recognised as men in the employ of the said count. Herr Bauer witnessed the men taking hold of the young lady by force; he then suffered blows by one of the said assailants which rendered him stunned and disabled for a time. When he recovered his senses and feet, the young lady was gone, and he had not been able to trace her.'

'And did Herr Bauer have corresponding injuries with his testimony, Chief Inspector?'

'He did. He had a lump the size of a pear on the back of his head, sir, and a pair of black eyes.'

'And was his claim fully investigated?'

'It was. But the young lady's mother claimed that it was all fabrication. She claimed that the young lady had left of her own accord with Herr Bauer, had eloped with him, to her very great *shame and to the distress of her family, who now disowned her, and that Count von Wuelffen had no connection to the family beyond that of general acquaintance and could not possibly have anything to do with the young lady's disappearance. If the young lady had indeed been carried away, it was most certainly by ruffians who were in no way connected to herself or the count.'*

'And did you interview Count von Wuelffen?'

'I attempted to, sir. But Count von Wuelffen declined to be interviewed. He said only a warrant from the Chief Magistrate would make him submit to being questioned on such ludicrous allegations.'

'And did you seek a warrant, Chief Inspector?'

'I did. But the Chief Magistrate said he could personally vouch for the character of Count von Wuelffen, and required greater evidence than the word of an uneducated youth who was likely of unsound mind following a blow to the head.'

'Did you inform His Majesty of this outcome?'

'I informed His Highness, Prince von Thorne, who was acting as mediator between myself and His Majesty.'

'And what did you do next?'

'There was little I could do, officially, sir. My hands were tied, so to speak, by the Chief Magistrate refusing to give a warrant for the interview of Count von Wuelffen, and also by the testimony of the young lady's mother, who likewise claimed that the count had no part in the young lady's disappearance.'

'But His Majesty has the power to overrule the Chief Magistrate.'

'Indeed, he does. And Prince von Thorne was to gain a written statement from His Majesty to that effect.'

'And did His Highness do so?'

'He did not.'

'That is surprising, is it not, Chief Inspector?'

'Nothing surprises me where folk are concerned, sir. I have seen it all, so to speak.'

'But why did His Highness not assist you in this?'

'I can only surmise, sir. I can only assume, I can only suppose, I

can only consider and ponder over the fact of His Highness's father being known to be as close an acquaintance to Count von Wuelffen as is the Chief Magistrate, as are most of the senior members of Parliament, as are most of the influential members of our kingdom's nobility, sir.'

'Order! Order!' shouted the Chairman as the crowd broke out into loud exclamations at these words. Fräulein Opel, who was now most likely Fräulein Schwan, who was now most likely Baronin von Winterheimer was looking very ill as she sat in the front row of the witnesses, listening to the Chief Inspector's testimony. Count von Wuelffen had to be restrained at the back of the room by the guards, and only the threat of removal from the room silenced him from his outbursts, as he protested against the lies being uttered, and made threats of what he would see happen to the Chief Inspector when he was done.

'You said, Chief Inspector,' said the Chairman, when the crowd had been quieted, 'that until recently you had very little to go on in regards to the investigation. What is it that you have recently learnt?'

'I said, sir, that officially my hands were tied, so to speak. But I am a man with no less than four young ladies for daughters, sir, and could not rest in the knowledge that there might be another young lady and daughter in distress, should the testimony of Herr Bauer be true, and I have always considered that no testimony can be considered untrue until it has been fully investigated.

'I considered it my duty to pursue this investigation as far as was in my power, even if it meant doing so unofficially, that I might find a way of pursing it officially, so to speak.'

'And what did you find in your 'unofficial' investigation?'

'I took it upon myself to gain two unofficial interviews with two servants at the home of the missing young lady. I spoke to a groom as he waited at the smithy in town, and I spoke to a laundry maid as she walked out on her half day off. Both persons were alarmed at being spoken to on the subject of their young mistress, but once I had introduced myself and my purpose and assured them of their anonymity until there was evidence enough for them to make a

257

formal statement, they both were very ready to tell me what they understood of the matter concerning the missing young lady of the house.'

'And what did they tell you?'

'They told me of a man of the name of Count von Wuelffen having made regular visits to the house, visits that did not accord with that of a distance acquaintance, as the mistress of the house claimed. Visits that involved dinner and tea and a proposal of marriage to the missing young lady.'

'A proposal of marriage, sir?'

'Indeed. A proposal that was not accepted. The laundry maid claimed that she overheard a conspiracy between the young lady's mother and the count to have the young lady forcibly removed and married. She claimed to have assisted the young lady in escaping the house, under the protection of a young man by the name of Herr Hans Bauer. And she had heard nothing of either the young lady, nor the young man since.'

'Order! Order!' shouted the Chairman yet again as the crowd erupted into loud exclamations at such revelations.

'Chief Inspector, can you identify the young lady you see, known to us as Fräulein Opel and also Fräulein Schwan. Can you identify whether or not she is the missing young lady you have been investigating the disappearance of?'

'I cannot, sir. For I have never met the young lady in the care of His Majesty. I was to interview her on two occasions, the first at the palace, the day following the visit of the Emperor of Österreich, which did not come to pass, for the young lady had removed to Swanstein Castle on my arrival. The second appointment was to be at Swanstein Castle, but His Highness, Lieutenant Prince von Thorne, telegrammed to say that she had been removed to New Swanstein, and as yet, no one was permitted to call without express permission of the king. Express permission was to follow, but it never did.'

'So we have no witnesses to the true identity of the young lady present, excepting that of Herr Bauer?' said the Chairman, turning to peer at the lady in question through his monocle.

'You have my own testimony, sir,' said the young lady. Her voice trembled, but was clear. 'My memory was restored to me very recently, and I do beg of you, Chief Inspector, that you will give me word of my brother, for he was unwell when I last saw him.'

'And your mother?' said the Chairman. 'You would wish to have word of her?'

'My stepmother is guilty of all that the Chief Inspector has described. She imprisoned me, colluded in my abduction, and has now cast me off with lies and infamy. The only wish I have regarding her is that she be brought to justice.'

The Chairman made no attempt to quiet the audience. He was worn out with shouting. He called for a intermission for luncheon. The count must remain under guard, and the investigation would continue in the afternoon.

CHAPTER 31
TREASURE

Workers had cut out crude steps down the mountainside to the waterfall pool below the castle, but it was still a steep climb. The king bounded ahead as surefooted as a deer, while Herr Haller and I slipped and stumbled a little, holding onto one another in places and laughing at ourselves, like children on an adventure.

When we reached the green pool where the waterfall fell from high above, the king had disappeared.

'Where did he go?' I asked, looking round. Herr Haller still held my hand, for the rocks we stood on were slippery with spray.

He pointed, and we saw a gleam of light from the mouth of a small cave.

We ducked into the cave, but in a few steps stood upright as the roof grew in height. A silver-blue glow lit up the walls, and the magic was tangible.

The passageway widened, and we rounded a bend to find a great cavern with a lake of water spread before us. Columns of pale stalactites and stalagmites gave the cave a strange and beautiful architecture; the lake was so green it looked as a meadow of still grass, but what made Herr Haller and I gasp was the light.

The king stood on a rocky ledge above the lake bathed in blue light that shifted into green, then yellow, orange, red, violet. Herr Haller gazed open-mouthed at the patterns of colour that passed over the walls and water, as though trying to fix their shades in his mind that he might paint them, though they were richer and brighter than any paint I had ever seen.

The great, white swan came gliding from the far side of the underground lake, its feathers reflecting the slow change of colours. We watched in silence as it halted before the king and bent its long neck as though in a bow before him.

'It's so beautiful,' I whispered.

The scene before us was dreamlike, and yet it felt more real than anything beyond the world outside, but it did not feel quite safe. Herr Haller and I stood close together, as though to gain protection from one another. There was great beauty before us, but I felt we were close to some invisible boundary that was dangerous to us as mortals.

The king glowed with a rainbow of colours, he seemed to be listening to the great swan, but I was too distracted by the colour and shifting light about me to concentrate and hear what was said.

The swan bowed its long neck once again, then moved away, gliding beyond our sight. The king moved to the cave wall, passing his hands over the rock, as though feeling for something. He gave a cry of satisfaction as part of the rock wall seemed to melt beneath his touch, as though some magical barrier had been removed. From the uncovered alcove in the rock wall he drew a chest of black wood bound in brass.

The king stood taller, more beautiful and unearthly than ever. His eyes were brilliant turquoise as he passed us by with long strides.

'Come,' he commanded. 'Now I know what is to be. You are my witnesses.'

We climbed back up the steep, rough steps, Herr Haller

tugging me up as my long skirts hampered me. The king had far more speed and strength than we did, even while carrying the wooden chest in his arms. and we were soon left behind, wondering to ourselves what treasure he held.

When we reached the castle grounds, we were met by a carriage drawing up outside the gatehouse. Wagons of goods usually went to the rear gate, so we knew it must be a visitor. A rare one, for few were permitted entry, and those that did come never liked to stay long.

'Herr Weimann,' exclaimed Herr Haller. 'Wonder what he's doing here.'

Herr Weimann alighted from his carriage like a squab, black cockerel, with his black-feathered cape and hat, contrasting unfavourably against the pale castle walls.

'Welcome, Friend,' greeted the king, looking tall and bright and magnificent beside Herr Weimann.

'Your Majesty, my heart rejoices to see you!' A flourishing bow was made. 'See how my eyes fill with tears to see our vision emerging!' He swept his arm towards the castle before him. 'Just as the Muse showed it! Happy day! And yet—'

'Yet what, Herr Weimann?' said the king.

'And yet here I stand before His Majesty a man of sorrow with a weeping heart.'

'Come inside and the king shall hear your woes.'

Another ornate bow, and Herr Weimann followed the king through the gates. 'Haller,' he said in greeting to him as he passed by. 'I trust you are preserving your master's reputation by continuing his work in all faithfulness to the vision?'

'Sir,' was all Herr Haller replied with a bow of the head.

Herr Weimann paused a moment to scrutinise Herr Haller's face. 'You look different,' he murmured, frowning. 'I hope you have not been indulging your pleasures instead of working.'

'I believe His Majesty is satisfied with my work,' replied Herr Haller.

'You mean His Majesty is satisfied with the work done in my name, Haller.'

'Sir.' Herr Haller bowed again.

Herr Weimann hurried after the king.

'Pompous fraud,' I muttered.

Herr Haller started, looking at me as though I had kicked him.

'Not you,' I said. 'Him. Taking all the credit for your hard work.'

Herr Haller shrugged. 'That's the lot of an apprentice.'

'Let's find out what he's here for.'

'It can't be good. The last time I saw him in black was when they closed all his credit accounts in Vienna, and we had to flee in the middle of the night to escape the bailiffs.'

Herr Weimann admired all he saw as he passed up the staircase and into the throne room. The murals were unfinished, but the beautiful mosaic floor gleamed, and the magnificent golden chandelier had been recently hung from the domed ceiling high above.

'Just as I saw it in the visions given to me,' Herr Weimann declared over and over. 'What excellent workmanship. Who would have believed such skill resided in the fingers of peasants?'

The king seated himself upon his throne, the bronze-bound chest was placed at his feet. 'What tidings do you bear, Friend?'

'Ah, Your Majesty, it is with a heart full and heavy that I come.'

'Why do you bring heaviness and sorrow before the king?'

'Your Exceeding Majesty, I have been sent as an unofficial envoy on behalf of your loyal and humble government.'

'There is neither loyalty nor humility in the king's government. Why do they send you?'

The king spoke evenly, but his eyes were piercing, and a sound like distant thunder rolled through the air. The room darkened and cooled a degree, and I thought of that fearful moment in the palace. Herr Weimann no doubt recalled it also. He stepped back, shrinking into his high collar and throwing out his ringed hands in a gesture of appeasement.

'Forgive me! Oh, that I could cast all words of trouble into the Danube where they belong! They said you might listen to one who has been called Beloved Friend by His Glorious Majesty.'

'Speak what you must,' the king ordered. The thunder abated to a softer growl.

Herr Weimann took a deep breath 'There are concerns, Your Majesty. Large bills come in daily from your suppliers. The treasury is weak from the cost of the war.'

'They desired their war. My work brings peace and prosperity to the land. Can you not feel it? Do you not see it in the beauty about you, hear it in the song of my people as they build?'

'There is dismay that His Majesty does not attend parliament at this time.'

'Parliament waits on the king, not he on them.'

'His Majesty will not meet with dignitaries and royal guests at the palace, nor will he permit them to his castles.'

'I permitted a great feast and ball for that fox of an emperor and how did he repay me? By demanding my royal swans!' The room darkened a degree more, and the rumble of thunder grew a little louder.

Herr Weimann took another step back. 'That is all I have to say, and it has given me no pleasure. I have repeated what I have been compelled to speak. My own heart honours the king's absolute right to rule as he sees fit. I am his humble servant.'

'Why have you brought this message?' the king demanded. 'Why did not you refuse?'

Herr Weimann made a gesture of despair, he replied in a strangled voice, 'They said if I did not speak, Your Majesty, they would… send in my creditors.'

'I cleared all creditors when I employed you!'

Herr Weimann squirmed. 'There are one or two new ones. It is the Muse, Your Majesty; I cannot refuse any request she makes. She is my mistress, and I am bound to obey.'

'Who are these creditors? What have you been bound to obtain?'

'Mostly jewellers, Your Majesty. The Muse takes great delight in the refraction of light, the fire of a ruby, the ice of a diamond, etcetera. They are most acceptable offerings to her.'

The king stood up and Herr Weimann gave a little cry of fear and dropped to one knee, for the king's eyes were dark as a winter storm. But the king said no more. I heard his footsteps cross the room; when I dared to lift up my head he was gone, and he had taken the chest with him. Herr Weimann struggled to his feet and shook out his coat tails.

'Haller,' he barked, 'gather up your things, and let us be gone. I have done my duty here.'

'Go where, sir?'

'To München, where else?'

'Will your creditors permit you to stay there?'

'Don't ask impertinent questions, boy, only do as you are bid.'

'But the work here is not done. The king daily asks for new designs to be sent to the weavers and goldsmiths and—'

'There will be no more tapestries or chandeliers sent from the workshops,' growled Herr Weimann. 'The government will not finance his work, and he has spent all his own fortune.' Herr Weimann looked about him at the six-foot candelabras, decorated with gold swans, and sighed. 'Magnificent,' he said sadly. 'But they do not understand. They have not art in their souls. They know not genius when they see it.'

'I cannot leave without the king's permission,' Herr Haller said. He stood tall and spoke firmly. I had never heard him speak up for himself before Herr Weimann before. I felt proud of him.

'The king does not own you,' said Herr Weimann angrily. 'He does not pay your wages!'

'No one pays me wages.'

'Why, you ingrate, you thankless cub! Did I not take you in? Have I not housed you, fed you, trained you?'

'And I have worked hard in return, Herr Weimann. I have given my all to show you my gratitude. But the king is my master now. I must do as he bids.'

'The king is about to be bankrupted!' cried Herr Weimann. 'Who will feed you then?'

'With all due respect, sir, most of the time I have been with you, you also have been in dire financial straits.'

Herr Weimann was growing purple. He thrust out his square jaw and his eyes bulged.

'This is insubordination! Defiance! Open rebellion! Insurrection! You will come with me, Haller, or you will henceforth be cast onto the streets whence you came!'

'Then we must part ways, sir,' said Herr Haller. 'I will not leave.' There was a tremor in his voice, but he stood firm.

Herr Weimann stamped his patent leather shoe on the mosaic floor. He swung his felt hat with the black ostrich plume around him as though it were a vicious-edged sword. He fumed and roiled and called Herr Haller very rude names, but Herr Haller stood immovable. His master stomped out in a cloud of black wool and streaming feathers and Herr Haller sought the nearest chair and sat down heavily.

'Well done,' I said warmly.

He gave a weary smile. 'I've had enough of being dragged about from city to city, working all hours for him. I can't go back to that life, though heaven only knows what lies ahead for me.'

I understood his uncertainty. What lay ahead for me also? My future seemed far more uncertain than his.

'You will be fine,' I said, feeling a little deflated by my own thoughts. I sank down onto the chair next to him. 'You have talent. You will find work.'

He nodded. 'Dare we ask the king what is in that chest?' he asked me, and the feeling of adventure returned to lighten our gloom.

'We can try,' I said.

'Come on then.'

CHAPTER 32
A WAY OUT

'HERR POPPE, tell the Committee your occupation and most recent position.'

'I am a cook. I worked for the king.'

'You were at New Swanstein Castle as the only remaining cook, is that correct?'

'It is.'

'This committee is concerned with gathering evidence regarding the king's state of mind prior to his mysterious disappearance. Did you converse with the king in your occupation, Herr Poppe?'

'Not directly. My orders came through the butler and housekeeper.'

'Were those orders of the usual nature, Herr Poppe? Was there anything unusual in the last months or weeks of the king?'

'The only thing unusual was that he did not eat in the last days that I was at New Swanstein.'

'The king did not eat? How is that possible?'

'I should say, the king did not eat of anything I cooked.'

'Who cooked for him?'

'No one.'

'I do not understand. Clarify your statement, Herr Poppe. The committee requires facts, not conundrums.'

'I did not ever see it happen myself, sir. I can only tell you that *the king had a magical cup, like a giant emerald. They said he only had to pour out this cup and as much food and drink as he desired flowed out onto his table.'*

'A magic cup. A magic emerald. Herr Poppe, are you mocking the committee?'

'I only say what I know, sir. And I know he did not eat, and I know the cup was as beautiful as a great jewel for I saw it once myself when I was passing by the throne room.'

'And where is this "magical" cup now, Herr Poppe?'

'It disappeared.'

'Of course it did. I suppose as a mountain dweller you retain all loyalty to the king, and thus there lies your collusion in the ridiculous fairy tales that surround him. Leave the chamber, Herr Poppe. You are wasting our time.'

THE DAY AFTER HERR WEIMANN'S BLACK VISIT, ANOTHER GUEST arrived. Princess Sophia swept up to the castle gates in her four-horse drawn carriage and was ushered into the throne room before the king.

'Dearest Ludwig,' she said upon rising from a curtsey before the throne. 'Such formality when it is only your old friend.'

The king sat upon his gilt throne beneath a canopy of blue and silver stars. The armrests of his seat reared up as life-sized swans.

'I perceive that you come on formal purposes, Your Highness,' replied the king.

The princess hesitated, seeming uncertain of herself in relation to the imposing, glowing figure before her. The soft growl of thunder began, and the air in the room cooled a little, as before a storm.

'Your Majesty, I speak with the urging of Her Highness, the queen mother.'

'Why does the queen mother not speak herself?'

'She is unwell. She has a dreadful cold. I speak both as friend and ambassador.'

'Ambassador of whom?'

'Your chief ministers and High Court officials. They are distressed, they say they are refused your presence. They claim to receive instructions from their king only through the mediation of your aide-de-camp, or on occasion, when the prince is not with you, your valet.'

'What of it?'

'Dear Ludwig you of all persons understand protocol! They feel it as an insult.'

'Recall your own sense of protocol in addressing the king rightfully. If the king insults them, they should look to their own actions for the source of his displeasure.'

'I know the war displeased you—'

'It disgusted me. As does all their ways. They are for war, I am for peace. They are for all that is monstrous, I am for beauty. I disown them!'

'Your Majesty—you cannot disown your people! Forgive them. Return to them, I beg you!'

'Have they changed their ways?'

The rumbling grew louder, and the darkness increased. I admired the princess's courage, for she did not seem deterred by the palpable anger and tension in the hall. She lifted the fine veil from her hat and took a few, slow steps toward the throne, then dropped to her knees before the king in a gesture of appeal. The king looked down at her for a long moment.

'What is your request, Sophia?' His voice was softened, but still powerful. The thunder died down; the light slowly returned to full daylight.

'Your Majesty, Prince Niklaus has taken it upon himself to stand in your place in all matters of state and royal function.'

'What of it? I have given him the authority to represent the royal house.'

'But there are those who say that if Prince Niklaus is bearing the office of king, then why should he not be king?'

'He is not appointed. And he has not the ambition.'

'He is not ambitious, but those who surround him are. The new Cabinet Secretary, Count von Wuelffen, is well known for his avarice for position, and seems to be working tirelessly for your removal, though I do not understand why. The Cabinet Secretary has called upon the government to have you declared insane and unfit to rule, even now he is garnering support among leaders and prominent men. He is a man of persuasion. Thus, my request on behalf of the queen mother is that you would return to München and assert your authority and quash such insurrection.'

'What you ask is impossible.' The king sounded saddened by this admission.

'How can you say so?'

'They are not my people, Sophia. I have never belonged here. And soon I shall leave.'

'Leave? What do you mean? Shall you abdicate? You will be playing into their hands if you do. You will be abandoning your people to those who are unjust and self-serving.'

'They are not my people,' he repeated. 'I have never belonged here. All my life I have felt so. All my childhood I have been tormented by it. But now I begin to know who I am. And I do not belong here.'

'Ludwig, you speak as an enigma!'

'And an enigma I must always remain.' He stepped down from his throne to take her hand. 'Rise up, my lady. He took from inside his coat an emerald cup. 'Hold out your hand. Princess Sophia looked distressed, but she did as she was bid. The king tilted the cup and from it poured a silvery stream shaping itself into a small flask. Princess Sophia exclaimed at the silver flask that now lay in her hand; she held it up and turned it round to examine it in wonder.

'Ludwig, what is this? What have I just seen?'

'Take it to the queen mother. It is wine that will aid her recovery. But take it immediately. Its efficacy is short-lived in this temporal air. There is one last kindness you can do for me, my lady: comfort the queen mother when I am gone.'

THE SNOWS CAME EARLY THAT YEAR. WHEN PAUL RETURNED from his latest foray in the city he travelled by sleigh up the mountain path.

He found me late on the afternoon of his arrival; I was gathering fresh flowers from the gardens, for the king liked to have vases and bowls of flowers all around him.

'Lilies in October,' Paul commented. I paused with my little knife mid-air at the sound of his voice. I had not seen him for some time. I did not turn around immediately. 'Lilies in the snow. And so many.'

'As fast as we cut them, they grow again next morning,' I replied. 'Crocuses in the forest,' I continued, 'larches in full bloom, this mountain is full of wonders.'

'Full of uncanny and unnatural happenings,' said Paul, his voice not bearing his usual warmth and humour.

I turned now to look at him, half expecting the familiar uncomfortable lurch of my stomach to occur as I met his smiling eyes and tall, golden presence. But something about him was different. There was no glow, no charismatic presence, no charm radiating out. He looked haunted, edgy, uncomfortable. His eyes darted about as though expecting someone or something to leap out from somewhere.

'You look well, Elsa,' he said, when his eyes returned to me. 'I've missed you.'

'You look tired,' I replied truthfully. 'And unhappy. Too much work, or too much entertainment?'

He attempted a smile. 'Little entertainment of late. More's the pity.

'Are you here to ask the king to return to court?' I said. 'Everyone else has tried and failed. Is it really as bad as they say? Is the king's rule threatened?' The words sounded unreal as I spoke them. Here, feeling the flow of power surging up from the depths of the mountain, spilling through the castle walls, through the gardens, down the hillside, it seemed impossible that any force could come against the king when such power surrounded him. The castle felt invincible.

'It is very bad, Elsa. It could not be worse.'

I was taken aback at his expression.

'What is going to happen?'

Paul stepped closer to me, dropping his voice to a low urging. 'Come away with me, Elsa. I leave tomorrow. I travel to Zurich on a diplomatic assignment before taking up my new commission. Come with me, there's nothing for you here.'

'There's nothing for me in Zurich. Except the shame of being talked of as your mistress. You don't want to marry me, do you?'

For one brief moment I almost hoped he would say, *Yes, I do. Marry me, Elsa.*

He faltered, his face showing a wrestling with thoughts and feelings before he answered.

'I cannot.'

For the first time since I had known him, he looked small and weak.

'My father would not permit it. I am the younger son. I have to marry money even if I would choose to marry for love.'

The last of my hopes regarding Paul fell away. How foolish of me to have clung to them in a part of my heart.

'I wish you well in Zurich, Your Highness,' I said, when I could trust my voice not to shake. 'One thing puzzles me, however...how is it you have gained a lucrative position without the king's permission? You are leaving him without him even knowing. Who has the authority to arrange this? And what have you done to get it?'

He looked stricken. Then he gave a short laugh. Not his

usual warm, sunny laugh that cast dancing lights about me, but a dry, tired laugh.

'It's a cruel world out there, my darling. Perhaps I understand why you like it here, hidden away from it all. I gave the king my best. I worked hard for him. But I can't afford to go down with him. My father has friends in high places: General Hogenstaller and the new Cabinet Secretary, and their ilk. Between them they've arranged a new position for me.'

I knew who the new Cabinet Secretary was, and it sent a shock of fear through me to hear that Paul was closely connected to him now.

'And what did you do for them?'

He shook his head. 'Nothing of any magnitude. Gave testimonies regarding the king's patterns of living, unusual behaviour, any concerns.'

'You have been a spy.' I felt anger surging up, but the prince looked so diminished and wrung out that my contempt was tempered with pity at what he had become, and what it had cost him. 'You have betrayed him,' I said sadly.

He made a strange sound, almost like a sob catching in his throat. He stretched out a hand to take hold of mine, but I moved so that all he grasped hold of was the heads of the lilies I held.

'Elsa, come away, let me take you somewhere safe. It's not just what is to come upon the king that endangers you, there's something else—I am sure you know.'

'Know what?'

But I knew.

'I know who you are.' His voice lowered as though he spoke a secret.

'So do I. I learnt it very recently. But who told you?'

'I...put the pieces together, from things I heard.'

'From things you heard from the new Cabinet Secretary. The man you have been feeding information about the king. The man who will use it against him. The man you have received a new position from. The man who wishes me harm.'

Paul could not answer, and he could not meet my eye.

'He's a wicked man.' I said.

'I know what he is,' he rasped. 'That's why I want you to come with me, out of his reach. I'll find somewhere for you to lie low, start a new life somewhere where he'll never find you. He doesn't want to hurt you, Elsa, he just wants to…own you. Come with me. If not to remain with me, then let me assist you to flee from here and take you to some place of safety. I want to help you.'

The words were tempting. Very. If the prince were right, if the king was to be usurped, his power stripped from him, there would be no king to protect me. Who would rule in his place? His uncle would. And he was close to the count. I had no chance. I had no hope. And here was hope. Prince Paul stood, pale as the lily heads that lay crushed in his hands, full of fear and foreboding, offering me a chance to flee a second time, but to what, and to where? The carpenter had said I had an aunt somewhere north, but he did not know her address; I could not remember either her name nor where she lived. My head swirled.

'I need to think,' I said finally. I turned away, letting go of the long lily stems.

He dropped the crushed flower heads and caught hold of me. 'You know, Elsa,' he said in a ragged voice. 'I could give the order and have you bodily removed. Carry you off.'

'Why would you do that?'

'Because it is what I have been charged to do.'

I stared at him, appalled at what I was hearing.

'I thought you were my friend,' was all I could say.

'I am! That's precisely why I have risked my neck coming here a day early, that I might warn you, and hide you from him before he gets here. He is coming, Elsa. Soon. Perhaps tomorrow. I leave at dawn. We can ride together. He is coming, Elsa, and there is no one who can help you.'

Paul dropped his hand from my arm. My flowers had fallen in a tangled heap of ruin in the snow. I left the garden, picking up my skirts so I could run along the swept path. I did not know where to, I just knew I needed to be alone with my thoughts. I had only one night left to determine my future.

CHAPTER 33
DECISIONS

I FOUND myself at the lakeside, which lay grey and mournful beneath the white sky. A few stray flakes of snow fell half-heartedly upon me, melting into my hair. Mist shrouded the far side of the lake as the evening drew in.

I couldn't think. I felt as numb as my hands and feet. Out of the mist ghostly shapes came gliding towards me. The only sound was a muffled, watery lap against the shore. An owl hooted as though greeting the shapes that now took the form of swans. I watched them pass by.

Was Paul destined to be my helper a second time? He had found me when I was in need and destitute, and had brought me into the safety of the castle; was he to pull me from the castle into a new place of safety?

I was more confused than ever.

There was a sudden shift in the clouds and the sky cleared above me as dramatically as theatre curtains drawn back to reveal a bright stage. The sky gleamed green at the lake's edge, flushing into gold, then crimson, as the sun set on the west side of the water. To the east the moon now appeared, low, pale, and full. It would be a spectacular Hunter's Moon that night. Perhaps the king would call for his golden sleigh that he might ride out beneath it. Perhaps for one last time.

The swans sailed away into the last of the golden ripples. An owl hooted again from the trees behind me. The burst of colour was fast fading; it was growing dark, and I was so cold.

'Elsa!' a voice called from somewhere beyond the owl. 'Elsa!'

'I'm here!' I called back, not wanting Herr Haller to waste time searching for me in the dark. I followed the glinting light of a lantern swinging amongst the trees until I met him.

'Elsa, I was worried! No one could find you and it was getting dark.'

'I'm fine.'

'You're shivering!' He threw a cloak about my shoulders. It was warm and heavy.

'You can't walk back in your shirt,' I protested. 'Here. It's big enough for two.' I held out one edge of the cloak that he might take it and wrap it about his right shoulder; his left shoulder abutted mine beneath the cloak.

'It's enormous, I wonder you could walk in it,' I joked through chattering teeth. The cloak skimmed the ground.

'I think it must be a castoff of the king's,' said Herr Haller. 'It's about right for someone nearly seven feet tall. I just grabbed the warmest looking one in the boot room.'

'You shouldn't have come out,' I said. 'You know I can look after myself.'

'Oh, be quiet,' said Herr Haller. 'There's so much odd stuff going on that I know nothing for sure anymore.'

We had to link arms to keep together as we walked.

'Thank you,' I murmured, feeling grateful for his presence.

'What do you think will happen?' I asked. The lantern light made swinging arcs of light on the snowy ground. The golden crocuses glowed brighter by moonlight than they did by sun.

'I don't know. But the prince is as jittery as a high-strung horse before battle. I reckon he knows what's going to happen. But he's not saying.'

'He says the king will lose his power.'

'I'd like to see them try to take it,' he said with surprising fierceness. 'They'll have to get past the Castle Guard first, and they're all mountain folk; they'll defend the king with their last breath.'

'The prince is leaving in the morning. I think he's fleeing before the trouble starts.'

'I bet he is, the lily-livered rodent!'

I almost laughed to hear the usually peaceable Herr Haller speak with such savagery. But nothing about the situation was funny.

Herr Haller stopped suddenly, holding me tightly so I would not walk on and pull our shared cloak away.

'Elsa,' he said in a tone of urgency. 'I think you should leave before anything bad happens. I don't want you caught up in it.'

'Don't be ridiculous. I'm not abandoning the king just because a few over-stuffed dignitaries are coming from the city. Like you said, they'll have to get past the Castle Guard first.'

'But if you are seen,' pressed Herr Haller. 'By *him.*' The lamplight cast his mild hazel eyes into dramatic dark orbs. 'Count von Wuelffen is one of the men coming. I heard the prince talking to his valet.'

I flinched back at that name and the cloak fell from my shoulder. Herr Haller picked it up and rearranged it. 'Come on, let's keep walking. I bet your feet are wet.'

I shivered at the thought of what would happen if the count found me. Perhaps Paul and Herr Haller were right. I should leave at dawn. Herr Haller pulled me closer, thinking my shiver was from the cold. He hurried me on, asking no more questions.

When I awoke next morning, I knew two things: I knew I had a streaming cold coming, and I knew that I was not going anywhere with the prince. I couldn't bear the thought of being with someone who put their own interests first and betrayed their friends. It made me sick and angry to think of it. Herr Haller with his dreamy, clumsy, kindness was more of a true prince and soldier of the king than Paul. And he had nicer eyes, I concluded. Paul's almost seemed to be laughing at one's confusion; Herr Haller would never laugh at someone, he would only laugh with them.

With this resolution I swung myself out of bed, wincing as my bare feet touched the cold, stone floor. It was colder today than yesterday, and my fireplace held only pale ashes. I dressed quickly and left my room.

There was a new feel in the castle. The exterior work had ceased when the snow came, but the ring of chisel and the grate of saw could be heard on the fourth floor, above the king's chambers. The workmen sang as they worked. It was the singing that was different, I realised. The words were the same, but the rhythm was faster, the voices urgent, the magic felt heavy as deep, deep snow, as though it were piling up and a mountain avalanche was imminent.

The horn, the horn, it calls him home,
The king must return to his land
Build a door, build a door
Let him now enter
The king now returns to his throne

'Elsa,' Paul's voice came out of the shadows; I turned to face him in the oak-panelled hall. 'I waited for you. I wanted to be gone at dawn.'

'You waited in vain, Paul. I'm not going with you.'

'Elsa, please.'

For one awful moment I wondered if he would carry me off, as the count had told him to. He came towards me, his face taut and without light—no candles were lit in the passageway, the window at the end of the hall was too far away to shed much wintry light, and Paul's inner light had dissipated.

Suddenly a surge of terror gripped my breath, as a rush of forgotten memories rose up and flooded me—I was in a room of rough wooden walls, instead of panelled oak; in the shadows were the forms of men—strangers, rough, ill-smelling—a scream rose up as Paul's face blurred into that of a man with bared, yellow teeth.

'Elsa!' called another voice, and I whirled round and ran into the arms of Herr Haller, who stood at the other end of the hall.

'Get away from her!' I heard him say in a voice so fierce it startled me. 'You've done enough harm.'

When the feeling of terror subsided, and I was no longer in a dark, shadowy lodge, I could look up; Paul was gone.

'Are you alright?' Herr Haller said, smoothing the hair from my face.

I nodded. Unable to speak. The memory had been so real. So awful.

'You know we can't stay,' he said. 'I've been thinking of it all night. We need to leave before *he* gets here.'

'Where will we go?' I whispered.

'I don't know. We must speak to the king. I won't leave without telling him.'

The footman in attendance on the king's chambers was authorised to let us in. The king was at his desk, the twenty-four candles in the chandelier above him were lit, and the pair of oil lamps at either end of the table glowed bright. The golden fireplace smouldered with orange flames. The figures in the murals on the walls seemed to live and dance in the moving light: kings signalled orders, knights held aloft their banners, fair maidens bent to give favours, and dragons threatened to devour them all.

But what caught and refracted light most of all was the

collection of jewels and gold objects heaped carelessly upon the king's great desk like the hoard of a dragon.

'The treasure from the cave,' Herr Haller said, as we surveyed the glittering spread. We had tried to find out what was in the chest, but had not seen it until now.

'I've never seen gemstones so big,' I said in quiet awe. And I had not. The jewellery was of an unfamiliar fashion; crudely shaped, rather than carefully faceted. There were great lengths of smaller gems, strung into necklaces, and brooches with stones the size of songbird's eggs.

'The hidden treasure of the wizard,' said the king. In his hand he held the green cup carved out of emerald.

'That is what you have been searching for,' I said, my eyes mesmerised by the light of the goblet. It pulsed with power; while the gemstones on the king's desk might have come from the earth, the emerald chalice in the king's hand had not. It was certainly from another realm.

'It must be returned from whence it came,' said the king, lifting it up so rays of green light flashed in the lamplight. 'It does not belong in this world. Even that which is good becomes a curse when it has been stolen. And these,' he gestured to the largest jewels, 'I leave behind. I send them to the queen mother with instructions. They shall recoup the cost of rebuilding this castle. I leave behind no debt. The mountain is healed from its treachery. The people of the mountain shall dwell in peace now. No darklings shall roam or pillage. Their crops shall fail no more. The misdeed is undone. The cup is recovered. I leave behind only blessing, and I go and tell them so this very day. The smaller gems I shall distribute among them as a farewell gift, for they have worked with one mind for me, and they alone of the people of this land have shown me love.'

'Leave behind?' Herr Haller repeated. 'Are you leaving?'

'We all must leave. Each to his own destiny,' was the king's reply. 'Wait with me this one final night.'

· · ·

THE SNOW MADE EVERYTHING STILL AND QUIET. THE CASTLE waited patiently. The workmen ceased their toil, but the songs continued, resounding through the singer's hall where they laboured.

'It seems fitting,' Herr Haller said, as we stood inside the great hall, watching the workmen passing round a flagon of beer as they sat or stood upon boxes of tools or piles of lumber singing heartily of dragons slain and battles won and lost. 'Fitting that they should fill this hall with song.'

Herr Haller's drawn-up plans had included balconies from which to view the hall below, candelabras twelve feet tall and great chandeliers, each bearing a hundred candles. The carvings of winged messengers and swans with outstretched wings were in place, but they were not yet gilded. The musicians' dais had four pillars supporting its three great arches, but the murals were not yet begun, and the walls were bare plaster. There would be no musicians taking their place with violin and cello and horn; no regal guests would sit in the balconies, basking in the mellow notes that soared to meet their ears. There were only crude oil lanterns to light the space, not that they were much needed, for the windows stretched the full length of the great hall, letting in that peculiar still light of snowy skies.

I agreed with Herr Haller. The bare plaster walls and unadorned wood was more fitting for the mountain folk, sitting as their descendants would have done in ancient times, among the walls of underground stone with tree roots as their seats, and tree trunks as their pillars. There they would have sung the very same songs in the same deep, full voices. Raising their flagons in a toast to the King of the Mountain, calling upon the power that brought snow and sun and flowers and storms to be at peace with them as they sought to live at peace with all things unseen.

But that peace could not last. For men of a different spirit were coming.

CHAPTER 34
THREE WISHES

'BARON VON FLEISCHMANN *and Dr Guttenberg, you are respectively the Master of the Horse, and assistant psychiatrist to Dr Mensdorff. You were both members of the government deputation sent out the night the king was last seen.*'

'*That is correct,*' *replied the tall, broad-chested baron. The thin, slight doctor nodded.*

'*Please describe to the Committee the events of that night, Baron von Fleischmann.*'

The baron cleared his throat and began.

'*The deputation was represented by ten persons: the Minister of the King's Household, the Grand Master of the Household, the new Cabinet Secretary, four doctors of psychiatry, including Dr Guttenberg here, two handlers experienced in the use of the straitjacket and chloroform, and, of course, myself, as Master of the Horse. We made our way to Swanstein Castle by the royal train, leaving at precisely eight o'clock in the morning, and reaching our destination of Swanstein at fourteen minutes past seven o'clock in the evening, where we were supposed to be met by Lieutenant Prince von Thorne, now Lieutenant-Colonel Thorne.*'

'*Supposed to be met?*'

'*He was not there. Had left that morning. Inexplicably. Miscommunication, one can only conclude.*'

'That was a long journey, sir.'

'Snow hampered our progress at eight different points of the tracks. On each occasion the snow had to be removed before we could proceed. Lieutenant-Colonel Thorne had informed us in advance that the king was not at Swanstein but was residing in the partially completed castle on the mountain above.'

'Did you go directly to the castle where the king resided?'

'We did not. The king's sleigh was absent from the stables, and we were informed that His Majesty had been seen visiting the peasants in the villages to distribute gifts of jewels, and give any person or animal who was sick a drink from a green cup. We concluded it would be best to wait until he had returned to the new castle. Then we would know his exact whereabouts.'

'Visiting the peasants? Giving sick animals a drink from a green cup? Distributing valuable gifts? What did you make of such actions, Dr Guttenberg?'

'It was the opinion of Dr Mensdorff that this was further indication of the king's diseased faculties. Kings of sound mind do not distribute caskets of jewels and valuable items of luxury to peasants. What would they do with them?'

'Quite so,' agreed the baron. 'Unpardonable waste. There'll be peasants with diamond pins on their braces, wearing gold watches and using pearl handled paper knives to spear their sausage. Disgraceful.'

'No gold watches,' said the doctor. 'The king was most particular about not having watches or clocks about him at the new castle. Claimed that time was a symbol of mortal decay, which he wanted no part in. Dr Mensdorff said it was another symptom of his delusional condition.'

'How did you proceed, Baron Fleischmann? Did you advance to the mountain castle once the king's sleigh had returned?'

'Not immediately. I wished to proceed, but some of the gentlemen were complaining of the effects of the journey. It was decided that we should dine first and "thaw out", as some members of the party put it.'

'It was an exceedingly cold journey,' said the doctor, giving a little shiver. 'There was no heating on the train.'

'If you and your fellow doctors had gotten out to help clear the snow with the rest of us, you would have warmed up admirably,' said the baron.

'I had not adequate footwear,' said the doctor.

'So you dined at Swanstein? With the queen mother?'

'No indeed,' said the baron. 'We had no wish for Her Highness to know of our arrival. She would have sent warning to the king. We dined at the inn in Swanstein village. Not bad strudel. Excellent goats' cheese. Passable cutlets. Shame about the wine. We claimed to be a party of travellers on our way to Osterlee.'

'That was Dr Mensdorff's idea,' the doctor said.

'At what hour did you leave the inn and make your way up to the king's mountain castle, sir?'

'Reached the castle at precisely two minutes to midnight.'

'Did you gain entry easily?'

'Easily! Hah! We were met at the gates by a great mob!'

'A mob?'

'A mutinous, vicious mob!'

'With pokers and hammers and all manner of dreadful weapons,' added the doctor. 'It was terrible. It was like the streets of Revolutionary Paris.'

'How many people were there, sir?'

'Hundreds. Rough, ignorant peasants, all of them.'

'So they knew you were coming?'

'Someone had informed them,' replied the baron.

'Likely it was the two old ladies,' said the doctor. 'They came into the stables while we awaited the return of the sleigh. In nightdresses and caps they were, beneath their cloaks, one in black and one all in white, they shrieked out that we were traitors and murderers. They were soon taken away, but I think they roused the castle household and someone ran up the mountain path to give warning.'

'Could they have been the king's great-aunts, who are likewise among the victims of this tragic mystery?' asked the committee chairman.

'Almost certainly,' replied the baron.

IT WAS ALMOST MIDNIGHT WHEN THE NOISE BEGAN.

A castle guard hurried through the candlelit halls, up the staircase to the king's chambers. A young lad accompanied him, red-cheeked, and panting hard, as though he had just run a good distance.

No one had retired to bed yet; we were all too apprehensive. I heard the stamp of the guard's boots on the wooden floors and joined the servants in following the guard to see what was happening.

The king was in his throne room, standing at the windows, looking out at the snowy mountains, beneath the full moon. He remained as serene as the view outside. I had often noticed that when moonlight fell upon him, he grew so fair and beautiful that it was almost painful to look at him.

'Your Majesty,' cried the guard, keeping his head bowed as though he too found the brightness of the king too much to look upon. 'The coachman's boy has run up from the stables, says there's a group of men come for you.'

'What men?' asked the king calmly. 'Did you hear their names, young man?'

The guard tapped the boy on the head to tell him to speak.

'I didn't hear no names, Your Majesty,' stammered the boy. 'They was in big long fur coats and hats and smelled like cigars. Some of them was called doctor, and some was called milord. They told Pa he had to give them two carriages or they'd have him thrown in jail on orders of the new king, 'cause you weren't the king no more, but I don't believe it. Pa said to tell you he'd get the carriages ready as slow as possible. I run up the hill as fast as I could, I used the deer track. My brothers got sent to the villages to tell everyone.'

'You have served your king well,' the king told him.

The boy beamed with pleasure, but then recalled why he

was there. 'We won't let 'em in, will we?' he turned to the guard.

'The Castle Guard has closed and manned every entry point, Your Majesty. No one is getting in.'

The king continued gazing out at the moon. 'I wish to go to the lake. Unseen by the city interlopers.'

'Sir?' the guard looked perplexed. 'His Majesty wishes to escape by boat?'

The king made no answer.

'I suppose we could escort you out through the east gate and through the forest, if the enemy could be distracted. But Your Majesty would have to go on foot.'

'Confine the men in the guardhouse when they come. I shall leave by the carriages they have unlawfully taken from the royal stables.'

'Very good, Your Majesty. It shall be done.'

The noise of the crowd that gathered outside the castle gates carried clearly through the stillness of the air. Every villager who could run or ride had made their way up the mountain path, each bearing a stout herding stick, or tool with which to defend their king. The musical songs of the workmen now became a battle cry as they called out against the strangers that dared to trespass on their mountain. They would defend their beloved king with their lives, they cried, and no one who heard the passion in their voices could doubt them.

'What if they've brought guns, or swords?' I asked Herr Haller, as we joined the servants, watching the gatehouse from the castle courtyard.

'They would have brought soldiers with them if they were expecting violence,' Herr Haller said. 'I think the arrogant mules thought they could just walk in, put the king in a carriage and drive away, without any fuss.'

'Can you feel the magic leaving?' I said, looking about the

walls where flowers had grown in profusion the past months. 'Why is it going now when the king needs protection?'

'Perhaps it goes before the king,' said Herr Haller. 'He seemed to know it was time to leave.'

I felt such a rush of pain at Herr Haller's words. 'I'm cold,' I murmured, and ran back into the castle.

I paced up and down the gallery on the third floor, trying to calm myself. I sneezed and sniffed, my throat tickled and my head throbbed. I did not know what to do, where to go next. This life, hidden away in the castle, was ending, and I had to leave before anyone from the outside world recognised me.

'Swan Maiden,' said a voice like the notes of a violin. I turned and followed the call. The king was in his study chamber. He looked different. The royal hairdresser had fled the castle yesterday, along with some of the servants that were not native to the mountain. Word had reached them, no doubt through Prince Paul's valet or groom, that things were about to go badly for the king. Without the usual arrangement of waves on the king's thick, black hair, it fell straight and smooth to his chin. His ears could now be seen, and they were pointed as an eagle-owl's.

The king's eyes blazed like lanterns of deep green glass. His pale skin was luminous as pearl. Whatever the king was, he was no ordinary man. He raised up the beautiful emerald cup. He tilted it, and silvery liquid poured out forming the shape of a small silver goblet. I stared in fascination and watched as he poured a second goblet from the emerald cup.

'You and one other have alone remained steadfast to the king, from among those who are not of the mountain,' he said. 'Make your request, Swan Maiden. The king shall grant three wishes.' He held out one of the silver goblets to me. I reached out to take it, my hand trembling.

The little cup held what looked like red wine. I held it with both hands while my mind tried to formulate the words to reply with.

'I wish, Your Majesty,' I said faintly, 'to remember who I am. To be reconciled to my brother, and be delivered from those who wish to do me harm.'

'What is your second request?'

'I thought I had made three.'

'Your memory shall return without my assistance. And what is in the heart of your enemies shall bring its own judgement upon them.'

'Can you heal one who has been ill a long time? The carpenter told me my brother is very weak in health.'

I thought he might pour out a vial or bottle from his emerald chalice and give it to me for my brother. But he did not. He only regarded me closely, as though he were searching my very soul. I could not speak while his gaze held me.

'Do not be afraid, Swan Maiden. Even in mortal death there is a deeper life.'

I did not understand him, but I could not speak to say so while he continued looking deep into my soul. It was unsettling to hear him speak of death when I had asked for the very opposite.

'What is your third wish?'

What else was there to wish for? I felt no assurance that he had granted me the first two. 'I suppose you cannot bring someone back from the dead?' I said sadly, thinking of my father, who the carpenter had told me had only recently died. I knew even as I asked that it was not possible. But what else was there to wish for except that I could be restored to my family, in memory and in person?

He shook his head slowly. 'I cannot bring a mortal back from the dead. But I see the three greatest desires of your heart, Swan Maiden. Now drink the cup to seal them as granted.'

He drank down the wine in his small goblet in one swallow. I obediently did the same. It tasted bitter and sweet at the same time, but I felt warmed and strengthened by it. The illness I'd felt approaching, now left me.

The footsteps of a guard were heard.

'Your Majesty, we have confined the enemy in the guard-house. The way is made clear. However...'

'Yes?'

'Two of the men got away. We are looking for them, sir. They were not in the carriages, but rode up behind the other men. They turned back when the crowd surrounded the carriages. They cannot be far. The roads are being watched.'

'The king leaves now. Before moonset begins.'

CHAPTER 35
MOONSHINE

'BARON VON FLEISCHMANN, *you and Count von Wuelffen were the only members of the Deputation who did not suffer incarceration in the gatehouse. You made a courageous escape from the violence, I understand.'*

'We did. The carriages only seated four each, therefore the count and I volunteered to ride behind.'

'Why were you such a distance from the carriages?'

'The count had taken the king's own horse, but the animal seemed to determined to throw him off. The count soon showed him who was in command, but it slowed our progress. That is how we came to arrive later than our party.'

'And upon assessment of the situation at the castle gates you negotiated your way back down to Swanstein that you might send for assistance. Is that correct?'

'Our intention was to fulfil our orders, either by gaining extra men, or by whatever means necessary. The count wrestled with the brute half the way down the mountain path, then the beast threw him and disappeared into the forest. The count suffered no breakages, so we let the second horse go, and continued our way by foot, surmounting all the difficulties of having no light about us, not to mention the cursed terrain that had a mind of its own in tripping us up and blocking our way.'

'A mind of its own, sir?'

'A manner of speech. I am a rational man, but strange things happened that night, and so strange manners of speech will at times obtrude.'

'When you reached the village of Swanstein, what did you witness next, sir?'

'A great procession. If I were not a rational man, I should say it was like a scene from a fairy tale. The king was riding the most magnificent horse I have ever seen. Where it came from, I cannot say. I had never seen that horse in his stables. Nor have I seen its size and quality before.'

'Was it from the villages, sir?'

'Certainly not. An emperor would desire such a magnificent specimen; no villager could own it.'

'So, the king travelled by horseback to the village, accompanied by a great procession, you say?'

'Not to the village. To the lake. With a great long line of peasants holding candles and lanterns, lining the path, throwing flowers before him in a most pagan manner.'

'No weapons, sir? They were a peaceful crowd?'

'No weapons. Only lights and flowers.'

'And what did you venture next, sir?'

'Our only thought was to keep the king from escaping. Should he reach the other side of the lake and cross the mountain border, he might reconcile with the emperor, amass an army and plunge the kingdom into civil war. We determined if we could get to the boathouse and commandeer a boat, we would follow him out onto the lake and force him to return with us to the royal train, and bring him to München.'

'Even with so great a crowd about him?'

'He went alone into his boat. Only the young woman accompanied him, and a servant to pole the boat. We decided that if we could get to the other side of the lake, we could apprehend him and take him to the station without the peasants seeing us.'

'The king was a man of great height and youth, did you not fear being overpowered by him?'

'I am a former captain, and so is the count. We are not men of fear.'

'And were you armed?'

The baron was silent.

'I asked, were you armed, sir?'

'I was not.'

'Was the Cabinet Secretary armed?'

The baron threw a glance across the room to where Count von Wuelffen remained held between two guards.

'I ask, because there have been reports of gunshot that night.'

'The count was armed,' admitted the baron. The audience gasped. 'Liar!' roared the count across the room.

THE KING IGNORED THE CARRIAGES AT HIS DISPOSAL. HE STOOD at the head of the mountain path, looking into the dark forest beyond as though waiting. All the power that had formerly coursed through the castle grounds now gathered about him, creating an invisible barrier between him and his subjects. We all hung back.

There was a rustling noise from the trees, and the crowd gasped as a magnificent white horse emerged to stand with head bowed before the king. I had never seen so large a horse. Its white coat gleamed as if made of moonlight. As it bowed, I saw a slender horn upon its brow. The king mounted in one graceful bound, and the horse walked majestically down the mountain path.

More villagers surged up the path: woman and children, and the men not young enough to reach the castle gates as quickly as those who'd acted as guardians. As the king rode by they snatched up handfuls of gold crocuses from the snowy ground and strewed them across the path before him. The air was so still that even bare candle flames hardly flickered as the people stood, lighting the way.

I followed in the king's train, Herr Haller close by; the

castle servants and villagers fell in behind. The moon was brighter than I had ever known it to be. All was white and silver; moonshine, snow, icicle, candlelight, lamplight and torch flame.

At the lakeside the steamboat was made ready, but the king announced he wanted his gondolier.

'You shall steer,' he said to Herr Haller. 'My Swan Maiden must accompany me, for I have not yet fulfilled her request.'

As the boat left behind the glimmering lights on the shore, I heard the soft plash of movement, and knew the swans had joined us, swimming in formation alongside the boat; we gained speed at their appearance as though they gave power to our movement. We skirted the Isle of Swans, heading for the bank on the north side of the lake.

There was movement on the bank as we neared it. A large white figure emerged from the trees. The king's horned horse had ridden along the bank of the lake and now it plunged into the water. As it moved towards us, it was no longer the head of a great white horse; the horn on its brow elongated into a long, white neck, and its head rose out of the water into the body of a great swan, with a golden crown about its throat. A mist now arose, curling across the water.

We reached the bank. 'You must alight,' the king told Herr Haller. 'You can go no farther.'

Herr Haller threw me a panicked look. 'I don't wish to leave Elsa,' he said. 'Please don't take her where I cannot follow.'

'He comes! He comes!' sang a voice from the trees along the bank. Out of the silvered leaves materialised Princess Marie with a crown of gold crocuses pinned to her hair. Princess Sibylle rushed to the edge of the water and plunged in.

'Help her,' I cried, 'The water is icy!' Herr Haller leaped from the boat, standing waist deep in the water as he reached for the princess, but she jabbed him with her cane, causing him to lose his balance and fall back.

'Pull me in,' she cried, floundering in the star-lit water. With one easy lift the king pulled her aboard while the boat rocked alarmingly, and I clung to the sides.

There was a second splash as Princess Marie threw herself after her sister. She too was lifted up. The great white swan had moved to the head of the gondolier and the king held a golden chain attached to the swan's crown. We were pulled away.

'Elsa!' cried Herr Haller from the bank. He flung himself into the water, striking out after us.

'Go back!' I called. 'You'll die in this cold! Go back!'

I did not know where we were going. The princesses laughed with glee and I was torn between the desire to leap into the lake, so Herr Haller would not risk his life for me, and the desire to know what the king had meant when he said he had not yet fulfilled my request. 'Go back, Christian,' I called again. 'I will return.'

But I did not know if I would. For I did not know where we were going. Even if the king could grant life to my sick brother in this world, it did not mean that I would remain in it also. That might well be the price of such a gift.

It was then that a shot rang out.

CHAPTER 36
ENDINGS

'Who's shooting? I cried. 'Christian! Are you hurt?'

The mist was dense now, obscuring everything. I heard a low roar, like that of an engine; I heard splashing—perhaps the splash of oars, or perhaps someone swimming, I could not tell, I only knew that we were now plunging onwards and I seemed to be the only one concerned.

'There it is, there it is!' cried Princess Marie. Her wet gown clung to her childlike frame, and her silvery hair was plastered to her head. This was madness—we were all going to die of exposure, and what of Christian—was he shot? Was someone coming after us?

But all thoughts were silenced as the mist parted and the mouth of a cave appeared. At first glance there was no cave to be seen, only stone and overhanging foliage, but in a blink there it was, lit up with lights, like the lanterns of the peasants, but far brighter, bright and startling and magical as fireworks.

A second swan-drawn boat sat within the entrance. At its prow stood a woman, tall and glowing, with hair pooling to her feet, studded with stars that flashed brilliant as she moved.

'There she is,' sighed Princess Sibylle. 'So fair. So lovely. Oh, Sister, we are home at last.'

'Welcome, Son,' said the tall, glowing woman, bowing her head. 'Do you return our treasure?'

'I do,' said the king, holding out the emerald green cup.

'Come, and take your true throne.' Behind her a throng of tall, glowing figures bowed in unison.

The king stepped from the boat into the shallow water and moved away. The princesses scrambled after him, and as they entered the cave I stared in awe at their transformation. Where there had been two elderly ladies, with a garland of crushed flowers and soaked nightgowns, now were two young girls, in gowns that shimmered, with fresh flowers crowning their heads. From inside the cave came the sound of music, a song so beautiful that I wanted to cover my ears, for it pierced me, as though I could not bear such beauty. The sisters danced away, bright and glad and laughing.

I did not know if I should follow. A second gunshot startled me out of my dreamlike state, and yet, the jolt did not entirely bring me out, for the light ahead seemed far more real than the dark lake and the violence of gunpowder behind me.

There was the sound of splashing and a voice cried out, 'Elsa!'

'Christian, you're alive!' I cried, his voice dragging my eyes away from the cave; I was so relieved to see him appear, his head like that of a seal bobbing above the water.

'Come no closer,' the king's voice ordered. 'You will lose your mind if once you enter Faerie.'

'Stay back, Christian,' I urged. 'Or you'll become as the aunts.'

'What about you?' he called back; his voice was desperate.

'You may come, if you wish, Swan Maiden,' said the king, holding out a hand towards me. 'You will never know death or ugliness or war in my kingdom.'

I looked towards the mouth of the cave where he stood. I

knew instinctively that if I stepped foot over the boundary between earth and Faerie I might never come back. But come back to what? To a life of hiding? To living in the shadows of fear and uncertainty?

I could live in beauty, far away from violent men. Away from death and sickness. My hand lifted.

No more Alexis. No more Christian Haller.

Alexis. That was his name.

A rush of memory made me gasp. A young boy with dark shadows beneath his eyes; eyes too large for his pale, gaunt face.

'My brother,' I said, pulling back my hand. 'Can you help him?' The king reached for something hanging at the mouth of the cave: a cluster of flowers, like glassy white lilies.

'Cast them to the Little Prince. He will get them to your brother. Forces shall align, and they shall reach their intended.'

So, I could have both. I could send aid to Alexis and still escape from all my troubles. I did not need to choose.

'Elsa!' called Herr Haller. 'Don't go!'

His voice sounded fainter. He would die if he lingered much longer in the wintry lake. I had to make a decision quickly.

'What is there to stay for?' I called back, feeling torn in two. I could not see him; a drift of mist had hidden him. My words sounded faint and lifeless. 'Why should I not go?'

'Elsa, don't leave!'

At his words I saw Alexis. I heard Alexis saying the very same—*Elsa, don't leave me*; the image jolted my attention from the lure of the cave. A third gunshot sounded—it was closer.

'I go now, Swan Maiden,' said the king. 'Which do you choose, Faerie light or mortal love? Both will endure beyond their worlds. Which world do you choose?'

I knew where I belonged.

I stuffed the precious flowers into my bodice, then leaped from the boat, my breath wrenched away at the shock of the cold as I paddled and kicked as hard as I could.

'Christian!' I called, the mist closing round me, the water seeping into my mouth and nose. Only then did I remember that I was not an experienced swimmer.

A fourth shot sounded.

'Faster!' bellowed a man's voice out of the dark. 'He's getting away!'

The unseen second boat now appeared, it's engine rumbling like a monster. The face at the helm was contorted with rage as the light of the cave fell upon it. The face was the one of my dreams. Count von Wuelffen was not going to let the king get away. Could he not see that what lay ahead was not something he could fight or control? There was a splash as the count dove into the water, I watched appalled as he thrashed like a man possessed, reaching out to snatch hold of the king's cloak just as he stepped into the cave.

As the count reached the border, he screamed as though arrows had pierced him, then flung himself backwards into the dark water, flailing like a drowning man.

'Christian! Where are you?' Were two men to die before my eyes that night? My worst enemy and my best friend? I saw the second boat draw close to the count; a broad man in fur leaned down and dragged the screaming man into the boat.

The light of the cave was dimming; as the music and light faded, I felt human fear rise up in me—had I chosen Christian only to lose him in the icy water, or to a bullet? Everybody I loved died. Mama. Papa. Alexis dying far away. I remembered them all so vividly now. What had I done?

'Christian!' I shrieked. Why did he not answer? I swallowed a mouthful of water and choked and spluttered. The light from the cave now faded, like the sun slipping down below the horizon. I thought I heard the faint notes of music. I thought I heard the gleeful laugh of Princess Sibylle. The sound was gone and cold was seeping into me like iron. I sank down, feeling the last vestige of strength slip away as I tried to reach the surface. I too was going to die.

'You there—grab the rope!' Something fell crudely before me, and instinctively I took hold of it, to be roughly hauled into a boat by the man dressed in fur.

On the floor of the boat lay an emptied four-barrelled pistol. Huddled in a corner with his hands over his ears and his eyes wide and blank was Count von Wuelffen. And opposite him in a shivering heap of blankets, lay Christian Haller.

CHAPTER 37
THE TRUE STORY

'Arrest him!' *cried every member of the committee.* 'Arrest that man on the charge of regicide!'

'Liars!' *screamed Count von Wuelffen. His face was contorted into a snarl of yellow teeth and bulging eyes.* 'You can't arrest me! Do you know who I am? Let me go! I have the ear of the duke! I have the ear of the general! I have the ear of the regent—I will bring you all down!'

His voice faded as he was bodily removed from the chamber by four guards.

'Dr Guttenberg, you have interviewed at length the two *persons, Herr Haller and Fräulein Opel, also known as Fräulein Schwan, and now, we have reason to understand, Baroness von Winterheimer, who were witnesses of the disappearance of the king.'*

'That is so.'

'And their testimonies concur with that of Baron von Fleischmann, who pulled them both out of Swanstein Lake, in affirming that the king was shot by Count von Wuelffen, and thus could not have survived.'

'I cannot confirm that their accounts exactly align with Baron *von Fleischmann's, but the circumstances were that of darkness and confusion. It is not to be wondered at if there are variants in testimony. Both young persons were disordered in their minds as a result of the shock, but we can safely dismiss all irrational statements.'*

'So, there is only one conclusion?'

'There is only one conclusion. The king was certainly shot at by Count von Wuelffen, repeatedly. All persons present agree to that fact. As does the number of bullets discharged from the count's gun barrel. Even if the king were only injured, his wound would be fatal due to the freezing temperature of the water. When the body is found, I am certain it will show that the late king either died of gunshot wounds, or by drowning. There is no possible way he could have survived or escaped.'

'And Count von Wuelffen has only just regained his faculties after his fall into the lake, but is refusing to supply the missing testimony?'

'He denies all charges, as you have witnessed. His mind is sadly disordered and erratic since his fall into the water. He spent a full twenty-four hours in a near-comatose state after Baron Fleischmann pulled him out of the water, punctuated with outbursts of ranting.'

'What did he speak of in these rants?'

'He talked of a girl who will not get away again, and of flogging and drowning various persons, and of a horse that could speak. He also talked repeatedly of a lady of bright light hurting his eyes. We are uncertain if the girl and the lady are the same person.'

'Does Dr Mensdorff consider Count von Wuelffen to be suffering from a condition?'

'He has diagnosed damage to the front cortex, most likely caused by the shock of entering cold water as he did when he leaped from the boat. Dr Mensdorff has seen similar cases, including a recent one he is working with. Generally, the most prominent symptoms are that of confusion and delusion. The Princesses Marie and Sibylle, the great-aunts of the late king, are two such examples of this condition. They fell into Lake Swanstein in their childhood, and

though recovered by their nurse, they had suffered irreparable damage.'

'And have they been found yet? It has been some time since they too were lost.'

'They have not been found. The worst is feared. They could not have survived long in such extreme cold wearing only their night-clothes. The queen mother is greatly to be pitied at this time.'

'Indeed. What tragedy our kingdom has seen in these days.'

'Truly unprecedented. But we look forward to better things to come, do we not?'

'Certainly, we do.'

It was unsettling to know that the same sanatorium where Christian lay, completing his recovery from hypothermia, was also where Count von Wuelffen had been treated before he forcibly discharged himself and made his way to the testimony chamber. The boat journey across the lake to Füssen had been short, but dreadful, as Christian and I huddled together at one end of the boat, numb and soaked and shocked, and the count, the man who had haunted my nightmares, sat at the other end, in a strange state of imbecility. The baron, in his fur coat and hat had expostulated all the way across the lake that he had never expected to get caught up in something like this—the king shot dead! That was not the plan—that was not the mission!

The royal train at Füssen had taken us to München, where we had been hurried to the sanatorium. There I had been separated from Christian, and from the count, who was ushered away between two orderlies, under the eye of Dr Mensdorff.

Alexis was all I could think of now. I had to get to him; had to give him the flowers from the cave. What he would do with them, I did not know. But first I must wait for Christian, I would not leave him; he was due to be discharged the next day, and I could not leave München myself until all the testimony statements had been signed and the interviews completed. It was a trying time. The Chief Inspector took statement after statement from me. I had to identify the four men in the employ of the count who had abducted me. I shook for hours afterwards, huddled in the little room the crown had given me as my accommodation during the investigations.

'What will happen to my stepmother?' I had asked the Chief Inspector.

'She will be interviewed. But there is little evidence to bring against her. It is her word against yours, my lady, unless Count von Wuelffen admits to her as an accomplice. But even then, his is the word of a proven liar. The allegation will not likely stand before a judge.

'So, she will get away with it? And I have to suffer her in my home.'

'I understand she is negotiating a sale of the family home,' the Chief Inspector informed me. 'Her debts have caught up with her.'

I stared in horror at him. 'I have to get back, I have to see my brother. When can I leave?'

'You are free to leave now,' the chief inspector said. 'But there is someone I would like to show you before you go. Someone who claims to know you, though it's a strange case, and we're still dotting the i's and crossing the t's on it, so to speak. An odd turn of events.'

But I could not wait another day. I didn't care who the Chief Inspector wanted me to meet; if it were not compulsory under law, then I was not going to be delayed one day further. I hastened to the sanatorium to talk to Christian of my plans.

CHRISTIAN HAD A VISITOR. HERR WEIMANN WAS DRESSED IN ROSE pink.

'I thought you had left München, sir,' Christian said, clearly surprised to see his master. 'Due to…er…the usual problem.'

'Mere trifles, my lad,' said Herr Weimann, flicking his money troubles away with his cologne drenched handkerchief. 'What a dreadful place this is. Reeks of antiseptic. We must get you out of here. There is work to be done!'

'I won't be working for you, Herr Weimann. I thought I had already made that clear.'

'What? Nonsense. You are my indentured apprentice. You have two more years with me. You cannot stay with the king, for there is now no king. You have to work.'

'Show me the stamped papers that say I have to work another two years, sir.'

'Papers? What have I to do with formalities such as papers? I am a man of my word. If I give my word that I will take you on for five years, then that is what I do, and you shall likewise keep your word.'

'You took every pfennig I had for my indenture and gave me no certificate in return. I have worked for three years for you without the legal rights I am entitled to.'

'Legal? Rights? What violent language is this, Haller? Have I not been as a father to you these three years? Did I not take you from the streets when you begged me to? Have I not shown you all of Europe and brought you into the presence of kings? What ingratitude is this?'

'I have repaid your kindness with many long hours, sir. I have followed you about the continent, assisting you in your evasions of debtors. I have gone against my conscience in lying for you so they would not find you. I have suffered lack of food and shelter and sleep as we fled from city to city.'

'And you have drank champagne and slept in feather beds when I have done well!' cried Herr Weimann.

'I don't recall there being much sleeping,' said Herr Haller dryly. 'In short, sir, you've worn me out. I can't go on with you any longer. I shall not.'

'But Duchess Tucher von Simmelelsdorf desires a summer schloss in the style of New Swanstein! The late king, Beloved Friend of my heart forever—he is so very fashionable now—romantic tragedy is so *a la mode*—everyone wants something built in the style of New Swanstein. You have to come!'

'Good bye, Herr Weimann,' said Christian. 'If you wish to pursue your claim against me, then you must take my stamped, signed, indenture papers, that do not exist, to the magistrate and sue me.'

Herr Weimann tried another tactic.

'Haller, as good to me as my own son. Come away with me, together we shall draw up beautiful plans for the duchess. She will pay in Österreichen gold, think of it! And you will be promoted, you shall be Assistant Architect to Herr Weimann—chief architect of Europe! You will receive a wage. And you may sleep all you want. Don't abandon me, my son. Together we make the most beautiful architecture—we make true art, do we not? The Muse she loves us because we love her!'

Christian looked miserable. I could see the inner wrestling he was undergoing. He looked at me from across the room. I don't know what he saw in my eyes, but it was enough to strengthen his resolve.

'I have other commitments now, Herr Weimann. Our time is at an end. There is nothing you can say to change my mind. I care nothing for Österreichen gold.'

Herr Weimann blustered. He was so vexed he threw his pink velvet hat to the floor and stamped his silver-buckled shoe on it. But Christian would not be moved. When an angry matron came to see what all the noise was, Herr Weimann stamped and cursed one last time and was bundled out in a cloud of fury and attar of Persian Rose.

'Well done,' I said when he had gone.

Christian gave me a weary smile. 'So why do I feel so bad? He did take me in when I had nowhere else to go.'

'He took you in because you offered him indenture money

for an indenture he never had drawn up. He kept you because you're a gifted artist. So what do you feel bad about? You're too soft-hearted.'

'I suppose we should all be tough like you,' he said with another wry smile.

'You should. Then the likes of Herr Weimann wouldn't get away with exploiting people. I'm proud of you. And you look much better,' I added.

'I can't wait to leave tomorrow,' he said. 'I hate being confined. How I miss the mountains. Don't you?'

I nodded. 'You've kept busy.' I picked up a sheaf of drawings from the bed and looked through them.

'Trying to get things down before they fade from memory. They're fading fast.'

The pictures were of a tall man, shining and golden; a faery king. Other sketches were of faery folk and creatures.

'They're beautiful. I'm glad you're drawing them. My memories are fading too. It all seems so dreamlike now. Where will you go tomorrow, when you leave?'

'That depends on you, Elsa.'

'Me?'

'I don't know what the future holds, but I know I don't want to leave you.'

I tried to smile, but I felt saddened. 'I have to see my brother. I have to go home.'

'Then I'll come with you.'

I shook my head. 'I don't know what will await me back home. Perhaps trouble. A lot of it.'

'I thought your problems were tied up with the count. He can't hurt you anymore.'

'No. But others can. There's not evidence enough against my stepmother to have her arrested. The word of servants is not enough, apparently.'

'Then I will come with you. I'm not going to let you walk away into danger. Again.'

'I can't turn up with a strange young man, Christian. What

would that look like? If it weren't for my brother, I'd never go back. I'd start a new life somewhere else. But I must go back to him.'

'Of course you must. Family is important.'

I pulled out the spray of clear lilies I kept with me at all times. I feared letting them out of my sight. 'Hansi says I ought to show this to his aunt. She's a gifted herbwoman. Otherwise, I don't know what to do with them, or how to use them to help my brother.'

'Then it's simple. Tomorrow we go to the mountains to see the herbwoman. Didn't I tell you we'd find a way through together?'

'I WONDERED WHEN YOU WOULD RETURN. I KNEW IT MUST BE soon,' said Tante Trudy, sitting by the fireside where a piney fragrance filled the room. 'Come, sit and rest. You are in time for supper.'

'Hansi kissed his aunt's lean cheek, then was hugged fiercely by a tall girl with blue-green eyes, who could only be the sister he had spoken about.

'This is m'lady, who I've told you of,' said Hansi, introducing me to his aunt and sister.

'Call me Elsa,' I said. 'I'm very glad to meet you.' So, this was the famous Tante Trudy of the mountain. The woman who could drive away trolls and had brought the king into the world. She examined me closely, but I was no less interested in her.

'And this is Herr Haller,' Hansi said, making the introductions.

'Call me Christian,' said Herr Haller, with a bow of his head.

Tante Trudy's green eyes examined him briefly but thoroughly, noting the hazel-green of his eyes. I had noticed myself that the hazel became greener when he was in the mountains.

'You are from this region?' she queried.

'No. But my mother was.'

'I see. Perhaps I knew her. What was her name?'

'Aveline. Klass was her maiden name.'

This was more information than I had heard from Christian before. He rarely spoke of his mother.

'Klass,' said Tante Trudy thoughtfully. 'There was a family of that name on the other side of the mountain. The youngest daughter was very beautiful.'

'My mother was very beautiful,' Christian said quietly.

'She caught the eye of a passing nobleman. The family had little choice but to agree to the marriage, though it was a fateful decision to let her leave.'

Christian was silent. He stared unhappily at the floor. My curiosity was aroused.

'Why was it fateful?' I couldn't resist asking.

'She was closely tied to the land, as mountain folk often are,' said Tante Trudy. 'Her fey blood was of a particular kind that needs constant connection to its ancestral lands. Some of us can come and go between places, but some must stay where they belong, or they wither away. I am sorry for your loss, Christian, son of Aveline.'

'Fey blood?' I repeated. But I was not surprised. Nothing of that nature could surprise me anymore. And it made sense. Only those of the mountain could bear the magic when it awakened. If Christian had fey blood, it would explain why he had thrived at New Swanstein, his creative gifts enlarged. But what of me, I wondered? Did I have fey blood? Did that explain my animal-speaking gift that I had hidden all my life? Did it explain Alexi's gift of knowing things, a gift our mother had shared?

'I brought this to show you, Tante Trudy,' I said, reaching for my bag to take out a wooden box. Inside lay the stem of faerie flowers. 'Do you know what it is?'

Hansi's sister gasped at the flash of light that burst out as I opened the lid.

Tante Trudy's eyes gleamed as the flowers lit up her face. 'May I?' she asked, putting out an eager hand.

'Of course.'

'Exquisite,' she murmured, drinking in the beauty of the flowers. They were shaped as lilies, their petals pliant and translucent as gossamer, yet strong as leather.

'They do not wither or fade, even without water or light,' I said.

'They need no water or light from this world,' said Tante Trudy, her voice low and full of awe. 'They have power and life of their own. They were given to you?' she asked sharply, her expression changing suddenly.

'Yes. The king gave it to me.'

'Good, good,' she murmured, looking relieved. 'It would be a terrible thing if you had taken them. Take even a single flower stem from Faerie without it being gifted, and a terrible price will be exacted.'

'He said it would heal my brother. But I don't know how. What am I to do with it?'

'An elixir must be made from it. A stem of a royal Faery rose has the power to break any curse, but the stem of a royal Faery lily has power to heal any ailment. What a blessed child you are to receive such riches.'

Me, blessed? Orphaned. As good as homeless. I almost laughed in reply. But it was near impossible to remain cynical in the presence of the royal Faery lily. Its beauty and light had a healing power just in looking upon it.

'Let Christian hold it,' I said impulsively, plucking it from Tante Trudy and laying it in Christian's hand. 'He has been unwell, and our journey has been tiring. It will strengthen him if it has such power, will it not? Can you make an elixir, Tante Trudy?'

'I'm not sure. I have never worked with so much power before. Even the powerful herbs and flowers we have gathered while the mountain was awake have not strength comparable to this. Never before have I touched something directly out of Faerie.'

'But you will try? Please. The king would not have given it if it could not be used.'

'If Tante Trudy cannot do it, no one can,' said Hansi decisively. 'Of course, she will do it. She will begin at dawn, will you not?'

'I will not.'

'But—' I began to argue.

'I will begin at moonrise. Moonlight is the closest we have to their light.'

Supper was a cheerful meal, and for a while I forgot my troubles, caught up in the pleasure and warmth of friendly faces and hearty food. Hansi's sister put the precious lily in a pottery cup, where it sat as a benign light in the centre of our table.

Hansi raised up his cup when the plates had been filled and said jovially, 'A toast! Our beloved King of the Mountain. Our Faery King. Our Swan King.'

We gladly raised our cups. 'To the King of the Mountain!'

A long-forgotten memory suddenly surfaced in that moment. I recalled sitting by candlelight around the table, with Papa and Mama, as a small child. Other people had been present, but I could not remember them. It was Christmas Eve, and everyone was merry and light-hearted. Glasses were lifted up, sparkling in the light and clinking together as the adults gave the Christmas blessing to one another.

'Happy Christmas, Sisi. May love find you always, and bring you home to feast,' Papa had said, clinking my glass with his and saying the traditional blessing. I had felt very grown up to have a glass of my own, with a little watered-down wine, to share in the toasts.

'Happy Christmas, Papa. Love bring you home,' I replied, making Papa laugh at my forgetting half the words.

'Something wrong?' Christian asked.

I shook my head and wiped a tear away.

'I'm fine. I wish happy memories weren't so sad sometimes.'

He nodded. 'Me too.'

'So how is it you ended up with Herr Weimann, when your father is a nobleman?' I asked, wanting to turn the attention from me.

'Same as you. I ran away.'

'Your father wanted to marry you off to an old harridan for her money?'

He couldn't quite manage a smile. 'I fell out with him. Over my mother's death. I blamed him. Though I should not have.'

'Oh. I see.' I would not press any further on what was clearly a painful subject.

'So, Tante Trudy,' said Hansi. 'Will you now tell our friends the true story of the king?'

'The true story?' I repeated eagerly.

'Tante Trudy knows more than anyone,' said Hansi's sister. 'She was there when he came into the world, and you were there when he left. She wasn't able to speak of it until he had gone again, is that not so?'

'That is so,' replied Tante Trudy. 'I was bound by promise not to speak of what I had seen that night. I kept my promise. Only a fool would not keep their word to the Fair Folk.'

'What did you see?' This was most intriguing.

'Let me eat, then I will tell you.'

CHAPTER 38
CHANGELING CHILD

'He was a changeling child,' Tante Trudy said, as we sat about the cottage fire. 'The queen's own son was born on the stroke of midnight after a long and difficult birth. The queen was so small, she was not well fit for childbirth. The baby never cried. It was too weak. Its little heart so faint. I did what I could, but there is a destiny to mortal lives that no power of healing can stop.

'I watched over his failing life, while the physicians attended to the queen. I was alone in the ante chamber where the cradle stood. They say it was carved from the last of the ancient mountain firs, I believe it was, for I could feel a faint hum of life in its polished knots and grain.

'I opened the window when the child had given his last whisper. I wanted to sigh my sorrow into the wind and not add to the grief that would soon come. I thought it must the Queen of Faerie herself who slipped through the opened window. She was so bright and beautiful I fell to the floor, knowing what power was visited upon me. She bore a child in her arms. A new prince.

"He must dwell apart from his people for a time," the faery said. She took the body of the mortal prince and laid the faery prince in his place.

"But the mortal child has no life left in him," I said.

"You are wrong. He has but one breath left. He shall grow strong in purer air."

"Will he return?"

"None can return and remain whole."

"Why leave your prince in this world of trouble? What life will he know here?"

"He must awaken the mountain one last time, and recover the treasure hidden there, stolen of old. He must restore the balance that has been disrupted."

'The faery wrapped the mortal prince in a gown that filled the room with the scent of lilies. "You shall not speak of this until the time has passed. Only because the gift of wisdom rests upon you have you been permitted to see and speak with me."

'I bowed to the ground again before her.

'She was gone, and I wondered if I had dreamt it all. Perhaps I had dozed off, having been up since the evening before, as the queen laboured. But the features of the changeling prince were not the frail features of the human prince. Before my eyes the light about him faded. His skin, pure as a white petal, coarsened, though still far finer than that of an ordinary child. His hair, shiny and rainbow-coloured as a starling's wing, faded into finer, less uncommon blackness. The point of his ears rounded almost to a human shape, but not perfectly so. And his eyes, they opened once and flashed as deep green jewels, then faded, to the blue of a new-born's, though a blue as bright as meadow gentians.'

Tante Trudy finished her tale.

'To the king,' said Hansi solemnly, reaching for the jug of herb-flavoured beer and topping up our cups. 'And to the prince that lives, but not with us.'

We all raised our cups and drank.

Tante Trudy sealed the bottle of elixir with wax. I was sad to leave the mountain, but I desperately wanted to see Alexi. I didn't know what I'd do when I reached home; I just knew I had to get there. I had given up trying to dissuade Christian from coming with me, he would not let me go alone.

'Will you come with us, Hansi?' I asked. 'The servants know you; you could find out how things lie. You could get the elixir to Ziller. She can get it to Alexis if I can't see him. Once he's well he can come away with me.'

'Where will you stay in the meantime?' Hansi asked. 'Have you money?'

'The crown gave me some money to cover my travelling expenses home.'

We left as a party of three, acquiring mules from the closest town to Füssen. We rented rooms in inns; Christian and I posing as man and wife, and Hansi as our groom. If anyone noticed that Christian took a pallet above the stables with the servants instead of sharing his wife's room, no one commented.

All was well, if cold and tiring, until we reached the town of Vogt, late in the evening, only eight miles from home. We would have completed our journey next morning, but one of the mules was showing wear on its front hooves, so we waited in town to get it shod. I'd taken care to conceal my face with scarf and hood, eating in the bedroom of the inns and not in the public dining room. Although my name had not been publicly revealed as part of the drama and scandal of the king's apparent murder—yet, there were still posters of my face pasted to notice boards in the towns and villages as we neared home, offering a reward for my discovery; presumably posters the count had put up after I had fled that night, though they looked puzzlingly fresh.

But I made an error, on leaving my room that day; my bag with the precious elixir had not been brought up from the saddlebags, and in fear for its safety I had rushed out of the room, with my head bare, to find it.

As I reached the entrance room of the inn I noted, with little thought, that a bearded man in a shabby coat and hat was staring at me. I peered into the dining room, then the smoking room, but could not see either Christian or Hansi. Perhaps they were still in the stables. I would run up and get my cloak and see.

I re-emerged from my room, too busy with the fastening of my cloak to realise there were three men before me in the hall.

'Pardon me,' I exclaimed as I walked into one of them. It was the bearded man in the shabby cloak.

'It's her all right,' he said to the others, holding out a torn-down poster. 'Image of her, right down to that mole, look!' My head reeled to see the drawing of my face upon the poster, and the words: *Reward Offered for Information Leading to Recovery of Missing Person* in large, black letters.

'Come along with us, Fräulein,' said one of the men. Only now did I notice he and his companion were in the uniforms of the constabulary.

'Wait! No—let me go!' I protested in vain, for they took me by both arms, one constable each side of me, and propelled me through the inn and out of the door into a waiting carriage.

'Where do I collect my reward from?' the man in the shabby hat called after us as the horses were urged on and they bore me away.

'You're making a mistake! You have to let me go!'

'Calm yourself, Fräulein. If we've made a mistake, we'll take you back. But you're the image of that missing baron's daughter. Once you've been identified, or dis-identified if it's just an uncanny likeness, then all will be well.'

'You don't understand!' I protested, 'Haven't you heard of

the trial and all that has happened. The Chief Inspector of Bayern spoke with me not more than ten days ago! I am not missing!'

The constable laughed. 'Chief Inspector of Bayern himself. A likely tale.'

'We'd sooner you're identified,' added the second constable. 'There's a grand reward on your head. There's been a fair few scoundrels making up stories about having sighted you in unlikely places, but none of them have led to finding you yet.'

'One fellow claimed the baron's daughter was a goat herder in the mountains, didn't he, Clodwig?'

'Geese actually,' replied Clodwig.

'No, it was goats.'

'I heard it was geese.'

'And then there was that lad who said he'd heard from some duchess's maid that the king's new mistress was the image of the missing girl, didn't she?'

'The last king,' added Clodwig. 'Rest his poor, young soul. Not the new one.'

'Every time someone gets sent out to investigate the claims, they come back no wiser than when they went out, don't they?'

'Got attacked by a vicious goose, the last fellow,' said Clodwig.

'I thought he got butted by a goat.'

Clodwig shrugged. 'Well, it put the reward up, anyhow.'

'I hope you're her,' said the constable wistfully. 'Wages are poor these days. Got another nipper on the way.' He sighed heavily. 'Are you her?'

I didn't answer. I was too busy racking my mind for ways to escape. The curtains were drawn at the small windows, so I could not see where we were. Perhaps when the carriage slowed, I could dart out and run. But that idea was put paid to, for when the carriage did draw to a halt, the nameless constable held on tightly to my arm. 'I do so hope you're her,' he said again. 'Be a shame for the old baron to lose both his nippers.'

'Wait, what did you say?' I asked sharply. 'The baron is dead. And what do you mean lose both his children?'

'His son's dying, and his daughter's missing,' said Clodwig. 'Are you sure you're not her? Perhaps we ought to let the servants have a look at her first,' he said to his colleague. 'The baron might get angry if we've brought another mistake and got his hopes up.'

'The baron?' I clutched my pendant at my neck as my heart beat rapidly. 'What are you speaking of? And Alexi is dying?'

The carriage door opened, and a rush of cold air came as a slap on my bewildered face.

'Upon my soul if it isn't the mistress!' shrieked a voice from the carriage door.

A large, furry muzzle thrust itself in and gave a deep bark of greeting.

Over Magni's furry head I met the amazed look of Zillah.

'Oh, my lady! Heaven be praised you've come home too!'

CHAPTER 39
THE THIRD WISH

'Papa, am I dreaming?' But the arms that held me were solid and not a dream. The smell of cinnamon and orange peel in his study where I had run to find him, was aching in its familiarity.

'I've been looking everywhere for you,' Papa's voice was muffled against my head. 'They told me you'd left München, but no one knew where you had gone. I hurried home, I thought you must be here, but you were not. That idiotic inspector! How could he let you go without an escort—and after everything you have been through!'

I pulled away to look at Papa. 'But how…?'

There was a bustle of noise and a voice that caused me to start back, looking with alarm at the doorway.

'What is she doing here?' I said, my voice shaking.

The baronin could be heard, saying loudly, 'What? How is it *she* is here?' Quick footsteps followed and there she was, in the doorway staring back at me.

'Returned to us, and safe, as you see,' exclaimed Papa. 'Is this not wonderful?'

'What has she been saying?' the baronin demanded. Her face had drained of colour, leaving two spots of rouge standing out as smudges on her cheeks. 'Whatever she says is a lie!'

'Elisabeth never lies,' said Papa, his hand tightening on my shoulder.

The baronin was not listening to him; she was staring at me as though she could not believe what she was seeing. Her eyes raked me up and down, the corner of her mouth curling in disgust as she took in my dishevelled hair and travel-stained gown. She took a step forward.

'Have you come back to watch your brother die? It's you who has killed him. He began to fade the day you left him.'

'Sabine, enough,' ordered Papa.

'You cannot hurt me anymore,' I said. I met her glare. 'Whatever lies you have spun about me will all unravel. The truth will come out now.'

'There is no evidence against me,' hissed the baronin. 'You have ruined *everything*.'

'It is you have ruined our lives,' I retorted.

Once and for all you must choose between us, Gilbert,' said the baronin, turning her eyes to Papa. I will not remain here with *her*. Choose. Choose now, Gilbert!'

Papa's hand on my shoulder drew me closer to him. 'I will not take your part against my only daughter, Sabine,' he said, his voice low and full of pain.

'You never did,' the baronin said. A look of anger and hatred now twisted her face. The same look I had seen on Count von Wuelffen's face before he threw himself after the king, and before they had marched him away under arrest for attempted regicide.

She made a growl and lunged to strike me, but I stepped away, she only caught my face by the tips of her fingers.

'Sabine, I won't have violence in my house!' cried Papa, pushing me behind him, out of her reach. 'Cease this instant! Have you lost your senses?'

Gerling and Griffin appeared at the door, drawn by the

sound of shouting. Brunn was ordering them away again, but they would not heed.

'Take her away,' Papa called to the footmen. 'Before she becomes violent—don't hurt her—bring the carriage—she is leaving.'

'Murderess!' the baronin shrieked as she was wrenched away. 'Liar! Do not listen to one word she says!'

'She has gone mad,' Papa said, looking after the baronin in distress. 'It is the only explanation for all that she has done. But I will hold her to her word, she shall not spend one night under the same roof as you.'

Papa looked ashen. He staggered to the faded couch, and sat down.

I waited with him, listening to the sounds in the household, until the baronin's voice could be heard no more. 'Papa, tell me everything that has happened to you.'

'I soon shall. But let me rest a minute more. All this trouble has worn me thin, though your return is the only comfort I wished for.'

Papa's story was as strange as my own. He had been thrown from the wreckage of the train, had been tossed down a hillside, falling into the lake, where he certainly would have drowned as other passengers had, had he not fallen only at the shallow edge.

He had only the vaguest recollections of being found by two passing workmen; foreigners who spoke no German, but helped him to their little hut and sought help.

'I awoke in hospital,' Papa said. 'I was disorientated; I could not even say who I was at first, and I had nothing about me to identify me. But someone recognised me. Count von Wuelffen was searching through the wards of the survivors, and when he saw me, he arranged to have me sent to Dr Mensdorff's sanatorium where I had all the privilege of an isolated room.'

I was so shocked at these words that they took my breath

away for a moment. 'The count knew you were alive, and he concealed it and shut you up where no one could see you?'

Was there no end to that man's depravity?

'He wanted you kept out of the way,' I said, putting the pieces together. 'If you had returned home, you would have stopped their plan, you would not have let me be married off.'

'My poor child,' said Papa, looking broken.

'You have suffered too, Papa. I wonder if she knew.' I meant my stepmother.

'She said she did not,' said Papa. 'But how can I believe any word she says anymore.'

'And how did you gain release? Why did they let you go?'

'I thought I would be killed. I heard the count telling Dr Mensdorff that it was all up, that someone called Fleischman was sure to talk and it would all be up. He sounded like a crazed man, and he wanted to do away with me, that is what I heard him say.'

'He wanted to kill you! Oh, Papa!'

'The doctor would not let him. They had a furious row. And then… and then the strangest thing happened.'

'What happened?'

'You will hardly believe it.'

'I don't think there is anything I would find hard to believe after all I have seen these past months, Papa.'

'There was a darkening of the rooms, a strange unnatural darkening. The count cried out that it was *him* come to get him. I don't know who he meant. The doctor was telling him to be rational, but as the air darkened the doors of the ward swung open—and this is the part you will hardly believe— though the doors were opened, there was no one there. And stranger still, the count was so paralysed with fear, rambling and calling out that they were coming for him, and the doctor was so busy in trying to restrain him, that I walked right past them, Elisabeth, imagine that, I just walked right out of the doors, it was as though they did not even see me. I gained my freedom, I expected someone to run after me and take hold of me, I expected the count to come after me, but no one did. I found a constable, I said I had been held hostage, and from there I was helped.'

'I wonder they did not arrest the count immediately, as they did the doctor,' I said.

'The inspector said he was putting the count under close surveillance. His supervisor, the regional chief, had already tried to investigate the count, but his high connections kept him immune from interrogation. The count was too clever and influential to successfully convict without irrefutable evidence. He wanted to let him make his way to the testimony rooms, for he was sure he would betray himself publicly when he heard the evidence given. The count did not realise he was closely followed by officers from that moment. If I had only known that you would be there, Elisabeth, at those very rooms, I would have found you.'

'Why didn't the Chief Inspector tell you of me sooner, Papa?'

'I did not see him until after the government enquiry was finished. He was out of the city gathering evidence until the last day of the enquiry. I only dealt with the local inspector who did not know of your true identity. The Chief Inspector had been conducting the investigation secretly, rather than officially, it seems. When everything came to light the Chief Inspector was to bring us together, but you were gone.'

I thought over all this for some minutes. And then my thoughts returned to the most pressing thing—Alexis.

'I must send Gerling to Vogt, Papa,' I urged. 'You have to believe me when I say it's a matter of life and death. He must find my friends, and bring them here.'

ALEXIS WAS SO PALE AND THIN I SANK TO MY KNEES AT HIS bedside at the sight of him.

'I warned you he was faded,' whispered Ziller.

Nurse took my arm and steered me towards the chair near his bed. 'He looks better since the master returned,' said Nurse. 'But he doesn't wake up much. He didn't wake at all yesterday.'

'He was worse than this?' It didn't seem possible he could be any frailer than he looked now. His breath came as a whisper, his sleeping chest barely rising.

'He knew you would come,' said Ziller. 'He'd tell me the dreams he had of you. Fancy dreams about castles and swan knights and things.'

'Dear Alexis and his dreams,' I whispered. I saw peeking out from under his pillow the carving Hansi had made him. I drew it out and put it inside Alexis' thin hand, closing his fingers over it. I took my swan pendant from my neck and put it in his other hand. Perhaps it would have some power to help him. He needed every bit of strength.

'Hansi,' I said decidedly, looking at the carvings.

'What did you say?' Ziller looked a little startled.

'Hansi. And Christian. They must come quickly. Tonight.'

'Hansi is coming here?' Ziller's cheeks coloured.

'I hope so.' I stood up again. 'He has to. He must.' It was impossible to sit quietly knowing that Alexis' cure lay somewhere between Vogt and his bedside. I had not the patience to wait a moment longer. 'Are there any horses in the stables, Ziller? Or has my—has that woman sold them all?'

'There's the last of the carriage horses,' said Ziller. 'They only put two to the carriage for the mistress, but you can't be—'

I flew to my bedroom. It was strange to see it again; happy childhood memories mingled with the trauma of my last days locked up in it, but there was no time to linger with thoughts, it was now early afternoon and there were not many hours of winter daylight left. I pulled on riding boots, snatched up a warm riding coat and hat and fled the room, Ziller following behind me like a worried spaniel.

'M'lady, where are you—?'

'I won't be long, tell Papa!' I called back. 'I have to find something!'

I OVERTOOK GERLING WITHIN HALF AN HOUR OF HARD RIDING. 'Follow me!' I yelled as I passed him. He looked startled, but urged on his horse after me.

We had to drop our speed to a trot after a couple of miles; I wished we could gallop all the way there, but it was too far, and my horse was complaining. I scoured the road at every turn and every bend. Why were Hansi and Christian nowhere to be seen? When we reached the inn, I threw the reins at the groom. 'Wait for me!' I ordered, rushing into the inn, snatching up the hand bell at the desk and shaking it violently.

'Hoy! You'll raise the dead making that racket!' scolded the hosteller, coming through the kitchen door, wiping his hands on his apron.

'Two men were here this morning!' I gasped out. 'Herr Haller and his groom!'

'Yes. What of it? You're Frau Haller. It's in the book. Have you lost your husband?' He laughed, and I wanted to shake him.

'Where are they?'

'Are you the girl they took away? You are, aren't you?'

I decided to pull rank. 'I am the daughter of Baron von Winterheimer, and I demand you tell me where those two men are—it's a matter of life and death!'

He regarded me doubtfully. My boots and coat were fine, but my unkempt hair and borrowed gown were not. I did not look like a baron's daughter at that moment.

'Don't know where they went,' he said. 'Took their three old mules and settled up. Come to think on it, they were asking everyone where *you* went.' He broke into a laugh again. 'Baron's daughter! Hah! I've got sixteen suppers to see to!' And he disappeared through the door to the kitchen. I could hear him laughing on the other side.

There was no time to lose. I flew round to the stables, interrogating the grooms—someone must know of where the two men with the three mules went! But no one did. One man said he thought they took the road to Kißel, a young lad said he'd seen them over at the magistrate's house, a third said he thought they'd headed south.

'Where's the magistrate's house?' I demanded.

I hurtled through the streets in the directions given me. A po-faced footman answered my hammering on the door. 'Servants' door is round the back,' he said, looking at my wild appearance before shutting it in my face.

I flew round to the back where an equally humourless serving girl answered the door. Yes, some man had come calling that morning. No, he had not been admitted, for the magistrate was not at home that week. No, she did not know where the man had gone next, only that he had gone. He'd wanted to know where a person would be taken if the constabulary had them, and he was told that as decent folk never got taken away by the constabulary, they could not say where they went. And then she shut the door in my face.

I felt deflated. Where else could I look? Where could they have gone? I could not linger; it would be dark soon. I had to return home in defeat. I was so bewildered—had not the king said the cure would find its way to the one it was given for? Did I believe him? Could I trust that it would be so? It was only easy to believe something when the life of one you loved was not at stake.

I returned to the inn, where Gerling waited.

'We can't ride home at the pace we got here, my lady,' he advised. 'The horses can't take it.'

'I know,' I groaned. 'Don't you think I know that everything is against me!'

We reached home in the dark. I trudged back into the lamp-lit hall. Ziller flew to meet me. 'Where have you been?' she cried. 'Hansi's been waiting for hours!'

CHAPTER 40
SOMETHING MAGICAL

I COULD NOT SPEAK at first when I ran into the drawing room. Hansi and Christian stood near the fireplace while Papa sat on the edge of a sofa.

Christian quickly crossed the room to meet me. 'We've been looking everywhere for you!' I wanted to fling my arms around him, but was aware of Papa's perplexed stare.

'Have you got it?' I gasped out.

'The nurse, understandably, would not let me, a stranger, administer it.' He pulled the small wax-sealed bottle out of his breast pocket and I snatched it up with tears of relief and ran to Alexis' room.

'What's this?' Nurse demanded, as I burst in, waving the little bottle.

'Don't try to stop me, Nurse,' I warned, struggling to loosen the seal. 'This will make Alexis well.'

'Don't you go giving him no snake oil potions!' retorted Nurse.

'Let me do it, your hands are shaking,' Ziller said, plucking the bottle from me. 'How much do I give him?' she asked. 'Oh, my!' she exclaimed, as she removed the seal and a powerful perfume was released. 'Oh my, I've never smelled anything like it!'

'Oh my!' echoed Nurse, and her fierce expression softened.

The fragrance was heady, and I felt myself revived a little.

'His eyes moved!' I said, seeing a flutter of movement on Alexis' face. 'Put the bottle under his nose.'

Ziller did, and his eyelids fluttered again. His nose twitched, his mouth parted, and then he gave a surprisingly strong sneeze— 'Achoo!'

Ziller drew the bottle away, kneeling down beside me.

'Alexi, it's me,' I whispered. He opened his eyes. 'Can you sit up and drink something? I'll lift his head, Ziller, you hold it to his lips.'

'I'll hold his head,' Nurse insisted.

'All of it?' Ziller asked.

'All of it.'

'Oh, the smell!' she exclaimed. 'And it's shiny, like something magic! What is it?'

I did not answer; I was too busy watching carefully to see that every precious drop was drunk down. One stray drop escaped from Alexis' pale lips and ran down his chin leaving a trail of lily-scented light.

I was holding my breath, watching for some sign of change. But nothing happened. He closed his eyes again, sank against the pillows and fell asleep once more.

Nurse felt his forehead and smoothed the hair from his face.

I slumped back onto my heels.

'It might take time.' Christian put a hand on my shoulder. 'Be patient.'

'But what if it doesn't work? Tante Trudy said she'd never made anything like it before. She said she didn't know what to expect.'

'She also said it was very powerful. Have faith. The king wasn't deceiving you when he gave you it, was he?'

'No,' I said in a small voice, my frustration evaporating under Christian's calm touch and words.

'King?' said Ziller and Nurse in unison?

'What's happening?' said Papa's voice, coming into the room. His eyes fell upon Christian's hand resting on my shoulder. He looked at me questioningly, but the look on my face subdued any questions for the moment.

'I gave Alexis the elixir,' I opened my clenched fist to show Papa the empty bottle. 'But I don't know if it has worked.'

'What is that smell?' said Papa, sniffing the air. 'Reminds me of the flowers your mother used to grow.'

My exhaustion and the tension of the day caught up with me now, and I feared I would break down sobbing in front of everyone, something I could not bear to do. The room seemed overwhelmingly crowded, and my emotions were about to spill over. I got up abruptly. 'I need to take a breath of air,' I said. 'Excuse me. I'll be back.'

'I'll come with you,' said Christian.

'No. I need to be alone. I won't be long.'

'Elisabeth, it's bitterly cold outside,' said Papa. But I fled from the room. I was still wearing my coat. I paced up and down in the stables, out of the chill wind that had risen. I did not care if the horses saw my tears.

My exhaustion must have overwhelmed me, for I fell into a strange half-sleep, sprawled across a hay bale.

'Elsa,' said a voice. Someone was shaking my shoulder. 'Elsa, wake up. Come inside, it's cold out here.'

It was Christian. 'My word, Elsa, I didn't think you could get any rougher looking than you already were,' he said, tucking a loose strand of hair behind my ear and plucking a piece of hay from my coat. 'You look like a wild woman of the forest. What's your brother going to think when he sees you like this?'

I stared at him, gripping the hand that had lifted my hair.

'Yes,' he said. 'Your brother. Who's sitting up eating enough pastries to fill a baker's shop and asking where you are.'

I shrieked, leapt from the hay bale, and flung my arms

around his neck, jumping up and down and laughing and crying into his shoulder all at the same time. He laughed with me and hugged me tight, keeping me from tottering over as we lurched about the stable in a wild dance.

'You smell like a stable hand,' he said, when I pulled away again. 'But if I don't mind, I don't think he will either.'

THERE WERE SO MANY GOOD THINGS IN THOSE DAYS. THERE WAS Alexis, bounding about the house and grounds as though making up for all his lost years of health. I suppose I shouldn't count the banishment of my former stepmother and her maid as a good thing, it was not a happy time for poor Papa, but I was glad her malignant influence was removed from our home. But life is never without some tension or difficulty. How can it be? There is no growth and new beginnings without the death of former things. And some things had gone and had to be let go of.

I loved my home because it was where Alexis and Papa were. But I didn't quite belong there anymore. I refused to heed it at first, pushing away the nagging, aching restlessness. What was I restless for? Christian had gone. It had been a shock when he had announced that he must go. He said he had personal matters he must see to. Old relationships he must repair. People to forgive and reconcile with, that he might move on with his life. I had stared at him in disbelief. What had I thought? That he would follow me around forever? Always be there when I needed him?

Hansi went with him as a kind of valet, which struck me as odd. Christian Haller the apprentice with a valet? But they left. I often caught Ziller lost in thought, with the same unhappy look on her face as I knew my own must show.

What had I to be sad about? I did not understand. I distracted myself, kept busy. Papa's affairs were not so bad as they had been thought. He'd had the foresight to take out a note of insurance on his last venture, an insurance that could only be payable to him, and not to his widow. The house did not now need to be sold.

'We shan't ever be as rich as we were,' Papa said, looking over his papers in his study.

'We don't need to be. I have no desire for ball gowns and fancy dinner parties. All I want is you and Alexi. Though I wish I could have Pumpernickel back.'

'You shall have your horse back,' said Papa. 'Gerling knows where he was sold. I shall buy him back directly. Will that cure you of your restlessness, Elsa?'

'Me? Restless?'

'As a caged animal. What's troubling you? You can't settle at anything.'

I was going to deny that there was anything wrong, but I couldn't. 'I don't know, Papa,' I said honestly. 'I really don't. It's like…it's as though…I'm not the same person I was when I left here. And I can't settle back to the way I was, even though I want to.'

'Is it that young artist?' Papa asked.

'Chris—Herr Haller? No. How could it be him?'

'Good. He seemed a gentlemanly young man, but he's not of your class. I should be sorry to see you lose your heart to a penniless man.'

'How do you know he's not of my class?' I countered, suddenly angry that Papa should think so little of Christian. 'His father is a nobleman.'

'What nobleman? What is his name?'

'I, I don't know,' I stammered. 'He never told me.'

'I'm glad to hear it. If he told you nothing of his family then he never had a serious thought for you.'

'Even if he's not of my *class*, what of it?' I cried, feeling as though my father had put a finger on something painful that I had not realised was there. 'What's so special about us?'

'Elisabeth, please, you're losing your temper.'

'We're not so rich anymore. I'm not even as well-educated

as Chris— Herr Haller. He has more talent and manners and, and everything that really matters in a man, should I ever consider marriage. Not that I am!'

'Of course you're not. And I would not part with you to a man who could not provide for you, no matter how talented or well-mannered he was.'

I had nothing more to say on the subject, so I made a swift exit from Papa's study before I said something I would regret.

THERE WAS AN UNEASY POLITENESS BETWEEN PAPA AND ME IN the days following. We skirted round the one subject that might cause friction. I had no wish to displease him, I was so grateful to have him and Alexis back, so I did my best to be good and push down unruly feelings. Life shaped new routines as Alexis grew in strength. Pumpernickel was returned to the stables, and I took great comfort riding out on him. Only when I was out in the open air, away from any sight of the town and the roads full of market traffic did I feel some release. But how I yearned for blue mountains, for meadows full of wild flowers, for turquoise lakes. For Christian's quiet and comfortable friendship.

Alexis never tired of hearing all my stories. I took pleasure in his shining eyes as I described palaces and magical castles and caves that led to Faerie. He longed to see blue mountains and turquoise lakes for himself. But still my restlessness deepened.

CHAPTER 41
KING OF THE SWANS

I HEARD the first cuckoo on my ride out the morning he returned.

Two fine chestnut geldings came trotting up the drive; I saw them from Papa's study window.

'Is that Herr Lenbach?' Papa asked.

'I don't think so,' I said, craning my neck to see through the ivy around the window. The sharp tat-tat of the door-knocker sounded in the hall. Jank, our old butler, answered the door, and I strained to hear the voices.

'Who is it?' Papa asked.

I did not reply, I was too busy listening. The timbre of the youthful voice could not be mistaken—it was *him*!

'Do I look all right?' I said anxiously, patting my hair and smoothing my skirt.

'Look all right for whom?'

'Come this way, sir. The baron and baroness are in the study.' Our butler neared the door, and I sprang away, feeling the colour rise into my cheeks. Until the moment I heard his voice again, saw his face once more as he followed Jank into the room—only then did I realise what had been missing in my life—the one thing my heart still wished for: Christian Haller.

'Elsa,' he said, and promptly walked into a side table, knocking two books to the floor. 'Sorry, I should say, Fräulein Schwan, no—Freiherrin von Winterheimer!' He picked up the books and smoothed down a bent page. 'Sorry,' he said, putting them back.

I laughed. 'Herr Haller, it's so good to see you!'

'Is it?' he looked about to teeter into the table again; he really was anxious about something. I was just overjoyed that he was here.

'Come in,' I said, gesturing towards Papa's desk. 'Papa is here. You should have sent word you were coming.'

'Should I? I'm sorry. Have I inconvenienced you?' He was bowing to Papa as he apologised and caught his foot on the fur rug between the door and the Papa's desk.

'Herr Haller,' said Papa, not smiling, but putting out a hand. He looked uneasily between my grinning face and Christian's embarrassed one.

'But where is Hansi? I thought I saw two horses arrive.'

'He is with me. He, er, has been taken to the kitchens.'

'The kitchens! He shall be treated as one of the family after all the kindness he has rendered me, is that not so, Papa?'

'I think, El—my lady, that he would be very pleased to be taken to the kitchens for the time being,' said Christian.

'Why...?' And then I understood. I beamed in delight. 'Of course. Ziller! Come into the drawing room and I will send for refreshments. You will stay and dine, won't you?'

'Actually, if I may,' stammered Christian, 'I would like to speak to your father. Alone.'

'To Papa?' I was flummoxed. 'Oh. Very well. I will arrange for tea for when you are ready.'

Christian gave a tight smile and stood twisting his cuff-links. It was only then that I realised how smart he looked. I had never seen him so well dressed before. His hair was trimmed and groomed; the last time I had seen him it had been overgrown and he'd had two days of stubble on his jaw.

'I will go then,' I said unnecessarily, still puzzled.

I looked back into the room before I closed the door. Christian still stood looking like a worried schoolboy, and Papa looked grim and uncertain. I shut the door, pressed my ear to it for a moment, then chided myself for listening in and turned away.

It was almost half an hour before Christian came to find me in the drawing room. Whatever his talk with Papa was about, it had not eased him, for he misplaced the cup of tea I handed him, sending it crashing to the floor instead of the table.

'Blast it!' he cried, 'I'm sorry!'

'Don't fret, it's only a cup,' I got up to ring the bell for the maid. 'I wish you'd tell me what's worrying you, Christian, you're being very mysterious.'

He sprang up and took my hand before it reached the bell. I looked at him in surprise. It was a little disconcerting to have him so close. It was also rather nice.

He drew me closer and bent his head towards me, cupping my face with one hand. 'I've missed you so much, it's been agony.'

'Then why did you stay away so long?' His hand was warm and I leaned into it.

'I had to settle affairs with my family. Reconcile with my father. Then the roads were too icy to travel on for a long time. I came as soon as I could.'

I was sure he was going to kiss me. I tilted my face to meet his.

'May I?' he asked.

Must he be quite so courteous!

'You once said you would never kiss me,' I reminded him.

'I did? No—'

'Yes. Those were your words, I remember them exactly. In the gardens at Swanstein, remember?'

He looked sheepish. 'What I meant to say is that I would never kiss you like *that*.'

'Like what?'

'In that sneaking way that *he* did. Trying to steal a girl's heart without honourable intentions towards her.'

'So, you would kiss me if your intentions were honourable?'

'I would only ever kiss you with such intentions, Elsa. You deserve nothing less. I've asked your father for permission.'

'To kiss me?'

'To ask for your hand.'

My stomach did a little flip at these words. 'And what did he say? That you're too poor for a baron's daughter?' In that moment I knew I could not let Christian go again. Not even for Papa.

'I'm not so poor. My father is Prince von Hallerstein.'

'A prince?'

'Not terribly wealthy. And I'm not the heir.'

'You're the son of a prince?'

'I will need to work, but there will be extra income, enough for a comfortable life, but not a city mansion, or a fancy carriage, or whatever other luxuries you are used to.'

'You're Prince Christian von Hallerstein?'

'We could settle in whichever town you choose. As long as we can go to the mountains in the summer months—'

'Why not all year round?'

'There are no balls or concerts in the mountains.'

'No—far better! There are mountains to climb and lakes to swim in, and meadows to walk though! How can we ever go back to the ordinary world, Christian, after what we have seen? I've been floundering around like a…a…'

'A swan in a goose pen?' finished Christian. We laughed. 'I've been the same,' he said. 'Of course we can't go back. We're not the same people. We will always have a foot in each world, I think. We're not the only ones.'

'Is it a curse or a blessing?' I wondered aloud.

'Would you choose not to have seen all you have?'

'No. I have seen such beauty. I never knew there could be so much of it.'

338

'Then it must be a blessing. Besides, we saw it together. It brought us together.'

'Yes. It did. Now are you finally going to kiss me?'

'We will live in the mountains,' he said as we sat close together, the tea grown cold and undrunk, our fingers twined together as we talked of our future life.

'What of your work? An architect must work in towns and cities.'

'I don't want to be an architect. I never liked all those straight lines and calculations. I shall be an artist.'

'You are an artist. A true one. You see the inside of things.'

'Shall you be happy living as an artist's wife on a modest income, Elsa? Won't you miss the comforts you've been brought up in?'

'We shall be ridiculously rich in the things that matter. But I don't know about being anyone's wife.'

'You don't?'

'How can I? No one has ever asked me.'

'I haven't?'

A second thing he had to remedy; and he did that very well too.

We returned to New Swanstein after our wedding. I promised Alexi he would see it when he came, but it was right for Christian and me to be alone the first time.

We wandered around the deserted courtyard. No saws, no hammers, no chisels, no songs.

The doors were shut up, so we could not see inside. I did not wish to. There were ghosts enough in the memories outside.

'I wonder if the new king will open it up and finish it,' I said.

'I think the new king likes the city too well,' said Christian. 'Not everyone likes to be so far from 'civilisation'.'

'The lilies are gone,' I said. We had seen a few drifts of crocuses as we climbed the mountain path from the village of Swanstein. But they had been very ordinary crocuses, as would be expected in April. The great, golden, riotous swathes of flowers had sunk back into the earth beneath.

'The magic is gone,' I said.

'Not quite. Look.'

One spray of silvery jasmine bobbed in the spring breeze. I put out a hand to take it, then drew it back. 'It should stay here,' I said. 'Nothing should be touched.'

We ventured down the steep stairs to the foot of the waterfall, looking for the door to the underground cave. But we were not surprised to find that there was no longer any door.

We traced the familiar walk around the lake; memories of the great-aunts made me smile, as I remembered their impish ways. The black swans seemed very ordinary. They came paddling up as I stood at the water's edge. 'I don't have any basket of bread and lettuce today,' I apologised to them. Christian tore up one of the bread rolls the innkeeper's wife had given us for our picnic lunch and threw it on the water.

'Let's build our house somewhere where we can see the lake,' I said. 'Not too far from Hansi and Ziller, when she comes. A guest room for Alexi, and one for Papa. And for your father and brother,' I added. I had yet to meet Christian's family. That was our next stop on our wedding journey.

We wandered slowly back to our lodgings in the village. It was amusing to see how many people stared at us as if they thought they knew us, but could not quite remember where from. Prince and Princess von Hallerstein were very different from the strange girl with no memory who had fed the king's birds, and the overworked architect's apprentice who had been there in the days of the king.

I woke very early the last morning of our visit to Swanstein Village. Christian still slept, so I dressed and wandered down to the lakeside. The early morning mist lingered above it like a cloud of tulle. I watched it lift, inch by inch. I heard the call of a duck echoing across the water from the little island where they nested. The sun gilded the horizon; the moon still lingered faintly in the west. A breeze blew across the water. A lone white swan sailed just beyond the curtain of mist. I could glimpse its long neck, its red-gold beak. I watched it, wondering if the mist was playing tricks on my vision, or if the swan seemed very large, with the gleam of a gold crown about its neck. I moved nearer, keen to see. The sun rose higher, the mist dissolved, but there was no crowned swan on the water. Only the spirit of one.

'Goodbye, King of the Swans,' I whispered. 'I will never forget you.'

ABOUT THE SWAN KING

Schloss Neuschwanstein in the Bavarian mountains is the archetypal fairy tale castle brought to life, not least because Walt Disney used it as the inspiration for his Sleeping Beauty palace. The builder of Neuschwanstein, King Ludwig II, is as famous as his creation, remembered as *der Märchenkönig* – the Fairy Tale King, also the Swan King, the Dream King, the Moon King…and the Mad King.

I've called *The Swan King* a historical fairy tale, with emphasis on fairy tale; many of the details, settings and events are biographical and historical, but ultimately it is a fantasy with dates, details and characters elided and altered. What is factual is that Ludwig was born in 1845. He was a sensitive, imaginative child who loved the heroic myths and legends that adorned the walls of his summer home at Schloss Hohenschwangau: a Gothic Revival castle by the Schwansee (Swan Lake).

Despite his privileged birth, he endured an austere childhood, with a gruelling regime of study, designed to toughen him up and make him fit to be a ruler. But no one could have foreseen that he would be suddenly thrust onto the throne at the age of eighteen. He was young, he was shy, he would rather immerse himself in designing fantastical retreats than dealing with endless government business and facing the harsh realities of war with Prussia, France, and the rise of the new German empire under Bismarck.

Ludwig worked hard to fulfil his duties, but his ministers eventually decided they'd had enough of their reclusive king, and when Ludwig decided he'd had enough of them, and was going to replace them all – a coup was hatched. Ludwig was forcibly taken from Neuschwanstein, certified as insane by a doctor who had never examined him, and incarcerated in Schloss Berg, south of Munich. The evening after his deposition, Ludwig went for a walk with the psychiatrist who had certified him. They never returned. Their bodies were found in the shallow lake. Ludwig was declared drowned, yet he was a strong swimmer, the lake was only three feet deep, and there was no water in his lungs. A tragic accident? An attempted escape gone awry? An assassination? To this day no one knows what happened.

One of the accusations against Ludwig was that he had bankrupted the treasury with his building projects. He had indeed spent all his own fortune, and amassed massive debt, but he had not spent the treasury's money. Immediately after his death his castles and palaces of Neuschwanstein, Linderhof, and Herrenchiemsee were opened to the public. The revenue from tourism quickly recouped the cost of the buildings and has contributed to making Bavaria one of the wealthiest economies in the world. Ludwig left his people a generous legacy, both artistically and financially, albeit perhaps unintentionally, in part.

Something about the complex, troubled life and person of Ludwig moved me enough to want to write a story about him, and to give him a happier ending than he had in reality.

He was a man of artistic vision, stirred by beauty, who believed in promoting the arts and advancing culture in his kingdom. As an introvert he struggled as a public figure, but he loved the Bavarian countryside and people. He might find ministers and dignitaries difficult, but he had no problem talking with the local farmers and villagers, who loved him in return, calling him their Fairy Tale King as he rode through the snow in his gilded sleigh, having moonlit picnics. He was certainly eccentric, and there was madness in the family, perhaps due to generations of inter-marriage; but I'm inclined to agree with his cousin, the Empress Elisabeth of Austria who declared, *"The King was not mad; he was just an eccentric living in a world of dreams. They might have treated him more gently, and thus perhaps spared him so terrible an end"*

"Alas, he is so handsome and wise, soulful and lovely, that I fear that his life must melt away in this vulgar world like a fleeting dream of the gods." So said the composer, Wagner, whom Ludwig was patron to, and who was my inspiration for the character of Herr Weimann (who was a lot of fun to write!).

As a deeply private person, Ludwig most likely would have been appalled at having his royal retreats filled with tourists, as they are today. But I hope he wouldn't mind being the Muse for a fairy tale and a loose telling of *Lohengrin* – one of the Arthurian legends he loved from his childhood and throughout his relatively short life.

I hope you enjoyed *The Swan King*

Sign up to my newsletter at
www.ninaclarebooks.com
to hear about new releases, special offers
and to download a free fairy tale

BOOKS BY NINA CLARE

REGENCY ROMANCE NOVELS

Beau Brown

Constance & the Inconstant Duke (coming 2022)

THE JANE AUSTEN FAIRY TALES

Magic and Matchmaking

Midwinter Mischief

Midsummer Madness

FAIRY TALE NOVELS

The Thirteenth Princess

Beck

The Miller's Girl

The Reluctant Wife

The Swan King

The Earl of Highmott Hall

The Stepsister and the Slipper

Printed in Great Britain
by Amazon